DANGEROUS DANCING

DANGEROUS DANCING

Julie Welch

Chatto & Windus
LONDON

Published in 1992 by
Chatto & Windus Ltd
20 Vauxhall Bridge Road
London SW1V 2SA

A CIP catalogue record for this book is
available from the British Library

ISBN 0 7011 3636 7

Phototypeset by Intype, London
Printed in Great Britain by
Mackays of Chatham plc
Chatham, Kent

To Ron, who went out and earned all the money so I could stay at home and write.

Acknowledgements

Special thanks to: Pippa O'Mahony, Patsy Plender and Richard Plender for help and information; Roberta and Vic Ziegel for use of the apartment; Alison Samuel for being rational, cheerful and sensible at all times when I added to 'Some problems of an editor', and above all to Cat Ledger. Without her encouragement and enthusiasm, this book would never have been started.

Chapter One

The Accident

As FLORENCE JOHNSON lay on the edge of life, pinned to the high hospital bed like a creature prepared for dissection, she dreamed of her childhood in France. Summer in the Hôtel Kikinette in the Gironde, the beaches where the Atlantic rollers reared and crashed, her uncle's cronies trying to catch her undressing, Aunt Laurence's boiled Friday fish, the big theatre in Bordeaux where she saw the dancing girls from England.

Waiting for Uncle Gaston to buy tickets, Florence had strayed round to the stage door and witnessed their arrival, crammed companionably in a limousine, giggling, eating, smelling beautiful; the tiny one who looked as if she slept in a shoebox, the smouldering one with hair the colour of strong tea, the blonde who was soon to be famous for marrying an American actor, the big one who to Florence's fourteen-year-old eyes seemed to have a foot in the grave already though she was actually only a rather jowly thirty-one. Sweet Fanny Addams; she knew them all by name and nature from the publicity pictures which preceded them – little Juliet, bad-tempered Alexa (known by everyone as Ratty), ethereal Collette, and businesslike Tina. The one Florence fell in love with, though, was Millie. Millie was different from the others; she was shy and dark with huge red hands and no one in a thousand years could have described her as beautiful. But Millie, almost as if she had known her for years, got out of the limo and smiled at Florence, and that was when Florence knew she would join a dance group. They would be friends, sisters, travelling together, supporting each other like the loving family she had never known. Later, as the dancers bobbed and

I

thrashed to *les tubes*, and Millie, transformed by the rhythm, wiggled around the stage like an eel evading capture, Florence noticed that Uncle Gaston, too, could not keep his eyes off her. Shortly afterwards, Uncle Gaston shielding his bulging lap with a newspaper, the pair of them were marched out by Aunt Laurence, who when purchasing the tickets for an improving night out had wrongly thought the English girls came from the Royal Ballet.

These dreams were so clear and accurate that it was as if Florence were actually a child again, though now she was filled with a joy and gratitude for her life that had been thoroughly absent at the time. Her mind was simply preparing in case of death. As it scanned her existence from twelve years old, when her mother died, to twenty-two, when she walked off the boat train at Victoria and Millie Fisher held out those ugly red hands to greet her, a strange thing happened to her sense of time. Everything seemed to take as long to happen as it had originally, though in fact she was only in a coma for six hours.

During those six hours, Joanna-Mary Reed-Herbert was happier than she had ever been in her entire life.

'I want you to be very brave,' said Greg Casdon. 'There's been an accident.'

They were in the residents' lounge of the Brijua Guesthouse in Hull (Your Hosts: Brian and Juanita Capstick. Thespians Made Welcome). It was eight o'clock on a dusty summer evening, and nearly a decade had passed since the night Florence set eyes on Sweet Fanny Addams. Since then the group had broken up and the dancers had gone their different ways. Now it had reformed with a new five-girl line-up:

Millie Fisher (36), choreographer, innovative, small and shy.
Joanna-Mary Reed-Herbert (21), spoilt, rich and proud.
Janey Sears (19), kindly, level-headed, a true friend, big bust.
Lily Smith (17), junior harpy.
Florence Johnson (23), sexy, bohemian, determined.
Greg Casdon (21), man.

The contents of Mrs Capstick's lounge had been winnowed from auction sales and the sort of shop which used the term 'antique' in a rather free-associating way. Outside the window was a huge variegated laurel which obscured the view of the street. The lounge was in darkness, which had seemed to fall very suddenly while Greg was speaking. Lily sprawled on a scratchy maroon sofa, Joanna-Mary perched on the edge of a stained armchair and Janey sat on the floor, her chin resting sadly on her knees. From where she was positioned she could count five lamp-posts in a row. Four of them were casting a yellow glow on the roofs of parked cars, but the fifth had failed to light up, which did not surprise Janey one bit. Things often showed themselves in ways like that. Greg moved restlessly around the room, carrying the ashtray with him. 'Millie is dead,' he said. 'Florence may not survive the night.'

Sweet Fanny Addams were in Hull because they were about to start a three-week engagement at the Scala in Summertime Special. Janey, Lily Smith and Joanna-Mary had travelled up from London with Greg, wearing his roadie hat. Millie and Florence were to join them later as Millie had a hospital appointment. The Scala engagement was important. They were appearing with the singer Spike Uttley who'd had a number one hit in 1986, and they had been booked as guests on a local television chat show (*Friday Night with Rocco Reeves*). They were young and promising and beautiful and in the days that led up to their journey enjoyed many private dreams of fame, money, good hotels and marrying well.

'We'll see you at the dress rehearsal,' Florence had said to Greg over the phone that morning. The bigger and bolder of the two, she often did the talking for both herself and Millie. 'We'll go straight there.'

Millie said something to her in a low voice. Greg hung on to the receiver while the two friends conferred urgently, huddled together. He was in the hall of the cavernous Victorian house where he lived in a bedsitter. The floor had brown and white tiles mottled with time and dirt. There was a pile of old newspapers by the stairs. A smell of tomcats seeped under the front door.

'Oh no, wait – ' 'Well, I say we should go for the – ' 'That settled, then?' 'Oh no, hang on, hang on, hang on!'

Presently, Florence resumed her dialogue with Greg. 'We want two rounds of prawn mayonnaise on brown waiting for us,' she said. 'Millie has a craze on them at the moment. Oof. Pardon. Millie has just broken my ribs.' Millie, who had merely nudged her, was overcome by giggles. Greg found it good to hear. Lately she had seemed even quieter and more secretive than usual.

There was more murmuring. Florence said to Greg, 'Don't let Joanna-Mary make a fuss about the room. She's to go in with Janey and don't you stand for any of her rubbish about don't-they-know-who-I-am.'

After this, Millie told Greg to collect their costumes from Miss Fluge, a Belgian lady reduced to a small flat in Wimbledon where she sewed rather fiercely on an ancient electric machine. 'I hope they're all right,' said Millie. 'She pulled a bit of a face when I wanted feathers. What if we start moulting on stage?'

'I don't suppose – ' said Greg.

Millie cut in, 'Must go. Someone's at the door,' and rang off. For a minute Greg sat by the phone, tipping his chair against the wall. Millie's face appeared in his mind – thin, beaky-nosed, with a glossy black fringe clipped just above her eyebrows which like everything else about Millie were neat and well cared for. Everything about Millie was shiny and clean – her shoes, her hair, her buckles. He felt funny, as though he ought to ring her back, but instead he returned to his tasks.

When Millie and Florence did not arrive at the Scala for the dress rehearsal, Joanna-Mary experienced feelings of rage, triumph and hope. The day before the journey to Hull, she had dragged Greg into a private corner of the musty Territorial Army hall they used for rehearsals. 'Something's happening,' she said. 'I think Millie is going to leave.'

Greg said, 'How do you know?'

'Because I followed them to the loo in Geronimo's,' said Joanna-Mary. Geronimo's was the nearby café bar where the girls took lunch. The smell from the drains was haunting but the owner (he boasted of Red Indian blood) let them eat half-price after

4

two forty-five and all the time in the case of Florence. Her soft brown eyes and thin arms aroused his protectiveness. 'That's where they always meet to do their plotting,' said Joanna-Mary. 'Millie is leaving, Florence is taking over, they're going to dah dah dah dah, which I missed because she pulled the chain, and Florence asked to have it in writing because of me. Not in so many um, um, words, but that's definitely what it boils down to.'

Greg, who was a diplomatic and somewhat proper young man who had refereed many of the girls' fights, said, 'I'll look into it. You should certainly be consulted. You may not want Florence to take charge.'

'Over my dead body,' said Joanna-Mary. 'Or hers, preferably.'

'BRAVE JOANNA-MARY VOWS TO CARRY ON.'

When the girls had returned to Mrs Capstick's guesthouse after the aborted dress rehearsal and there was still no sign of Millie or Florence, psychic Janey Sears knew they would never arrive. At the time of the accident, and for the hours that intervened till receipt of the news, she had been visited by the most terrible pangs of fear and loss. These caused her to phone her mother and father, younger married sister and grandparents in Norfolk, and the elderly neighbour in Shepherd's Bush, West London, who was keeping an eye on her flat, to check on their well-being. Later, outside the hospital where Florence lay, she said nothing of this to the man from the *London Age*, thinking he would find her silly.

Joanna-Mary suffered no such qualms. No lover of either Millie or Florence, and a firm believer in the idea that people were responsible for their own fate and no one else's, she was unimpeded by any feelings of grief or guilt and her thought processes were distinguished models of calm and clarity. Her quote to the man from the *London Age* – 'At five past three when we were just coming into Hull, I felt a dreadful shock pass through me' – was given in a spirit of generosity to the public, who liked to read that sort of thing.

The press were at the Herts and Middlesex General Hospital on the northern edge of London where the crash had taken place.

Most were breezy boys and girls from the tabloids to whom Millie seemed as *passé* as a dinosaur, but they perked up on finding out who Joanna-Mary's father was. They weren't a bit bothered about Janey, who hired a cab out of Hull the minute she could get away, flinging her old man's mackintosh over her feathers, leaving all her things behind including her make-up box, slipping dowdily unrecognized into the hospital in the early morning gloom to begin her vigil beside Florence's bed. The ride came to more money than she had, so she let the driver feel her bosoms. She didn't really mind. He'd been telling her about his wife, who wouldn't let him except with the lights off and then a fortnight till the next time. She felt quite sorry for him, really.

'Don't go, don't go,' he said, making little whimpering noises and thrusting his crotch at her like a trayload of canapés. People never liked to part with Janey.

Janey, motherly and stalwart. She was the soul of the group. She was rounded, yellow-haired, broad-backed, as though ready to take on all the burdens of the world. Her family lived in a farm cottage miles from anywhere, with cabbages growing in the front garden and a yard full of washing and hens and tumbling Labrador-cross puppies. She was the oldest of six children, possibly more by now as there wasn't much to do in the evenings in her village. There was a fuss when Janey went to London to be a dancer. She was the first of her family to move away. Her mother called in Lady Edwina from the big house to try and talk her out of it and her dad weaved around in the lane in front of home-going tractors. 'Take the clothes off the backs of your own people,' he said. 'Off you go to Sodom and Gomorrah.'

'Look, I'll be able to give you something every week. I'll be able to get you a proper toilet.'

She had had trouble getting away from Hull because Joanna-Mary wanted to go on with the show. 'Millie was a *professional*.' Flipping through her filofax for the names and numbers of replacements. 'Who was that girl, Janey, who came with you from the Pepita Vasquez School to the audition? She'll jump at the chance.'

'You said she had a squint.'

'No, um, um, I certainly didn't. You're imagining things.' Even

6

as Janey opened the door of the cab, Joanna-Mary was still clinging to her hopes. 'Lily, *think*.' 'Wheee,' said Lily, who had taken Ecstasy in the Scala ladies. 'Hee haw.'

Janey sat by Florence's bed like a madonna in a motheaten leotard dotted with blue feathers. There were screens around them, and beyond that a flimsy-looking partition with tall double doors leading on to the corridor. She listened to the hospital sounds: a dripping tap, a phone ringing far away, the brisk footsteps of the night staff. A policeman came to the nurses' station, asking if Florence had come round. Janey could hear his shoes, squeaky on the lino. 'I don't think she will come round,' Janey heard the nurse say.

She turned back to Florence. 'I've brought you some Pez,' she said, burrowing in her bag. Pez were Florence's favourite sweets. You put them in a small rectangular dispenser with a flip-top. The tops came in all different shapes, like teddy bears' and cats' heads. Janey's was a poodle, which was the closest she could find to a Labrador-cross. She thought the sweets looked really pretty and neat, like miniature tablets of soap. They were made in Austria.

'You probably don't feel like them now,' said Janey in her voice which was cooing and sometimes wistful. 'I'll leave them beside your bed. Right, my love? There's lime flavour in there and the refill's cherry. It was the last cherry in the shop but go ahead, have it. Cheers ears.' She turned the packet over. 'Frugt-Pastiller. Ingredienser: sukker, glykose, syre: E330, emulgator: E471, plante fedt, aroma.'

The nurse put her head round the screen. 'Oh,' she said, 'I thought I heard someone talking.'

'It's to trigger off something in her unconscious,' said Janey. 'Like you read in the papers. You know, when the doctors have given up but the person's fiancée or sister or whoever it is keeps going and going for weeks and then it happens, the person wakes up.'

'I wouldn't get too excited,' the nurse said. 'These things don't come about very often.'

'Yes, they do,' said Janey. 'You just have to have faith.'

7

'What about a nice cup of tea? There's a kitchen right by us, go on, get a bit of rest.'

'I could do,' said Janey. 'In a minute.' She turned back to Florence. Her face had been hit by flying glass and there was a deep red line across her forehead. Janey took out a comb and gently tidied Florence's hair. She dipped a Kleenex in the water jug and washed the blood out of her fringe where it had stuck together. She was going to start talking again, but everything she thought of saying had Millie Millie Millie in it. Pez Hedelmamakeisia. Valmistusaineet: sokeri, Millie, tarkkelyssiirappi, kasvisrasva, Millie, Millie. So instead she hummed quietly over the blip and whirr of the monitoring machines and the far-off swing of doors and clatter of trolleys, a song they could never dance to because it was too slow, but it was one of Florence's favourites. She was always playing it on Geronimo Cohen's juke-box. Something about when you were sweet sixteen and I first saw you on the village green. Janey thought it was very romantic, and often wondered who it was that Florence was thinking of when her face went so dark and sad.

And as Janey sang, Florence dreamed on, of Millie all those years ago, walking towards her down the steps of La Poste in Bordeaux.

Chapter Two

Bordeaux, 1980

MILLIE WAS WEARING an old fur coat with a bit of torn lining hanging out of one pocket. This despite, firstly, the hot sun and secondly, her high earnings. Millie had bought the coat from a junk shop in the excited poverty of her early days as a dancer. She kept that coat like a talisman and called it Horatio. She wore it at the testing moments of her life, and this tour in France in August 1980 was proving extremely testing. Everything seemed on the brink of falling apart.

She had always been the one who held the group together, but this time she could not. 'They're all at it,' she had confided down the phone in La Poste to her boyfriend Curtis in England. 'Juliet v. Tina. Ratty v. Tina. Worst of all, Collette v. Tina.'

'What else is new?' said Curtis. After all, Collette and Tina had rows every day. 'It's a formality,' came Curtis's opinion down 600 miles of cable from the London office of Plantagenet and Schwartz, Theatrical Agents. 'Its a tradition, like the State Opening of Parliament. One couldn't exist without the other. Collette, therefore Tina. There's probably some biological or scientific explanation for it – some gravitational pull operating between them. As for the other girls, you're always saying Tina treats everyone like a lump of shit.'

Millie said, 'That was the cold war. This is the real thing.'

'Come back to England,' said Curtis. 'Let's get married.'

'Are you still going on about that?' said Millie. But for once she didn't think it sounded such a bad idea.

She told Curtis how, in the restaurant after Friday's show, Collette left the dinner table. 'Must have a pee,' Collette said.

As she disappeared from view, the waiter arrived with their first courses. The waiter was wearing fusty black trousers and a dark red jacket of a shade between hotel porter and Warsaw Pact general. The tablecloths were lacy and laid with lots of shiny glass. The windows were curtained with soft pink plush. At the front of the restaurant as you came in was a high wooden counter with a cash till on the end, behind which perched Madame on a tall chair. She was dressed in a blouse of some slippery fabric in an abstract pattern of blue and white. She sat very still, a Frenchwoman in late middle age with hair dyed dark blonde and a big proud chest. The door to the kitchen was open and from it came bright light and the hiss of pig's liver being thrown into a hot pan. There were two other diners in the restaurant, a couple who sat silently with their hands clasped over plates of empty whelk shells.

The waiter placed the girls' food on the table. There was a *salade aux lentilles* for Millie, a *salade aux haricots verts avec foie gras* for Tina, *soupe aux poissons avec rouille* for Juliet, a plate of *radis beurré* for Ratty, thin and white with livid red tips just like her fingers, and for Collette, a *salade aux lardons*, into which Tina spat.

'Oh no,' whispered Juliet.

'Oh yes,' murmured Millie, almost admiringly, as Tina leant over, her big cheeks working to fill her mouth with saliva which she then spat on to the curly green *frisée* that was Collette's favourite. Tina then looked challengingly round at everyone else.

'Are you going to say anything?' mouthed Juliet to Millie, eyes fixed on her soup.

'What?' muttered Millie between her teeth. 'I'm more interested in Tina renewing my contract next month, thanks very much.' They glanced sideways at Ratty, who simply looked pitying in a bored way. Then Collette returned from the loo. She studied the little silvery puddle on her lettuce and, picking up the spoons, tossed the salad again, all the while giving Tina a long hard stare. Then she ate the salad. Still staring at Tina. Mopping up the leftover vinaigrette with her bread till the plate was so clean it squeaked and still all the time with her eyes on Tina. 'Mm,' said Collette, putting down her fork. 'Delicious.'

'And,' said Millie on the phone to Curtis the next morning, 'and that's not the end of it. Juliet has been funny all week. I'm afraid she's gone all religious. She gave me a frightful-looking pamphlet called *The Wheel*. And Ratty's in love.'

'But that's what you hoped for her,' said Curtis. 'Ratty to fall in love and become a happier person.'

'With a woman!' shrieked Millie through tears of laughter.

Ratty, radiant with love and novelty. 'Get yourself a woman,' she kept saying, in the tones of a games mistress exhorting the second eleven at lacrosse to improve their cradling. Ratty was the daughter of a public school housemaster and in times of extreme emotion tended to lose her carefully cultivated egalitarian accent. 'You should all get yourselves a woman.'

Watching Millie stroll down the steps of La Poste that morning, Florence of course did not know any of this.

Florence was sitting with her back to the wall, beside a pile of luggage. Fourteen years old trying to pass for eighteen. Her brown hair was long and thick and straight with a fringe obscuring her eyebrows. There was a beaten-looking beret in front of her which contained a few coins of small denomination. The wall against which she was sitting belonged to the Banque Nationale de Paris. She was trying to raise money for her train fare out of France. She sang an old Françoise Hardy song, years out of date:

'All over the world, people are falling in love . . .'

Millie recognized her as a face from the crowd at the show's opening night. She laughed and gave her a 50-franc note as you could not buy a decent beret for less.

'Take me back with you,' begged Florence, who spoke good English, Millie was intrigued to hear.

'I don't think so,' said Millie gently.

Florence was running away from Aunt Laurence, the relative from hell. She was tired of Uncle Gaston looking through the keyhole when she took a bath, and had no desire to eat any more boiled fish. 'Or anything else cooked by Aunt Laurence,' Florence told Millie.

'What?' said Millie. 'But French food is so good! Do you

know, I counted seven different kinds of lettuce in Auchan. Seven! Back home in Safeway they think they're being cosmopolitan if they get in the occasional Webbs Wonder.'

Perhaps because so much of their dancing was erotic, Sweet Fanny Addams tended to retreat into infantilism off duty and concentrated mainly on food. Millie loved to go to France. She could linger for hours in the markets, gazing at the creamy-white piles of cauliflowers, the purplish heaps of aubergines like body bags, huge bunches of fresh coriander and mint, mountains of celeriac and bags of almonds, the stalls selling offal that the English would never look at, cow heels and tripes of three different kinds, brains, pigs' trotters and tails to be simmered till they were falling apart tender and embalmed in mustard sauce. She longed to be French herself, to go to the market every morning with a stout misshapen bag, to buy poultry off the *volailler* plucking old hens for the pot, to squeeze and plot.

'French food is not good at all as dished up by my Aunt Laurence,' said Florence. 'The woman boils vegetables till they're dead, and she gets special supplies of slimy flageolets from a secret source. I think they're rabbit turds myself, rabbit turds in disinfectant. And I've given up asking when my father is coming back for me.'

Ever since her mother died, Florence and her father had travelled through Europe, relying on the kindness of friends. It was a sad but romantic time, Florence being at an age where she loved having her father all to herself. When they could not find friends to take them in, they slept under bridges and lived off baguettes and cheap wine. Her father was tall, blond, bony and vague, an actor from England. He was not a very successful actor. It was Florence's mother who had the money. She came from a rich family of plumbing engineers and manufacturers in Limoges. 'But,' said Florence sadly, 'all that money couldn't save her life.'

Florence's father Gervaise Thomas picked up odd work in bars as a singing pianist. All over the world, he sang, people are falling in love. Fifteen years before, in the summer of 1965, it had been the song he sang to Florence's mother, the shy but pretty Solange Castaing of Limoges.

Florence and Gervaise wandered along the coast to Boulogne where Gervaise auditioned for a job in experimental theatre. The job did not materialize, but a lady friend did. Paulette was the director of the early evening news programme on TV Nord-Est, a local station which encompassed the Pas de Calais. At thirty-one, she enjoyed success in her career but was beginning to get a bit desperate where men were concerned. She emptied half-bottles of Opium over her front and hung on the words of male colleagues in bars, who were frightened by the look in her eyes and bolted home to their wives. She had black frizzy hair and big flapping feet and a long, thin nose like a runner bean, and she was always snapping the clasp of her handbag shut. But Gervaise Thomas had no wife to hurry home to and was caught like a rabbit in her headlights.

At first the three of them shared a hotel room but as Paulette said, it was really out of the question on a permanent basis. 'This is no life for her,' said Paulette. 'She needs a mother's guidance.'

Uncle Gaston and Aunt Laurence were duly contacted. Laurence was actually Solange's cousin but had been given the title of Aunt as one of those courtesies people bestow on the fierce and spiteful in the hope of placating them. She and her husband Gaston ran a hotel on the south-west coast. More accurately, Gaston sat with his cronies playing cards in a corner of the bar while Laurence did all the cooking, cleaning and serving. Left to himself, Florence's father would not have thought of palming Florence off on them, but Paulette was made of sterner stuff. That is why Gervaise Thomas needed her. She washed his under-wear, made him get his teeth fixed, bullied him into going for auditions, turned him into a man of sorts, using sex as a weapon. In return, she got a weak but handsome actor for a lover. They were ideally suited. Poor Florence, no place for her there.

'A hotel in the Gironde!' exclaimed Paulette. 'Most children would be grateful!'

'I am not most children,' said Florence. 'I am not a child, come to think of it.'

'Oh! You are just a kid. You know nothing.'

'I know what disgusting things you and my father have been

doing every night,' retorted Florence, 'when you creep off to the shower because you think I won't hear, and with Maman not cold in her grave, even.'

'It is only for two weeks,' said Gervaise to Florence. 'Paulette needs a break. I'm going to take her to Lyons. I will come for you in two weeks.'

The Hôtel Kikinette was in a side street on the edge of town. Pine needles blew down from the dunes and covered everything. Sand got between your toes and in every crack and crevice of your body. Florence's bedroom was the worst in the hotel, on the top floor right next to the *toilettes*. The bedspread was the colour of bolognese sauce. Aunt Laurence had combined it with wallpaper featuring a design of bloated pink lilies, and curtains which were white with a pattern of blue and red hearts. Behind a partition was a sink choked with coiled hairs. Apart from the bed, the only bit of furniture was a lopsided chair with peeling varnish and a little metal plate on the back which said *F. Durand, Fabrique de Meubles, Saint-Pol-sur-Ternoise*, though Florence could not for the life of her work out why F. Durand would think the making of this object was anything to boast about. From the window there was a view of an old *droguerie* selling faded pink trusses and grubby plastic toilet seats.

'Are you happy with your room, Florence?' asked Uncle Gaston, who used the conversational opening to rub his hand down the small of her back.

'I would prefer something a bit less cramped,' confessed Florence.

Two hours later she was following Aunt Laurence across the hotel courtyard. 'So!' said Laurence. 'You would like a bigger room.' She opened the door of the old laundry, which contained a mangle, an early example of a spin-drier, and a china sink with a crack in the middle. 'We have been intending to decorate this but everything costs money. Feel free.'

Afterwards, Laurence said to Gaston, 'Business is business. The other room will be needed for guests now that we have her as an extra expense.'

'Surely not,' said Gaston. 'Does she not have her income from the trust Solange set up in her name?'

'Little better than small change,' said Aunt Laurence, 'and in any case, Gaston, you are not to tell her about the trust. It would not do for a young girl to fancy herself an heiress. She would grow up lazy, arrogant.'

Uncle Gaston always had a roll-up dangling from his lower lip, and a brown channel of nicotine bisecting his chin. He wore a beret and was small and jolly, not at all like his surname, which was Mortureux. But the name suited Laurence very well. She was long, narrow and humourless, with greyish-yellow hair and a thin mouth which was pulled down at one corner like the elastic of a catapult when you stretched it back. In the hotel bar was a visitors' book into which all the hotel guests were invited to write glowing testimonials while Laurence loomed over them. They all wrote how traditional the cooking was, because although it was horrid it was still better than everything else about the place.

In the old laundry Florence slept on a mattress on the concrete floor. Beside her was the airer where Aunt Laurence washed her plastic flowers and hung them out to dry upside down. Sometimes Uncle Gaston's cronies would try the door, mistaking it for the adjacent *lavabo*; at least that was what they mumbled when Florence shouted at them to go away. She stayed awake most nights, even after the bar emptied. Then she would creep out and sit in the courtyard, at one of the new white plastic tables with integral sun umbrella that Aunt Laurence had just bought. Beyond was the kitchen, which since Florence's arrival had gained white lace curtains and a coat of bright blue paint, as well as a new radio which hour after hour played Aunt Laurence's favourite religious music. Here in the courtyard Florence would dance alone, under the blue-black sky.

Every time Aunt Laurence addressed her as *vous*, every time Uncle Gaston and his cronies touched her up, Florence comforted herself with her father's promise. Two weeks. It is only two weeks. As the time grew near, she packed her round grey dressing case and waited for him to open the little door into the courtyard. Just wait till Papa found out where they had made her sleep! He would never let her go there again! . . . But the night Gervaise Thomas came back, it was when she was in bed. He left some things for her and was gone. Significant, permanent things like winter clothes.

'Why doesn't Papa take me home?' she asked at lunch the next day. They were having the stewed cod which all the hotel guests had very sensibly rejected. Aunt Laurence's cod had miraculous properties. The longer it cooked, the whiter it became. Nothing left a stain on its purity, neither oil nor tomato, not red or green pepper. The bones gleamed. 'Mon Dieu!' said Gaston. 'This is like eating someone's corset.'

'When he came here last night,' continued Florence, 'and Uncle Gaston and his friends got out the kirsch he is making in the cellar and everyone started to sing, and you said to be quiet because I was sleeping.'

'Not that there is anything wrong with corsets,' said Gaston. 'They can denote sensuality and generosity of spirit in a woman. Do you ever wear a corset, Florence?'

'Gaston!' said Aunt Laurence. 'Remember it is Friday.' Uncle Gaston had given up trying with the cod and was spoon-feeding himself milk pudding from a stainless-steel bowl in the fridge.

'Since when did puddings have meat in them?' demanded Gaston.

'Ah non, il contient des oeufs!'

'Merde! Are you a religious fanatic? Was Our Lord made of eggs?'

Nothing more was said about the visit of Florence's father.

Turning somersaults on the pale thin sand of Cap Ferret that afternoon, Florence discovered that the thought of her father made her eyes fill with tears. As she gazed out over the flat dreary inlet towards the featureless sand dune opposite, she felt a sense of utter desolation. It was like looking at a picture with its face turned to the wall. My mother is dead, she thought. My father has gone. Now I am utterly alone for ever.

'Aimez-vous Pez?' said a soft voice behind her.

Florence turned to see a boy in blue trunks with his bony male feet encased in old tennis shoes. He was offering her a sweet. The fact that her eyes had flown immediately to the trunks made both of them blush. They had red fish swimming around them. Florence wished she still had a best friend so she could tell her about this encounter afterwards, but all her schoolmates had been left behind when she and her father set off on their wanderings. 'I said to him, Lucky fish,' she imagined herself telling Véronique Durr behind the bicycle shed. And having her words passed round the classroom. 'Florence said, Lucky fish!' 'Oh, there's Florence for you!'

'Cheer up,' said the boy. 'Are you on holiday here? Maybe I could show you around.' He was Moroccan; golden skinned, curly haired and tall. His leg muscles were pronounced. His long face and flared nostrils reminded Florence of a horse. Florence had seen him before, at church where her aunt had dragged her for three hours that Sunday. He was the cantor. She had been filled with both sweetness and melancholy as that gentle boyish voice filtered through the crumbling stone walls and evaporated among the pine trees like the smoke of a forest fire. Behind him was a window of blue-stained glass on which St Matthew was depicted floating with arms outstretched against a backdrop of hills somewhat out of scale, so giving the impression he was ski-jumping. In front was an eagle carved in dark glossy wood. The cantor had worn white cotton robes and around his neck was a starched ruffle.

Now he said, 'Would you like to swim underwater with your eyes open?'

Florence swam behind Yusuf in the warm green sea. Later they sat on the beach and exchanged autobiographies. Yusuf had a way of saying things seriously that made her want to laugh. He told her how he lived in a children's home attached to the church. He would not, he said, dream of singing in church if he had a normal family life. As it was he shared a room with a *noir* called Bob who was into all sorts of ruses and rackets and would either fetch up a millionaire or dead before he was twenty.

'Don't you have anybody else who could look after you? Any aunts or uncles?'

'No idea. They're all wandering about the desert, I expect, wearing hankies on their heads.'

'Oh,' said Florence. 'I suppose anything's better than that.'

'I'm going to be a sports star,' he said. 'Rugby or football, I don't know yet.'

Florence said, 'One day when you're famous perhaps I'll come and watch you play.'

Sitting by Yusuf at the edge of the water where the waves made little frills round her long brown legs, she felt consoled. She absorbed some of the noises and sensations that would remind her for ever of the year she was fourteen. A man playing a guitar and singing in English on a radio in the back room of a café: And when I grow old, let me dream of yoo-hooey-you-hooey-you. The distant flap-flap of the nets round the oyster beds. The cherry flavour of the sweets. The smell of Gitanes, the brilliant blue of the packet; Yusuf cupping his hands round hers as she lit one of the stubby white cigarettes from a crooked match.

'Come inside, Florence,' he said as she bent her face towards his flame. Florence ran her finger across her upper lip, aware that it was suddenly beaded with sweat. He kissed her and after a moment of surprise and fear she found she liked his wet, warm, cherry-flavoured tongue. She closed her eyes then opened them to find him looking at her. She could see his fingers digging holes in the sticky sand.

Suddenly Yusuf broke away from her. He said: 'Who is that thin ugly woman waving her arms at you and shouting?'

'Come here this minute!' shrieked Aunt Laurence from the promenade. Despite the weather she was encased in a long black dress, thick stockings, black cardigan and black headscarf. Girls in bikinis wandered past her like tropical fish around the hull of a wrecked ship. Either side of her were carrier bags containing the ingredients for her famous dish, Corsets Lyonnaise. These banged against Florence's legs as Laurence marched her back to the Hôtel Kikinette. 'You are just like your mother. She was immoral too.'

'You don't know anything about what Maman was like.'

'Hah! Your grandparents should never have sent her to England in the first place. I could have told them what would happen – sports cars, drink, no-good actors.' Shy, brown-haired Solange Castaing who had seen something long ago in Gervaise Thomas;

kindness, good looks, vulnerability, or perhaps it was just simple despair on her part, alone at eighteen in a strange city.

'He *is* good,' said Florence. 'It's just there aren't many suitable parts for him.'

'Be grateful I don't throw you into the street,' said Laurence, who in Florence could see her cousin's warm intelligent look and sideways banana mouth.

'Throw me out, why don't you, its clear I'm a terrible nuisance to you.'

'I promised dear Solange that should anything ever happen to her than I would look after you,' lied Laurence, who had just given the go-ahead to her builders for extensive improvements to the bar.

That night there was a religious procession through the town. Pubescent girls in cream tussore marched in rows towards the church. 'I won't go,' said Florence, but Aunt Laurence whacked her with a wire coat hanger. Florence at fourteen was still too small and light to resist. First she put elastoplast on her legs where the blows had broken her skin, but looking at the patchwork effect she knew she couldn't possibly go out like that. If Yusuf were to be there. . . . Hunting among the clothes which her father had left for her, she found a pair of Paulette's black tights packed in error, and put them on.

During the procession, Florence fell in with Yusuf and his room-mate and friends. She led them, creeping, back to the Hôtel Kikinette, where they siphoned off the kirsch that Uncle Gaston was making in the cellar. They were all very sick in and around the sacristy of Notre Dame des Douleurs where they had retired to drink it. At Florence's instigation they all got their *zobs* out to see who had the longest. The winner was Yusuf. Florence had the idea he was sober. He beckoned her into the church. 'Come inside, Florence,' he said.

Florence felt a violet kick of pleasure in the pit of her stomach as he pulled her towards him. 'What are you doing?'

'Don't you like it?' His hand was creeping under her knickers.

'Oh, oh, yes.' She thought she'd better back this up with action so she stuck her tongue in his mouth, which was something

Véronique Durr had told her about one afternoon in the *cabinet* when they were cutting geography.

Yusuf broke away from her, spluttering and coughing. His throes went on for some time. He kept looking at her wide-eyed and trying to say something but all that came out was coughing, which made her giggle because he looked like one of the fish on his bathing trunks.

'You're not meant to do that,' he said crossly, when he'd recovered.

'No?' said Florence, blushing.

'The man's meant to do it first.'

'Why?'

'Well, ah, because . . .'

'Does the girl get to do anything first?'

'No!'

Footsteps sounded on the stone floor of the dark church.

'Bloody hell,' said Yusuf. He opened the narrow dark-brown door of the confessional and pulled Florence inside.

'Who is it?' Florence whispered.

'Sh!' They huddled against each other as the intruder passed the confessional. Florence sniffed the peculiar fusty air. Perhaps it was the distilled breath of people like Aunt Laurence.

After a while Yusuf opened the door half an inch and peeked out. 'The priest's housekeeper,' he said. They heard a door open and close in the distance. Yusuf kissed her and put his huge hand inside her knickers again. Florence whispered, 'Are you . . . *experienced*?'

'Yes,' he said shortly.

'Who with?'

'Don't be so nosy.' But he couldn't help saying, 'My friend Bob's got an older sister.'

She sighed romantically. 'Will you do it to me?'

He started to tear her knickers off and got his hand all tangled up in her tights, which made her giggle again. Suddenly he drew back and looked at her with his eyes narrowed. 'Here,' he said. 'How old are you?'

'Eighteen,' said Florence. He continued staring at her. 'Well, go on then.'

'Calm down, for God's sake,' said Yusuf. 'I'm not a complete bastard. You're far too young. Eighteen! You've hardly got any tits yet. Hey, don't cry. You're very beautiful but I can't risk it. If your father found out he'd blow my balls off.'

'He's not that kind of father,' said Florence. 'He's not any kind of father, really.'

Yusuf said, 'Come on. Let's go back to my pals.' But even as he spoke, Florence heard a voice that seemed to echo round the church though it was merely an inspired intervention from her own subconscious.

'*Give him a bit of a flash!*'

So she lifted up the skirt of her cream tussore dress, and for the first time Yusuf really saw the black tights underneath.

The next morning, Florence was hurried round to the surgery to be examined by old Docteur Pichard. He was not the doctor whom Aunt Laurence normally attended but some years ago he had dealt promptly with a little Algerian chambermaid with whom Gaston had been very foolish. His surgery was the other end of town, wedged between a couscous restaurant and a shop which sold lampshades speckled with dead flies. 'Which passage did you use?' demanded the doctor.

'We didn't,' said Florence, who in many ways was still very innocent. 'We did it in the confessional.'

After leaving the church the previous night, the priest's house-keeper had popped back in to offer up her suffering caused by having to wash all the priest's garments by hand including his underwear (he was inclined to be absent-minded about personal hygiene). Before her thoughts could wander, as they sometimes did, to a washing machine, she was alerted by unfamiliar sounds from the towering dark-brown kiosk. She shone her torch on it. It was rocking from side to side.

Yusuf had fetched his cantor's robes from the vestry and laid Florence on them tenderly. They had just been laundered and were cool and soft under her skin. As he moved on her they rippled. Lying in the surgery the next morning, Florence thought of Yusuf's lovely hairy legs and the smell and warmth of him.

She started to weep stoically at the memory, of the priest's housekeeper screaming the place down as Yusuf with his trousers round his ankles tried to chase her off. Then her aunt and the housekeeper holding up the white robes, searching them it seemed for bloodstains, arguing over who would boil them, for each wanted to offer it up. Yusuf was even now in a train, transferred from the children's home of St Matthew, Bordeaux, and on his way to something more corrective and severe. And here was Florence with her legs in the air on the couch of the fanny doctor of Cap Ferret.

'No, no, my dear,' Pichard was saying, his eyes more red and watery than ususal as he yanked off her pants. 'Did he use your back passage?'

'Quoi?'

'Did he have anal intercourse with you?'

'Quoi?'

'Did he bugger you?'

'Florence, listen to me,' said Aunt Laurence. 'If he used another entrance all is not lost and you can still find a decent Catholic boy with some money, as you will still be *une vierge.*' To the doctor, she said, 'There was no blood on the surplice. Not a drop.'

'I am not a virgin any longer,' said Florence, grabbing her pants back from Docteur Pichard, 'and it's the only good thing that's happened to me since I was dumped here.'

From dawn to twilight every day Florence had to wash the hotel bedlinen as a punishment. Locked into the unlit laundry room by her aunt. But souls are all Houdinis. Florence made her plans. One day she would find her father again and never let him leave her side, but first she would make England her goal and become a famous dancer.

'I'll be a waitress in a cocktail bar,' she said to Millie outside the steps of La Poste. 'Anything to pay my way.'

'I don't think so,' Millie said again, 'but come for a walk with me.'

Florence showed her the darkest, most unvisited jewellery shop in town, two doors down from the *droguerie*, where you could buy antique rings for next to nothing and necklaces with stones of black and white. 'No cruelty is involved in their making,' said Florence who like all fourteen-year-olds could be terribly pompous. 'The black ones have ink in them and the white ones are milk.'

Millie, who had just bought a darling little black-and-white dress from Anastasia in the Rue St Germain in Paris, chose two, one for herself and one for Florence. 'I'd love a ring,' she said, 'but don't you think my hands are too ugly?'

'Ugly?' said Florence. 'They're distinctive.' She picked out an old silver ring with a stone of greeny-grey. The colours (there were many greens and many greys) all spiralled outwards from the middle so that when you traced the spiral back it would always end up at that mysterious green centre like the bottom of the sea. 'Like your eyes,' said Florence. 'Your eyes are the colour of the sea.'

Millie bought the ring, and wore it often, especially with a black-and-green checked suit and sea-green flatties from a terrifyingly expensive shop in Covent Garden. She wore it to meet a lover. This, and many other things, she told Florence, and sometimes did not tell her, in letters and later face to face, during a friendship which began that day in Bordeaux when Florence was fourteen.

Chapter Three

When Curtis Met Millie

THE DAY AFTER Millie died, Joanna-Mary arrived at the hospital to be photographed with flowers in her arms. In those summer months at the turn of the decade she made a lovely subject.

Joanna-Mary was a beauty. Slim, upright and tall, she had long silky hair that was almost naturally the colour of gold-top milk. This she liked to toss with a jerk of her head and raising of her hand as though reacting to an assault on her face. Never, of course, had she actually experienced such a thing. From babyhood she had owned a cold, glittering, confident prettiness and was accustomed to unstinting praise and worship from her father, who from this prettiness posited other desirable human qualities such as intelligence, discernment and warmth. It was sheer laziness on his part, but he was famous and powerful, so her mother and everyone else took their tone from him.

'I knew at once that something dreadful had happened. I kept it to myself because I did not want to worry the others. Then when they told me that five past three was the time of the crash, I just fainted.' To the man from the *London Age*, who was writing all this down, Joanna-Mary said, 'Don't say I fainted, will you? It sounds so awful and feeble,' knowing full well that he would.

When she was satisfied that the press had had enough, she terminated the photo-opportunity and went inside the intensive care unit. She lacked a sense of humour, and the gravity of the occasion suited her.

As Joanna-Mary entered the hospital, Curtis Fisher, Millie's husband, was high above her. He was watching out of the window of a Qantas 747, looking forward to seeing his wife after the 22-hour flight from Sydney.

The plane was banking sharply, about to make its landing approach to Heathrow. From the sky, the view of London was misleading. His eyes could take in only the gross, the out of scale, the architecturally misbegotten. High-rise office buildings shot out towards him. The London of Curtis's marriage – south-of-the-river London, Victorian terraces with cherry blossom snowing on the pavements and frilly stonework picked out in white, laconic two-tone cats on old grey walls and giant blowzy rhododendrons shouldering their way through iron railings – considered from a plane, that London did not exist at all.

Curtis felt an urge to define it properly for his fellow passengers, some system of labelling such as his mother had used at the parties of his suburban youth: little paper flags on cocktail-stick flagpoles waving festively on top of piles of sandwiches – cheese n'chive, chicken n'ham, sardine n'cucumber. Mrs Fisher was the very first mother in their North London neighbourhood to abbreviate 'and' to 'n''. This, in addition to the fact that she went out to work, gave Curtis his own doorkey from six years old and expected him to iron his own clothes, caused people to think of her as fast and neglectful. Her parties, aimed at introducing herself to the neighbours when she first moved down from Leeds, were poorly attended. In fact, she was a good mother and to be congratulated, since Curtis's upbringing made him an exceptional husband who did half the housework without even having to be told.

The first paper flag would have 'Our Restaurant' on it, he decided. Our Restaurant – what a lot of time they had given over to eating and drinking in 1971, the year he met Millie. Lunches that began at midday and closed at tea-time, followed by bed. In 1971 they seemed to spend so much time in bed. And then got up and went out for long dinners, while a group called the O'Jays sang a song called 'Back Stabbers'. What had the words been? He couldn't recall exactly. He seemed to think there hadn't been many. It was mainly a case of, 'Back Stabbers,' and 'Whoo-hoo-oo'. But the tune still haunted him.

Millie Francis as she was then, fresh out of stage school, still in her teens, holes in her knickers but with all her life before her. She had a room in a house on the borders of Maida Vale, with coconut matting on the floor and a stone vase full of rushes in the fireplace. They made love on a lumpy mattress while Laura Nyro played on a record deck balanced on an upturned blue plastic milk crate. 'Stoney End', 'He's A Runner', 'Wedding Bell Blues'. In summer when the windows were open the music flowed out into the warm dusty air, mingling sometimes with Millie's cries of ecstasy.

Curtis was a twenty-four-year-old theatrical agent, all cosmopolitan sophistication in Fu Manchu moustache and mildly flared trousers. He met Millie for the first time in the waiting room of Plantagenet and Schwartz, theatrical agents to the stars. 'I'm going to be a star,' said Millie, 'but in the mean time, can you get me some work?'

She was small and self-contained. She wore a hat from Biba with a wide floppy brim, a cream vest with red stripes and size 8 wide-legged jeans. Over the next few months he took her to French restaurants, Italian restaurants, chophouses, brasseries, fish restaurants, bistros, Chinese, Greek. He got his money back on his expense account by claiming to have lunched the cream of British theatre. Their Restaurant was in a green-painted Victorian villa in Putney where the owner recited the menu at them while they were in the process of (they thought) breaking up.

'Starters. Mr McGregor's Soup. Lettuce lightly sautéed in butter than simmered in a delicate rabbit stock with chopped chives, tarragon and sorrel and topped with a whirl of cream. Tailor of Gloucester pâté.'

'If you're taking the New York job I'll never see you again so we might as well finish now,' said Millie, stubbing her cigarette out and lighting another one.

'Come with me,' said Curtis. He realized with a terrific sense of fatality that she was the one, that she had to stay with him for ever. 'I want you to be with me out there.' Seeing Millie's look of contempt and fury. Helplessly. 'Look, I know I'm not particularly good-looking . . . or, or very rich . . . but I love you.'

'Double Gloucester cheese pounded in a pestle and mortar with shalots, borage, sea salt, freshly ground green peppercorns and cream, and served with crisp wedges of lettuce and toasted herb bread.'

'What about my career?' exploded Millie. When she was indignant her chin jutted out. 'All the years I've trained, all the hours I've worked, I'm just to chuck that in to be your transatlantic fuck?'

'What career?' said Curtis. 'Wobbling your tits in fleapits is a career?'

'I don't do that.'

'You haven't worked for weeks. You owe rent. You can see the road through the floor of your car. Where else are you going to get the money?'

Millie picked up her bag and walked out. Curtis had to chase after her with her junk-shop fur coat with the torn pocket hanging out.

'Millie, Millie, I'm saying let's get married.'

'I don't want to get married. I want to be a dancer and if I have to wobble my tits in fleapits to get there, so be it. But I won't have to. Something's going to happen for me soon, you'll see.'

'All right, then,' said Curtis. 'I won't go to New York.'

Millie was crying. 'I don't want you to do that on account of me.' She opened another packet of cigarettes, her second of the day.

'Don't you love me?'

'I do, I do, but I haven't done enough with my life yet.'

'When you have.'

'I don't know. Maybe.'

Their Restaurant. Now pulled down along with the rest of the block to make way for a Sainsbury's. 'Starters. A giant heap of broken window frames nestling on a pile of rubble, surrounded by corrugated iron and patrolled by guard dogs.' Like Where We First Made Love, in Curtis's Ford Capri in the secluded driveway of an empty mansion south of the river at two o'clock

27

one morning. Millie's left leg dangling out of the front near-side window, her right foot switching on the push-button radio in her passion.

Place a flag there now and it would fly on top of a Development of Exclusive 4 and 5 bedroom homes, First Phase Now Complete. Curtis wondered if the Breakfasting Kitchen was haunted by the sound of their lovemaking. Floating up through the waste disposal unit. 'Yes! Yes! Oh God, yes!' 'Sweetheart!' 'Aaargh!' Shy Millie losing all sense of self at these times. 'Ooh, I'm coming, ooh, ooh, ooh!' she shrieked like a backing singer. Back Stabbers, Whoo-hoo-oo.

Jointly, they bought a flat in a mansion block in Battersea, just by Albert Bridge, which with its iron frills and furbelows resembled a wedding cake designed by Isambard Kingdom Brunel. Curtis's share of the flat was obtained with a mortgage. Millie reached into her bag and wrote out a cheque for £10,000. For that day outside Their Restaurant, Millie had been right. Something was about to happen for her.

A weekly spot on a variety show on telly, a West End musical, an American tour; that was how it was for Sweet Fanny Addams by the middle of that decade. Millie with alternatives to junk-shop fur coat and colander knickers. The love letters they got. Dear Millie, Will you marry me? The clothes they bought, the cigarettes they smoked.

A man slightly known to her took Millie out to lunch and during the course of conversation said, 'You would make the perfect dominatrix.' Her with her black bobbed hair and pointed shoes. 'That sounds quite interesting,' said Millie. 'What would I have to do, exactly?'

'You must dress all in black leather and carry a whip. The men would like it if you hid in a cupboard, then emerged from it at an appropriate time.'

'What,' said Millie, 'would the appropriate time be, I wonder?' The vodkas they drank, the limousines they purred around in. There was something about them, which was not perhaps a true representation of their real hearts and lives, but which was nevertheless there; rustling, virginal, in bud. They were chaste and erotic at the same time. There were other groups of girls who danced, but none evoked such mysterious yearning as Sweet Fanny Addams in their prime.

As far as Curtis could remember, the group started to fold up long before that terrible moment at the wedding. It had been eroding away for a couple of years. Blonde Collette Sweet, who had the kind of hair you wanted to go to sleep in – she was the first to leave, on the arm of her famous American film star. Tina Addams, who by dint of being the oldest and the only one who could ever talk about money without stammering or hesitation, was acknowledged as leader of the group. She brought in a couple of replacements but neither really worked out. The wedding; that was when there was the disaster with little auburn-haired Juliet. And the sullen one with hair the colour of office tea, the one who started the disaster, what ever happened to her? Ratty, they called her. He remembered now. Alexa was her real name, but nobody ever used it. Even the fans called her Ratty. She had a really funny surname, too – Cuntface or something. Ratty Alexa – the world's worst-tempered girl.

In the autumn of 1981, Curtis and Millie got married. She wore a long cream dress of embroidered silk and tulle (Anastasia again) with a little straw hat. It rained from the minute she stepped out of the car, which made the hat smell bad. He would never forget her as a bride, sitting on the synagogue steps in her French frock with her chin uptilted defiantly towards the streaming water. 'Behold, you are consecrated unto me by this ring, according to the law of Moses and Israel.'

Tina Addams was her maid of honour, Ratty her page, and Juliet her Best Woman, having after prolonged prayer realized that it was her duty to represent Jesus at a Jewish wedding. Collette wasn't anything. She had been long gone by then, swimming lazily up and down a blue pool in the Beverly Hills morning.

The girls got Millie ready in the bedroom of the flat in Battersea. Curtis had to dress in the bathroom, or it would have been unlucky. He had eyes and ears, though. 'How could you?' said Ratty, bottom lip stuck out as she sewed fresh flowers into Millie's head-dress. Hennaed hair sprang in a fierce wobbling tuft above Ratty's strange domed forehead. She wore a grey velvet knickerbocker suit and a white lawn shirt with a huge frilled ruffle that made her look like a saucepan of milk boiling over. 'After all you've achieved, just to throw it away on a man. You're as bad as Collette.'

'I *did* invite Michaela,' protested Millie. 'You said you wouldn't insult her by expecting her to –'

'You made it very clear that she wasn't welcome.'

'I only said that I hoped it wouldn't make her feel –'

'Now look 'ere, Ratty!' said Tina, adopting the good-humoured sergeant-major manner to which she resorted when wishing to impose discipline without any crockery being broken. 'It's Millie's wedding and the girl's entitled to invite 'oo she wants.'

'I wasn't talking to you.'

Tina's tail started to swish. 'Millie asked you to be her page out of kindness because she thought you felt left out, so just you leave off giving her a hard time, darling.'

'Oh, just fuck off the pair of you, why don't you.' Ratty stabbed her finger with the needle and blood spurted on to the lilies. 'Fuck it!'

Juliet's face went all solemn and churchy. 'Look at those clouds,' she said. 'I do hope the weather's going to hold out.'

'Up your arse.'

'I think we all ought to read the order of service quietly,' said Juliet, 'and remember what we're here for – a wedding.'

'Oh drat,' said Tina in a lazy kind of way, 'and I thought we were off to the World Basket-Weaving Championship.'

'God has a lot to offer someone like you, Tina.'

Ratty curled her lip. 'A new Ford Sierra? Two weeks in Morocco? A wall clock?'

'It's all right, Ratty,' said Juliet, smiling brightly. 'God can take a joke.'

'And your middle name is Puke-making.'

Tina said, 'Now then, Ratty, I don't think you should talk like that.' Something in her tone of voice made Millie try frantically but unsuccessfully to catch her eye. 'You see, Ratty,' said Tina earnestly, 'I've been thinking lately about all that Juliet's told us about God, and how happy and peaceful she is now she's found him, and I do believe there may be something in it.'

'Is that right, Juliet?' said Ratty, turning to her.

'Oh, Ratty,' said Juliet, 'if I could just *convince* you of God's relevance to your *life*.'

'I must seem really stupid,' said Ratty, 'but how can She be relevant to my life?'

'You could ask . . .' Juliet smiled indulgently, 'you could ask *Her*. Why don't we pray together? Let's kneel.' She got a little bible out of her red dorothy bag. 'What do I ask Her for?' said Ratty.

'Anything you like.'

'Oh. Well. God. Haha. Hi. It's me. Alexa. You can call me Ratty if you want. I'd, um – I say, Juliet, are you quite sure this is on?'

'Oh yes!'

'Okeydoke. God, I'd like to ask you for a *big soft girl with a tongue like a boa constrictor and a great huge bottom.*'

There was a long, long silence. Millie passed her hand across her forehead and realized she had been sweating for quite a while.

Juliet said, 'I feel sorry for you, Ratty, truly I do.'

Millie turned to Tina and said, as though the last few minutes hadn't happened, 'I've had a career for six years. I've been quite famous. I've got half a flat, a new Renault 5, a spare room full of clothes, and nearly a five-figure sum in my bank account. You know, and I wake up every morning and my life seems silly and empty. I want children . . .'

Tina banged the tray of buttonholes she was making on to the floor and ran out into the street in her cherry-pink maid of honour's dress with the basque front barely containing her magnificent breasts. She hadn't told anyone, but she'd just had another abortion. She was going to get into her car and drive away very fast in it but when she tried to open the door she dropped the keys. She was kneeling on the pavement, scrabbling around in the gutter for them when some skinheads came by. At the time, Tina was no longer as famous as she used to be, and anyway, it was her backside not her face they saw.

'Out of the way, fatty!' one of them said. 'Cluck-cluck, cluck-cluck!'

Tina sprang up and roared like a lioness. She pulled the basque front down and swung her breasts at the boys, who scattered, terrified. Quietly, Tina tucked herself in again. Difficult times required difficult solutions, she always thought.

Meanwhile, back in Millie's flat, Ratty was chasing Juliet round the bedroom.

'You feel sorry for me?' gasped Ratty. 'You presume to feel sorry for me? Listen, you sex-starved pill, I feel sorry for *you* that the only way you can get through life is to kid yourself that up there some old bloke in pyjamas, some filthy old *man* who can't even be bothered to use a shaver, is taking time off between throwing aeroplanes at mountainsides to talk you through your piddly little existence. How egotistical can you get? I'm telling you! Take this away and you've got nothing! You're just some plastic doll with a silly smile!' Ratty got her cornered by the wardrobe and grabbed the bible.

'Ratty – Alexa – *please.*' Juliet's voice was quiet, pleading.

Ratty brayed, as though cheering on the Lower Fourth at hockey. 'What would you do if you didn't have this?'

She jumped on a chair, and ripped pages out of the bible while Juliet tried to grab it back from her, but Ratty was much taller than Juliet and just waved it out of reach. 'What are you going to do now, Juliet? Hadn't you better fetch God, quick? Run along now. Tell him what wicked Ratty is doing. Tell him there's a sin going on. No, hang on a sec. Isn't he meant to be up there listening? You say all I have to do is ask and he'll be there? Right. Sit yourself down, Juliet. I'll tell him myself. God! God, are you watching? Can you stop killing thousands of babies in a famine for a moment and tune in to us? Arr, come on, God. Give me a sign. Make my hair fall out. Turn me into a parsnip. Let's hear it from you, God. A bit of thunder. A jolly old flash of lightning. Where are you, God? Juliet needs you right now. Turn up and strike me down!'

'Uh,' said Curtis, emerging from the bathroom. 'Is there anything I can do?'

'What the *hell* are you doing in here?' demanded Ratty. 'Juliet, tell Millie there's an intruder in her bathroom.'

'I'm only the fucking bridegroom, missus!' Curtis shouted,

pursuing a squealing Juliet down the stairs. Millie was already in the street, running to Tina, the hem of her beautiful French dress trailing on the pavement. 'What's wrong, Tina?'

'Wrong, darling?' The experience with the boys had invigorated Tina and calmed her. 'Why should anything be wrong? I just remembered I left my car unlocked, that's all.'

Slowly, everyone else came down the steps and into the street.

Engulfing Ratty in a busty hug, Tina drew her to one side. 'Now then, young Alexa,' she murmured, 'I forgive you almost everything for the stand you took against the Virgin Mary back there, but don't think you've got away scot free. Any more carrying on and fuck this and fuck that from you and you're finished. Got that?'

'Yes,' Ratty snapped. 'Message understood.'

Tina said, 'And Juliet. Less of the toilet-face please. In my opinion, you've been asking for all that and more for some weeks. Right?'

Juliet sniffed, smoothing the creases out of her bible. 'Right.'

'Good,' said Tina briskly. 'That's all sorted out, then. This is the happiest day of Millie's life and no one is going to spoil it. Now, are we ready to go?' She looked around. 'Millie? Curtis?'

Curtis and Millie were muttering in private either side of an adjacent pillar box. 'So you're getting married because you've nothing better to do, huh?' Curtis said.

'What?'

'Not because you love me, oh no.'

'I *do* love you.'

'A bit late to start all that now.'

'Come along now, my darlings,' ordered Tina, trying to push them into the wedding car. 'No time for that.'

'Would you leave us alone, Tina?' said Curtis.

'Curtis!' hissed Millie, who had not yet negotiated a satisfactory new contract with Tina. But also she loved Tina dearly and knew that she was not immune to hurt. She looked at her now and realized how bowed her shoulders had become in the past few months. 'We'll only be a moment, Tina,' she said.

'Very well,' said Tina, 'If you insist on playing his pathetic game it's nothing to do with me. When you're carried into casualty on a stretcher with your face bashed in, a victim of male violence, don't blame me.'

'Don't go,' Millie said pleadingly to Curtis, tugging his sleeve. She knew he was trying it on but she still felt a bitch. In the occasional moment of great cold clarity it would come to her mind that she might not have married him had Sweet Fanny Addams been as big now as it was in 1976. 'Don't go,' she said.

'Well.' Curtis hunched his shoulders and stood sideways on to her. 'Well, I don't know.'

After two years of marriage, Mr and Mrs Curtis Fisher moved to a house in Wandsworth, and Our First Flat was demolished under a road-widening scheme. The synagogue where they were wed was turned into studio apartments with a tactfully designed hamburger restaurant on the ground floor. When Curtis looked back, his past with Millie had disappeared like the wake of a ship.

Disappearing. That was something he had always been frightened of Millie doing. A Sagittarian with the moon in Virgo; footloose and restless, practical, urban and shy. Even after they were married he sometimes had the feeling that they were only tied together by a strand of cotton. He found himself doing things he didn't really want to, just to keep her happy. He did not much like their house, for instance, with its dark Victorian rooms and sunless back garden patrolled by two self-absorbed shag-pile cats. He would have preferred the country. He dared not tell Millie this, because she would say, 'Then we must live in the country.' Millie in the country – it would be like trying to grow orchids in Piccadilly.

'Then we must live in the country.' Sometimes in one of his gloomier moods, when in the grip of some recessive genes bestowed on him by his Russian forebears, Curtis knew that Millie did not love him: she was too willing to do what he wanted.

She missed the group, that was the trouble. No, it wasn't just missing the group, she was cruelly bereaved by its sudden disintegration, she mourned it. 'If we could just dance together again it would be all right,' she said.

'It's over now. You'll have to accept it. It's gone – like England's world supremacy at football.'

'I miss them so much.'

'But you all hated each other by the end.'

'I'd still do anything to have them back again.'

Curtis always thought she would calm down once they had the baby she longed for. Five years of trying. No joy. Millie started seeing specialists, then they had a joint appointment. Curtis had to provide a sperm sample. He was given a pile of *Playboys* and shown into a cubicle. He managed the best part of a teaspoonful. 'That's not very much, is it?' said the specialist. Curtis felt humiliated and would not go back with Millie to hear the results.

'He says there's nothing wrong with either of us,' she reported on her return. 'It's just a question of relaxing and letting nature take its course.'

'Don't leave me, will you?'

'Oh, for heaven's sake.'

For two more years their childlessness was like an uncovered well. They couldn't bear to approach it closely, either to throw a lid over it or to look down into it. The well was in a garden, and because the garden reminded them of the well, they could not go into the garden either.

Then Florence came to live with them.

It was in the summer. They went to meet her off the boat train from Paris. As they drove back to London she spent half the time laughing and half crying. She had fled Paris in a hurry and consequently had only 250 francs and a bicycle to her name. They couldn't get the bicycle into the car so they left it on the pavement for someone to steal. Millie and Curtis both had to lend her some of their clothes.

She moved in with them, became their child, their friend, their project. They started drinking lots of wine again and had proper sit-down dinners with home-made French dressing on the salad, and side plates on the table, and bread, and coffee. 'It's important,' said Florence. 'It's a family thing.'

Curtis wasn't sure, but he thought she'd probably saved their marriage.

At night, Millie sat on Florence's bed and watched over her sleeping. She had put Florence in the little room at the top of the house. It had green flowery wallpaper and an iron fireplace that Millie had coloured white. The brush had left three long black bristles in the paint. There was a basket of dried flowers in the grate. Here Millie remembered the girl she herself had been. Just starting out and everything new and exciting. She remembered arriving at parties in December, standing expectantly in doorways in Willesden and Brent, wrapped against the cold in Horatio. She always seemed to be in the shadow of someone bigger; first her mother, then girls she'd met at auditions, old friends from stage school, later Tina and Collette. 1970, 71, it would have been. She'd have a bottle of Lambrusco in her hand and under Horatio would be a jumble-sale frock, a sagging low-waisted thirties thing, a profusion of flowers on a background of black. She looked so good in that frock. Maybe she still had it somewhere. Maybe Florence would like to wear it.

Oh, those long ago days. There was that old-fashioned blue phone book she'd kept beside her bed, full of names of men she'd almost forgotten. Andrew, Richard, Tony, Stuart. All married now, probably, with children called Tom and Hannah. Days of worrying because her period was late, and whether the post would bring one of those windowed envelopes from her bank manager. Dear Miss Francis, I notice that your account is at present £175.23 overdrawn against the agreed limit of £100. Will you please arrange to place the account within the limit or go and fuck yourself.

When she wasn't worrying about money she'd be thinking about sex, at least ten times an hour it seemed. Sex and clothes; wandering through Ossie Clark's shop in the King's Road, ready to die for an electric blue crêpe skirt. Clothes, and nights out; driving home behind a milk float, a misty morning beginning to dawn over the city. Sleeping till midday then lying in bed smoking dope while the afternoon came and went.

'We'll re-form the group,' thought Millie to herself. 'Sweet Fanny Addams II.' She had something else to think about at last.

One morning she nerved herself up to go to Legwork

(London), Tina Addams's dance studio and company head-quarters by the river at Fulham. It was the first time she had seen it except in newspaper photos. Tina had certainly done well for herself since the group fell apart. Millie pushed her way through the plate-glass doors, wondering whether she was still loud and terrifying. They hadn't spoken for seven years. For some reason Millie had a sudden recollection of Tina striding into the kitchen of the flat they used to share. Tina was always a girl who liked to lead with her tits. She was wearing a pale pink T-shirt and nothing else, and roaring, 'All right, which of you fuckers has got my knickers?' at an audience consisting of the meter man, the builder and Collette's mother who had stayed overnight after coming up to town for Christmas shopping.

Millie was so unnerved by the memory that she hardly noticed the Legwork décor, beyond a general impression of black and white. Behind the reception desk was a middle-aged man wearing a checked lumberjack shirt. He was working the switchboard. 'Hello, Legwork London, can I help you? Just one minute, please.' Switch, click, plug. Ring, ring. He had a pleasant, sing-song voice, like a vicar leading a congregation in responses. 'Hello, Legwork London, can I help you?' There was a cardboard box on the floor by the desk, packed with crisps. 'More' – than a – 'snack'! it said on the side. 'Tomato sauce'! 'Indian tandoori'! 'Mexican chilli'! A slim black youth with a blue headscarf tied neatly over his hair leant against the counter, talking to his friend. 'You can get really stale, can't you,' he was saying sym-pathetically, 'night after night like that.'

Disco music was playing somewhere. Millie tracked it down through some double doors and along a corridor which had windows set in the wall. Of course, the rehearsal room. Millie stood on her toes and peeped in. She saw a big woman of forty with dark flying hair, working out alone. Millie's eyes took in a black leotard and tights with all sorts of bits and bulges straining to get out. As she turned the corner and stepped into the rehearsal room, there was a ripping noise and a white circle of flesh slowly broke through the tights like the moon from behind clouds.

The woman looked up before Millie had time to retreat into the corridor. Millie said, 'Hello, Tina.'

'What the fuck do you mean by barging in on me like this?' screamed Tina, leaping for her towelling robe.

Millie figured she wasn't going to get very long to state her case, so she said, 'I'm here to ask if you'll let me re-form the group.'

'Are you,' said Tina in a voice full of iron filings. In the hurry to pick up her robe she had landed heavily on her ankle and sprained it painfully. 'Well, now you have asked me and if you don't have any more questions there's the door behind you.'

'I don't see why you've got to talk to me like that,' said Millie.

'Don't you jut your chin at me, Millie Francis or Frobisher or whatever you call yourself now.'

'Me? It wasn't my fault what happened.'

'Did anything happen?' said Tina. 'I don't remember.'

'Tina, will you stop that! Have you any idea what it's taken for me to come up here today? If I could have asked this of anybody else but you, I would have. And don't say your heart bleeds for me.' Abruptly, the disco tape came to an end. A police siren wailed a long way off. Millie said pleadingly, 'A new group could really take off. It's the right time, the right mood. Four girls and me. I'll dance for a year to get us re-established, then – '

'Who dreamed this up? The Airhead?' Tina had turned her face away from Millie's. She was combing her hair, roughly as if it didn't belong to her.

'I haven't seen Collette for years. Juliet either.'

Tina went on combing. Millie waited, then said, 'I swear to God.'

'Ouch! Shit!' Tina threw the comb across the floor, then looked round at Millie again. 'I don't want to know,' she said. 'It's a really stupid scheme, plus I'm too busy.'

'Tina, you make me so sad. Really you do. What happened, everything, it's such a long time ago.'

At that moment a girl with white-blonde hair launched herself into the rehearsal room. 'Tina, what the hell is going on? I've driven miles out of my way to see you and you're not even in your office. I've just been waiting in there like a fool.'

Tina said, in the lazy way in which, Millie remembered, she

used to quell riots in the old days, 'Joanna-Mary, this is Millie Fisher.'

'Hello.' Joanna-Mary turned back to Tina. 'I can't believe you made me go to that audition. It was a total farce. I don't know why they bothered to hold it. They'd already decided to use those fucking cows who danced on the *Smart Money* programme.'

'Joanna-Mary,' Tina said to Millie, 'wants to be a dancer.'

'Talk to me!' shouted Joanna-Mary. 'I've been working my guts out all morning in front of a bunch of fucking cunts and you just sit there like a great black beetle!'

'No swearies, darling,' said Tina. 'Its not at all clever.'

'Oh Tina, I'm, um, um, sorry, it's just this whole business is getting me down.' Joanna-Mary burst quite attractively into tears.

Millie said, 'Well then, I'd better be going.'

'No,' said Tina. She put her hand over Millie's. 'Millie's come up with an idea,' she said to Joanna-Mary. 'I think you'll be interested.'

And now . . .

Now Curtis was a director of Plantagenet and Schwartz, with special responsibilities for their sports interests. He represented footballers, athletes, some boxers and a woman who cycled. He had just concluded some business in Australia. He had a jersey for Millie which he worried she would not like, and a suitcase full of toys. They were for the baby which Millie had told him, on the eve of his trip, that she was expecting. 'Nature has taken its course,' she said.

'What about Sweet Fanny Addams?' said Curtis.

'Florence can take over everything,' said Millie. She paused. Thoughtfully. 'Everything.'

But the suitcase full of toys triggered off a surprisingly enjoyable chat about fatherhood with a customs official, and Curtis was thinking about the future, not the past, as he left the customs hall. There, outside, a policeman and a chaplain were waiting. They seemed to be walking his way. For a moment Curtis thought they were there to tell him someone had broken into his car in long-term parking and stolen the Blaupunkt.

Chapter Four

A Theft

IN THE INTENSIVE care unit of the Herts and Middlesex General Hospital, Joanna-Mary was bollocking Janey. 'Well, I um, um, think it's a bit off, actually. You might have waited and come back to London with us. Lily was in a hell of a state. She kept trying to push me out of the car because she didn't like my earrings.'

'I'm sorry.' Janey hung her head. Being a kind person, as well as not terribly confident, she tended to get bollocked by everyone.

'No, well, really, you know what it looks like, don't you, it looks like some sort of attempt to ditch the rest of us and grab all the publicity for yourself.'

'Oh no,' wept Janey, who all that strange and sleepless night had staved off her tears, and who consequently had a great number of them all dammed up and waiting for a small breach in the wall. 'Joanna-Mary, I promise, I went out of my way to avoid the press.'

'Well, I could have done with your help back there, actually. I had to beard them all on my own.'

'Sorry,' said Janey.

'I suppose you haven't been to her flat, either.' Joanna-Mary glanced at Florence, as if for confirmation. Florence's face was turned to the wall, and her eyes were in any case closed. Scabs tufted with stitches stuck out like grass from a sand-dune. Joanna-Mary counted them anxiously.

'Oh dear,' said Janey. 'Should I have?'

'Well, someone's got to get her things. Don't you think she

might like some of her favourite tapes and um, um teddy bear? It never changes. I'm the only one who thinks of these things.'

Janey said, 'I'll go now.'

'Oh, stay where you are. Where's her handbag?' Joanna-Mary plunged her hand into the bedside table and fished around. Her hands were trembling so much that the keys jangled, but she presumed that Janey was too much of a dope to make anything of it.

By then it was half-past eleven in the morning.

Lily Smith was meant to take over the bedside vigil from Janey but the taxi taking her there went via the King's Road.

'We got held up in the traffic,' said Lily, dragging half a dozen susurrating carrier bags into Florence's cubicle.

'I never heard of a flipping traffic jam lasting half the afternoon and all of the night,' said Janey indignantly. 'You were meant to be here yesterday.'

'Oh, you know how it is,' said Lily. 'I just sort of had one peep in the window of Russell and Bromley, where sadly I saw the pair of tan calfskin boots without which my life would be but a walking shadow.'

'Don't start on one of your audition pieces,' said Greg.

'And Yves St Laurent was practically next door so it seemed silly not to look at their jackets, which you have to regard as an investment. The T-shirts were a silly price, but you only live once. Oh, Greg, don't look at me like that.'

Greg was twitchy because they weren't allowed to smoke in the intensive care unit. He was so tired his skin was the colour of his Reeboks. He was pacing up and down the best he could in the space the cubicle had to offer. He said, 'Lily, I know you better than to impute any sinister motive to you, but it looks so bad, as if you didn't care.'

'Oh well,' said Lily, 'Florence never thought much of my conversation while she was all there, so she's going to get even less out of it now she's a vegetable.'

Greg turned to Janey. 'Where's Joanna-Mary?'

'Gone to pick up Florence's things.'

'I'll go over now. She may appreciate a hand.' He glared at Lily and went out.

'Yeah, well,' said Lily, 'I can't hang around. I've got a tap class at one-thirty.'

Greg rode down the escalator and crossed the foyer, lighting a cigarette. He whistled to himself, more for reassurance than anything. There were three old people in wheelchairs lined up just inside the doors, not doing anything, not even breathing as far as he could see. Greg went over the road and started up his car. The cassette was loaded with a Tina Turner tape. He fast-forwarded it to 'Private Dancer' and moved into the traffic stream.

Greg was slim, fair and handsome, though almost completely without vanity; he used mirrors to check that his collar was straight, his jacket neatly buttoned, his trousers properly moored. He had just finished at university, where he had bonked and overslept and drunk enormous amounts of spirits in a con-trolled sort of way. His aim was to go far in his career so he could ensure a comfortable widowhood for his mother. He was, said his mother, desperate for a job connected with the theatre.

'In that case, you're for us,' said Millie, and welcomed him aboard.

Greg was their PR, agent, roadie, agony aunt, secretary, bag-gage-carrier, chauffeur, Tampax-dispenser, lawyer, psychiatrist, archivist, umpire, surrogate brother and whipping-boy. He was in love with all the girls, in the most latent kind of way. He had always succeeded very prudently in depressing any sexual stirrings he felt for them. Much of the time, he carried a serious newspaper into which he could plunge when they drifted past him naked from the shower or murmured to him to do up zips or buttons over sweet-smelling downy flesh.

But sometimes he wondered whether there was more to it than that. Whether in some way he was saving himself for Collette Sweet, the toast of the Naughty Club.

The Naughty Club. At nine years old, Greg and his friends Duncan and Daniel, and Jonathan Waddell if he truanted from his piano lesson, had carefully clipped pictures of Collette Sweet out of newspapers and magazines for the collection that Greg kept in a suitcase under his bed. Along with photographs show-ing headless torsoes advertizing bras, and some of the racier

42

vests in the Damart Thermawear catalogue, and pages torn from copies of the *Pictorial*, for which they trawled litter bins and gutters on their way home from school. The Naughty Club. There had been a constitution, a list of rules and regulations. Places Where Items of Intrest Can Be Found:

1. The Pictorial.
2. The Grattan Catalogue.
3. Woman's Own.
4. Sometimes in Good Housekeeping.

All their pictures showed Collette Sweet dressed, although over one of them Jonathan Waddell had drawn the approximate contours of the female form, added nipples and pubic hair, then in a fit of terror that his mother would find out, concealed these biro-coloured charms under a stout all-in-one corset with plenty of gusset. And that was quite apt in a smutty sort of way, for Collette was not really there for what she showed, but what she hid, like the rest of the girls in Sweet Fanny Addams in the 1970s. Their stock in trade was little flashes of flesh, an ankle, long legs, young round bottoms in lace. And of them all, Collette was the most beautiful.

How Greg's heart had ached when Collette went away to America to get married. First he daydreamed of the film star treating her very badly, of Collette in a locked room in a burning building from which he would rescue her. Later he realized this was immature, and went around with his hands in his pockets, slamming his shoulder into neighbours' garden fences and muttering, 'Women!'

Greg had all but buried this until the morning after Millie's death when he watched breakfast television and saw her again. The accident was already taking hold of the national imagination. Old lags from Fleet Street, who had once been young and hopeful and able to get into tight jeans, lamented their lost youth. In one paper was a picture of the girls in a dressing room where knickers had been laid out to dry on hot-water pipes and a cigarette burned unclaimed in an ashtray. Greg studied it for a while. It must have been around 1972 by the look of the clothes. Juliet was in bra and pants in the foreground, reaching for a can of hairspray, her lips slightly parted, her eyelashes hard and black with mascara. Behind her, Collette bent forward in concentration, staring herself down in the mirror, a thin band of dark ribbon tied round her hair. Tina leant against the vanitory unit in a satin housecoat, applying lipstick to her mouth. The vanitory unit ran the length of one wall and there were mirrors all the way. At the far end, Millie lolled on it, curled up, perhaps sleeping. On the adjoining wall was an ancient radiator. Ratty was sitting on it. All around them were kitbags and suitcases, giving Greg a sensation of rootlessness and imper- manence that left him close to tears. Meanwhile on breakfast television, snippets of film from the seventies played twice an hour, of Sweet Fanny Addams in those long-ago days much loved by Millie. She was towards the left of the stage. They were dancing to a bouncy tune called 'Young Hearts Run Free', by Candi Staton. And Greg's heart ached again, not for Millie but for Collette Sweet.

Joanna-Mary let herself into Florence's flat more quietly than she needed to, since she was legitimately there. Her eyes raked the dark, untidy front room decorated with arty posters and chipped Deco china. The place was stale with smoke, and some of Florence's discarded dresses lay on the carpet as though they had crawled out of the bedroom seeking help. The teacups on the floor by the hearth had a half-inch of liquid at the bottom of each one in which cigarette ends floated wanly. An unwashed plate bearing half a slice of toast and a little caterpillar of ash completed the décor. 'A slut.' She actually said it out loud. Florence ate, slept and God knew what else in this dirty place. It gave Joanna-Mary a kind of angry thrill.

She helped herself to a shot of whiskey from the bottle of Jack Daniels on the hideous oak sideboard. Maybe it would stop her hands shaking. Through the grimy window she could see the parade of shops opposite. There was a Greek grocer selling wrinkled black olives and wooden cartons of old mottled peas. Cars roared past, dredging them in petrol-tainted dust. Next door Rushey Green Electrical Supplies featured a display of orange extension cables and a toaster packaged in drab cardboard. A man ran across the street in a break in the traffic, carrying a ginger-haired child in his arms. She leant against the wall and listened to the thumping of her heart.

Joanna-Mary had met Florence for the first time at the inaugural meeting of Sweet Fanny Addams II in the Territorial Army hall. There was a kind of chemical disturbance as soon as they saw each other. It was one of those relationships where people hate each other immediately and instinctively. Sulphur smelt and water hissed. There was nothing that could be done about it.

It was a dull day in late November 1988. The windows were high on the wall and misted up. They filled the room with a sad, waxy light. The girls were larking around to a scratched recording of 'You're So Vain'. They bent forwards with one arm outstretched and the other on the side of their waists and sang to the music,

I had some dreams but they were clouds in my coffee,
Clouds in my coffee,
Ooh . . .

Millie dragged a paraffin stove on to the floor and used her fur coat to block the draught from under the door. She hated standing up and giving speeches. She fiddled with her straight black hair and said, 'Anyway, hallo everybody, welcome to Sweet Fanny Addams. This is Lily, this is Janey, this is Joanna-Mary, this is me, Millie, and this is Florence.'

Joanna-Mary glanced at a slim young woman in a purple polo neck and black leggings. Her watch strap was fastened over the sleeve of her jersey and she hadn't bothered to comb her hair properly.

'Hi,' said Joanna-Mary. She'd heard all about Florence from Tina. Florence was funny. Florence was French. Florence was this. Florence was that. She'd already heard enough about Florence to last her till the other side of next Christmas. She turned to Millie and said privately, 'We're not just going to get jobbing dancers, are we? Tina was very keen that we'd get some names.'

Taken aback, Millie said, 'Lily has done six months in *Les Mis*. Janey's just danced on the Basilica tour.'

'Great,' said Joanna-Mary. 'And Florence?'

'Florence has been working as a dancer at one of the top theatres in Paris.'

Joanna-Mary could swear she saw Florence and Millie catch each other's eye and try not to laugh. Millie went on, 'And she has a teaching diploma from ballet school. We're very lucky to have her.'

'You don't mind my asking? I feel a responsibility to Tina. I want us to have the best.'

Florence said, 'And you, Joanna-Mary? Tell me all about what you've done.'

Joanna-Mary turned her back on Florence and said to Millie, 'Did you get the ideas I sent you for routines? They're only suggestions. I have plenty more.'

Florence could sense Millie's agitation. She knew how Millie hated to upset anyone. Millie was the kind of person who would go through agonies herself rather than cause pain. Her house was full of bugs she couldn't bear to kill.

'Yes,' said Florence, 'Millie and I had a good look at them.'

Joanna-Mary stiffened.

There was a pause.

'*And*?' said Joanna-Mary with an encouraging smile.

'Thank you,' added Florence politely. She put some more music on. 'And now I think you should warm up, yes, like the rest of us have been doing?'

Joanna-Mary was damned if she was going to be told what was what by some lost fucking dog of Millie's. She said to Florence. 'A teaching diploma? Well, I hope you aren't going to try and teach me to dance.'

'No,' said Florence. 'That would be a waste of time.'

After the rehearsal was over, Millie and Florence went to Geronimo's. They sat at a table with a gravy-stained tablecloth under some autographed photos of celebrities which Geronimo had picked up at a book sale in a church hall. Millie and Florence sometimes tried to guess who they were.

'Look,' said Florence carefully, 'if you would rather she was your number two, please say. I wouldn't make it hard for you. It's heaven to be in the group at all.'

'You what? Blimey, the only hope I have is that she'll grow on us.'

'Warts grow on you,' said Florence. 'You don't ask them to join your group.'

Millie said, 'Florence, I swear that if she was dancing at the bottom of my garden I'd close the curtains. But we have to keep her nice.'

'Really? You didn't tell me there was a set of house rules.'

Millie said, 'Don't think I brought her into the group. She was Tina's little present to me. I tried to change Tina's mind but Tina's a big girl, it was like pushing a steamroller uphill.' She sighed. 'I've got a bad feeling about this group. Florence. Sometimes I wish I'd never started it.'

'It'll be all right.' Florence put her hand over Millie's wrist. 'Try not to let that girl get you down. You've got me.'

Millie smiled lovingly. 'Yeah.'

That same night, Joanna-Mary ate out at Tina's invitation. They went to an Italian restaurant in a basement in Covent Garden. The diners ate at round tables covered in stiff white cloths. The tableware was blue and had flowers and dots and small creatures painted on it in yellow and red. Tina had spaghetti carbonara, T-bone steak and apple tart with cream. Joanna-Mary had spaghetti carbonara. There was pink champagne to drink, and capuccino afterwards. Tina had two capuccinos, and a marc.

'How did it go?' she said.

'Super,' said Joanna-Mary. 'Millie was really, really nice.'

'And Florence? Do you get on with Florence?'

'Oh yes. I'm going to learn a lot from Florence.'

'That's great,' beamed Tina. She put down her knife and fork and unwrapped the cellophane from a fresh pack of cigarettes. She was trying to cut down and now allowed herself only six a day, none to be smoked till dinner. Her wavy black hair disappeared temporarily behind a cloud exhaled in bliss. 'Your dad will be really pleased you've found something you like at last.'

'Daddy's filming in New York for the next three weeks. I'm stuck with stupid, boring Mummy.'

'Poor lovely. You've got me.'

'Millie was really interested in all my ideas.'

'Good,' said Tina caressingly. 'Well – work hard. Millie won't be the leader for ever.'

Quickly, too impatient even to check that she had fastened the front door properly behind her, Joanna-Mary went to the desk and started searching but it was in the hall, on the doormat with the other post, that retracing her steps she found what she wanted – a large brown foolscap envelope. It yielded a letter and contract from Millie, handing over control of Sweet Fanny Addams to Florence.

Another girl might have crowed. Joanna-Mary's self-control, however, was like the door of a bank vault.

She was about to start packing some of Florence's things into a case when a shadow discoloured the front door's frosted glass. As the door swung open, she stood like marble.

Greg said, 'Janey told me you were here. Do you need any help?'

In the delicious fear and relief of the moment, the knowledge that she was alive while Millie lay dead, and the suspicion that Greg might want to do something laboriously correct about the brown foolscap envelope if he got a long look at it, Joanna-Mary began kissing his hand. Then, writhing, she dragged him to the hall floor and unpeeled his jeans and boxer shorts. 'Gosh,' she said, and sat on him.

The girls had all speculated about Greg, during long nights backstage in Stoke-on-Trent and Catford, waiting to go on behind the International Magic of Dave Stromboli and Nadia. 'Perhaps he's gay,' said Janey.

'Pah!' said Florence. 'He has a two-inch willy.'

'I bet you it isn't,' said Lily.

'Do you know something we don't?'

'I spied on him in the dressing room,' said Lily. 'It's quite a pretty one, bigger than average with a sort of waist.'

'Oh Lily,' Janey said.

Meanwhile, back on the hall floor, Joanna-Mary pretended she was riding her palomino Rob Roy through the forest.

'No, no, stop,' moaned Greg. Then he groaned and shuddered.

'Sorry,' said Joanna-Mary, and went to fetch Florence's things, leaving him crumpled on the floor. Afterwards she realized that she had been clutching the brown foolscap envelope under one arm the whole time.

Curtis went from the airport straight to the hospital. There he had to identify Millie's body. It *was* Millie's body. There was no more hope. She was lying on some sort of trestle table covered by a white sheet with the name of the hospital stamped on it in purple. There was a hole in the sheet through which he could see a tiny bit of her arm.

In recent months he had often found himself calling Millie Florence and Florence Millie, and the shock made him even less able to draw the distinction. 'Yes, that's Florence.'

'We have a name of Millie Fisher.'

'That's my wife.'

They would only let him see her head. There was a patch of flimsy gauze on her brow and nothing more, as though she had only died of a graze. He stroked her cheek. It was cold. He desperately wanted to warm her, comfort her, take her in his arms, bathe her wounds. But they had told him not to remove the sheet. It was for the best, they said. Best for them, maybe. 'Don't you realize I'm her husband?' he wanted to say. Didn't they know he had cared for her when she was sick, cleaned up the vomit, kissed her better, woken sometimes in a lake of her menstrual blood? Now she was lying on a cold, cold table, covered with a sheet, and the one remaining way he could express his tenderness and care, the one last act of love and commitment he could bestow on her, was denied him.

'We have a name of Millie Fisher.'

'That's my wife.'

'Do you mean Millie Fisher is your wife or this is your wife?' they said gently.

'Both are my wives. 'Wife.'

After that the worst was over except for one moment when

49

they gave him the black plastic bag that contained Millie's belongings, and he cried because when he went to Australia he had had a wife and now all he had was a black plastic bag full of clothes.

Curtis sat on a bench in a park on a hill and tried to imagine what Millie's baby would have looked like. He hoped that, inside Millie when the crash was happening, it would not have suffered, that no pain or violence attended its passing, that it simply ebbed away, safe inside its mother till the last heartbeat.

He could not think of that other thing, of Millie dying, dying, dead.

When he reached home, he found a letter on the hall table, propped up, with his name on it, in Millie's writing.

Florence had waited in the car, outside Millie's house. They were late setting off for Hull. 'Can I help?' she said. 'Shall I come in?'

'No. Don't. I won't be long.'

Millie had been strangely preoccupied all through her ante-natal appointment. She had demanded that Florence come to keep her company, but why, Florence couldn't imagine, as hardly a word passed between them. Florence, who had lots to tell Millie, felt constrained by this invisible portcullis of silence.

I hope we are not going back to the bad time, she thought.

Then, when they left the hospital, instead of heading for the motorway straight away, Millie spun the car round and went speeding for home.

'No,' Millie said. 'Don't come in. I won't be long.'

Florence sat in the car and watched as Millie appeared in each and every room. What on earth . . . ? Millie seemed to be reaching out to touch each wall. She even kissed one of them. It's pregnancy, thought Florence. Pregnancy is doing this to her. She is hungry for the wall, the way that other women want prawns or coal.

Millie disappeared from view. Florence, for want of anything better to do, looked for a tape to put on the car stereo. Opening the glove box, she found 'Head over Heels' by the Cocteau Twins and put it on. In the glove box there was also an empty Marmite jar. Pregnancy, thought Florence again.

Then Millie came out of the house and they set off for the motorway.

'Did you get the contract I sent you?' said Millie. 'Are you happy with it?'

'I haven't opened the post yet. But I know it'll be fine.'

'If there's anything you want to change it's on the Amstrad. I only have to print it out again.'

After that, there was silence. Florence, looking across at her friend, thought, 'Why, she is wearing Horatio.'

The accident wiped all this from Florence's memory, so that even if Millie had told her everything she would not have realized it, would have had no chance to warn Curtis about the letter that Millie had propped up on the hall table. It was to say she was leaving him.

Chapter Five

Joanna-Mary Has a Tantrum

STEALING FLORENCE'S MAIL was not the only unethical thing
Joanna-Mary did.

At a meeting called by her in the Territorial Army hall the
future of the group was discussed over a catering-sized jar of
pickled onions, two pounds of extra-strong Cheddar cheese and
four French sticks. They were unable to eat at Geronimo's,
which had been temporarily closed by the Health and Safety
Inspectorate after one of the regulars found a rat looking up at
him when he went to the toilet.

Janey felt she ought not to be hungry, but she was. She ate a
whole French stick on her own, wishing she could be like Joanna-
Mary, who simply glanced at the feast with an expressive little
shudder. 'We must audition for two replacements,' said Joanna-
Mary.

Janey said, 'Let's wait for Florence.'

Joanna-Mary said, 'Millie shouldn't be allowed to die in vain,
Janey. This accident has increased public awareness of the group.
We must strike while the iron is hot.'

Greg observed Joanna-Mary fumbling in her bag for a piece
of paper and said, 'It's pretty hard to say this, Janey, but Florence
may not recover, and if she does it's going to be a long time
before she can think of dancing again.'

'So I've put an advertisement in the *Stage*.' Joanna-Mary
started reading from the piece of paper. Janey eyed it over her
shoulder. 'Wanted. Two pretty girl dancers for top group. Open
audition. Top salary and conditions. No toples.'

Joanna-Mary had been to a private school on the Sussex

Downs which taught her how to fold table napkins and indeed to say napkin, not serviette, but not how to love her fellow human beings, and not how to spell.

Janey said, 'It only happened last week. It's wrong not to wait for Florence.'

She looked at Lily for support, but Lily was trying on that morning's trawl of new shoes. The Territorial Army hall was fatally close to Oxford Street. 'Oh Lily, I wish you'd listen.'

'What's that?' Part of the trouble was that Lily had nine GCSEs and found Janey's conversation soporific. 'What do you think?' Lily mused. 'Would they be better in ivory? Should I take them back and change them?'

'Florence is going to get better,' said Janey. 'I asked the cards.'

'I don't suppose the cards told you Millie was going to be leaving,' snapped Joanna-Mary, 'or that um, um, Florence was going too.' She tossed back her hair and stroked it. 'They were going to steal all the bookings and go off together, leaving us all in the lurch.'

Greg stifled a gulp.

'Florence would *never* leave,' retorted Janey. 'She lives and breathes the group.'

Joanna-Mary said, 'Millie promised me I could take over from her yonks and yonks ago, actually. Sweet Fanny Addams was to be a vehicle for me. Tina Addams let her re-form the group strictly on this understanding.' She tossed back her hair jerkily. 'This group wouldn't um, um, exist without me because Tina and Millie weren't ever going to speak to each other again after what happened at the wedding.'

'Well,' said Greg. 'Let's have a compromise. Let's audition for one replacement now and keep our options open till we know what Florence is up to.'

Joanna-Mary rushed out of the hall and threw a tantrum by the bus-lane. 'Agh! Gar! Fuck!' she screamed, lying on the pavement. Janey bent over her to try and calm her down and got kicked in the bust. Then Greg tried to get her into a taxi, but she picked up Lily's shopping and hurled it at him. 'I-want-an-audition!' she gasped. 'Audition-for-two! Audition! For two! Audition-want!'

'Bitch!' hissed Lily, picking shoes off the road. 'Look. Look. Are Russell and Bromley going to let me return *those*?'

Greg, pinned down by Joanna-Mary's rage just as surely as if she had sat on him again, took the decision to audition for two replacements. And Joanna-Mary was calm again.

In her high-walled hospital room, Florence began to drift in and out of consciousness.

Sometimes she heard the voice of the Sister, a squat woman with a head of tight thin curls who bullied the gentle first-year nurse from Ireland. An old man was dying at the other end of the ward. He came originally from Romania and was spending his last days on earth there, while his middle-aged son sat beside him, trying to engage his attention on the matter of a missing post office savings book. An orderly was sweeping the grey unwashed lino around the cubicles, her brush banging against the furniture.

Sometimes Florence could sense the presence of the sun and would turn towards it as though returning from the bottom of the sea. At those times, she became aware of how much pain she felt. Her head, her leg; something had happened to her, brought her to these strange surroundings. A man came to mind. Something about this man that caused more pain than anything. But what it was, old wounds or new, true or imagined, she had no idea. Soon she forgot even that the thought of him had made her feel bad, once or now.

Florence had met the young man in Geronimo's. He was a footballer.

It was one of those times in a girl's life when absolutely everything had been a disaster, no work, no money, no men, and then suddenly it looked as if it was going to be perfect instead. They had been out of work for five weeks, ever since Honeybuns Club in Macclesfield went bankrupt two days into their run, and when they came back to London it was too late to get anything else. Lily began acting up because her mate Jacci had told her there were spare places going in the chorus of *South Pacific* in Eastbourne and she wanted to back out of the group.

'Florence,' said Millie, 'if you lose Lily the group's going to fall apart. If I tell them I'm standing down too, everyone else will start wanting to get out.'

Florence spent twenty minutes grovelling to Lily in the rehearsal hall kitchen.

'You're such a great dancer, Lily. You'd be wasted in the chorus. You're too big a talent.'

'I've got a living to earn. I'm very overdrawn. The assistant manager has started sending me shitty letters.'

'Look, Millie's driving over to Aldershot right now to see if Pavarotti's can let us have a spot. She'll be devastated if you pull out.'

'I can't afford to be sentimental.'

Janey came in to find Florence practically on her knees to Lily by the gas stove. 'Lily, you don't want to get involved in that *South Pacific*,' said Janey firmly. 'It's a very unhappy production.'

'Says who?'

'I've got a friend in it, Annie Easterfield, she says they take the stage crying every afternoon because the director's so nasty. That's why they've got so many spare places.'

'Oh, well, Annie, she's just the absolute end,' said Lily. 'You should hear what Jacci says about her.'

Janey crossed her arms thoughtfully. 'What's Jacci been saying about Annie?'

Florence said hurriedly, 'Nothing, Janey. Please let's be adult about this. Lily, if you go to Eastbourne you'll be breaking your contract. And besides, it's so shabby after everything Millie's done for you.'

'You ought to see someone about your little twosome with Millie,' said Lily. 'It's really unhealthy.'

'It's *what*?' said Florence.

'You heard.'

Florence was so angry her eyebrows almost joined together. 'Words aren't possible to describe how low I think you are,' she said. 'I don't want to see you around here again. You're fired.'

'No I'm not,' said Lily in a singsong voice. 'I've resigned. And now if you'll excuse me, I must go home and phone Eastbourne.'

Florence was just about to chase Lily down the street and kick her up the arse when Greg came in looking as if he'd just heard he was going to get a knighthood.

Greg said, 'Where's everybody else?'

'Joanna-Mary's left early to have her teeth polished,' said Janey, 'and as to Lily, it's a long story.'

'I don't think Millie will mind,' said Greg, 'if you two know before her. The Scala in Hull have phoned. They want to book us for Summertime Special. Eight weeks, a spot either side of the interval and the finale, two hundred a week each. We're to go up there to start rehearsals the day after tomorrow.'

'That's amazing,' said Janey. 'I've only just stuck a pin into Lily's photo and she's lost out already.'

Florence threw Janey a look and said, 'Well, we've got to get her back. We haven't got time to audition for anyone else.'

They tried calling Lily at home in Chelsea but her line was engaged all the time because whenever anything went wrong for Lily she rang round all her friends and told them about it in detail and with plenty of background material. The Radio, they called her. Radio Lily.

Greg and Florence set off for Chelsea in Greg's car. The sky had clouded over and the windscreen was smeary with dead bugs. Greg drove slowly along, trying to penetrate it with a fierce gaze.

Florence said, 'Oh Jesus, Millie is going to kill me over this.'

'I have to say,' began Greg in his worst sort of parliamentary voice, 'that in firing Lily you exceeded your remit as Millie's assistant.'

'I don't know what a remit is,' said Florence, 'and you're such a pompous twerp.'

Greg's face went all long and pointed and he made a furious pecking motion with his nose. The car jerked to a halt in Lily's street. 'You'd better leave this to me,' said Greg. 'Unless you think the occasion calls for your diplomatic skills.' He slammed the door and set off up the path to the council flats.

Florence leant over and wound down the window. 'Why don't you clean your fucking windscreen?' she shouted, 'or is that exceeding your remit?'

She watched Greg climb the concrete stairway to the second floor and bang on a royal-blue door. No one answered.

Florence got out and went up the stairs to join him. 'Lily,' she called through the letterbox. 'We've got a show. Much better than *South Pacific*.'

'She's in there all right,' said Greg. 'I saw her through a gap in the curtains.'

Florence called, 'Lily? I'm sorry, OK? I was being really stupid. Please come back.' She waited. 'Millie might let you do a solo,' she coaxed.

Nothing happened at all. Five minutes went by. Greg leant over the balcony and watched a large ginger dog shitting on the communal grass.

Florence sat on the doorstep and had a little cry while his back was turned because she was so disgusted with herself. 'I feel terrible,' she said. 'This is all my fault.'

Greg put his arm out and pulled her up. 'You and I know it isn't,' he said warmly.

'I'll leave her a note,' said Florence. She fetched a Sainsbury's receipt out of her bag and wrote on the back of it that Lily was to be at rehearsal the next day, three o'clock sharp. She even signed her name with three kisses, which nearly killed her. After that Greg walked her back to the car. She nudged him and said, 'Well, anyway, I've learned my lesson. I'm going to keep my temper from now on.'

At six o'clock the next day, Florence was getting mad at Lily in Geronimo's.

Geronimo's was in a cellar on the route to Goodge Street station. It didn't have a name on the front so how people discovered its existence was a mystery. Sometimes they were passing by already drunk, and fell through the open door and down the rickety staircase. The place was decked with cobwebs and you couldn't see much of the walls for all the pictures hung on them. Florence's favourite was a portrait of the Queen. Her Majesty had been young at the time and was smiling girlishly next to the Duke of Edinburgh.

Behind the bar was an old drink-splattered photo of Sweet Fanny Addams (1976 vintage).

In 1976 Tina, Collette, Millie, Juliet and Alexa looked so naive and vulnerable that it was impossible to imagine how they had survived so long. They were posed in a country garden. Collette leant against a white painted gate with her eyes modestly lowered and her curiously sated smile. Her dress was unbuttoned to show the tops of her breasts but she was keeping her knees firmly crossed. Her hair was long and soft and her skin the colour of creamy yellow roses.

Tina wore a black crochet frock, the holey sleeves of which looked like seaweed washed up on the beach of her pale plump arms. She was having problems with her weight even then. The camera had caught her kneeling forward and to one side, rather uncomfortably, as though she was worried she was going to sit on a thistle. Or perhaps she was just trying to shake off Juliet, who was lolling against her with her neat auburn head resting on Tina's arm.

Juliet wore a loose purple dress with gold braiding, and looked as fragile and luminous as Tina looked big and miserable. People always said she was the prettiest of the girls, and she couldn't walk ten yards down the road at times without some man rushing up to give her a bunch of flowers or ask her to marry him. It all got to be a bit of a strain. Well, she was very young when she joined Sweet Fanny Addams, hardly sixteen and very ladylike because her mother ran a beauty salon in Harrogate. Then she got thrown into this life of travelling and loneliness, fame and temptation, and there seemed to be no good reason any more for saying No because there was the pill, the Abortion Act, the example of her sisters. The only way out the poor girl could see was to take up religion. She became a prig to get a bit of personal space.

The photograph showed Millie in a rather severe stripy pinafore, one bare arm clasped defensively to her side, the other resting on the knee of Alexa, who, much taller than her, was curved around her protectively like a letter C. Alexa was in dungarees with a lumberjack shirt and floppy red hat. She was scowling because Tina had just told her to stand up straight and stop looking like a spiv.

Mrs Geronimo appeared in front of the photo carrying a pile of plates. Supper time was approaching, and she headed for a trestle table which was already spread with a white cloth, giving the proceedings a slightly Eucharistic atmosphere. Soon she began to bring forth giant Pyrex bowls filled with her home-made salads. These were usually created by chopping up what-ever didn't shift at lunch, and mixing it with bottled mayonnaise.

Anyway, you didn't go to Geronimo's to eat salad. You went there to start love affairs, preferably illicit. At corner tables lit by dusty bulbs, after one too many bottles of Côtes du Rhône.

Florence had just finished a rather dull romance with a man from the advertizing agency up the street. He wore shirts with stripes the size of airport runways, and red braces, and he kept a mobile phone in his jacket pocket which always seemed to ring if he kissed her. He went around with a lot of other guys from advertizing and they all owned things: fast cars, compact disc players, apartments. Florence really only wanted the guy for his Porsche but after six weeks she still hadn't got hold of the steering wheel and her patience ran out. Anyway, there was a new intake of footballers using Geronimo's, now pre-season training was starting at the club beyond Regent's Park.

Florence was already mad with Lily before she reached Geroni-mo's because Lily hadn't shown up at the rehearsal hall. Florence came clattering down the stairs with Janey and there she was, cruising footballers. Lily was lurching a bit but taking care not to send any tables crashing, and singing 'Una Paloma Blanca' in a tinkly mezzo-soprano.

Florence jerked her head. 'Over here, Lily.'

Lily was high on two doobs and half an acid tablet with vodka chasers. She had been that way since the night before, when she had fallen in with a party of students from the University of Manchester on the pavement outside a transient café and got swept up in their reckless mood of immortality. She looked at Florence and turned away, draping herself over the bar like a bra drying on a radiator. There was a good-looking guy next to her, lean and tall, dark-eyed, with brown curly hair and a golden skin.

'I'm busy talking to Joe,' said Lily. 'He's a footballer. He's famous for his long balls. Hic.'

Florence and Janey dragged Lily into a corner. 'Did you get my note?'

'No,' said Lily with the sort of wide eyes she made when she was lying.

'Millie wants to see you. She's in the rehearsal hall, waiting for you.'

'Let her wait.' Lily took a swig of vodka and coke.

'How can you be such a fool?' said Janey.

Lily said, 'Don't call me a fool. I'm perfectly sober.'

'I believe that like I believe that's Nescafé you've got there.' Florence paused. 'So – when are you starting at Eastbourne?'

'This weekend. The director adores me. I've got a six-month contract and I'm in the front row.'

'What, in *South Pacific*?'

'Of course, dumb brain.'

Florence put her face very close to Lily's and said, 'Such a lie!'

'Are you accusing me?'

'*South Pacific* has closed,' said Florence.

Janey said, much more kindly than Lily deserved, 'I'm afraid it's true, Lily. Annie Easterfield phoned to tell me last night.'

Florence glanced at the bar. The golden-skinned guy was still there. She caught his eye and gave him a little smile.

Lily said to her, 'Why should I take any notice of you? I've danced in *Les Mis*. You're just a silly French bitch.'

'I meant what I said yesterday,' said Florence. 'You *are* a great dancer, better than anyone I've seen. It's the only reason why I put up with you being such a Grade A pain in the neck.'

'You're so mean to me!' Lily threw her arm in front of her face and started sobbing loudly.

Janey took her elbow. 'Come on, Lily,' she said, 'Let's go and see Millie. We'll get it all sorted out.'

Florence went back to the bar and introduced herself to the footballer because for five minutes he had been watching her without speaking.

His name was Joe Daniel and he was French. They marvelled at the coincidence – two French people with English names.

'It isn't quite my real name,' he said. 'I changed it so people could say it more easily.'

It was so exciting they grabbed a bottle of Piat d'Or and went over to a corner table where it was quieter. Then after all that he didn't seem to be able to talk about anything except long balls, so she stared into his eyes to make him stop. When that didn't work she realized there was nothing else for it. She put her glass down on the table, took his glass out of his hand and kissed him.

After that he held on to her hand and took a long look at her as if she were a poem he was trying to learn and said, 'I know you. I can't think why, but I know you.'

Florence thought that was one of the oldest lines in the world but one of the most beautiful when spoken by a French footballer with golden skin.

'I know,' she said. 'I mean, I know you, too.'

She couldn't believe it when suddenly he let go of her hand and shot out of his chair. 'Maybe I'll see you again,' he said and left her sitting there.

Just then Janey came back in. Florence beckoned her urgently over to the table.

'Ooh,' said Janey, picking up the wine bottle. 'Pete Door. Aren't you being grand.' She helped herself to a slug.

'I can't make sense of this,' whispered Florence. 'Is he crazy?'

Janey glanced over her shoulder to Joe, who was standing by the bar again. 'He looks as if he's waiting for someone,' she said. 'He's probably meeting his wife or girlfriend in here.'

'Oh, I can't bear it,' said Florence, 'he's so gorgeous and talented that every woman in the room is going to want to bonk him.' Just then Joe stole a look at Florence and looked away again quickly. 'It's no good,' Florence said, getting out of her seat. 'I've just got to act.'

Janey said, 'Oh Florence, that isn't sensible at all. You don't know anything about him.'

'Yes I do. I know everything about him. I can just feel it.'

'He might be an axe murderer.'

Florence went over to Joe and said, 'I suppose a fuck's out of the question.'

Joe choked and spilt his drink down his sweatshirt. 'Jesus Christ,' he said, wiping tears from his eyes. 'Do all the girls in London carry on like this?'

Florence lowered her eyes modestly and murmured, 'I'm sorry. You do something to me. I can't seem to help myself.'

He said hoarsely, 'It's not a good time at the moment. You'd better give me your phone number.'

Florence shrugged and picked a paper napkin off the trestle table. She scribbled Janey's address on it and tucked it into his pocket. 'I'm going back to my friend's for coffee now. I'll wait for you there half an hour exactly. After that, the offer's closed.'

Janey lived some way behind Shepherd's Bush Green.

The journey seemed as if it was never going to be over. On the tube they had a mysterious wait between stations while the train sang to itself with a ding-a-ding-a-ding-a-ding-a sound. Janey felt doused in sweat from head to foot. 'I'm burning,' she whispered.

'Me too,' said Florence, 'with lust.'

'I don't know what's got into you,' Janey scolded her when they came out of the station and crossed the green. 'I never thought you'd be the one to behave this way. It's so dangerous. Now where are you going?'

Florence was diving into the chemist's. 'I'm out of ribbed Durex,' she said, loud enough for everyone passing by to hear.

Janey hung around outside the window, pretending she was looking at bubble baths while Florence studied the display of condoms on the counter. The careful way she was inspecting and selecting reminded Janey of the time her school went on a day trip to Calais. They'd walked through a market full of French housewives with their baskets and scarved heads, poking away critically at the piled-up fruit and vegetables.

When Florence came back they walked to Janey's flat in silence.

Janey made coffee in her narrow little kitchen. The window overlooked a cracked patch of concrete that served for a garden. She had prettied it up with a big mossy flowerpot of white geraniums. Inside, on the tiled windowsill, was a jam jar full of greenish water and an avocado stone with one little shoot.

Florence went past her to use the bathroom. Janey's greying pink dressing gown hung on a hook behind the door. Florence sat on the toilet, feet swinging, and called out, 'Where's Pete?'

Janey set up a clatter washing some pots and pans, as though she didn't hear.

They went into the sitting room to drink their coffee, and on the way Florence looked past the open door of the bedroom which had always been strewn with Pete's things but was now ominously tidy.

Janey stared at a crack on the wall and said, 'He's gone to Leeds to find himself.'

Florence snorted so hard she blew a bubble in her coffee. 'Oh,' she said angrily, 'That Pete never did deserve you.'

Pete liked to think he was a rock musician. He'd spent most of his days holed up in Janey's bed while she worked mealtimes in a pizza bar to support him. Then she would hurry off to class, to auditions, hoping to be seen by people who would make her famous. Even after she got her contract with Millie, Florence knew that in secret Janey did a small amount of topless. Florence thought of her, arms round a brown bag full of delicatessen goodies, returning late at night to cook Pete's supper, which he would eat to the sound of her cooing small talk that was entirely free of reproach.

What really got to Florence was that even now, as Janey confided her loneliness and longing, she spoke of him only with awe and tolerance. 'You should have seen his face,' she said, 'when I bought him the guitar.'

'You did what?' exploded Florence.

Janey, defending him, said, 'His old one just wasn't any good. Pete wanted a Fender if he was going to be taken seriously.'

Florence said, 'A man like that doesn't want to be taken seriously, he wants to be taken away. You spent everything you had on him and he took the guitar and left you. He's a git.'

'He doesn't want to be in a relationship at the moment. If he did want to be in a relationship, I'm the only girl it'd be with.'

'Bloody hell, the guy can't even come up with an original brush-off.'

Janey's expression gave Florence a terrible feeling of pathos, like seeing a cat that had been run over. 'Oh God,' she said, 'I'm sorry, Janey.'

'Oh well,' sighed Janey, 'you're only telling me what I know already, but what can I do? I've never been very good at making men behave themselves.'

Florence took hold of her hand the way French girls do and said, 'Now it's my turn to scold you. You're too nice a person to be hanging about waiting for him. He couldn't get a job as a free gift in a Cornflakes packet. And never buy a man anything unless you're prepared to break it over his head when he leaves.'

Janey caught sight of the clock on the mantlepiece. It was a 1930s one left to her by her great-aunt Dot and she loved it because of its big round dial and solid wooden case. She realized it was eight o'clock.

'Well,' said Florence, following her gaze, 'seems like Joe's not going to come.'

'Oh Florence,' said Janey, 'are you terribly upset?'

Florence said enigmatically, 'Not really, because if it had been him he would have come.' She kissed Janey's cheek. 'I'd better go.'

She washed out her coffee cup in the sink and went to the door without saying anything more.

Janey thought, well, she oughtn't to have done it in the first place but it's a real shame, even so.

She stood in the sitting-room window bay and watched to make sure Florence got down the street safely. The evening was still light but you got some odd characters about.

Florence had only got halfway up the street when the taxi drew up beside her and the door swung open.

'Hello, Joe,' she said.

'Well – ha – hello there, *chérie*. Fancy seeing you.'

'Such a coincidence!'

She got in and pulled down the little seat behind the driver's cab so she could sit and look at him on the way. They were going to the football ground. 'There's a supporters' club there,' Joe said. 'That'll be open.'

Florence didn't think it sounded very promising though she was ready to be wrong. The club was empty and silent. It was beginning to get dark. In the supporters' lounge they were served by a man with a brown overall and scowling face. Florence's forehead ached. She asked for a lemonade and followed Joe over to a formica-topped table with dried blobs of ketchup on it and an ashtray the size of a boat. On the wall was a team photograph with Joe grinning in the front row, his arms crossed and his hair slicked down with a wet brush. Underneath the picture was a fruit machine with a notice on it saying Out of Order. The floor was carpeted in maroon and pocked with cigarette burns.

Florence sipped the lemonade. It was warm. She tucked a stray lock of hair behind her ear.

'So,' she said. Her voice sounded high and nervous to her. 'How long have you been in England?'

Joe was just about to speak when the barman switched off the lights.

'Oh shit,' he said, 'I knew this was a bad idea.'

'Show me the pitch,' said Florence desperately.

By the time they got out there darkness had fallen and it was completely quiet. Florence left her shoes at the edge as though it were a mosque, and padded across the turf. 'It's lovely,' she said. 'It makes me want to dance.'

'Topless?' he said teasingly. Out in the open air he seemed happier. He took her arm and twirled her around.

'Watch me,' she said.

And Florence took off her clothes.

Afterwards, when Joe had kissed her goodbye at her front door, she let herself in and leant against the wall. Her hand hovered over the telephone to call Millie but then she changed her mind. She wanted to hug it to herself for a bit. Tomorrow, on the way up to Hull. She'd tell Millie everything tomorrow.

Janey and Lily stood outside the intensive care unit, waiting for someone to let them in.

Janey was wearing a baggy brown T-shirt and jeans, an old

tweed jacket, and a little brown hat with the brim turned up. Lily had on a white lace shirt and a black leather mini. It was mid-afternoon and nothing much seemed to be happening. The door-bell shattered the silence like a fire alarm. Janey was so impatient she was hopping from one foot to the other. 'That Joanna-Mary's a fast mover,' she said. 'We haven't got much time.'

'What are you going to do?' said Lily, as though it was funny.

'Take industrial action,' said Janey. The door opened and she darted in. They couldn't find Florence at first. She had been moved further up the ward, to a bed without so many gadgets round it. A junior doctor led them to it. He looked as though he had been awake for a week and his eyes were the same pink as his eyelids. 'Good news,' he said. 'Your friend's out of danger.'

'Pardon me,' said Janey fiercely, 'but she's in even graver danger than she was before.'

The junior doctor looked taken aback. Lily caught one of his pink eyes and giggled. She put one finger against her forehead and waggled it to make out Janey wasn't all there.

There was a washbasin on the wall by the bed with a mirror over it. Janey caught sight of herself and felt ashamed. She hadn't had time to wash her hair since Hull, it was plastered against the sides of her head. No matter how thin the rest of her was her face always stayed round, and when her hair got dirty like that she looked as if someone had taken her head away and put a ball of yellow knitting wool in its place. She flung her hat on the bed and shook Florence's arm gently. 'Florence, wake up, wake up. You've got to do something.'

Florence dimly became aware of two people beside her. Janey, and who else? she thought drowsily.

Lily spread herself on the edge of the bed where the junior doctor could see her. 'It's no good,' she said. 'She can't hear you. She has outsoared the shadow of our night.'

'Yes, all right, Lily,' said Janey hurriedly.

'Envy and calumny and hate and pain.' Once Lily got going on her audition pieces she was like a car with failed brakes. 'And that unrest which men miscall delight, Can touch her not and torture not again.' Lily turned with a winsome smile to include the junior doctor in the last two lines. 'From the contagion of the world's slow stain, She is secure. Well, go on, then. Take industrial action.'

Janey said, 'Whose side are you *on*, Lily?'

'Oh, yours and Florence's, that goes without saying.'

Lily! That snaky bitch! Florence was so indignant, so concerned to warn Janey not to trust her, that she willed herself to become conscious. Live, damn you, live, damn you, live.

'She moved!' said Janey suddenly, grabbing Lily's elbow. 'She knows we're here! Florence, listen. Joanna-Mary's trying to hijack Sweet Fanny Addams. She swears she's got Tina's backing. Tell her what we're going to do, Lily.'

Lily yawned. 'We're going to . . . what is it?'

'Withdraw our labour till Florence comes back,' said Janey.

'Oh yeah, there you go, Flo.'

'No Millie, no Florence, no Lily, no Janey. I'd just like to see how Joanna-Mary gets on. A dance group with one member, ha ha ha.'

'Here, Janey,' said Lily, suddenly lively again. 'I've just thought of something. Florence won't know what you're on about.'

'What?'

'She doesn't know what's happened, silly. Someone's going to have to tell her about Millie.'

Janey paused, then got a grip. She took Florence's hand. 'I've got some bad news, my lovey,' she said, stroking Florence's forehead gently, hoping somehow that her touch would make the scars disappear.

Florence dreamed she was talking to Janey, comforting her. 'It's all right,' she was saying. 'I know Millie's dead. Don't put yourself through this. I've had time to get used to it.' The dream turned into one about her mother. Florence was walking along a street in Tours with her, towards the house where they had lived till Florence was about eight years old. The house was tall and thin, with pale grey walls and big, peeling shutters that never quite closed properly. The porch had ivy growing round it, and there was a long, narrow front garden, two strips of parched green grass bisected by a path of cracked flagstones. Florence's mother wore a blue dress splashed with white and yellow daisies, the one she always wore when Florence dreamed about her. They were probably returning from Florence's ballet lesson, and would soon be pushing open the high iron gates and walking up the path to the dark-green double doors. But every time they reached the doorway in this dream Florence's mother would be unable to find her key, and would set off retracing her steps to look for it and never come back. Florence would then find herself hunting for her mother all over the Paris métro. This time, unusually, Janey was on a platform with her in a dented brown hat, explaining haltingly that her mother had died. 'Don't worry,' Florence reassured her. 'I've known all along.'

But now Janey seemed to have broken off to talk to Lily Smith. Florence listened.

'Anyway,' Lily was saying, 'I'll have to be off now. I've got to book myself a cut and colour at Daniel Galvin.'

'Lily!' said Janey reproachfully.

'Well if I can't get an appointment on Saturday I'm fucked.'

Janey turned her back, but capitulated as Lily was on her way out.

'Lily . . .'

'What?'

Janey said, sternly, 'You are with us, aren't you?'

'Yeah, all right,' said Lily. 'But don't let's ruin everything. We're only just beginning to get straight.' She slipped a piece of paper with her name and phone number into the junior doctor's pocket and went out into the North London evening. She liked doctors best of all. They were always very good about giving her the pills she wanted. The blast of traffic noise hit her after the lullaby of Janey's conversation.

'It's all right,' said Florence.

She realized she really was talking to Janey, and opened her eyes.

'Hello, Janey,' she said.

Janey looked at her astounded, then burst into tears. Florence tried to say, 'Don't cry.'

'I'll fetch the doctor,' said Janey.

'No. Listen to me.' Florence's voice was weak and halting. Janey's head was almost on the pillow, trying to hear what she said. 'On the floor of my flat. Just inside the front door as you come in. There's some post there. It came just as I was leaving for Hull and I didn't stop to pick it up. There's a big brown envelope with Millie's writing on it. That'll sort out everything.'

Janey blurted, 'But Joanna-Mary didn't say anything about . . . I mean, when she went to your place and picked up your things to bring here . . . I mean, she would have brought your post to you, wouldn't she?'

'*Merde*,' said Florence, and closed her eyes again.

Lily took the tube to Sloane Square and walked the rest of the way to her flat.

She lived there with her mother, who had had her at fourteen. Her mother was now thirty-one and consorting with an enormous Turk by whom she was thinking of having a baby. Any time Lily brought people home her mother sought advice from them, complete strangers, even. On the other hand, she often seemed to forget that Lily was her daughter and was surprised to see her in the flat. Lily came and went at will.

Before Lily reached home she stopped off at a pay-phone. From where she stood, she could see a break in the grey high walls of the estate. She watched container lorries move slowly along the main road as if pushed by scenery shifters. The grass round the phone smelled of dogs' pee. Lily's head and shoulders were reflected in Perspex behind the Telecom sign; some powdery looking hair, a full lower lip, the slightly too close together eyes. Looking down, these eyes fell on a shiny coin. She picked it up. It was a peseta.

Joanna-Mary was on a sunbed in a Floral Street beauticians. She took the call on her mobile phone.

'Oh, I might not be able to come in for a few days,' Lily said in her little silvery voice. 'My synovitis has flared up again.'

'What's going on, Lily?' said Joanna-Mary.

'Nothing.'

'Yes, um, um, there is, I can tell by your voice.' Joanna-Mary had just received a rather unsettling call from Janey, who practically accused her of tampering with Florence's mail.

'I don't know what you mean,' said Lily, giggling.

'Stop messing about,' said Joanna-Mary. 'I can't have people in the group unless they're completely committed to what I'm trying to do. Either you're one of us or you aren't.'

Radio Lily, who had the discretion of a billboard. 'Oh, you know what an ass Janey is,' she said, 'she wants us all to go on strike or something.'

After she put the phone down she made her way across the grass, past the hospital and the shopping parade beyond it. A young woman with roughly clipped black hair sat on the front steps of a house, a child in her arms. The child was large and lay stiffly, legs protruding. In the woman's hand was a polystyrene cup containing a few coins of small denomination. She held it out to Lily, who dropped the peseta in it and hurried on.

Chapter Six

The Knife-thrower's Assistant

IN THE LADIES' lavatory of Crabbs, a department store in a seaside town in Essex, Manon Cole was getting ready to go out to her evening job. She was called Manon because her mother had been walking past the Royal Opera House a few days before she went into labour and been struck by the name as it appeared on the posters outside. Manon Lescaut. It sounded posh and distinctive, a cut above Mandy which was the other name Fidelma had in mind for her.

Manon had to have an evening job because she was paying her way through dance classes. There was no grant available to the pupils of Mrs Studebaker's International School (Flamenco and Disco a speciality), and her parents did not have much money.

Crabbs was three floors high and had brown exterior paintwork. On the left-hand side was a window display of lawn mowers and garden shears, on the right were pink nylon sheets and in the middle were three mannequins in day dresses of the hard-wearing kind. There were SALE notices stuck on the glass. A woman with high-rise ginger curls stood behind the make-up counter, staring out into the street. She and Manon seemed to be the only people in the store.

Manon was a knife-thrower's assistant.

A pony-tailed athletic girl, she had won prizes throughout her childhood for gymnastics and throwing the javelin. As a girl she had dreamed of Olympic gold on the beam but then her genes took over and she grew a foot in height and put on six inches round her bust. Now she was tall and striking, with big cheek-

71

bones and a strong chin and one of those traffic-stopping walks. She'd had to stop wearing her black Lycra shorts because men kept driving their cars into things when they turned to look at her.

Every night in the summer season she strode to the Cavern down by the seafront caravan site and stood motionless among the raining blades, for which she earned £25 a session plus tips. She wore an old rose leotard with washed-out sequins over it which winked and blinked under the Cavern's tinpot lighting. It wasn't what she had planned for herself but at least she didn't have to strip down to her tits. Everyone else in the show had to do topless, and sometimes if business was bad the owner would pay off the local cops and make the girls dance naked on the tables where lay preachers, law enforcers, masons and councillors would contort themselves into ever more bizarre sitting positions in order to glimpse a fleeting slit.

As Manon got ready that night, she realized her hands were shaking. Paolo the knife-thrower had started looking at her in a way she didn't like, but somehow she had to hang on till she had saved enough money. Then she was going to get herself out of here. London, that was where she was heading. All the top dancing jobs were there.

Her Dad didn't know she was the knife-thrower's assistant at the Cavern. 'Tell him you work at Knockers, I would,' advised Fidelma. 'You know what he's like.'

Knockers was a joke-shop on the seafront. It sold plastic willies to wear on your nose, and false teeth made of rock. Her father, who was strict and inhibited in a violent sort of way, thought working there was bad enough. If he'd known about the Cavern he would have wept and then tried to smack her about. He never learned. He hadn't been able to land a punch on her since she was fourteen.

She didn't hate him, though, he hadn't been a bad dad to her. But it beat her why her mum had fetched up with him. Fidelma could have done a lot better for herself than a little geezer with a bald head and squeaky voice. He was a night watchman at the biscuit factory. They couldn't afford a car or holidays and

Manon never had many new clothes. They got a good discount on biscuits, though.

It seemed Fidelma had already been pregnant with her when she got married sixteen years ago. Fidelma was a teenager and Liverpool Irish and there was a lot of trouble.

'You should have had an abortion,' said Manon.

'Manon! It's against our religion.'

'You always said you didn't believe in all that crap.'

'If I'd had an abortion, you wouldn't have existed,' said Fidelma triumphantly.

'How do you know? Maybe my soul would have jumped out just before everything landed in a bucket.' Manon couldn't stand it when Fidelma went pious on her. 'Then hung around over some other people shagging till it found a couple it fancied. I could have been born into a different family. My dad might have been a famous heart surgeon or something and my mum a top model.'

'I could have been a top model. I had no end of offers.'

'Well, pity you didn't take them up,' said Manon. 'I bet Twiggy isn't living in a cruddy council flat.'

When Manon said things like that her mum stormed off into the kitchen and washed up loudly to the sound of Tammy Wynette. Manon thought longingly of getting out of Eastleigh. If she didn't get out soon she'd go whizzing and banging all over the place, like when someone puts a match to a box of fireworks.

After she'd changed into costume, Manon had twenty minutes to spare so she stopped off at the newsagent and bought a copy of the *Stage*.

There were some interesting-sounding dance jobs in the Situations Vacant and Auditions. Manon drew a ring round one for Starburst International Agency which was offering three-month contracts and £300 a week for work in Greece and Italy. It said it was with or without sitting at tables, and you could choose whether you stayed dressed or did ten seconds' topless. 'Flights paid for, accommodation arranged,' Manon read. That seemed all right, although she wasn't sure about 'No consommation'. Did that mean you didn't have to sleep with customers? Surely there wouldn't be any question of that anyway, not for an agency that advertized in something as respectable as the *Stage*.

She was still reading the small ads as she stood behind a curtain at the Cavern, waiting to go on stage.

'Members and genitalmen, just look at her! Lady Leopardina, the wildest of all the she-cats in the jungle! Only one man can tame her!'

Manon dropped the paper and cartwheeled across the dirty floorboards. *Rod Stewart's Greatest Hits* was emanating from the birdshit-splattered speakers on the walls. She had incorporated a backward somersault and tumble into her routine, perfected at her gymnastics class. It was more for her own entertainment than anything else. The dust and fag ash, formed into a glue with beer and spirits, always lodged in her nails however hard she cleaned them. She hardly ever bothered looking at the audience. Half a dozen tables occupied by local businessmen paying £15 a head for the privilege of looking absolutely joyless through the four hours of goosepimpled female exhibitionism on the makeshift stage, plus Barry Christopher, Self-Contained Country & Western singer, a dull man with a beard and machine-washable cowboy suit. He plugged his pearlized guitar into some kind of box which simulated the sound of a 16-piece band. He had the same taste in songs as Fidelma.

One reason Manon never liked to look too long at the audience was in case she was spotted by someone who might know her boyfriend Ray.

Ray worked in a bar in the next town down the coast. He was a stocky youth, not quite as tall as Manon, but fit and strong. His hair was as bristly as a nailbrush. Unlike her dad, he was still big enough to hit her if he chose, although he'd only done it a couple of times. Other times he was all right, good fun. Well, if your idea of good fun was watching him pick fights with any bloke he thought was looking at her in a certain way. Manon was beginning to think there might be more to it than that. But Ray had a Ford Escort and they would take it inland, far away from the flat brown beaches and junk caravan sites of seaside Essex, screaming up the motorway till the lights were the size of pinheads behind them, and then they would turn off and go skidding down to the end of a lane where he would undress them both and pound into her so hard and urgently you'd have thought he'd been imprisoned on an island without women for years on end. But the quietness of the summer night and the softness of his hair against her face and the caressing words he always spoke despite the wildness of his thrashing excited her so much that even the first time he did it to her she had an orgasm before he was even halfway there himself.

Not long after that he hit her, because he couldn't believe she'd been a virgin, coming like that, even though she'd bled like a pig all the way home and had had to walk upstairs sideways so her mum couldn't see the back of her skirt. 'Don't lie to me,' Ray said. 'I'll take anything from a woman except lies.'

That was what Manon couldn't understand about men, how they chased after you and showed off to you and told you nothing was any good without you till they got your trust and you opened yourself up to them, and then they hurt you.

Famous and rich on her own account, that was what Manon was going to be. Her mum had told her so, and Manon didn't argue. Famous and rich so she'd never have to mind what a man thought again.

But first of all she had to get out of Eastleigh alive.

> There was an old man of Belgrave
> Who shafted a whore in a cave

Youthful, brave Manon who got through her routine by the recitation of limericks and poems learned in elocution class, and dirty jokes. Normally this would pass the time but tonight she could not prevent her fear from seeping through the boredom.

That evening she had told Paolo she would be leaving at the end of the week. She'd been doing her sums. Four more afternoons and nights at £25 per session gave her a train ride to London, a room with a view of chimneypots and air-conditioning ducts at a cheap hotel while she found work. She didn't mind living on burgers and chips for a while. She imagined herself walking to auditions to save money and keep fit, through the wrapper-strewn parks of summer.

Paolo had been sitting in his caravan when she told him. He was very aggravated. The caravan stank of the fried fish he was eating, plus stale pee from where he urinated against the tyre outside. It was a long walk to the toilets. 'You aren't going to an audition,' he said, pouting. 'You've got a job at some low-down dive. But if Paolo can't have you no one will.'

'Oh, yeah, what you going to do about it, throw all your knives at me?'

'I wanna be your husband.'

'You owe me a hundred in back money which I'd like before Saturday night.' Manon realized that Paolo was even more drunk than usual. He always went into his Joke Italian mode when he'd been on the bacardi and cokes. He wasn't a real Italian at all, his mum ran a dry-cleaner's in Margate. She added up what she'd got saved already and what she expected to make for the rest of the week. It wasn't enough. She would have to work tonight. 'Anyway, you've already got a wife.' Concepta was behind the curtain that separated the kitchen from the living area. She yanked the curtain closed so Manon knew she was listening.

'She is not my wife, she is my cohabitee.'

I'm gonna whack the tosser right now if I don't watch myself, thought Manon. 'Concepta wants to be your assistant again,' she said. 'She's fed up with sitting on her own in the caravan while you work all hours.'

Paolo tried another tack. 'I can get you hundred-and-fifty a night,' he said. 'All you have to do is dance on tables.'

'With all my clothes off and fellas trying to look up the top of my legs, no thank you.'

Paolo's knives were displayed on the table. He arranged them in an angular pattern. 'No auditions,' he said. 'I'll make sure you don't get through no auditions.'

What a prat.

Now Manon stood with her back to a plywood board and the knives thudded into it beside her. Already three had her pinned by the fabric of her leotard. She told herself that soon she would walk away as usual, leaving the shape of her body traced out as though the police had been working on the scene of a murder, and the half a dozen businessmen out front still sitting there like cardboard cut-outs. 'Don't let the bastard know it's hurting,' she thought, 'don't even twitch.' The last-but-two knife leapt through the beery air and landed so close to her cheekbone you couldn't get an eyelash between them.

Manon stared steadily at Paolo. He grinned back at her. The penultimate knife came and with it a stinging feeling as the skin of her scalp was breached and a trickle of blood began to meander down past the back of her ear. Oh, the bastard. With the last knife he would pierce her heart, the grinning shitbag wop.

She thought, I should've whacked the cunt while I had the chance, and to hell with the money.

Now that she was about to die she was not afraid but filled with melancholy about all the things that she would never do, like marrying a sixties pop star who could be her grandad, or driving very fast down a motorway in her own Lamborghini while drinking champagne from the bottle, or walking on the moon.

She hadn't even made it to London.

Still grinning, Paolo released the last knife and it flew not towards her heart but to its allotted place in the crook of her neck as though nothing had been amiss.

Manon pulled a handful of knives from the board. Sashaying off to the sound of 'Tonight's the Night', she chucked them at his feet. 'I hope your brain caves in,' she said. Then she walked round the corner of the building and threw up against the side.

'My money,' said Manon later in the shadow cast by the bloated and silent inflatable fun castle.

'Hold out your hand,' said Paolo, struggling for something in his trousers.

Manon stepped back. 'Oh no. I don't want to do that with you.' She was tall and strong for sixteen and she had the confidence of a winter's course at the self-defence classes for women backed by the local council.

'It's good. Once you do it with me you'll want me to do it to you all the time.'

'Piss off, Paolo. I'm not interested, piss off, sew it on your forehead.'

'Ah, come on, Manon. Give it a rub.'

'I wouldn't give it a dog biscuit.' Manon sprang sideways as she glimpsed a half-hidden blade of dull grimy steel in Paolo's hand. Her foot connected with his chin, a piece of luck that spurred her on to sidefoot the knife away from his grasp. He dropped it with a wheeze of surprise. Her readiness and capability amazed her. There seemed to be time to do everything. Months of smiling through his pisspoor jokes and sidestepping his wheezing lunges spurred her on. In her pocket she found a set of rock false teeth from Knockers. She brought them crashing down on his head, then kicked him in the balls and as though she was on the inflatable fun castle trod on his stomach for good measure.

She stood over him and, fingers trembling, took the £100 he owed her in tenners from his wallet plus the night's earnings and £32.50 to cover the cost of a new leotard. As she walked off, he stirred. 'That's you finished,' he gasped.

Over her shoulder she called, 'I'm wetting myself.'

'I know where you live.'

Manon, in a prudent moment, had given Paolo a false address, claiming she came from Marbella Drive, a row of jerry-built bungalows up near the refuse site.

'I know where you live.'

'Prat.'

She walked off quickly down the seafront. Everything looked so normal there. A woman walked a corgi past a flowerbed full of sweet william. Water trickled from an outlet pipe near the iron-framed placard bearing the table of tides, which had never been painted since Manon was little and was a soft rusted blue. Beside the outlet pipe lay half a crab. The smell peculiar to Eastleigh, fishy with bass notes of raw sewage and gorse, wafted in on the breeze.

Manon's fingers felt like salamis as she checked her money and realized she had taken twenty pound notes instead of tenners from Paolo. She went to stuff what was not hers by right into the RSPCA plaster spaniel with a slot in its head outside the rock shop, but then decided against it. Ahead of her was the station where, as if for the first time, her eyes took in the signs advertizing limos and cabs, glowing and blinking in the dark.

'Is that you, Manon?' her mum called out from the kitchen.

'Yeah.' Manon hurriedly closed the bathroom door, having crept up the stairs. She peeled off her sequinned leotard and stuffed it behind the cistern, then shoved her head under the tap. The water ran pink out of her hair.

'Did it all go all right?' Her mum was following her up the stairs. Manon's heart sank. She'd want one of her girl-to-girl chats. What sort of crowd did she get. Did she recognize any of them. Fidelma cleaned houses for some of their wives.

'So-so.' Manon could hear the couple who lived in the next-door flat arguing about what to watch on TV. The walls were as thin as the biscuits her dad brought home. Up by the ceiling there was a peninsula of black mould which never scrubbed off. In another flat along the corridor a baby cried and someone else flushed a toilet.

'Did you tell him you were packing it in?'

'Uh-huh. Where's Dad?' Manon could sense her mother standing behind the door, a short woman with good ankles and a fake suntan. She was wearing a pair of fuschia-pink trousers from Manon's Freeman's catalogue, and a white acrylic top. People told her they were more like sisters than mother and daughter. She had a rather startled hairdo with frosted blonde highlights, and round white earrings like big pills. She always wore heels, even to do the washing up.

'Dad's not in yet. He's on late shift. I was just looking at your *Stage*. There's a job there you ought to go for. A box ad. Phone and ask for Greg. I'll get on to them tomorrow morning if you want.'

'No thanks, Mum. Matter of fact . . .' Manon came out of the bathroom, the blood-streaked leotard bundled under her arm and a towel round her head. 'Matter of fact, Mrs Studebaker told me about it. I'm going to London tonight.' A car hooted outside the front gate as she spoke. 'That's my minicab.'

'Oh well, if that's how you want it. I thought we'd go together.'

'I'll phone you from the audition. You could come down if I get anywhere.'

'I'm not without connections, you know. I could have helped you out.'

Into her backpack Manon put her toothbrush and Walkman and a photo of Ray behind the wheel of his Ford Escort. You could just see the back seat where she'd had it for the first time. Over the top of her backpack she laid her denim jacket and Aran sweater. At the door of her bedroom she turned and looked back at it, the damp shoebox where from childhood she had lain awake at night wondering who she was really, and plotting her escape. She thought of Paolo with contempt and Ray with a pang, but she knew that she would never go home again.

Chapter Seven

Wedding Bell Blues

B<small>Y THE TIME</small> Joanna-Mary's advertisement appeared in the *Stage*, ten days had elapsed since the accident, but still Millie's funeral had not taken place.

In normal circumstances, of course, it would probably have happened within a week of her death. As she was Jewish, it might even have happened the day after, since Millie's mother Mrs Francis had a tendency to swan in and take over; furthermore you had to be very determined not to be buried religiously, and Millie was in no position to be determined. She was on a slab at the mortuary having undergone a post-mortem.

There were mysteries about her death. Why should a woman apparently in the best of physical and mental health concede her life on a near-empty motorway on a day in midsummer so hot the horizon shimmered and the sky was almost transparent? What caused her car to end up in a tree two fields away? Mystery upon mystery; had she really, as was claimed by the driver of the juggernaut that sent it spinning there, performed a U-turn on the carriageway? How could she, a first-rate driver with not one blemish on her record, have done such a thing? How could it not have been the fault of her car, which a police examination deemed innocent: tyres, steering, brakes, all blameless as far as they could tell from the cage of misshapen metal and fittings dappled with spilt blood.

Meanwhile, the insurance company was waiting eagerly for the opportunity to express their regrets; 'This poor woman . . . just one of those terrible accidents, we're afraid.' The insurers' attitude was no mystery; the law relating to third-party insurance stipulates that if negligence can be proved on the part of the insured then the company is obliged to pay out to the victims. In other words, the company needed Millie to have suffered a brain haemorrhage or a heart attack or a massive fit, so that they would not be liable for the handsome compensatory sums due to both Florence and the driver of the juggernaut who had suffered memory loss, two broken arms and double vision, as well as the shakes for two days.

It was not one of those terrible instants of destruction where parts of the body are sliced off or torn away. Millie was recognizable, there was some comfort in that; her skeleton was simply cracked into many thousands of pieces inside her skin, like a very old piece of china held together by the glaze. But the post-mortem showed nothing: no heart attack, no stroke, no traces of drink or drugs in blood or urine, no history of epilepsy. Not all post-mortems need an inquest but there it was; mystery upon mystery, an unnatural death. So, on the tenth day after the accident, the inquest took place. It was no different from any bog-standard murder case. The coroner formally opened the proceedings. He gave permission for burial to take place. Then he announced an adjournment so that the police could look for witnesses.

It was with the burial in mind that Joanna-Mary revved and lurched her big red Toyota sports car into a parking spot in the underground car park behind Legwork (London). While doing this she scraped the paint off someone else's vehicle with her bumper then chipped a rhombus of paint off the wall as the engine stalled and the car jumped forward. Joanna-Mary could not spell, and neither could she drive.

Legwork had started off eight years before as one dance studio in an abandoned church hall at the very edge of the shadow cast by the Post Office tower, when with the loan of £100,000 from a friend, Tina had boarded up her broken heart and opened up for business.

Since then she had come a long way. Soon Legwork came to be regarded as the best studio in England. It was young, friendly and fashionable. Word of mouth brought dancers to Tina's classes not only from all over Europe but even from America and Japan. All the West End musicals began to use it as their pre-theatre venue. Without spending much on advertizing, Legwork's fame spread all over the world.

Tina began to think of franchises, own brands, concepts, videos. Why leave it at dancers? Everyone wanted to be fit. They needed places in cities where they could work out during the lunch hour, or spend a day pampering themselves. They needed clothes to look good in while they were doing it. Why not have a haircut while you were there, and eat at the salad bar, and get a tan, and swim in the pool?

Before long, Tina was leaving most of the classes to her staff while she concentrated on building up the company. Tina could make businesses grow in the way that green-fingered people can rear plants. She was hopeless about men but terrific with money. In negotiations she was tough not only on her own behalf but on that of her employees. Millie had always liked to recall the time when she and Tina called at the Associated British TV Centre to discuss contracts for their next series of shows. The producer offered her, Tina and Collette a rise from the previous year – £800 per show, plus a retainer of £100 a week while they were resting between series. The next name to come up was Juliet's. The producer offered the same per show, but only £80 a week retainer.

'Juliet must have what we're getting,' said Tina.

The producer said, 'But you're better dancers than Juliet.'

'Not when we're resting, we're not.'

So successful was Tina that later she was able to buy and convert a tall Victorian warehouse beside the Thames at Fulham. Branches of Legwork had also opened in Manchester, Glasgow and Birmingham. In all important respects they were alike: a colour scheme of black and white, with lots of glass, a gym, a pool, a shop. Tina was also planning on opening in New York. But Fulham was her palace; it was her company headquarters, her main studio and her London home. This was the building outside which Joanna-Mary had just made such a pig's ear of parking.

The office was run by Kit, a middle-aged gay with close-cropped grey hair and a round gentle face. He wore horn-rimmed glasses and had been an opera singer. His partner, Geordie, was small and tubby with brown hair styled rather medievally. He drove a white van round London delivering things. Kit and Geordie lived in a two-up, two-down with a green onyx suite and gold taps in the bathroom, close to Battersea Park. Here they had lots of spectacular rows late at night, with much slamming of doors and shouting and stomping down the stairs. They were very happy together. For Tina, Kit fixed the lights when they fused, planned her diary, co-ordinated the classes, hired and fired the staff. Since the break-up of the first Sweet Fanny Addams and the loss of all her woman friends, Kit had grown to be her closest confidant.

He stood in reception, a cigarette burning between his fingers, and looked out into the street.

Outside the main doors a taxicab filled the narrow alley, its engine ticking away. On the side was painted an advertisement for *The Phantom of the Opera*. A thin woman with a cigarette perched upon her pendulous lower lip bent to get in, letting the door swing behind her.

Joanna-Mary, on her way in to the building, gave this woman a wide smile, recognizing her as Betty Trout, the Associated British TV light entertainment producer who attended Tina's body condition and stretch class on Wednesdays. It was the only class Tina now took, and although it was never articulated you usually had to be rich or successful to get in.

Betty Trout was wearing a couture jacket over leggings. Her red hair was as short as a boy's. She had the silhouette of a nineteen-year-old, though close up her face was sallow and wrinkled like skin on cold rice pudding.

'Joanna-Mary Reed-Herbert,' called Joanna-Mary, noting the absence of light in Betty Trout's eyes. 'Roger's daughter.'

'Of course, darling. Are you making progress at the, what was it?'

'Dancing.'

'Super!'

'Sweet Fanny Addams!'

'Gosh!'

'Thank you for a lovely lunch,' called Joanna-Mary, 'lunch' being a somewhat loose term for a brief encounter in the ABTV bar in the company of her father's producer, floor manager, assistant director, make-up lady, continuity girl and film editor, two of whom knew Betty Trout well enough for her to stop in passing and exchange pleasantries.

'We must do it more often!' called Betty Trout, for whom this was a euphemism for We must never do it again. She waved and the taxi bore her away.

Joanna-Mary took the lift to Tina's top-floor apartment.

In the living room she found her mother, draped in a grey towelling robe, having also attended Tina's Wednesday class. The robe looked simple and dull, and had cost well over £200 at a shop in Sloane Street. 'Hallo darling, you're looking wonderful today,' said Valerie Reed-Herbert, who was in her early fifties, attractive though she had big lips that turned down at the corners. Joanna-Mary was the youngest of the family, Vallie's other children being a son and married daughter who were neither of them very interesting. To occupy her hours respectably Vallie organized social events for charity and took courses in various skills she did not need. 'Tina, doesn't Joanna-Mary look wonderful?'

Tina poked her head round the door from the shower. Her wet, heavy hair thumped on to her shoulders. 'I think you both look wonderful,' she said. 'Don't you think Vallie looks wonderful, Joanna-Mary?'

'Doesn't she always?' said Joanna-Mary, slipping into the conservatory kitchen where she helped herself to coffee from a cafetière. A fat girl was ironing Tina's knickers by the window. The river rolled past outside. 'Hallo, Tracey,' Joanna-Mary greeted her warmly. 'You're looking smart today.' The fat girl, whose name was Michelle, said, 'How tanned you're getting.' The apartment ran the length and breadth of the old warehouse. There was a spritz bath, and a guest suite where Joanna-Mary's parents would sometimes stay overnight after theatre visits. Tina, a woman on her own, had some years ago been hoovered up into the Reed-Herbert family. Now she did very few things in isolation; there was almost always a Reed-Herbert element attached.

From the living room the discourse of the two older women filled the air like the chatter of rooks. On the air wafted a variety of scents: the asexual floral favoured by Vallie, the cloying blast of 'Tina', a perfume marketed under the Legwork franchise which was worn by fat Michelle, the hired help. She received rather a lot of it in gift form. Its smell was spicy and as intense as turpentine. Tina herself wore Joy. With these smells came others, each recognizable and distinct though without sequence or structure, like the jumble of notes of an orchestra tuning up: the smells of the company of women – creams, lotions, lipstick, varnishes, the soles of slippers, bathrooms left warm and steamy, a haze of talcum powder sinking to the floor.

'I'm waiting for a woman from the *Pictorial*,' said Vallie. 'Doing some article on the secrets of staying married. I've never heard such a load of bosh.'

The Reed-Herberts were what Vallie tended to call 'a high-profile media family'. They were a good-looking, successful bunch and they liked to present their good looks and success to the world. It was comforting to see what they were in print. If a month went by without some external manifestation of their good-looking, successful existence, they would start to feel oddly troubled, and a growing sense of insubstantiality.

'Oh, go on, you'll do it wonderfully,' said Tina. 'You're the only happily married woman in London.'

'God, no one else would put up with the old twit,' said Vallie. Joanna-Mary re-entered. Vallie patted the empty space next to her on the sofa. 'Well, darling. Come and sit down and tell me all about it.'

'I think Tina and I ought to pop round to Wandsworth and see poor Curtis,' said Joanna-Mary.

'Of course you should,' said Vallie.

'Mmm,' said Tina carefully.

'It's just we've all sort of been caught up in our own um, um, things,' said Joanna-Mary, looking diffidently at her knees through the filmy cream curtain of her hair. 'I think we've sort of forgotten about him. And Tina, it was so great to see you and Millie together again and if you let that go, well, I think it would be such a shame if you let it slide. Maybe you could help Curtis do a nice sort of funeral service for her.' She firmed up her voice. 'So I told Curtis we'd pop round about six.'

'I'm a bit tied up tonight,' said Tina, sitting at the dressing table and nestling into a satin dressing gown as though she were the centre of a chocolate. 'For a start, there's a business meeting.'

'It won't take long and really it is important, don't you think, Mummy.'

'Indeed it is,' said Vallie, hugging her.

'Have your business meeting, Tina and then we can go,' said Joanna-Mary into Vallie's shoulder. Vallie was speaking simultaneously. 'So glad I've got such a thoughtful daughter.'

Tina rang round and left messages for her lover. Owing to the circumstances of the relationship, these messages had to be somewhat obfuscatory. Then she went to her business meeting in the boardroom on the fifth floor, directly under her apartment. There was a table you could have performed Holiday on Ice on, and some paintings chosen to match the blinds. Tina sat at the head of the table, her accountant on her left, her lawyer on the other side. Kit brought them tea and chocolate biscuits on a tray covered with embroidered linen. The lawyer said, 'As your legal adviser, I must tell you that if the balloon payment is not honoured you will lose the premises and be declared bankrupt.' The accountant said, 'As your financial adviser, I must tell you that the bank are not prepared to accept our forecasts for company profits and have refused to grant an extension to the loan. It is imperative that you persuade your backer of the necessity of providing the sum of money involved.' Tina ate nine chocolate biscuits and broke her rule of not smoking before dinner. After the meeting was over she rang and left more messages for her lover.

'Curtis!'

Framed in the doorway, Joanna-Mary held out to him a sober species of potted plant. She was wearing a little magenta hat with a veil and matching summerweight gloves. Behind her, Tina was both doubtful about the advisability of this visit and despairing as to its timing, but remained strangely incapable of contravening Reed-Herbert family policy. 'I'm so terribly, terribly sorry,' said Joanna-Mary.

'What've you done?' said Curtis, sounding slightly bewildered. 'Oh! Yes, I see what you mean. Thanks!'

Tina followed him into the front room, which was very neat but had a black plastic bin bag abandoned in the corner which she feared contained things worn by Millie at the moment of her death. 'Have a look in there,' suggested Curtis, following her gaze. 'Might be something you like.' He leapt over and rummaged in it, returning with some sort of bedraggled fur coat. 'This any use to you?'

'Oh no, I . . .' Tina cleared her throat. 'I have enough furs, thank you.'

Curtis made a pot of tea, talking of arrangements for the funeral at Hoop Lane crematorium in the brisk, conversational tone of a breakfast television presenter announcing that highlights of last night's snooker quarter-final will follow after the break. He brought the tea on a tray through to the front room and placed it on the floor, where he and Tina knelt to drink it silently.

Curtis had round brown eyes and a bushy moustache. He was quite a bit plumper than Tina remembered him, but still an attractive man. Despite having lived in London since childhood, he still had traces of a Leeds accent. That was sexy too. And Tina had always liked the way he looked at you when you were talking to him – firmly, shrewdly, listening to all you had to say. He was naturally a cordial man, but this impression was probably strengthened by his hair, which though now duller and greyer retained still the reddish colour that people associated with welcome. 'Like real flame gas fires,' thought Tina, with a terrible urge to giggle. She cleared her throat again and said, 'This is the first time I've seen you since the wedding.'

'That would be whose . . . ?'

'Yours. To Millie. You know, at the synagogue.'

'Oh. Oh yes. Haven't I seen you since then?'

'No. No.'

'Well, that's a shame. But here you are now.'

Joanna-Mary's tea was cooling on the tray. On arrival, with a sharp intake of breath and clutching her stomach discreetly, she had disappeared upstairs.

'Curtis,' said Tina, 'Are you all right?'

'Yes, yes, I'm fine! Which one are you, by the way?'

'I'm Tina.'

'*Tina*. I didn't recognize you. You've put on some weight.'

'Maybe this isn't a very good moment,' said Tina, 'but all this time I've tried to pluck up courage to tell you how bad I feel about what happened.'

'Did you fly over specially?'

'Say again?'

'You're still living in the States, aren't you? Oh no, that's Collette, isn't it? Sorry, not quite myself at the moment.'

The mention of Collette brought it all back to Tina – what happened at Curtis and Millie's wedding in September 1981.

Everything went all right till halfway through the reception, which was in the bar of the Shaw Theatre, Euston, where Millie and Curtis had just reappeared after changing into their going-away outfits. They wore His and Her gangster suits with wide-brimmed hats which were impressive although in retrospect made them look both touching and mildly ridiculous. Millie was rosy with exhilarated drunkenness. Nearby, Juliet was standing with Roscoe, her boyfriend, who was about ten times her size, a big bear of a man who had formerly produced their programme at the ABT. She was wearing a yellow Fiorucci skirt, narrow at the hem, and was clutching Roscoe as if frightened he would float into the air like a barrage balloon if she slackened her grip. Near Juliet and Roscoe were Ratty and Tina, who both, like Millie, had been at the buck's fizz, and it was here that the trouble started, with raised voices over the issue of Ratty's contract, and Ratty's cry over the languid murmuring of guests and the clink of champagne glasses: 'You're trying to get rid of me because you're trying to get rid of the lesbian in yourself.'

'Roscoe!' trilled Tina. 'Ratty thinks I'm a lesbian!'

Everyone's attention was on Roscoe, who was doing a sudden

imitation of a woodworm hunting for a hole. Juliet looked offended, a little mystified. 'We're just going,' she said.

Curtis's mother Mrs Fisher came bustling forward with an oval plate piled with sandwiches. 'You can have chicken n'mayonnaise, cheese n'chive or smoked salmon,' she offered, twirling the little flags around for Tina to see.

Tina said, 'Tell her otherwise, Roscoe.'

'No, honestly, it's been lovely but I think we must,' said Roscoe.

'Look at the two of them,' said Tina, 'Cosy, eh? Well, while she's been preaching at us about the wickedness of our ways, lover boy was humping me on your futon.'

Juliet let go of Roscoe's arm. She turned slowly to him. Looking up at him, she whispered, 'Is this true?'

'True?' said Tina. 'He made me pregnant. But I got rid of it.' She turned to Roscoe. 'I thought you'd like to know you're out of danger. Since you were so petrified at the time.' To Juliet she said, 'I got rid of it for you, Juliet. So you wouldn't have to see it. I hope I get some thanks.'

Tina had gone to Roscoe some months before to take up the cudgels on Juliet's behalf.

Roscoe was going off Juliet because Juliet wouldn't have sex with him. 'I mean,' he said, 'this is 1981. I think I'm entitled . . .' However, Juliet was in love with him and because he was treating her so casually her dancing was going all wrong. Oh, Tina meant well, all right. But her ego was about an inch high at the time and when Roscoe started coming on to her she couldn't help herself. Anyway, another part of her was angry with Juliet, the sanctimonious little wretch; served her right, her and the pamphlets she tried to press into your hand, and saying that she'd pray for you in that silly wispy voice of hers, and looking so pained when anyone said fuck or cunt.

And when Tina saw them standing together in the bar, Juliet looking up at Roscoe with that hurt expression, hanging on to his hands, the hands that not so long ago had grabbed and pawed and scrabbled in his urgency to part Tina's legs as though he were ripping open a parcel, she was overcome by a rage and anguish so strong and terrible it almost had mass, she could almost touch it and lift it high above straining shoulders.

'Where are your manners now, Juliet? Don't I get some thanks?'

Juliet just went missing. Practically in mid-sentence, a canapé made by Mrs Fisher halfway to her mouth. They walked around the streets of Bloomsbury calling her name as though she were a lost cat. Ratty walked with Millie and Roscoe walked with Curtis. They caught themselves looking up for her, half-thinking they would spot her in the branches of a plane tree, just a little glimpse of her yellow Fiorucci skirt. The Georgian squares and terraces became Tottenham Court Road with its electronic shops and ethnic restaurants, every building exuding its own burst of sound or blast of pungent air. After an hour, when they still had not found her, they gave up and went their separate ways. There did not seem any point in going back to the wedding party. They never saw Juliet again, and to all intents and purposes Sweet Fanny Addams was finished.

'Joanna-Mary's being rather a long time,' said Tina to Curtis. 'I'd better go and see if she's all right.'

Curtis followed her upstairs. He heard a sound from Millie's office and opened the door. Joanna-Mary was gazing raptly out of the window.

'The roses are dying,' she said. 'So sad.'

On the way back down the stairs, she whispered ruefully to Tina, 'Terrible curse pains. Couldn't find an aspirin anywhere. You don't think he realized do you?'

She had not quite finished.

When, earlier in the day, she told Janey she had Tina's backing, she was not speaking the strict truth. Her words were more by way of a prediction. Now she needed to establish it as actuality. 'The group,' she said, driving away from Curtis's house.

'God, is that the time,' said Tina. 'Look, just drop me here. It'll be quickest if I take a tube.'

Joanna-Mary said, 'Here's what you have to do.'

'Darling, why don't we get our diaries out and make a date for lunch and we can sort it all out then.'

'Listen to me!' shouted Joanna-Mary.

'Sweetie-pie, I'd love to but I've got to *be* somewhere.'

'I'm in a hurry too,' said Joanna-Mary. 'Daddy's away filming and I've promised Mummy I'll be home early because Jonty's gone to a party in Hertfordshire and she hates spending the evening all on her own in our great big house. I wish she'd get a flat. No one wants her any more.'

Sitting in the car in the rain on Putney Bridge, Joanna-Mary lit two cigarettes and passed one to Tina. A lamp shone through the window on to her hair. From somewhere a Madonna song was playing over and over again on a juke-box. 'Florence hated me,' said Joanna-Mary. 'She would do anything, say anything to get me out of the group.' She opened the window and slowly waved the smoke away. The Madonna music filled the car. 'I have to have the group,' she said.

There were two flushed spots on Tina's cheeks. 'You as leader?' she said. 'You're talking real pressure there. Shouldn't you give yourself a bit more learning time? You've only been in the biz a year.'

Joanna-Mary appeared not to hear. 'You've got to back me against Florence. It's the only way we can see this through.' She started the car again, as if to move off. 'I want you to come in and help me manage the group on a temporary basis, please.'

'Look, I'll have to think about it.' Tina tried to open the door, only to realize that the car had central locking, and Joanna-Mary's hand was on the release switch. She heard the sound of a train coming in alongside the river, the rattle and singing of rails.

'I can't believe you're doing this to me!' said Joanna-Mary with a catch in her voice. 'I thought you were my friend!'

'I am your friend. Just give me time to take this on board. I mean, last time I heard from you, everything was great. Millie loved you. Florence loved you. The punters loved you. In fact the way you were talking there was nearly a wave of national hysteria.'

'I never said any such thing.'

'Can I please get out?'

'Wait. I, I wonder . . . Millie did say to me some days ago that she was going to prepare a contract for me giving me control. She may just have had time to do that, I, I don't know, perhaps it's worth a look. You'll have to ask Curtis if you can see what's on her Amstrad. I don't know how to work them, I'm afraid.'

Free of Joanna-Mary at last, Tina took a taxi to Heathrow airport, where her British Airways jumbo had left several minutes previously.

Tina adored to make, and was adored for, theatrical gestures. She had planned to fly to New York and greet her lover in his hotel room when he returned from filming. She badly needed her lover to be charmed and moved. After finding out her flight had gone, she tried despite being almost dyslexic with panic to speak to him on the telephone. He was not in his hotel room. She bought a ticket on Concorde with her Gold Card.

She arrived at seven in the evening New York time. A cab whose driver was eating a chicken took her to the Algonquin where it had always been her pleasure to make love in one of its brown warm bedrooms with creaking floorboards. On her arrival she learned that her lover, Roger Reed-Herbert, had checked out some hours ago.

Tina ate a pastrami on rye at the Stage Deli and wandered off along Seventh Avenue. She had no idea whether her body clock was on morning or midnight really. After walking some more she passed the Buffalo Roadhouse and reached her favourite Greenwich Village bar. Through the door she could see the regulars hunched. There were a couple of sportswriters who met there before Yankees games, a blond man in a striped jacket and his friend who was bald and plump. A snub-nosed woman with abundant black hair sat one side of them, holding up a book in her red-nailed hand. A man called the Weasel was punching buttons on the juke-box, a cigar jammed in his mouth like a cork in a bottle. The juke-box was made of imitation teak, with blue and gold circles picked out in black on the fascia, and runnels of beer dried on the glass. There was a shiny old-fashioned phone at the end of the bar, and a doorway on to a dark corridor leading nowhere you'd want to finish up. Tina sat down opposite Wes the barman and put her money on the table. She sighed and said, 'How are you, Wes.'

Wes reached behind him for the vodka bottle and mixed her a bullshot. He was a tall man with a stoop, and a moustache that looked as though it had been stuck on in a party game. He said, 'I got some very bad news. Buddy Berrigan's "I Can't Get Started" has disappeared from the juke-box.'

She went into the john and repaired her make-up on tiptoe at the Wilt Chamberlain Memorial Mirror, which was so high that the punters had to jump up to sniff coke at it. A certain pride made her straighten her shoulders under her brown raincoat and smooth the fur of her collar. She stroked out the wrinkles in her tights. Her hair spilled over her eyes as she bent to clean the dust of New York off her shoes, like a cat washing herself after a fight.

When Tina got back, the piano player was getting set up.

Tom McCall was a lean, laconic man of forty-six. He performed at the bar every Tuesday and Thursday, with the band, except when he was on tour; he made his main money travelling with rock stars as a backing musician then came home and spent it on drink, women and making records with the band. His hair was curly and brown-going-grey, and his voice was rich and hoarse. On his forearm an anchor had been tattooed. Tina, who was a fool for curly hair, had sneaked into Tower Records on Broadway and 66th last time she was in New York, and bought two of his albums on cassette, feeling silly and full of yearning like a fourteen-year-old.

Now she moved silently through the drinkers towards him and put a whiskey sour on top of his piano. Then she went back to her place at the bar, from where he could see her and she him.

She didn't know this, but Tom McCall just about fell in love with her there, the sad-eyed lady with the fur-collared raincoat and stockings slightly wrinkled over ankles as small as a girl's. When he had done playing he wandered over to the bar next to her and asked her name. He said, 'Let me know when you're coming back to New York and I'll take you to dinner.'

She said, 'I'm never coming back to New York, but thanks.'

He said, 'Well, then, but I'm going to record a song about you.'

'Of course you're going to,' she said, 'and I'm the Yeti's daughter.'

Later that night, she set off back to England. It was hard blue morning when she arrived. She got off the plane with a headache and a churning stomach. As she walked from the customs hall, her heartbeat suddenly became rapid and violent. It seemed so loud to her that she thought others must hear it too. She leant against a wall under an advertisement which said IT'S ALL OR NOTHING. The arrivals lounge was a babel of voices, a blur of faces. Placards were waved by disembodied hands. See You Soon Vacation Tours. Mr G. DeForest Stubbs (Anglo Freezers). A woman pushed a trolley with one hand, slowly, holding her baby who was plump and round with reddish blond curls and a baleful expression. Tina yearned to be that woman and have that baby in her arms. An Asian man in a grey overall swept the floor by her feet.

After half an hour her heart began to beat properly again. She moved off. She went to the short-term car park to pick up her BMW. It was new, delivered to her the previous week, and she was thrilled to bits with it: she was a woman in a BMW, her own, paid for by the sweat of her hands; she owed it to no company, no man. The paintwork was racing car green and it had a sun roof, leather upholstery and compact disc player. It was heavily alarmed, but she had also taken the precaution of tipping the car park attendants £20 each to watch over it. She got in and rested the back of her head against the seat. In the car next to hers a man and a woman were arguing. Their car was dun-coloured and scratched, and had a pink candlewick cushion on the rear window-ledge. Occasionally words from their argument became audible, as if in little phrase balloons – UP! PEACE! DON'T! The man flung open his door. It banged against the side of Tina's car. She jumped out and yelled at him. He yelled at her. She threatened to call the police. He threatened to hit her. In the passenger seat of the dun-coloured car, the woman wept. Tina jumped back into her car and drove away with a screech of tyres and rage, rage sticking in her throat. The journey home was nine miles long and took one hour.

Five minutes after Tina got home, Joanna-Mary was at the front door. 'Have you asked Curtis yet?'

'Asked him what?'

'About Millie's Amstrad, silly.'

Curtis let Tina back into Millie's house. She went up the stairs and sat down at Millie's desk in the little silent room. An oriole window looked down over the lilac tree. The leaves were speckled and dusty. A clump of marguerites grew by the peeling wooden fence where a passer-by had left two empty plastic bottles and a baby's shoe. The marguerites were scrawny and uncared for, like the kind of women left lining the walls at dances. For a while Tina listened to Curtis moving around below, making man sounds – a cough, the clumsy dropping of some utensil he was unaccustomed to using, the male animal's carefree urination. She had never cohabited with a man apart from her father. She was overcome for a moment by a feeling of yearning and great sad aloneness. Then she shook her head briskly and got on with it.

In the top drawer of the desk she found the disc marked Sweet Fanny Addams 89 and went through the files, half-hoping she would find nothing, because finding something would raise certain unpleasant possibilities; but it was there, she found it: a letter and contract addressed to Joanna-Mary, handing over control of Sweet Fanny Addams. Tina ran her eyes over it. It was the pro forma contract so familiar to her from the old days of the group, except for a paragraph, never seen before in any contract Tina had ever sent out, and surely unnecessary – peculiar by the very fact of its inclusion – 'You will have sole rights over who is in the group and can change the personal without notice at any time. This contract overides all previous contracts.'

Tina could only marvel at Joanna-Mary's will, the way one might marvel at any great elemental force such as the sea. She debated wiping the disc but knew that she would not. Joanna-Mary pleased was Roger pleased, and she needed Roger to be pleased.

While she was printing out the contract, Curtis stood in the doorway. He said, 'Can you find everything? Millie never kept things in the places you'd expect them to be. I looked for ever once for the teapot and she'd put it in the fridge. All her things are still in disorder. I found a turkey baster in her dressing table.'

Tina gathered up the printed contract and put it in her bag. Then she followed him down the stairs and went out into the day. She felt as though she had been awake for a week, and alive for a thousand years.

Chapter Eight

No Consommation

BACK IN THE summer of 1980 Florence thought at first that her life had ended, but was eventually given hope. A boy who was black and had curls tight to his scalp like scorched earth stood on the beach at the spot where she had first set eyes on Yusuf many weeks before. Studying the girls of the town as they went gliding by in their bikinis, he in time approached Florence and identified himself as Yusuf's friend Bob *le noir*. Yusuf, he said, had been moved to Auxerre but had asked him to give her this. He handed over Yusuf's Pez dispenser. When Florence flipped the top it appeared to be empty, but peering inside she found a piece of paper torn from an exercise book, on which was written Yusuf's brief, smudged letter fierce with love.

Yusuf made an attempt to see her, running away from the house with barred windows and bolted doors in Auxerre. He hitched along the Route Nationale – Orleans, Tours, Poitiers, Saintes, Bordeaux – walking when there was no willing driver. This Florence also learned from Bob, who went on to say that Yusuf had been stopped by the gendarmerie and roughed up when he tried to jump out of their van. Not long afterwards, Bob was arrested for illegal possession of firearms, the first incident in an enterprising and audacious career, and with his imprisonment there went Florence's last link to Yusuf.

Life went on. Florence spent three more years with her aunt and uncle, while the Hôtel Kikinette expanded into the next building and the next, gaining three stars and the head of a cherub in gold leaf above the main door. Though pine needles still worked their way into every crevice. Florence served in the bar and brought food to the tables of loudly holidaying families. She worked late, often till two or three, and had to be awake and dressed again at six to prepare the breakfasts. One night she saw her father's face on the television screen fixed to the wall above the bar. Having learned by now to keep everything secret, she said nothing to her aunt and uncle, merely noting the name of the programme and the television station.

She wrote to Gervaise Thomas, care of the television station, which was Associated British. She told him the bare bones of the life she was living, taking care that her words contained no blame. It was still her dream to become a dancer and she asked him only to find out about any dance schools in London or Paris that might take her. She understood that actors did not have much money and she wanted nothing from him except perhaps some letters of introduction to people who might give her the work she needed to pay for her tuition.

For some weeks nothing was heard from Gervaise Thomas. Then one morning at seven she was woken up by her aunt beating her with a coat hanger. A torn letter stuck out of the pocket of Laurence's synthetic crepe blouse. 'So,' shouted Laurence, 'this is how you repay us.'

Florence had to decipher what her aunt was saying. It seemed that Gervaise had written to Laurence demanding to know the whereabouts of Solange's money, and now he was coming to see her.

'I only told him the truth,' said Florence.

Mean, shrieking Laurence, the sound and fury of her indignation drowning out the voice of her conscience. As for Gervaise, he thought he was a fine fellow, championing his daughter's rights. Little Florence whom he missed so much. He admired his unselfishness in renouncing her, all so that she could enjoy a better, richer life. He was moved by the tears he wept while remembering her, the thin trusting child. And when he read her dignified letter that had meandered from department to department of the television company and then on till it found him, he was impelled by pride at his own sense of outrage. So it came about that he spoke angrily to Paulette, not something he ever did lightly.

'If it hadn't been for you I would never have left her there. You bear a lot of responsibility for this. You could have looked after her.'

'Oh, that's very noble of you,' retorted Paulette. 'Here we are, sitting in our airy apartment in Paris with a separate shower. How do you think these things would have been paid for had I not worked? Has your career as an actor been so successful that you could afford to keep us in this comfort? And a growing daughter greedy for clothes and ballet lessons as well? Some vision of fatherhood you have!'

'I wish you had been able to accept her as your daughter,' he said sadly. He felt resentful; he had tried his best after Solange died, taking on a suitable mother figure; why had she not fulfilled her part of the bargain? 'I can't see why you wouldn't accept her as your daughter.'

'I made every attempt but if she wouldn't accept me as her mother, what was I to do?' Paulette paused to straighten the cloth on the reproduction Louis XIV telephone table. 'And remember who paid for your teeth.'

Gervaise felt he had gone as far as he wished to go. If there was one thing he feared more than anything else it was unpleasantness. He nerved himself, however, to enquire of Laurence what had happened to the money that Florence had been left by her mother.

'It's more than enough to pay for her dancing tuition,' he wrote to her, 'and there should be enough left over to cover the rent on a small flat.'

Gervaise was unprepared for the wrath that this released in Laurence, who after laying into Florence with the coat hanger, catapulted herself downstairs and got on with the breakfast very noisily, banging lots of chrome jugs together and bestowing terrifying grins on the small children of hotel guests. She sent Florence into Bordeaux to dispute a bill that had just arrived from the plumber, and stood waiting in the doorway to welcome Gervaise.

'I'm sorry,' said Gervaise after wave after wave of bombing had passed. 'It was quite thoughtless of me.'

'And if you wish, at this late stage, to do anything for your daughter, you could perhaps repay me the 5,000 francs I have recently spent on redecorating her bedroom,' (She had not.)

'Of course,' said Gervaise. 'I'll let you have a cheque by return.' (He did not.)

'And don't ever come here again disrupting my routine and making malicious accusations.'

'I gave her a piece of my mind,' said Gervaise, returning to the apartment he shared with Paulette after this conversation.

'Good. Don't let her think she's off the hook.'

'Oh, you can be sure I won't let her get away with anything of the sort,' said Gervaise.

Some time after this, Associated British TV were casting for a costume drama about an English family living in France at the turn of the century. It required a year's filming in Manchester and the Camargue, and Gervaise landed a leading part as the family's high-principled and devoted father.

Gervaise felt very at home in the role. After a few months he thought he might send Florence some money.

It arrived on the 12th of June, a little after her twenty-first birthday which was on the 2nd, but Gervaise had always been confused about the day. Florence was in the hotel bar, cleaning the marble-topped counter. There was an old man in blue overalls by the football table, staring ahead of him with an untouched glass of brandy, as still and upright as a bird on a telephone wire. He had been one of Uncle Gaston's cronies and still came to the hotel every morning, although Gaston was now dead. He had suffered a heart attack in one of the maids' rooms, where, Aunt Laurence claimed, while mending a curtain rail he had fallen backwards in a six-feet arc onto the bed, unaware that the maid was in it at the time.

Florence's brown hair was cropped like a boy's. There were soft bristles at the back of her neck. Her skin was white because she worked indoors most of the time. Her eyes looked dark and huge. She opened the letter without recognizing her father's writing. A cheque for 10,000 francs fell on to the floor. She stared at it down there for a moment, taking in the signature, Geoff Thompson, her father's real name. There was a short letter with it. 'Just a drop in the ocean, I know! Not a word to Paulette, mind!' She remembered Paulette dimly, a sharp-faced woman with a nose that was long and sort of pulled away from her face, as though it had been shut in a door.

Aunt Laurence came stomping in and Florence hurriedly stored the cheque in the front pocket of her dungarees. After she had finished work, she went to the Crédit Lyonnais on the corner of the street and banked it. A week later she came downstairs with her bags packed and told her aunt she was leaving. There was a sudden rush of air in the bar as the night-shift workers came in for breakfast. Aunt Laurence didn't seem to understand what Florence was doing. 'Bring some more glasses in from the back,' she kept saying.

Paris at the end of June was rainy and full of tourists in macs. Florence walked through St Denis, looking for a room she could afford. The pavements were narrow and sticky with dust. At the cafés you could eat couscous with everything. She found an attic in a thin grey building with slogans spray-painted on the walls in Arabic. The front entrance was dark and nicely private for people to use as a *pissoir*. Trains rumbled all night, heading for the Gare du Nord. Kept awake, she knelt by her window and watched the neon signs on hotel rooftops. Her eye was then caught by a sign saying Au Pied de Vache, and three cows in tutus which changed from green to red to blue. When the neon went blue, the tutus fell off.

The next night Florence went round to Au Pied de Vache and sat through the floor show. There were dancers, boys and girls, and a flame-headed woman who sat by the entrance, checking coats. When it was over she stood outside a door marked Artistes, hoping to see the manager. After some time, the flame-haired woman shot out of the door, hissing, 'These are Polish teeth and they are mine!' From inside, a man shouted something back at her. The woman shot a gaze of extreme hatred at Florence and whirled round to leave, hitting Florence in the knees with her handbag.

Florence went on in and came face to face with a small Algerian smoking a cigar. 'Yes?' he said.

'I'm looking for work.'

'Are you prepared to do topless?'

'No.'

He shrugged.

'Listen,' said Florence, 'I'm such a great dancer you won't even notice you haven't seen my tits.'

He looked her up and down, then told her to go out on stage. The place was empty. He put on a disco tape and sat at a table, watching her in the dark. She writhed and wiggled, pretending she was in a courtyard at the Hôtel Kikinette all those years ago. After two minutes, the tape stopped. She waited on stage, hoping his heavy breathing was due only to the cigar.

'What's your name?' he said.

'Fanny Addams.'

'Flanny Addons. OK. You can check coats. Sit by the door. You're pretty – you'll bring in the punters.'

Florence stepped down from the stage. Her knee was hurting. 'What about the other one?' she said. 'The one with the flame-coloured hair.'

The manager made a dismissive gesture. 'Marika goes on the booze too much,' he said, 'and then her teeth fall out.'

As Florence was leaving he shouted after her, 'Hey, Flanny. You're too flat. Stuff some ST's down your front.'

Florence had to get there for six o'clock and work through till two the next morning, but the hours were not nearly as bad as those she had put in for Aunt Laurence. Also she enjoyed the busy-ness of Au Pied de Vache, the flirtations and quarrels, the noise of someone singing in the dressing room in the early evening, the crash of beer crates being humped into the cellar. The only problem was Marika, who had taken to standing on the pavement outside, shouting at her in a form of Polish.

She made a friend of one of the boy dancers. He liked to sit with her in his mid-evening break. He was a tall American called Cal Johnson, who had mousy close-cropped hair, a moustache and a big nose. She learned that he took ballet classes in the daytime.

'That's what I've come to Paris for,' confessed Florence, 'but how am I ever going to afford it?'

'I've got plenty of money,' said Cal. She knew that because he always came and went by taxi. 'I can lend you some till you find your feet. By the way, where did you get your dungarees? They're a fabulous cut.'

Cal always talked to her in a certain way, as though they were two girlfriends together.

One night Au Pied de Vache didn't close till four, and she was worried about going home on her own because now Marika had found out where she lived and was going around with a brick in her handbag. 'Come back with me,' said Cal. 'I need someone to talk to right now, anyway. I can cook you breakfast.'

It was a very long taxi ride. The streets of St Denis became the three-lane avenues alongside the Seine. It was just beginning to get light and an empty *bateau mouche* glided along the water as silently as a swan.

The taxi swung left away from the river and after a while turned into a narrow street full of darling little shops and hotels. Florence just caught sight of the name: Rue Jacob. They stopped outside an apartment building with white paintwork and a trellis full of flowers growing *inside* the lobby. The concierge saw her and raised his eyebrows. Florence blurted 'How can you afford—'

'Sh,' said Cal, propelling her into the lift.

They went up three floors and then stopped. Cal opened the door and Florence walked, not into a corridor, but into an enormous living room painted cream and full of real antiques and old books and rugs and paintings.

While Cal went into the kitchen and got some eggs from an avocado-green fridge and made omelettes with them on the matching cooker, Florence looked around the rest of the flat. Off the living room was a big bedroom with a double bed, a smaller bedroom with a divan piled high with junk, and a bathroom more than twice the size of her attic. It had a separate shower, two washbasins, a bidet and a big bath with gold taps, all set in panelled mahogany. On the other side of the living room was a study with bookshelves from the floor to the ceiling, crammed with huge learned books about law.

'My friend' – there was an unspoken 'er' between 'my' and 'friend' – 'who owns this flat is a British QC,' said Cal. 'He specializes in international law.'

'No kidding,' said Florence, 'I thought he was probably a dustman or something.'

'Pardon me?'

Florence said, 'Where is he?'

'He has a place in London and Brussels as well. He, uh, tries to visit Tuesday, Wednesday every other week. Godfrey is very well known in the legal and government world. He can't afford any scandal.'

'Poor Cal,' said Florence, 'having to make do with so little of him.'

Cal burrowed in a low cupboard set into the wall and came out with two bottles of Juliénas. 'It's my fault,' he said, 'for getting involved with a married man.'

Cal's omelettes were characterized by terrific attention to detail. He sprinkled them with chopped tarragon and served them with little circles of fried bread topped with sour cream and freckles of pepper. They took him the best part of an hour to get right, but the Juliénas was so beautiful and flowery that Florence was tipping it down like cola. 'Why do you need someone to talk to right now?' she said.

'My parents are on my back. They want me to come home.'

'Where's that?'

'Ohio. My family have a business there. It makes tractors.'

'Someone has to,' said Florence, 'but not you, I don't think.'

'There's a girl involved,' said Cal. 'She's called Courtney. Older than me, but very nice, a very good local family. I'm meant to marry her so they can stop worrying that I might be a faggot.'

Florence said, 'Can't you just tell them how it is with you?'

'I can't,' he said, 'no, I mean, my father, my mother too, no, I just can't do that to them.'

He looked so careworn sitting there that Florence had to get up and put her arms round him because if she thought she had problems they were nothing compared to Cal's. He put his big bony hand over hers. 'Don't go home,' he said. 'Stay here with me the rest of tonight.'

Florence lay in the double bed with him, on the edge, wanting to lie close to him but afraid it would be misconstrued. The Juliénas soon put her to sleep. When she woke up it was bright daylight and the phone was ringing.

Florence looked at Cal, who was still well away. She leant over him to answer it.

'Hello?' An American woman, confused at Florence's greeting. 'Is that 40614378?'

'Oh, you want Cal,' said Florence. 'He's right here beside me.'

'Excuse me? Who are you?' The voice rang round the room. Cal woke up with a start.

Florence said, 'Cal really hasn't told you? We're getting married.' Cal was fully awake now, jumping up and down trying to grab the receiver from her. Florence pushed him back on to the bed. Cal's mother meanwhile let rip with a piercing shriek in which there was perhaps a hint of relief. 'Well, I don't like to wake Cal,' said Florence through the screams, 'so I will just tell him you called.'

Afterwards, when Cal had stopped shouting at her, Florence said, 'Don't you see, it solves both our problems. You can stay here and get your family off your back, and I can have somewhere decent to live. No one's using that little bedroom. We can be like flatmates, and I'll keep out of the way when Godfrey comes.'

'What,' said Cal with his head in his hands, 'is Godfrey going to say?'

Godfrey, as it turned out, seemed quite amused.

He was a tall man in his fifties with long thin lips like a letterbox, and a taste for cashmere coats. Cal said he was very clever and Florence thought he might well be, though possibly not in a very nice way. She felt a shiver of danger every time he looked at her with his pastel-blue eyes. Nevertheless, he was very polite and charming to her, and to Cal's family when they came over for the wedding ceremony at the *mairie*. Godfrey's wife Lorna, a large woman with a firm jaw, came too. Godfrey had told her Florence was his secretary. They rolled up in a dark blue Jaguar. Lorna looked even more terrifying than Godfrey, particularly when he began to do rather strange things to Florence in front of her, like pinching her bottom and giving her a loud sloppy kiss.

Almost a year later, Florence came back one afternoon to find Cal on the phone. He saw her and shut the bedroom door.

Everything had gone very well since the wedding. Cal was very good-natured, a bit bumbling sometimes. He reminded her of Gervaise in their pre-Paulette days. He taught her to drive and now she spent some happy hours circling the Arc de Triomphe, carving up fat men in BMWs with Cal's Renault 5 turbo. When Godfrey visited she stayed away, curled up in a corner at an all-night café or sleeping under her coat on the dressing-room sofa at Au Pied de Vache. Meanwhile, she had used the money she saved on flat rental to pay for dance classes. She had just received her teaching diploma and was holding it in her arms along with a large brown bag full of groceries. The agreement was that she shopped and Cal cooked.

Cal was on the phone a long time and when he came out of the bedroom he said, 'Oh, I was talking to Godfrey,' and was looking rather tight-faced.

'You look as though something's wrong,' said Florence.

'No, it's nothing,' he said.

The next day she happened to look out of the window and see a dark blue Jaguar parked over the street. There was a big woman behind the wheel. She called Cal over and he peeked out. 'It's just a coincidence,' he said. 'Lorna's in England. There you go. Two fat women in the world who drive blue Jaguars.'

However, next time he spoke to Godfrey on the phone he closed the door behind him.

A few days later he said, 'I'm taking a couple of days off work. I'm going to Brussels.'

'OK,' she said, feeling that he didn't want her to ask questions.

'Godfrey's concerned about leaving the flat unattended. Make sure you get back at night.'

'Why wouldn't I get back?'

'Oh, you know, if you felt lonely and . . . Well, you just make sure you get back now, I don't like to think of you wandering round Paris all hours. I'm going to be ringing you each night, now, make sure you're back safely.'

Florence said, 'What's brought this on? You've never worried before.'

'I'm very fond of you,' he said. 'You remember that.'

The first night after he went, Au Pied de Vache closed a little late and the phone was already ringing as Florence walked out of the lift into the living room at Rue Jacob. It was Cal. 'I'm OK,' she said. 'You can go to sleep now.'

She made herself a cup of chocolate and got undressed, thinking she really ought to consider cleaning out her room some time. There were half a dozen cups and glasses full of liquid mould on the floor. A hot shower made her drowsy. She fell backwards into bed and didn't know anything else till the sound of breaking china woke her. A man was swearing in a plummy British accent. She opened her eyes and could just make out Godfrey in the gloom, stark naked except for his socks, trying to get mouldy coffee off his Italian suede shoe. 'Godfrey,' she shrieked, 'You've got the wrong – '

He put his hand over her mouth and swung himself on to the bed, at which the door burst open and a man started taking photographs of them. As Florence dived across the floor for her clothes, Lorna appeared in the doorway and in a deep, cultured bellow said, 'My terms, Godfrey, are these. Half your earnings for the last twenty years, the Jag, the house, the château and the Wimbledon debentures. Otherwise the photographs go to every newspaper in the free world.'

Florence didn't hear Godfrey's response; she was too busy running round the flat picking up everything that was hers and stuffing it into cases and carrier bags. By the time she'd got it all together, Lorna and the photographer had gone and Godfrey was pacing round the living room looking quite smooth, considering. 'Ah, hello, Florence,' he said, 'Perhaps some explanation may be in order.'

'You don't have to explain anything,' said Florence. 'You and Cal set me up and you're an oily shit.'

'You're taking a very extreme view, if you don't mind my saying. I realize that you are a rather unsophisticated girl but perhaps you can consider Cal's position, if not mine. Lorna had suspected for some time that I, ah, had been having an irregular liaison and, having traced me with the help of a private detective to this flat, was determined to, so to speak, catch me in the act. A divorce may be inevitable, but in the circles in which I move you may understand that it is infinitely preferable to be branded a womanizer than a practising homosexual. Where are you going?'

'I'm getting out.'

'I really can't permit that. I may need you to appear in some capacity again. I am not at all sure that Lorna is entirely convinced. After all, I have allowed you to live rent free in one of the best flats in Paris, so with respect, my dear, I believe you owe me something.'

If there was one thing Florence hated more than anything in the world it was the kind of man who called her 'my dear', so she threw all her cases and bags at him one after the other, jumped into the lift and banged the doors shut while he was hopping over everything trying to reach her. When she got to the ground floor she ran all the way down the Rue Jacob and across a few streets till she found a call box, hoping that Millie wouldn't mind being phoned at six o'clock in the morning.

Millie was so agog at Florence's story that she made her reverse the charges because Florence's money kept running out every time she got to a juicy bit. At the end of it, Millie said, 'That settles it. You've got to come to London.' Three hours later Florence was on the Boulogne train as it pulled out of the Gare du Nord. The last thing that went through her mind as she left Paris was to wonder whether Marika would get her old job back.

'How long have I been here?' said Florence to the junior hospital doctor on the morning after she woke from unconsciousness.

'Almost as long as I have,' said the junior doctor, who was not so fuddled through lack of sleep that he could not remember his usual joke.

'Did anyone call to see me while I was sleeping?' asked Florence. 'A young guy with golden skin and dark eyes.'

'Plenty of nice young ladies. I wish I had more patients like you. My working life would be much improved.' He yawned. He had a felt-tip pen and a comb in one pocket. As an after-thought he said, 'No men.'

'Someone with reddish hair, an older man?' said Florence. 'The husband of my friend who died. He must have called, surely.'

'Nope.'

But the gentle Irish nurse who was passing said, 'Florence Johnson? There was a young man who came here asking for you last Wednesday night, the day after the accident.'

'Oh,' said Florence quietly. 'Did he see me like this?'

'He didn't want to see you, just to leave something for you.'

The nurse brought Florence something folded in a silk tie. 'He asked me for wrapping paper,' she said, 'but it isn't issued on the National Health. So if he didn't take off his tie right there. Oh, and here's some post for you. Your friend Janey brought it in.'

'I'll have that tie if you don't want it,' said the doctor, 'I'm off duty tonight.'

Florence inspected her post first. Something prevented her from tackling the present wrapped in the tie. The post included an invitation to watch a video on time share, and a letter which she knew from the handwriting was from her landlady, Mrs Gardam. Mrs Gardam had been taught from the same book of spelling as had Joanna-Mary.

'Dear Miss Johnson, Since you still havent paid the rent owed to me for May and Jun as well as july I am giving you notice to quite. Please forward to me a cheque for the £330 owed to me by return of post or I will have to put the mater in the hands of my solicitors.'

A second letter was from Joanna-Mary herself.

'Dear Florence, As you may have heard at the time, Millie and I had already been planning some changes in the line-up of Sweet Fanny Addams before her sad death. Now the contract she promised me is in my posession I feel after much heart-searching that the time has come to go ahead and act on her wishes. Putting together the 'right mix' is always tricky and one never knows till its time to go out there and dance who is going to be right for the group's ethos and who's face doesn't quite fit. But might be absolutely 'the bee's knees' for some other group! What I'm trying to say, Florence, without wanting to hurt you, is that though Millie and I valued your contribution to Sweet Fanny Addams very much at the time, 'enough is enough' and sadly I do not feel you figure in our plans for the future. I am sure it wont be long before you find a group which is right for 'Florence' as opposed to 'Joanna-Mary' and needles to say, I will recommend you to anyone who has work going begging. Have you tried Starburst International? They are always wanting girls for Italy, Greece etc. Do keep in touch.'

Carefully Florence unwrapped the tie. Inside, she found a Pez. She turned it over in her fingers and looked inside, finding nothing. The dispenser was in the form of a football. She knew it meant Joe had gone. She doubted that she'd see him again. She doubted that she'd see anybody again. Ever.

Chapter Nine

Young Hearts Run Free

LONDON WAS COVERED in a hazy sunlight that made ghosts out of the buildings on the other side of the river. There were people going to work with dingy grey suits accessorized with dingy grey faces. On the roads, traffic rattled and droned. Police sirens sounded from a long way off. The interiors of vehicles smelt of heat and sick. Two men with the veins standing out on their faces howled and bayed at each other through the rolled-down windows of their cars.

Kit looked up from the reception desk at Legwork as Janey came through the swing doors. He smiled at her in recognition. She smiled back. 'She's just come up from the gym,' he said, dialling the inside line. Janey glimpsed her moon face reflected in the glass door. She worried she wasn't looking smart enough to confront the great Tina Addams. Should she have worn her hat? There was a bleep of the call signal and then out boomed Tina's breath-starved Hello. 'Tina? Janey Sears would like a word with you. Shall I send her up?' His face changed and he turned with the receiver away from Janey. 'Ah. OK. Sorry.' To Janey, he said, 'I must have got my wires crossed. She's not having any meetings today.'

'When is she having meetings? What about tomorrow?'

'I don't have a diary on me, I'm desolated to say.'

Janey was a helpful girl who since childhood had believed that older people knew best and that they had their worries and it didn't become you to add to them, but Kit was a friend of hers and when he said that, as though she'd just come to him as a total stranger, as though she'd asked him if he'd got any mushrooms in stock, or two tickets for the show, something inside her went *Excuse Me*.

'Save your tears,' said Janey in her soft Norfolk burr. 'I'll wait for her.'

She sat on the white-painted bench with her arms folded. A large lazy fly put its feet up on the window-ledge. Janey looked around her. So this was what you got for being clever and mouthy and for not doing what people said you had to do. So this was what happened if you said, I'm not taking this shit. I'm not thick and obliging like you want me to be. Well then, Janey Sears, she thought. Well then. Now you know. What are you going to do about it?

Presently there was a clatter of heels and Tina poked her head round the inner door.

'Kit, can you – ' She saw Janey and turned back to Kit. 'Bring it to me in my office,' she said, disappearing behind the door again.

Janey ran up the stairs behind her and caught her up halfway along the corridor. 'Tine, it's *me*. Janey.'

'And?'

'It's about Florence.'

Tina pushed her into her office and banged the door behind them. There was a bright pink rug on the floor, two sofas covered in Designers' Guild print, and a fifteen-year-old portrait of Tina in a rumpled leotard and leg-warmers, staring at herself in a dressing-room mirror. Her gaze was open and unhurt. 'Florence, Florence, Florence. I'm sick of Florence,' said Tina angrily.

Janey said, 'Ten days ago Florence had a job, a friend, a flat and her health. Now she hasn't anything. One or maybe two of those things she might learn to manage without, but four out of four, that's going to be awfully hard for her.'

'If Joanna-Mary says Millie nominated her to take over, that's good enough for me.'

'Oh, Joanna-Mary's lying and cheating, they're good enough for you?'

'Please don't speak about my friend like that.'

'Your friend? I'd rather have headlice than Joanna-Mary as a friend.' Janey decided to sit down on her own initiative as Tina didn't look as though she was about to issue any invitations. 'I wasn't ever much good at my school books,' said Janey, 'but it doesn't take whatsisname, the geometry bloke, to work out Joanna-Mary couldn't run a whelk stall. She doesn't know how to make people work for her, her ideas are all the kind of stuff people were doing twenty years ago and they weren't very good then, and . . .' Janey looked at Tina accusingly, 'well, I've seen this contract Millie's meant to have done for her, but you and I know, *personally* speaking, that Joanna-Mary can't *spell*.'

There was a coffee percolator in the corner by the window. Tina got up and switched it on. The room filled with sporadic gasps and sighs, like someone with toothache catching their breath. Janey said, 'You're a sensible woman, Tina, and so was Millie. You can't tell me that she was going to pass her group over to someone like that.'

'Joanna-Mary's got hidden qualities,' said Tina lightly.

'Yes,' Janey said, 'she's even nastier than people think.'

There was silence. The building began to vibrate slightly, the thump-thump-thump of the brass from the disco class in the rehearsal room. 'How do you want your coffee?' said Tina in her clear, magisterial voice. 'Black? White?'

'I only have decaff, thank you very much, Tina.'

Tina said, trying to lighten things a bit, 'Decaff? That's for cowards.'

'Oh well,' said Janey. 'Takes one to know one, in my opinion.'

Tina went red. 'Janey,' she said, 'I always had you down as a sweet little thing.'

'I always thought you were a nice type of person, come to that.'

After a pause, Tina said, 'Yes, well, don't think I wanted this to happen.'

'It doesn't have to happen,' said Janey, 'All you've got to do is put a stop to it.'

'Things aren't that easy,' she said.

Janey said, 'Why aren't they?'

'Doesn't matter. Nothing to do with you, and nothing to do with Florence.'

'I hate it when people tell me it doesn't matter!' Janey suddenly shouted. 'As though I'm stupid to be bothered with. Well, I'm telling you, I . . . I'm just telling you, I hate it,' she finished, because if she'd said any more she would have cried. Tina sat there looking into her coffee and not answering, and after a while Janey got up and let herself out.

It was too fine a day to go down into the underground. Janey rode on the top floor of the bus, looking out at the people scurrying along, ten wide on the pavements sometimes but still desperately managing to avoid touching. She'd been in London four years now and she still couldn't get over how scared of getting involved with each other everyone was. In her village, if someone knocked on your door you invited them in. In London there could have been a 90 m.p.h. hurricane blowing and you still kept them standing on your doorstep.

The intensive care ward was on the ground floor of the hospital. Janey had to walk through casualty to reach it. There was a pile of torn dirty sheets waiting to be moved, next to a row of stained chairs, where a woman was kneeling to mop the bit of floor where her child had been sick. On ordinary days Janey would have stopped and helped, but today she was feeling too upset to notice anything.

Florence was sitting up. She was looking in a hand mirror at the scars on her forehead, trying to cover them under a scarf. Janey did her hair and helped her knot the scarf at the back. It was lime green with things written in French on it in black, and some weird pale-blue diagrams. Then she sat down and brought out a box of Maltesers.

'How's it going?' Florence asked. Janey noted the studied unconcern in her voice.

'I went to see Tina Addams,' Janey said.

'I suppose,' said Florence, 'she was wearing the usual heap of old rags.' Carefully she bit all the chocolate off the outside of a Malteser.

'It was a Jean Muir,' said Janey gloomily.

'Oh well,' said Florence, 'haven't I always said it, Tina doesn't know how to dress.'

'Huh! She doesn't know how to be an honest woman, that's for sure.' Janey looked in the water jug. There was a little black fly in there, drowning. Janey fished it out, then washed the jug in the sink and filled it again. The cleaning activity made her feel better. 'I told her,' she said to Florence, 'that Joanna-Mary knows twiddle-twat about management.'

Florence's face was too patched to make laughing comfortable, but her eyes were amused. 'That might have been unwise. You know she and Joanna-Mary's old man are meant to be an item still.'

'I thought to myself,' said Janey, making herself comfortable on the end of Florence's bed, 'you've got to think the best of people. Appeal to their sense of fairness. But she wouldn't budge. She's a cow. I'm going to put a spell on her.'

'Janey, I'm so touched that you're doing all this for me. But you must stop. This is my fight.'

'Look. I'm just a dancer. There's not many other things I can do. I can tell fortunes, I can make banana bread and I can stick by my friends. So that's what I do. Would the world be a better place if I walked out on you and lied to everyone?'

'Do you want to work again?'

'Oh,' said Janey, 'that isn't fair.'

'Well, but you won't work again if you take Tina Addams on,' said Florence. 'Janey, you've got forty years to go before you can get your pension from the Artistes Benevolent Fund. They're going to be pretty empty years if Tina puts it around that you're a troublemaker. You get on the phone to her now and tell her you're sorry for all you said.'

'I'd rather eat a bat full of maggots.'

'Besides,' said Florence, 'I need you to stick around, I want to know what they're up to, Joanna-Mary and Tina, I want you to tell me every move they make because I'm going to use that knowledge somehow to get even.'

As Janey left, Florence was lying back with her hands underneath her head, frowning.

Janey flung pebbles at the bedroom window of Greg's room in Acton. A light came on and Greg looked down at her. She stood in the orange glow of a street lamp, her hair hastily crammed into her hat. The midnight buses rattled past behind her, causing their conversation to be conducted in a shout. She said, 'I've run all the way from Shepherd's Bush. When you went to Florence's flat to help Joanna-Mary, was she doing anything suspicious?'

It had come to Janey as she lay in bed, in the moment before dropping off to sleep. Over the chaos of the last few days she had been going like a pianist repeating arpeggios: Joanna-Mary's perfidy, Lily's treachery, Florence's anguish over the missing contract, Tina's evasiveness. She thought of Greg in the hospital room, soon after the accident, in his fawn jersey of scratchy wool, slightly pop-eyed and spotty with tiredness.

'Joanna-Mary's gone to pick up Florence's things.'

'I'll go over now. She may appreciate a hand.'

Now Janey stood on the threshold of the gloomy Victorian mansion where Greg had a bedsit. A cistern flushed unwillingly at the back of the house. There was a strong smell of curry. From behind a door came the sound of someone practising a flute.

'Let me in, Greg. Then we can talk.'

'Out of the question. You're a member of the opposite sex and it's after eleven.'

Janey barged her way into the hall. She pulled her old tweed jacket tightly around her, hoping he wouldn't notice that it was her nightie that was tucked into her jeans. 'Something important of Florence's has gone missing,' she said. 'Her rightful property.'

'I'm awfully sorry to hear that, but it's got nothing to do with me,' said Greg politely.

'Nothing to do with you? When you were at her flat same time as Joanna-Mary?'

'Why don't you go and ask Joanna-Mary about it, then?'

'Because,' said Janey, 'I'm acting on *instinct* and my instinct tells me you know more than you're saying and my instinct is never wrong.' She'd hit on something, that was for sure. Greg had moved away from her and was now pressed against the wall, hands in pockets, finding something terribly riveting in the pattern on the lino.

'You look just like our little brother,' said Janey disgustedly, 'when he was caught nicking money from our Mum's purse.'

'You're reading too much into this,' said Greg. 'I wasn't there long enough to see anything.'

'She's got at you too, has she?'

Greg had on his long, pointed look and was making little pecks of anger.

'She's very pretty, isn't she?' said Janey. The other night she'd heard her favourite soap opera heroine say something like that, trying to stop her best friend's boyfriend leaving her best friend for a girl whom the best friend thought was her friend. For some reason it had Janey crying because she believed in that sort of loyalty. 'But don't think you'll get any thanks for helping her out. She'll use you and use you and use you again and then when she can't use you any more she'll dump you just like a load of rubbish.'

'I don't know what you're talking about,' said Greg, 'and unless there's anything else I've got a bath running.' He held the front door open for her.

'Anything else?' said Janey. 'Oh, yes, Greg, where could I find some old newspapers.'

'What for?'

'Oh, I don't know,' said Janey, 'Why would I?'

'You're acting very peculiar lately,' accused Greg.

'Not half as peculiar as you,' retorted Janey triumphantly. 'I can read all the old newspapers I want, if I want.'

'Yes, but why,' said Greg, 'why do you want to start reading old newspapers? When you don't really read new newspapers, either.'

'How do you know what I do or don't read,' said Janey. 'You wouldn't know, you've always got your nose in some newspaper yourself. People with their noses in newspapers *all the time*, that's peculiar. Then having the cheek to ask questions when people say they're going to read old newspapers, what's more peculiar than that?'

'Oh, for God's sake,' moaned Greg, 'go to the fucking British Newspaper Library in Colindale.'

Going back to sleep for four hours just didn't seem worth the trouble, so Janey cooked herself a bacon sandwich with mayonnaise and sat in bed and ate it watching the horror film. Compared to what Florence was going through it was pretty tame stuff, she thought. Eventually she fell asleep and dreamed of waiting at a station somewhere for a train, which arrived on a different platform and left without her. Florence was in her dream, sitting in the buffet wearing Tina's big-brimmed hat and chestnut brown coat with fox-fur collar. Only it wasn't Florence, or Tina, it was a woman with blonde hair and a strange smooth face without contours, as though it had been drawn on a hard-boiled egg. 'You won't get far without me,' she was saying. In the morning Janey climbed on to a double-decker bus and headed up the Oxford road to Colindale.

The library was housed in a building so anonymous you could work in it all your life and have trouble remembering it afterwards. It looked down on to a narrow street with almost no identifying characteristics, as though whoever built London had had a few odd houses left over afterwards and rather than waste them had turned them into Colindale.

Janey hesitated at the bottom of the steps leading up to the main entrance. There was a pink-skinned man in a dark blue uniform up there. He was sitting on a straight-backed wooden chair, and his silver-rimmed spectacles glinted in the sun. Janey pretended to look for something in her bag. She'd never been to one of these places before. She didn't know what you were meant to do at all. The only library she'd ever been near was the mobile one run by an Asian who came out from King's Lynn and also did videos and dry cleaning.

The pink-skinned man leant forward and said, 'Do you have a pass, young lady?'

'A pass,' said Janey. 'Oh dear.' She delved in her handbag again, as if she expected one suddenly to materialize in there.

'If you haven't got a pass,' he said, 'you'll have to go along to that little window over there and see about it.'

He was so grand and terrifying that Janey was half inclined to turn round and go home. Then she told herself to get a grip. 'It's only a silly old library,' she thought. 'What kind of person is frightened of a library?'

She went in and filled in a slip of paper which cost her £5.50.

Her handwriting looked large and childish on it, like a row of balloons. Apart from learning to spell, she'd never got very far at school. Too busy helping her mum and dad on the farm. Well, someone had to pick apples. People couldn't all be professors and suchlike. The microfilm room, that was what the person behind the little window said she needed. What was she looking for? She didn't know, exactly. Reasons. An explanation. Joanna-Mary and Tina.

There was a young-looking guy at the booth next to hers in the microfilm room. She watched what he did, slotting in the roll of film, switching on the light, bringing the columns of print into focus. She squared her shoulders, popped a piece of Endekay in her mouth and presently found herself looking at page after page of early seventies back numbers of the *Pictorial*.

SWEET! FANNY! ADDAMS!

Ask any boy who he'd like to date and a dancer with Sweet Fanny Addams is bound to be pretty high on the list! We thought it would be fun to take a stroll down the King's Road one sunny afternoon and meet the girls from 'Music Box' who've taken the viewers by storm!

Sixteen-year-old Juliet is pretty lovable by any Romeo's standards. Just five feet tall with long ultra-feminine hair (she has it kept in shape by Tony at Ginger Group) she told us that at the moment her ideal boy should be smart and clean shaven, although she did point out that her ideas about boys change all the time. 'I'm fairly quiet by temperament – that's why I need a boy to be lively and fun to be with!' Not unnaturally, Juliet takes great care over her appearance and likes to buy clothes for her size 8 figure at Biba and Bus Stop. She prefers an informal 'spag bol' supper with a few close friends to clubbing and all-night parties. Her favourite music is instrumental and she's a great fan of Cliff Richard.

We couldn't help admiring Collette's outfit from Paris – she's so much like Brigitte Bardot, and to judge by the attention she was receiving as we chatted outside the Chelsea Drug Store, lots of boys think the same!' A very sophisticated young lady, and it's hard to believe she's only twenty-two. 'My ideal boy is tall, composed and well-spoken. He must be slim and preferably have blue eyes and fair hair.' Collette spends as much time as possible in and around the

King's Road and South Molton Street where she can visit all her favourite shops. 'I'm very lucky – Daddy gives me a monthly allowance but I still have to budget like everyone else!'

With her lovely slim legs and tiny face crowned by an ultra-fashionable 'Italian Page Boy' mop, Alexa could easily be mistaken for a top fashion model! She drives the latest mustard yellow Italian sports car and her favourite outfits are from French Connection and Sonia Rykiel. There are lots of boyfriends and a lot of weekend parties – but there's another side of the story! 'When we're on tour we have to wake up early to travel to our next gig and I find those 7.30 calls pretty awful!' laughs Alexa. 'But I never forget it's a super life!' Seventeen-year-old Alexa likes a boy who's not too short ('With my height I have to be careful I don't look down on guys!' she quips) and has a definite preference for the dark-haired ones!

Twenty-four-year-old Tina is from cosmopolitan Manchester and shares a flat with Collette and Millie. 'We act like twits but it's all great fun!' Tina seemed to be in a terrific hurry when we took this picture of her outside Granny Takes A Trip. She explained that she was on a whirlwind tour of the shops before meeting a friend at the Associated British TV Centre, so we asked her what she thought of London and our boys. 'From all I've seen, the guys are great. They dress with style, most are good-looking and nearly all have the nice, slim hips I go for!' But Tina isn't ready to go steady with anyone right now so don't raise your hopes too high, boys! 'I'm a swinger and no one's going to tie me down just yet!'

Janey turned to the next roll of film, and the next. She hadn't found what she wanted yet but she knew it would come. The bits about Sweet Fanny Addams seemed to be from another century. When all these things were taking place, she hadn't even started school.

She looked out of the window at the mean little high street. A lorry driven by a man and a Volvo driven by a woman came from opposite directions and met halfway. Neither was prepared to concede the space necessary for one to move past the other. A line of cars built up behind them. You could just see clouds above the blotched green trees, flimsy pale grey as though cut out of rice paper. Janey was overwhelmed by a feeling of sadness. Then she turned back to her desk and carried on reading.

*

Collette Sweet and Tina Addams came out of the Italia Conti school the same year, as thick as thieves, in fact twice as friendly. They holed up in a damp flat in Kilburn where once a line of toadstools sprang up on the rotting carpet. They also (this they never told anyone) drank milk out of baby bottles for comfort, these two young girls looking for fame, love and money in a merciless world. Tina the bold one from Manchester and Collette the company director's daughter from Berkshire trawled together for men. They danced on cruises together, and got caught up through sheer naivety in weird scenes in Italy and Greece, and pooled tips and hints about directors at auditions, and boosted each other at times of failure – 'Well, what does he know about anything?' 'The one he picked won't see thirty again.' 'I wonder how long *they've* been sleeping together.'

After four years of this, a mop-haired toothpick called Millie Francis came to the flat in answer to their advert in *Time Out* for someone to take the spare room. (Two girls seek similar for informal household borders Maida Vale. £48 per month plus usual outgoings. Dancer preferred.) They were actually going to pick a burly secretary called Somebody Spoto because she had a sewing machine, but then Tina said, 'Sweet. Francis. Addams. We must have her so we can have it above our doorbell.'

Sweet Francis Addams –

Which became Sweet Fanny Addams –

Millie turned out to have a sewing machine too. It was she who made Sweet Fanny Addams' costumes, until they got so busy that she had to delegate. Even then, Millie still designed the costumes. She drew them on a soft white sketchpad. They were run up overnight by Miss Fluge who was kept sweet by little private confidences and liberal gifts. The girls learned to dance on through hems descending and pins piercing their skin. The costumes had to be left that late because it was never settled till the last minute what music they would be dancing to. The worst thing was choosing something and rehearsing it all week, only for it to go down the hit parade instead of up.

Tina's affair with Roger Reed-Herbert began in 1971. One day she walked through the doors of Associated British wearing a floppy hat and market-stall blazer made of chintz, patterned with deep red blotches on white like blood on snow. Her hair was cut like a boy's. She was a leggy big-busted but slim young woman, with the look in her eyes of something lusty and searching like a young stag.

She was innocent of the Associated British security system, which even in those days was complex, insolent and slow-moving, and she had not tried to book an appointment. There would have been no point. He did not know who she was.

'Hello, Mr Reed-Herbert. There is a young lady here to see you. What did you say your name was, miss?'

'Nemesis.'

She strode up the horseshoe-shaped drive in front of the Centre and walked past the reception desk as though she'd worked there for years. She took a lift to the top floor and worked her way round and down the endless corridors like a silver ball in a slot machine until she found his office.

At first Tina did not get over the hurdle of his secretary, a creature with a terrifying voice who looked like a wart in a ginger wig. She'd come up with some sort of ploy – she was a colour supplement journalist, she'd booked this interview with him weeks ago, how *could* he have forgotten – but the woman did not wear it.

However, Tina's luck was in. Stepping out of the office and heading for the lifts was Roger Reed-Herbert, presenter, popular novelist, producer, later controller of the lot, on the way to lunch.

She was twenty-two years old, he was thirty-five. He had an Oxford degree and a halo of gold hair that made his head look large and brainy. He was tall, slim, eager-looking, with wire-rimmed spectacles that he removed before he went on air. His talk show was a mixture of guests, consumer affairs and light entertainment. He had big cheekbones and a general air of being rich, young, petted and powerful, which he was.

Tina went up to him in her floppy hat and nature-red-in-tooth-and-claw blazer. Between bouncing off the wart-woman and sighting Roger she had undone her top button. A kind of instinct born out of observing him on the screen had told her to wear nothing underneath.

Tina had no time for boy meets girl, her giving him a look you could pour on asparagus, him turning to jelly from neck to ankles, bells ringing, violins swelling, bluebirds darting and so on. She just wanted someone on top of the world to lean over the side and throw her a rope ladder. If it had taken longer than five minutes to get Roger interested she would have tried someone else.

One minute was all it took. She said, 'My name is Tina Addams, I belong to a dance group called Sweet Fanny Addams, we are all terrifically sexy and young and beautiful and you must put us on your show.'

He looked down her front and said, 'Let's talk about it over dinner.'

Roger, who saw girls like that as just so many cakes to be devoured, took her in the back of his E-type Jaguar in the Associated British underground car park. She wrote down her phone number in navy eye pencil on the back of a torn-off check stub. Being a careful man as well as one who did not have to work hard for sex he threw the scrap of paper away but was nevertheless haunted by her. Two weeks later, having ransacked his memory for details of the encounter, he tracked her down to the night-spot off Shaftesbury Avenue where she, Millie and Collette were working.

'I'm going to put you on my show,' he said.

Some instinct made him pull back at first from her invitation to more kisses, more sex, but aroused by her angry tears he screwed her against a lawn roller in the open ground at the back of the Temple car park. One leg twisted about his waist, the other pawing the concrete, she shrieked out her pleasure in the open air. It was 1971, it was that sort of time. Roger felt a kick in the pit of his stomach every time he thought of Tina talking dirty to him in her low lazy northern voice. He had been married to Vallie for seven years by then. For just one of these years, the first, she was the only woman he made love to. She was hopeless in bed, posed there with her frilled nightie and styled hair as though between the covers of a magazine.

1971. It was a far-off time, an innocent time. It was before people fired off guns at pop singers or left bombs in litter bins that blew strangers to pieces, and even most world leaders could feel confident that they would not die until they were old or ill. On the streets of London girls patrolled in trousers belted at the hip and flared at the ankles so that when they walked the excess material flapped like sails. These girls wore drawstring T-shirts without bras underneath and posed for pictures against the bonnets of two-tone cars. Platform soles. Loons. Clogs. They wore shorts held up by a bib and brace; floppy hats and matching jackets; frilly pinafores and smocks. There were no women newscasters. Some people still had black-and-white TV.

Some women enjoyed a state of hysterical romantic uncertainty called Being Involved with a Married Man. They sat around in sweaters that no one caressed, and dolled themselves up in outfits that their lovers hardly noticed in their rush to remove them before the allotted time for illicit copulation ran out. These women had flatmates who went out with dull bachelors whose clothes were never as clean and skin never as clear and smooth. The married men made statements such as 'Sandra's a very nice girl but I've outgrown her' and 'My wife and I don't sleep together any more.' Roger's favourite was ' I don't love Vallie any more, I just like her.'

At the start when Roger came out with this kind of claptrap, Tina scoffed and told him, 'What a fucking stupid thing to say. I've heard second-hand car salesmen tell better stories to women customers.' She had no interest in wedding dresses and lead-crystal decanter sets. She did not want babies or a house with a double garage. She bought herself a flat in Fulham so that she could entertain Roger as she pleased without complicated negotiations about shagging rotas with Collette and Millie. Life was good, for a while.

These things never last.

Tina had a memory of herself as a child, sitting on a wood bench at a circus which had pitched on the common near the Cheshire village in which she grew up. Of all the acts, she remembered only the girl in the threadbare leotard who had danced on a tightrope, in one hand an umbrella, in the other a book. It was not the girl's prowess that engaged Tina, but the apparent uselessness of the objects she was carrying were she to miss her footing and fall off the tightrope.

When completely against her will she fell in love with Roger Reed-Herbert, when she fell off the tightrope with no arms to catch her, all Tina's fame and money felt like the book and umbrella.

Oh, Tina could tell you everything about love with a married man. How, after their lovemaking he would spring out of bed and head for the shower to scrub every bit of her off him before he went home to Vallie. It was Tina's catastrophe not that she loved him but that he loved her, – too much to let her go, too little to sacrifice what he already had. Sometimes he tried to end the war raging in his heart by leaving her. Tina learned to decode his remarks and anecdotes. Instead of talking about his activities in the normal first person, he would start using the marital 'we' as in 'We had a great time at Adrian and Kate's last night.' He eulogized the oven they'd had for thirteen years which had never needed repair, and went into quite unnecessary detail about their new rockery.

There were halfway good times and halfway bad times. The bad times included those when he noted down other girls' phone numbers at parties, not always surreptitiously. These were only phases, though. They happened when he was feeling wistful, remembering his former uncomplicated life, girls on tap, no Tina.

He never tried to break free by leaving Vallie.

What with burst condoms, chances taken, disappearing coils, he made Tina pregnant twice. Not that this was much more than an additional passing nuisance for Tina, who really didn't want babies at the time and took herself off in the usual prompt, businesslike way to the abortion clinic. She didn't agonize or suffer, she didn't feel guilty, she had no subsequent problems with her fertility. All she felt was an immense relief.

Meanwhile, back she went into the fray with Roger. The whole thing went completely barmy when Tina and Vallie met, and Vallie decided to make this by now rich and glamorous young woman her confidante. The two women went up to Kensington for shopping and lunch, followed by a swim and massage at Tina's club. They lay on adjoining sunbeds, Tina's moundy old-fashioned breasts in contrast to Vallie's smart pointy things. 'I'm so afraid Roger's having an affair,' Vallie confessed.

'Oh, what if he is,'said Tina. 'These things always blow over.'

Tina found it good to have Vallie as a friend: efficient, motherly, non-competitive, flattering. It was before Vallie reached middle age, when she atrophied into a certain kind of Associated British wife, with designer clothes, flat stomach and brave smile. 'There just doesn't seem to be anyone for me,' Tina would sigh. 'All the decent men are married.' 'Don't talk such rubbish,' said Vallie. 'There are plenty of men out there and you could have anybody you wanted.'

Vallie would invite her to dinner parties at the Reed-Herberts' exquisite though tiny Victorian cottage in Putney. (Later they moved out to a proper country house; staff flat, tennis court, swimming pool, paddock for Joanna-Mary's palomino.) In Putney, Vallie carefully ensured that there would be a succession of unattached men for Tina, and Tina tried desperately hard to please them, biting her sharp tongue when they bored on and on about car insurance, feigning patience when these poltroons mispronounced the wine or knocked it over. Later, if the occasion had ended late, Tina would stay overnight in the spare bed in Joanna-Mary's room and Roger would creep to her and expertly lick her into a silent frenzied climax. Joanna-Mary was four at the time.

The friendship between the Reed-Herberts and Tina flourished. Often Roger asked her to intercede for Joanna-Mary – 'She's having a hard time with Vallie.' Vallie would say, 'Joanna-Mary is impossible. The only person she'll listen to is you.' After a while Tina understood that they were giving her Joanna-Mary, both as a consolation to her who had no one, and as a short-term car park so they could have a bit of time to themselves.

What kept Tina going was sheer competitiveness. She knew Roger loved her more than he loved Vallie, and understood his reluctance to involve himself in scandal; at the same time she did not want to concede defeat to her inferior. 'Divorce, giving up the kids, it isn't me,' he said. 'What *is* you?' Tina always wanted to demand. 'Lies and deceit?' But she never did.

Oh, there were good times and bad times, and there was the worst time of all, when he might have left both of them.

He had been Tina's lover for two or three years by then. The episode began normally; days passing without a phone call, a meal together spent staring at other diners, an eagerness not to be alone with her. Another bout of rockery-itis, thought Tina gloomily. However, some weeks later Vallie rang her in tears.

Tina took the call lying on her bed in the Fulham flat. The room was small and odd-shaped – the door to the bathroom was on a diagonal. The television was on without volume, offering up pictures of horses racing endlessly round some green, oak-fringed track. It was a bank holiday weekend. Tina with nowhere to go, no one to see. 'Vallie,' she said jovially. 'How's the rockery?'

Vallie's voice sounded as though she was swallowing a glass of water and talking at the same time. 'He loves another.'

'*What?*'

'Roger is in love with someone else.'

'Oh,' said Tina. 'Oh. Well.'

On the television screen, a row of horses jumped a fence in silence. Vallie's sobs came down the phone. 'Well,' said Tina.

'He's made her pregnant.'

Every feeling emptied from Tina like a massive loss of blood. Her life seemed to become suspended. Then she could feel her majesty take over, the calm, the command.

She said, 'What's she worried about? She can easily get rid of it. It's 1973.'

'Doesn't want to.'

'Oh, that's the way of it, is it? She's trying to trap him.'

Vallie said, 'Roger doesn't know if he wants her to get rid of it.'

Tina got through the next few weeks by pretending she was the Archbishop of Canterbury. Most days Vallie would either call or come round and obsessively rake through developments. 'He says he's just much sexier than me.' 'He says he wants both of us.' 'He says it's not my fault. 'I'm a good wife.' The front window of Tina's flat overlooked a large sooty church. Underneath the soot, the bricks were yellowish like the colour of old women's skin. A few gaunt birds flew over the roof. She could see the tops of people's heads as they walked along beneath. Afterwards, she remembered that time as nothing but rain and mist, falling, guttering, obscuring, floating, though in fact it was spring. Vallie curled up tense and spiky on the sofa like a dead lizard. Tina listening to the scrabble of her fingers searching out cigarettes, matches. 'You see, Tina,' puff, puff, blow, sigh, grind out cigarette, 'I've always regarded sex as something to be revered.' Tina said nothing. Vallie continued, 'I don't enjoy it. None of my friends enjoy it. Do you enjoy it?'

'Oh,' said Tina, 'Up to a point. You know. I'm more interested in business.'

One lunchtime Vallie came round looking more cheerful. She was carrying bags from Harvey Nichols and Harrods' Food Hall. There was a bottle of wine and some smoked salmon. 'Well,' she said, 'I've won. She's gone.'

Vallie and Tina ate at the table by the window, looking out at a mild early summer day. Vallie said, 'I feel awful about all this. I've droned on and on the last few weeks and never once asked how you are. I'm so sorry darling. I must have driven you mad.'

'Don't worry,' said Tina. 'Don't even think about it.'

'Really? You deserve a great big hug, my darling, and you shall have it.' Vallie knocked the wine bottle off the table on her way round to Tina's seat. Fortunately, there wasn't much left in it. She embraced Tina, patting her back and saying, 'Mmmmmm.' When she'd returned to her seat she lit a cigarette, offering Tina one as an afterthought. She said, 'By the way, we're going on holiday.'

'Ooh. Lovely.'

'A couple of weeks roughing it in France. It's where we honeymooned. We're going to make a fresh start.'

'What a good idea.'

'Actually, my darling, I've got a huge favour to ask you. Could you have Joanna-Mary?'

Tina spoke to Roger on the telephone and told him she never wanted to see him again. She had that much pride left. The worst thing was that he didn't beg her to change her mind. She consigned him to the special waste-paper basket that she kept in her head for people who had offended her, one with spikes in the bottom and lurking viruses, and wished disgrace and death on him. Her anger gradually dispersed like the imagined mists of recent weeks, but there was a wound inside that could not be healed. Summer passed, and autumn. She began to look beyond her career as a dancer, and realized that what she would like most of all for herself would be lots of money. She began making plans; concepts, premisses, logos. Towards the end of the seventies she looked around for finance, but found no one who would take a chance that enormous on a dancer.

In the summer of 1980 Delaney Ward came along. He took her to race meetings and Paris for the weekend. Tina wasn't fooled for a minute; he just wanted someone glamorous and interesting to dangle on his arm while he was promoting his latest film. She was witty, enchanting and above all tantalizingly elusive, since didn't really give a damn whether he got leprosy or went to the moon. Delaney was absolutely hooked. He had to have her. There were more flights to Paris, and flowers delivered to her daily, and desires expressed to show her to his parents. She shelved her business plans. They made film-star love, crossed oceans to be together, were chronicled in gossip columns, for a while.

He had fallen for her lightness, her detachment, her apparent lack of need. He did not realize, ardent cloth-head that he was, that her independence was a relic of agony. Slowly, she began to trust him with her feelings, and these feelings were often unattractive; she could be bossy, angry, cloying, possessive. In her ecstasy she had overlooked the fact that he was a shallow egocentric. In truth, she should have been grateful that Collette was about to take him away.

During a quarrel they had one day at rehearsal Tina screamed at Collette for some misdemeanour so trivial that its nature could not easily be recalled. Except that for some reason she was becoming more and more irritated by Collette – her lazy smile, the way she never rinsed out her coffee mug, her inability to execute a thorough flush of the loo. It is even possible that unconsciously Tina knew what was going on. She screamed at Collette, and mentioned the subject of the loo and various other offences. Then she walked out of the rehearsal hall with a bang of the door. Millie, Juliet, Ratty and Collette looked round at each other then carried on dancing. Six hours later, a red-eyed Tina turned up at Collette's flat.

'Look,' she said, 'I'm sorry. I don't know what's wrong with me. I should be on top of the world, I know.'

'You should see a psychiatrist,' snapped Collette.

'For fuck's sake.'

'Well, Delaney thinks so too.'

'What do you mean, Delaney thinks so too? Have you canvassed him about this? When did this great meeting of the minds take place? Was it just minds, might I be forgiven for asking?'

'Oh, *do* give over, Tina. I can't help speaking to him if he speaks to me.'

It was the discussion that was the betrayal. Oh, the fact that he had put his prick up Collette's cunt was not to be dismissed, but it was overshadowed by the usurping of Tina's rights as Collette's friend, Delaney's confidante. Tina could not get it out of her head, the vision of them lying there in the intimacy of rumpled sheets, bonded by their mutual problem – her; reducing her status to that of some difficult child, some sort of unwanted ornament.

'I'm sorry,' Delaney said helplessly to Tina. 'She was just so beautiful.'

Rory Cromarty of the *London Age* broke the story in his Diary in the summer of 1980. Articles followed, of the bleeding-heart variety: WHAT DO YOU DO IF YOUR BEST FRIEND STEALS YOUR MAN? Tina Addams, dancing boss of Sweet Fanny Addams spoke exclusively to the Daily This, the Evening That, about the love tangle between her, Delaney Ward and best friend Collette Sweet. 'There is no rift between me and Collette and never will be,' she told the Sunday Something-or-other exclusively yesterday. 'Collette and I have known each other for more than ten years. Our friendship is the most important thing in our lives. We would never let anything trivial like a man break us up. I wish her and Delaney all the best. The only message I have for Delaney is, I hope he knows he's the luckiest man in the world!'

Tina got into Collette's flat and put a dead rat inside her bed.

She left a doll stuck with pins on Delaney's doorstep. When they got married in a cloud of rose petals and real old-fashioned confetti, she stood at the church gates veiled in black. She drank a lot, and took to sweeping up and down motorways in her white Triumph Stag, flashing her lights at selected motorists and inviting them to pull off into service areas where in dark corners of car parks she would get them to fuck her. Unsolicited items would be delivered to the Wards' new Holland Park address – a range of hand-painted thimbles commemorating British victories in battle, a size 24 trouser suit in lilac Crimplene, a truss. There were various unpleasant scenes when Delaney and Collette requested her to stop, ending in solicitor's letters and the threat of prosecution.

Millie and Curtis got married, and Tina ruined their wedding. She went through weeks of shame and anguish alone. Perhaps Roscoe might have phoned her up, for after all he was in part responsible, but from him there was nothing – no balm, no cautious enquiry, not even the acknowledgement of reproach. Some nights Tina would slip early into bed and lie there crying, not for her reputation or her misadventures in love, but for the baby she had lost. The first two had no importance for her, they were like flies on windscreens, but for some reason this one was real. In her mind's eye Tina could picture her face (she knew this baby was a *her*), a little crumpled red thing with a black mop of hair; she was my baby, Tina cried at night, she was my baby.

One day Roger Reed-Herbert rang her up and asked her to lunch. They went to talk of this and that and she remembered the ease and mutuality of their past. He missed her, he said; she was as beautiful and sexy as ever, and so on. 'Blah blah blah,' Tina thought, 'heard it all before,' but in the end she could not help herself; she was comforted by his expressions of warmth and interest, and hey presto, they ended up in bed again.

He said: 'You know I can never leave Vallie, don't you.'

She said: 'I don't want you to leave Vallie. I want you to set me up in business.'

And so Legwork was born . . .

So that was why.

Janey was getting near the end of her stock of microfilm when she found what she was looking for in one of Rory Cromarty's Diaries. Roger Reed-Herbert was Tina's backer and a major shareholder in Legwork. No, Tina would never take a stand against Joanna-Mary.

The pink-skinned guard was still sitting on the straight-backed chair, though now he had turned it round to face the late afternoon sun. 'Find out what you wanted?' he said.

'Oh,' said Janey, 'yes, thanks.' She didn't add, What good it'll do me I don't know.

It was past suppertime when she got off the bus at Shepherd's Bush Green. She dawdled on the way home, looking in the windows of shops selling white nylon shirts with puckered seams and fawn polyester trousers. She had no one to get home for. At the fast food concession next to the tube entrance she bought a burger and fries and stood eating them by the news-stand, idly reading the headlines of a discarded evening paper. 91! IT'S OFFICIAL. Janey thought, There must be something pretty horrible going on, like millions more people losing their jobs, to make them pretend the weather's important. She chewed on the burger. It was tough and sour. Might as well have put those nylon shirts in a bun, she thought. Wouldn't have tasted any worse.

There was nobody about in Janey's street. It was too dark even for the kids' football game that went on most summer nights. The houses were tall Victorian boxes with peeling paintwork and weird-coloured badly fitting doors that on hot days were left open to reveal smudged babies dozing in rickety pushchairs, and big dogs with heads the size of suitcases, stretched out across sunbeam-dappled halls. The front gardens featured a crop of broken-down motorbikes behind wild and dense privet hedges. A couple of roads along, the road was lined with BMWs and Golf GTIs and the doors were white with brass fittings, and a burglar alarm above, but Janey's road had got missed out. For some reason she was glad about that.

There was a light on in her flat. She tried to remember if she'd left it on that morning, but she was prudent about things like wasted electricity and it was almost an act of religious observance with her to go round switching everything off.

She let the door swing open quietly.

'Old lady?'

'Oh,' said Janey slowly. 'You're back.' Quietly she walked into the bedroom where Pete was lying on the bed, curled round an ashtray containing ten cigarette butts and an apple core. His backpack was lying on the floor, spilling out dirty T-shirts, shit-smeared pants, stiff socks and a pair of jeans that filled the whole room with their smell. He'd gone to her cupboard and put on one of her big clean shirts. Apart from that he had nothing on. He was flapping around with his prick and balls in a bored sort of way. Janey wanted to sit down because it had been a bit of a shock, thinking her house had been broken into, but his guitar, the Fender, was propped up on the only chair.

'What does a guy have to do to get a meal in this place?' he grinned.

In the morning, Janey took the Fender to a shop off the Charing Cross Road and sold it back to them. Then she went home and threw his backpack into the road and told him to get on out after it.

Chapter Ten

Breakfast with Collette

MANON WAS UP early, so it would still be cool enough on the streets to walk. She was wearing her cut-off jeans and her Lynx T-shirt. She'd washed and dried them overnight as best she could on the hot pipes of the third-floor bathroom of the Albany Hotel, King's Cross. They were creased and a bit damp but at least people would want to stay in a room with her.

The owner of the Albany Hotel had bought up the entire world supply of wallpaper embossed with flattened string. There was a spiky cactus plant in the door as you came in, and an electric fan with two dead flies sticking out of it. The girl at reception was wearing a black jacket dotted with fluff.

Manon had breakfast at a table covered in imitation teak formica in a little alcove off the reception area. Around her, travelling salesmen stared into nothing, tapping spoons against chipped white china cups. Three cops coming off night shift ate together in formal and gloomy silence.

At the reception desk, Manon stood for two minutes while the girl pursued a long conversation on the phone. Finally she hung up and made as if to leave the desk. Manon said, "Scuse me. Can you tell me where there's a pay phone working?'

'Down the corridor, by the toilets.'

'It won't work.'

'It was all right last night.'

'It isn't now.'

'Nothing I can do about that, sorry.'

'Well, can I reverse charges on yours?'

'Not allowed.'

Manon walked to King's Cross station and phoned Ray from there. 'Where the fuck are you?' he said.

'London.'

He started cursing her so loudly that people walking past turned their heads. 'You're telling me porkies again, aren't you?'

'Ray I've never told you anything that hasn't been the truth. I've come uptown for some auditions. I've got to be at this place called Starburst International at ten o'clock.'

'You're having an abortion, aren't you, you fucking cow.'

'Jesus, Ray, can you just talk sense for a change.'

'I can find you, you know. You can't get away with it. I'll be waiting at the door of the clinic.'

'Well you'll have a long wait, you big tosspot.'

'Let me know what we would have had.'

'Oh, fuck off, toilet paper.'

He slammed the phone down just before she did. When she got out into the street the sky had clouded over and she could feel the first few spots of rain on her burning cheeks. Unwilling to return to the hotel she kept going, letting the drops seep through her T-shirt. She felt as though she'd been physically hit. It wouldn't have mattered so much except that when she had been scared she was pregnant once, he'd been on at her to get rid of it right away and even asked how did he know it was his.

Starburst International had an address in Soho. She looked at the A-Z in her bag and decided to walk it. She went along the Euston Road, past the blotchy red façade of St Pancras Station, then crossed the main carriageway and turned up a side street past a row of shops. There was a VIP Mini cars, Kleenest Dry Cleaners, Wax Cleaning supplies, Mad Malc's Army Surplus, an insurance consultant's decorated in shades of grey, and a chemist's with a sun-bleached window display featuring two faded packets of Durex and an add for karate classes.

Starburst International Artistes Agency was down a set of steps in a basement. There was a dingy metal sign on the wall, and an arrow pointing at the bell which said Press. The bell was broken. Manon kicked the door and it swung open. A man sat inside at a desk veneered in blond wood that was starting to fall apart like overcooked chicken. There was a door behind the desk with a poster reproduction of the Moulin Rouge taped on it, and another door at the end of the room was half ajar and showed a lavatory with the seat up. The man had greasy black hair and designer stubble and he was scraping his front teeth with a thumbnail.

'What can I do for you, darling?' he said without taking his thumbnail from his teeth.

'I've come about your advertisement in the *Stage*,' said Manon. 'The one with jobs in Greece and Italy.'

He got up from behind his desk and jerked his head towards the door behind it.

Manon followed him into the back room. The windows were barred and made of frosted glass. One wall was partly obscured by a metal-framed screen hung with fabric like the ones at hospitals. Behind it was a daybed with some misshapen cushions. There was a tourist picture of Greece sellotaped on the wall above a trestle table with a phone and a pile of folders. Next to the table was a sofa that had begun life as beige. On the sofa sat another man, around forty years old and a bit too fat to be wearing a Borsalino hat. He was smoking a cigar.

Borsalino grinned and motioned her to sit alongside him on the sofa. He was wearing a pair of cream trousers and a belt saying Gucci. He was obviously very fond of the trousers; he kept looking down at them and brushing off imaginary specks. It occurred to Manon that she was completely alone with two unknown men, neither of whom looked as though they'd been hand-picked for their extraordinary resemblance to Sir Galahad. She turned to leave, but Designer Stubble had closed the door behind her. He leant against it with his arms crossed, baring his teeth in a grin. They were teeth that needed more than a thumbnail to get him the Smile of the Year Award.

'She wants something in Greece,' he said.

Manon felt in her bag and brought out a folder. 'I've got my qualifications here,' she said, handing him her certificates from Mrs Studebaker's saying she had Grade 8 movement and dance and a gold medal in modern rhythmic gymnastics. There were some photos of her doing jazz dance at a county festival, one of her receiving a cup for throwing the javelin, and one of her wearing a bikini on the brown-pocked Eastleigh sand.

He flipped through them then motioned to her with the cigar. 'Stand up,' he said. 'Turn round.' Manon wondered why he didn't take his hat off. Perhaps he didn't have a top to his head.

'Good legs.'

'Thanks.' She put her folder back in her bag.

'What I can see of them. All right, Mandy, Jerry here is going to tell you what we at Starburst do.'

'It's Manon.' She looked at the tourist picture on the wall. It featured a group of people laughing uproariously around a restaurant table bearing a bowl of olives and a bottle of Retsina.

'We act as a booking agency supplying dancers for clubs, nightspots, hotels.' Jerry spoke very fast, as though he was anxious to get through it before he missed his train. 'We pay all your fares and expenses out there deductible from your first month's wages. Accommodation is provided by Starburst in combination with Kudos Entertainments as a special one-off rate of 10,000 drachmas. You'll be paid a basic weekly retainer of 3,000 drachmas which with overtime and commission can give you an overall salary of something like 20,000 drachmas. With me?'

Manon said, 'How much is 3,000 whatsits?'

'You'll understand if I don't talk in pounds. It's a very unreliable guide with the exchange rate going up and down the way it is. Starburst provides the costume but you'll be responsible for cleaning, and there will be a deposit of 6,000 drachmas returnable on fulfilment of the 6-week contract.'

'You haven't told me how many whatsits, zlotys there is to the pound.'

Borsalino said, 'What we're saying is, you stand to make around £150-plus a week overall.'

'That's with overtime and commission?' she said.

'It is,' Borsalino said.

'What's the overtime and commission for?' asked Manon.

'Well, it's up to you of course, but most of our girls think it's worth it,' said Jerry.

'Topless,' said Manon.

'You guessed it.'

'What if I don't want to do topless?'

Jerry pursed his lips. 'You're a very nice girl, a very presentable girl, but . . .' He looked across at Borsalino.

'Starburst International wouldn't frankly be able to offer you work,' said Borsalino.

Manon hesitated. She'd been in London three days now and wasn't any nearer to finding work. She could get out there on their money, do a runner, look for something else.

'All right,' she said.

'Good,' said Borsalino. 'Let's see you posed, then.'

'There's some of me dancing and that in those pictures I gave you.'

'Like for a beauty shot,' said Jerry. 'You know.'

Manon said again, 'Topless.'

'As a sign of your good faith, you understand. We need to know that you're suitable for this sort of work,' Borsalino said.

'Stand up, darling,' said Jerry.

'Well – ' Manon stood up, hands crossed protectively in front of her. She worked it out; Jerry was about five-six tall and scrawny and Borsalino must be around five-eight of blubber. She was five-eleven.

'If you won't do it for us how are you going to feel about doing it in front of a couple of hundred punters?' said Jerry.

'You really are a pair of dirty bastards,' said Manon, shaking her head.

'Hear that, Jerry?' said Borsalino. 'Did you hear what she called us?'

'I did,' said Jerry, 'I did and I think we're going to have to teach her not to do it again.'

Borsalino leant forward and grabbed her breasts with both hands. 'Nice tits,' he said. 'Ever thought of doing photographic work?'

Jerry said, 'Could be falsies.' He lifted up her T-shirt and felt underneath.

'If you don't take your hands off me,' said Manon, 'I'm going to throw you across the room.'

'What makes you think you can do that, darling?' grinned Jerry.

'Because I'm bigger than you.' said Manon, remembering how she'd dealt with Paolo and realizing she was never going to be afraid again because she knew what to do. 'Because it's something I'm good at.' She knocked Jerry's hand aside, ducked and tipped him over her shoulder on top of Borsalino, who staggered back and fell, bringing the trestle table down with him. Jerry was getting up again. She lifted him to his feet, rushed him backwards and slammed his head against the wall. He slithered to the floor. Manon checked him out. His eyes were shut and he wore a soppy smile.

Borsalino lay with the table upended on top of him, trying to prop himself up on his elbow. He watched as Manon bent down and removed Jerry's trousers.

'Now yours,' she said.

'Huhhh?'

'Get on with it.'

He struggled out of his trousers. She said, 'Goodbye,' and walked with them over her arm, out of Starburst International. Ideally she would have liked to set fire to them but on the whole it seemed best just to stuff them in the rubbish bags outside a Chinese restaurant. She bought some plums from a greengrocer and bit into them so hard the juice ran down her chin as she went on her way in the London morning.

Curtis was staggering out of his house, hidden behind a pile of laden cardboard boxes. When he saw Janey he put them down and did a little sort of shuffle in front of her, looking at her with his eyes twinkling as if to say, 'Which way are you going, love?' He was like some of Janey's uncles when she was a little girl, nice safe smiley men. When Curtis looked at her Janey always felt like a little girl, though she wasn't much smaller than him.

He said he didn't feel like going back to work yet, and it was something to do. Janey helped carry the boxes out through the front gate. They left them against the fence. Janey caught a glimpse of Millie's things – hats, half-finished knitting and a roll of bright cotton lawn with a pattern of flowers.

It was lunchtime and the street was very quiet. She didn't know how to talk to Curtis about what had happened. But he seemed so mystified and wounded. She put an arm round his waist and they went back towards the house. The front door was pale green with 60 in white numerals on dark blue enamel above the letterbox. The 6 wasn't quite straight. There was a stunted lilac bush underneath the bay window, and a stone model of a sleeping cat, painted black and white.

Janey said, 'I'm looking for Collette Sweet's phone number.'

He opened a drawer in the hall table and flipped a little leatherbound book in her direction. Millie's name was on the flyleaf. 'Do you know who she was going to?' he said suddenly.

'Pardon, Curtis?' Janey looked baffled. She doesn't know Millie was going, he thought. 'Ach, never mind,' he said.

Janey looked at Millie's contacts book but couldn't find what she wanted. She handed it back and gazed at him helplessly. It had seemed a good idea at four o'clock that morning. She was going to ring Collette Sweet in America and tell her everything and maybe Collette would be able to intervene. After all, Sweet Fanny Addams had been a limited company. It was wound up in 1982, but perhaps Collette as one of the three founder members retained some rights over the name. And Collette was married to that film actor. They'd have lots of money. Collette would be able to afford a good lawyer to get everything sorted out . . .

'Collette,' said Curtis reminiscently. 'Collette with her film star.'

'Lucky devil,' said Janey wistfully. She longed to go to America. Millie, who had travelled there, used to tell her stories of how it looked. 'Tell me about Los Angeles,' Janey would say as she and Millie sat squashed in the front seat of Greg's car, Joanna-Mary, Lily and Florence in the back, as they hurtled down the motorways from late-night gigs. 'Tell me about the airport.'

Millie, freshly-showered after her exertions. She smelt of carnations. November 1988. Where were they, Wales, Cardiff, the Severn Bridge rising out of the blackness at them, the unknowable river beneath. 'It's just an airport. The first thing you see is a man at a desk. You hand him your customs declaration card – '

'What's that?'

Joanna-Mary farted in her sleep, head lolling against the quar-

terlight in the back of the car. The car was an old and
uninteresting Renault coloured misty green that had for several
years belonged to Greg's mother. The head-rests smelt of lacquer
from being nestled into by hundreds of perms. Joanna-Mary's
hair spread over the back window-ledge. Behind her, headlights
appeared in the distance as pinpoints and grew slowly larger,
filling the car with their glare. Then darkness again.

'Oh Janey,' said Millie. 'It's just to say you haven't brought
in an animal or sausages or £300,000 in cash.'

Florence said, 'Sausages. That's what I want. Greg, stop at the
next café.'

'You're not really hungry at all,' said Lily. 'It's all symbolic,
this talk of sausages. What you really want is a penis. Greg will
oblige.'

Greg said, 'I believe there's a service station within the next
five miles. You can eat at the all-night facility and I'll take the
opportunity to fill up with petrol.'

'Spoilsport,' said Lily.

'He is not to make love to any of us,' said Millie. 'It would
be bad for team spirit, and anyway I promised his mother.'

In the service station café the lights were dim. Drivers of long-
distance lorries sat together and chewed midnight breakfasts in
serene silence. The girls ordered bacon, eggs, kidneys, tomatoes,
mushrooms, fried bread, laver bread, toast, but no sausages as
Millie did not want Greg to be embarrassed. 'He's very young.'

'Tell me about Los Angeles,' said Janey. Where she came from,
on the east coast of England, it was flat, endlessly flat and cold.
You could hear the mournful sound of foghorns across miles
and miles of fields. Great frozen heaps of mangel-wurzels and
cow dung carpeted the earth.

'You come out of the airport and it's just a non-stop circular
swirl of traffic. Buses. Pick-up buses to hotels. Marriott bus,
Hyatt bus, Holiday Inn bus, Radisson bus, you wouldn't think
there were that many buses in the world, let alone hotels. Lots
of women who aren't quite nuns come up and shake tins at you.
There's another woman who's holding her nose saying, "*No
parking other than to unload. No stopping other than to dis-
charge passengers.*" Last time I went there it began to rain and

people started dancing in the street because for so long there hadn't been rain. There are mountains in the background and they're brown and gold.'

'Where is Collette's house?'

'Beverly Hills.'

'Have you been there?'

'Once, when she had her first baby. She's got three now, all boys. Aaron, Jason and Rory. The house is big enough to get three ordinary houses in and still have room for an indoor swimming pool.'

Janey couldn't remember where the conversation went after that. Florence fell asleep curled up on two red plastic chairs. The tea came in white china mugs sized for a man's hand. Outside the lorries roared past on their way to everywhere in the world.

'I can't find it,' said Janey.

'Here, let me have a go,' said Curtis. 'Someone at Plantagenet's is bound to have it.'

'You're a good person, Curtis.'

'I wish I was, love. I wish I was.'

Janey went into the kitchen and made them some coffee. The kitchen was white-walled with units made from old wooden cupboards and floorboards. There were a couple of faint greyish squares where photographs of Millie had been. She put a handful of beans in the grinder and whizzed it round for a few seconds. When she switched it off she could hear Curtis murmuring down the phone. He rang off then tried another number. She found a tin of biscuits and put the nicest looking ones on a blue china plate hand painted with white dots. The tea trays were propped up against the wall behind the breadbin. She pulled one out, with an accompanying heap of scraps of paper. She nosed through them. They bore scrawled phone numbers, times of hair appointments, the beginnings of shopping lists. One piece of paper had 'J'ai envie de toi' on it. Florence? No, surely it was Millie's writing, with all those doodles around it. Janey held the paper in her palm and shut her eyes. She felt tugging, tearing, yearning, confusion. Goodness me, thought Janey, I'm not meant

143

to pry into this. She shoved the papers back where they came from. Well, she thought. Well, well.

When she went back to the living room with the coffee Curtis put his thumb up, and held the receiver out to her. 'On the line now. It's ringing.'

Janey held it to her ear. It rang once, then someone picked up the phone the other end. 'Collette?' said Janey. 'You don't know me, but – '

'Get your fucking enormous arse out of here.' This was said not to Janey but to some invisible presence at the other end.

'Mrs Ward – '

Something smashed on the floor. '*Shite*!' yelled Collette. There was silence, then the receiver was taken up.

'This is the Ward's housekeeper. Mrs Ward is resting at the moment.'

The imperious voice said, 'I am *not* resting. How *dare* you lie to people about me.'

'Mrs Ward, don't you think you should lie down now?'

'*No!* Hallo? Hallo?' Delaney Ward might have taken Collette out of Berkshire, but he had been unable to take the Berkshire out of Collette. Janey whispered to Curtis, 'Has she had something to drink?'

A big smile appeared on Curtis's face and he said, 'Quite a few somethings.'

'What time is it in Los Angeles?' Janey said, agog.

He looked at his watch. 'They're eight hours behind us. About seven in the morning.'

Janey couldn't help feeling impressed. It wasn't easy to get that drunk at that time of the morning. What would you do, pour gin on your cornflakes? 'Collette,' she asked, 'do you remember Sweet Fanny Addams?'

'They're trying to have me put away,' said Collette. 'Make out I'm a lush. That way he and his floozy get to keep the kids.'

Janey gestured to Curtis. He bent his head round the receiver and listened.

'They keep talking about my Problem,' said Collette. 'Shit, I hardly touch the stuff. He and the floozies are my only problems. Did someone say something about Sweet Fanny Addams?'

Curtis said, 'Collette? This is Curtis Fisher. Remember me?'

'Curtis, do you know what I found in our bed this morning? An earring, a really cheap earring, he can't even screw anything with any class.'

Janey said, 'I called to find out if you still had any legal rights over the name of Sweet Fanny Addams.'

'I was in a group called Sweet Fanny Addams once. With my two friends Millie and Tina. If you see them, tell them I miss them. Tell them I'm sorry I left and I hope they're having a good time.' There was a clunk, probably the receiver dropping. Janey said, 'Hallo? Collette, are you there?' She waited, then hung up. There didn't seem much point in redialling. It was hard to carry on a conversation with someone who was having trouble matching up their ear with the receiver.

As Janey was leaving, she said to Curtis, 'Florence is out of a coma now. You could go and see her if you like.'

'I don't want to see Florence,' said Curtis. 'The way I feel I don't ever want to see her.'

It's because of Millie, Janey thought, It's because Florence reminds him of Millie.

So she just hugged him again and went out into the afternoon. An old woman had already excavated the cardboard boxes by the fence. She was tottering off down the road wearing one of Millie's hats.

Chapter Eleven

Don't Give Up the Day Job

THE DAY BEFORE Millie was due to be buried, Sweet Fanny Addams auditioned for new dancers.

Tina allowed herself an extra hour in bed because she was still washed out from the New York trip. She wasn't sleeping well for worrying. About Janey and Florence, about Joanna-Mary and Roger, about where the money was going to come from to secure the property in New York. Worry and anger, fear and loneliness.

She woke herself up with three cups of coffee, thought better of her plan to take a run along the waterfront, put on her dressing gown and had Michelle the fat help bring her breakfast on a silver tray. She sat out on the terrace eating it, lit her first cigarette of the day, opened the post, lit her second cigarette of the day, and wondered what she was going to do. A dead bee lay on the quarry tiles. Tina wondered how it had ended up there, what mission it was flying at the time. Probably there was another bee still waiting up for it, hoping to see it soon. On the horizon a small aeroplane went buzzing above the rooftops towards London City Airport. The sky over there had a yellow and luminous quality, like raw silk.

She checked her watch. Ten o'clock. Roger would be at work by now. She had been trying to speak to him for the last forty-eight hours, ever since New York. She was unable to get past his secretary, a dumpy woman like the Queen only more self-important. Secretary was rather a feeble word for her, like calling the Pope a clergyman. ABTV was full of these women, half chatelaine, half pit bull terrier.

No, said the Queen, he wasn't in his office. No, they didn't know if he'd be in this morning. Why didn't she leave her name and number and he'd get back to her as soon as he could?

Twenty years had gone by and she was still trying to get past Roger's secretary. Tina put the phone back on the table. It took maturity; maturity and a high degree of restraint. Her entire being was aching to throw the thing over the balcony into the river. Instead she lit another cigarette though she really wasn't meant to smoke till the evening these days, and tried finding Roger on his car phone.

Joanna-Mary answered. 'Hallo, Teens!'

'Joanna-Mary,' said Tina faintly. She rallied. 'How nice to hear *your* voice, my darling. Are you on your way here?'

'Yes,' said Joanna-Mary. 'Daddy is driving me in, though he's very busy.'

She sat in the front seat of Roger's Jaguar wearing a tight calico skirt and a white lace blouse under a baggy cream jersey. A cigarette stuck out from her lips. The seat was upholstered in soft sandy hide.

She said to Tina, 'I've got a gig.'

'Clever girl.'

'Yes, we're going to open both halves of the floor show. Two hundred a night for twelve nights. Starts next week.'

'Where?'

There was a pause. Joanna-Mary's voice became distant. Tina heard her say to Roger, 'Where is it, Daddy?' and Roger say at the same far-off level, 'The Waterside Club, Trimmingham Green, darling.'

Joanna-Mary returned the phone to her ear. Tina said, 'I heard that.'

'It's owned by Daddy's friend, Billy Wenders the tycoon,' said Joanna-Mary.

Billy Wenders was always Billy Wenders when the Reed-Herberts spoke of him to others. All their acquaintances were similarly designated (those that were suitable for such treatment); Christian name plus surname, sometimes several times in the same anecdote. 'Billy Wenders' – so you would be in no danger of mistaking him for Billy Bloggs. The Reed-Herberts would often bring these absent friends into conversations: 'When Billy Wenders came for lunch he couldn't get his Bentley through the gates.' This profusion of names left the impression that you had strayed into an advertorial or commercial, though the product being advertized was not fruit gums or insurance or even Billy Wenders, but the Reed-Herberts.

'Splendid fellow,' said Tina.

'Wait till you see his son,' said Joanna-Mary. There was a wink in her voice. She had met the son of Billy Wenders at a dinner. He was a lawyer who played rugby for recreational purposes. His chest muscles bulged and his hair sprang like gorse under his silk shirts from Burberry. He had enormous amounts of money for one so young, and drove a large shiny Mercedes which smelt of mud and cologne. 'He's taking me to a charity ball,' she said.

'His *son*,' said Tina. 'What's his name?'

'Like a saint,' said Joanna-Mary. 'Nicholas or Michael or something.'

'How exciting. Anyway, my darling, what I rang about was, can I speak to the old man?'

'Greg is such a wanker,' complained Joanna-Mary. 'He um, um, didn't think we ought to take on the Waterside gig because it was so close to Millie's funeral.'

'Boring old Greg. Boo. Can you put me on to the old man?'

Tina heard Joanna-Mary and Roger far off again, but could not decipher what was said because Joanna-Mary's hand was over the mouthpiece.

Joanna-Mary came back on the line. 'He says he'll call you as soon as he gets to the office.'

'I'd really like to speak to him now, sweetie.'

'What about?' said Joanna-Mary.

'A business matter.'

Joanna-Mary said, 'I'd rather leave it, Teens. The traffic's frightful and Daddy's such a pathetic old fart he's not safe driving and phoning at the same time.' Tina heard her give a little giggling squeal, as though Roger had jabbed her in the ribs. then Roger's good-natured bellow: 'I may be pathetic and a fart, but I am *not old*.'

Joanna-Mary said to Tina, giggling, 'Did you hear that? See you at Legwork. 'Bye!'

Tina put on a grey cotton sweater over a grey crepe skirt with kick-pleats and a waistband which she could get within half an inch of fastening. She got Michelle to tie her hair in a thick loose plait, liking the way it thumped between her shoulder blades when she moved her head. Then she shut the door of her apartment behind her and headed down to the ground floor.

Reception was crowded with dancers. There were dancers who were top of their year at the Arts Educational, dancers who'd failed to make it at the Royal Ballet, young actresses not doing so well at acting, child models no longer children, no longer models. There were the kind of dancers you hope the rival group's got, dancers who were good enough never to be out of work, dancers who just scraped along making up their income as waitresses and cleaners. Mothers towed girls behind them and stopped anyone who didn't get out of the way fast enough. 'This is my daughter, fifteen years old, isn't she beautiful?' She might be beautiful to the mother. To anyone else she was a plain scowling teenager who needed to lose a stone. There were women of thirty pretending to be sixteen. Girls of twelve claiming they were twenty. Girls with no clothes on underneath their coats. Girls who arrived too late and cried in the doorway. It was sweatier and worse-smelling than a changing room full of men after the football game's gone to extra time. Everywhere you went you'd hear someone say, 'If you don't buy a ticket you can't win the raffle.' And among all the sweat and the showbiz clichés you'd hope to find one or two or maybe three girls who'd make it all worth it.

Tina went into the little office behind reception where she found Kit. She shut the door behind her and lit another cigarette. She smoked it with her back against the door, eyes half shut, breathing out fumes like a dragon.

'We have about a thousand girls here,' said Kit. 'I have taken the liberty of cancelling your four o'clock acupuncture appointment and re-booking it for five.'

Tina was undergoing acupuncture sessions to help her give up smoking. 'Thank you, Kit,' she said.

'One girl was sitting outside here when I arrived to open up this morning,' said Kit. 'She's very interesting. You should watch out for her. She'd look very good next to Joanna-Mary. Manon Cole is her name.'

'Thank you, Kit,' said Tina. She glanced out of the window on to the narrow street beyond the front steps. A large expensive car drew up. The driver got out to open the door for his passenger. He was a man in late middle age, with unnaturally bright hair, dressed in a linen-look sweater that wasn't a very nice colour, with a pair of pale-piss trousers neither tight enough nor baggy enough. This was the first time Tina had ever seen Roger from an aerial view, and as a stranger might see him, a trick of her mind which confirmed what she had suspected for a while. '*Jesus*,' she said involuntarily. 'His hair is dyed.'

Kit looked out of the window with her. Roger was pecking Joanna-Mary's cheek. He closed the door behind her and she went wiggling out of view. 'You don't love him any more,' Kit said in a singsong voice.

Tina ran out of the office and barged through the crowds of dancers in reception. Her heels clattered on the stone steps that led down to the street. Roger was getting back into his car.

'Not so fast,' said Tina. She jumped in beside him. 'What about the New York money?'

'Can't do it, ' said Roger.

'*What?*'

'All right, all right.' Roger waved his arms in the air as though at gunpoint. 'I know I was going to but the money just ain't there, old girl. I rue the day I became a Name at Lloyds. Ever since, planes have fallen out of the sky, boats have sunk, oil rigs have blown up. We've taken a terrible pounding. We're terrified every time the postman comes. We're due to hear how much we're in for this year. It could be £200,000. And we're the lucky ones. Vallie's friend, Lucinda Drairey the novelist, has had to sell her country house.'

'If you pull out as a backer I'm going to lose two million.'

'Look, I'll talk to you about it later. I must go. They're screaming for me at the office.'

'Later isn't good enough. I've got to tell the bank – '

'What is it, darling?' Roger wasn't talking to her. Tina looked to her left and found Joanna-Mary's face at the car window, all smiles. Tina wound the window down. Joanna-Mary said, 'Come on, Teens. Time to start the audition.'

'I'll see you in there. I just have to – '

'Has Daddy told you he's going to put up the money so I can take on three new dancers?' said Joanna-Mary.

Tina said, 'No.'

'Let's go, Teens.' Joanna-Mary opened Tina's door. 'So exciting.' To Roger she said, 'Thanks, Daddy.'

Roger said to Tina, 'I'll pop in later.'

'Of course you will,' said Tina. As she followed Joanna-Mary back into the building, it was just beginning to rain. A sharp wind blew up the street, scattering a cluster of small, dried dog turds. 'I'll be right with you,' said Tina to Joanna-Mary. She went into Kit's office and put the door between herself and the day. 'Sorry,' she said, 'You were saying . . . ?'

'You heard,' said Kit.

'I don't love him any more.' Tina tried on the words. 'Perhaps. You could be right.'

'Well?'

'Well what? I'm stuck with him, baby.'

'How can you be stuck with him?' demanded Kit. 'He's not married to you.'

Tina said, 'Oh, of course I love him. He just fucks me around from time to time. Most of the time. I'm used to it. I feel at home, being fucked around. Stability. That's what I like. Give me a drink.'

Kit poured her a vodka and tonic. He said, 'You're only forty.'

'I might not find anyone else.'

'You never will while you're with him.'

'Oh, and just *what* will I find. Here is a selection of men who will have me. Men with one-inch willies. Men with reindeer on their woollies. Men who like hamsters up their arses. Mother-fixates. Men with AIDS.' She caught the expression on Kit's face. 'Jesus Christ,' she said, 'Me and my mouth.'

Kit said, 'No, sorry, it's just . . . I think I'll join you in that drink, if you don't mind. Rather tough times, these.' He poured himself a vodka, found the tonic had run out, and topped up with vodka instead. Then he sat down again. 'Geordie has had some tests,' he said.

'Oh . . .'

'It isn't that,' he said. 'There are other things we can die young of.'

Tina said, 'What might it be, Kit?'

'Oh, something trivial. Or some moderately awful disease that you can get better from. Or perhaps MS. Multiple sclerosis.'

'MS,' said Tina. 'AIDS. We're all dying from sets of initials these days.

'Yes,' he said. There didn't seem to be much to say after that. They didn't feel like being funny and it wouldn't have done to be sad. They finished their drinks and then Tina left to watch the audition.

Greg stopped Joanna-Mary in the corridor on the way to the rehearsal room. 'When you went to Florence's,' he said, 'you didn't see anything, did you?'

'I didn't see anything,' said Joanna-Mary. 'No one had tried to break in, if that's what you mean.'

'Janey seems to think – '

'I wouldn't take any notice of anything Janey says, if I were you. She is educationally subnormal, and meddling with the occult has given her delusions.'

'Ah,' said Greg. He paused, then lowered his voice. 'About what happened – '

'Nothing happened, Greg. Did it? Did anything happen? I didn't see anything happen. Did you?'

'It is simply that if the other girls were to think something improper had taken place – '

'What *do* you mean?' blazed Joanna-Mary. Her face had somehow lengthened and tautened at the same time and her shoulders were straight as though they carried the weight of an impressive wingspan. Greg half expected her to descend on him with a squawk. There was something deadly about her eyes.

Greg was afraid that Joanna-Mary would cry rape. He was, in fact, quite wrong. Even if he had committed such a violence on her, Joanna-Mary would not have made the matter public; she was too proud to admit to any circumstances that would show her as weakened or humiliated. But he was not to know.

'I meant nothing,' said Greg. Joanna-Mary tossed back her hair and walked to the rehearsal room. He stood in the corridor for a moment, then followed her.

The rehearsal room stretched from the front of the building to the back. It was floored with narrow strips of blond wood and the paintwork was stark white. There was natural light on three sides, from windows high in the wall. The back view was of the paved gardens leading to the pier where the riverbus began its shuttle downriver to Greenwich, though even if you were as tall as a basketball player you would have had to stand on tiptoe to see out.

Under these windows was a raised platform for viewing. Most of each day there were people of power, or at least with something in their gift, standing there. They were perhaps overseeing rehearsals for West End musicals. Some watched the three o'clock class, where dancers worked out hoping to be seen, to be stars, to be put on stage or in videos or on tour with singers. Among dancers, Tina Addams's three o'clock class was famous. Ask any dancer about it, she'd tell you the same thing: *Out of six people backing Smart Money's tour of Europe, five were unheard of and came from Tina Addams's three o'clock class.*

Tina joined Greg in the corridor, and they joined Joanna-Mary on the raised platform. Janey and Lily arrived. Kit got the girl who ran the health food bar to stand in for him on the switchboard so he could watch too. The dancers filed in one by one. Greg started the music. One by one, they danced.

So another audition at Legwork got under way. An audition completely different from every other, yet exactly the same as well. An enormous list of people to get through, most of them much of a muchness, from all wrong to all right but no more than all right, the whole process so cumulatively tedious that you end up picking out all the peculiar names and clapping them really hard. Celandine Tongue. Yolande Rowlands. Minty Dick. Somebody called Claire Yonge gets the sort of thunderous applause normally reserved for a Nobel Prize winner. Her teeth stick out and she's so thin she could hide behind two sticks of rhubarb, but she's last.

We'll be in touch, Thanks for coming. Don't give up the day job. Girls weep in the loo, mothers threaten legal action. If you don't buy a ticket, you can't win the raffle. Oh well, there's an audition at Pineapple Studios/Riverside/London Weekend tomorrow. Another day, another dollar. See you there.

You come up with a short-list. Say fifteen, twenty out of the hundreds that originally walked through these doors. You see how they look next to the people they'd have to dance with. You interview them in your office, one by one. Do you like them? What does your instinct say? Will they fit into the group? Can they cope with fame and hard times equally? Are they disruptive, depressive, lazy, moody, devious? Or cheerful, reliable, adult, sociable, kind?

An American girl with blue eyes and thick chestnut hair shows you her c.v. She's done everything. Ought to be in movies. 'I see you had a part in *Starlight Express*,' you say. 'Why did you leave?'

'The director had a real down on me. I wasn't prepared to work with someone like that.'

'And,' you say, 'you also left *Rocky Horror* after a month.'

'A load of bitches. The worst company I've ever been in.'

Thanks for coming. We'll let your agent know.

A curly-haired half-pint with more personality in her little finger than a whole chorus line put together. She's not quite what you need, but she'll make some company a great soubrette, a little character dancer. You put her in touch with your friend the director who's casting for a West End show. You may need him to do you a favour one of these days.

And so the audition at Legwork went on. They'd got halfway down the short-list when Manon Cole walked in. The girl Kit told her about, Tina remembered. She looked her up and down, head to foot, and it was a long but pleasurable journey. What did Joanna-Mary think? Tina glanced her way. 'Lovely,' enthused Joanna-Mary in a whisper. 'So natural. But *so* tall. Not for us, Tina.'

'Stand back to back with her,' said Tina suddenly.

'I don't think . . .' Joanna-Mary was enjoying queening it on the Liberty print sofas.

'You asked me to run this audition,' said Tina. 'This is how I run auditions.' She put Joanna-Mary back to back with Manon. Manon was the taller by a good three inches, but their hair was the same colour, almost the same style. Their features were unalike yet similar – faces with good cheekbones, noses perfect in different ways. Manon's mouth was soft and pinkish-red like a peony. Joanna-Mary had Vallie's lips, not so big but like her mother's turning down at the corners. At this stage of Joanna-Mary's life, her lips suggested gravity and depth. Later, perhaps, they would merely indicate someone who snarled.

As Joanna-Mary and Manon stood back to back, Roger walked in. Tina looked round at him. 'I told you I'd come back,' he said to her, quietly. Then he looked up at Manon and Joanna-Mary and said, 'Wow.'

'I can't make any snap decisions,' said Joanna-Mary. 'I have masses more people to see.'

Tina sent for Janey and Lily and they lined up next to the other two. Roger whispered to Tina, 'Is she the one you want?'

'Mm.'

Roger said to Joanna-Mary, 'This is the one you must have.'

And Joanna-Mary shut up.

It was noisy in the ward because some people from a train crash had come in. The corridors were full of nurses flying up and down with things on wheels: beds, machines, chairs. Wires that had been attached to Florence were now attached to someone else. There was a lot of telephoning, a quiet well-ordered chaos, and not enough of anything – not enough things on wheels, nurses, beds, things with wires.

Florence sat in her dressing gown on a bedside chair that was upholstered in frayed PVC and had a chipped metal frame. She had come to a decision. Tomorrow was Millie's funeral and she wanted to be there. Covertly she reached into the locker where her clothes and bag were stored. She hid them under her dressing gown and shuffled out. Why she bothered to be secretive, she did not know. Right then she was the last person the nurses were interested in. She could have driven out in a dodgem car for all the notice they took.

Getting along the corridor was slow work. Every few yards she had to rest against a wall. She found a lavatory to dress in. She must have lost half a stone. Her jeans and T-shirt hung on her. She was weaker than she'd thought, and walking was more painful. By the time she got to the ground floor the sweat was running down her face like tears, or maybe it was the other way round. She made it to a pay-phone and called Janey. There was no reply. She remembered; it was the audition today. She phoned for a taxi. When it drew up, she told the driver to take her to Shepherd's Bush. She'd just have to sit outside till Janey came back. There was no point going back to her own flat. The locks were changed, her furniture had been impounded and her clothes were probably in the street.

The driver was a squat grey back who talked. 'Just come out, have you?'

'Yes.' She was so tired she had to force herself to answer. She looked out of the window at North London, hoping the driver would get the message. He said, 'Tch. You don't look well enough. They throw you out because keeping you in costs money. My cousin, she was in there one week after her hysterectomy. Three weeks they should keep her, then three weeks take it easy at home. Take it easy. Married to a schlep.'

Florence said, 'I've changed my mind. Head for Oxford Street, please.'

Two blocks behind Oxford Street, she got him to stop at Geronimo's. There was only one other customer in there. It was so quiet you could hear the bubbles detonating in his Pils. She sat at the bar. A young guy was stacking some bottles at the back. 'Where's Geronimo?' she said.

'On holiday.' He had a pleasant Scottish accent, was tall, slim and good-looking, and wore a wedding ring. Geronimo must have had to scrape the barrel. Normally he refused to employ anybody less rococo than a gay former fire-eater or a Polynesian dwarf. The barman said, 'What can I get you?'

'A bottle of Juliénas and two glasses.' Florence watched as he set the glasses in front of her and filled them with the dark red wine. She emptied hers in one go. The barman poured her out some more. 'Your friend had better get here quick,' he said, 'or it'll all be gone.' He went over and switched on the juke-box, then came back. 'Going anywhere for your holidays?' he said.

'I've just come back.'

'Where've you been?'

Florence said, 'The Isle of Wight. Parkhurst.'

'Ah,' he said. He moved off, down the other end. Florence lit a cigarette and listened to the traffic go past. She thought of Millie, wondering if she would ever see her again or whether all that stuff the church told you about harps and heaven was just sales talk. Somehow she thought it probably was. You only got one chance. So it was important to do the best you could with it.

Millie had been her closest, longest-standing friend. She had known her for nine years. She had been a child when they started and an adult when they ended. In between, they played together, plotted, drank and dreamed big dreams. They did not tell each other everything; there were other people in their lives; they were not dependent, unhealthy. But she was the one Florence went to in the depths of despair. She had loved Millie with a passion.

She would miss all the things that Millie did for her. But she would also miss what she did for Millie: the acts of friendship small and big, the absolutions from guilt, the reassurances of worth, gladly given, that reinforced her image of herself as a good and successful friend. 'Of course you didn't make a fool of yourself, you were inspirational.' 'Of course your hands aren't ugly.' To Millie, Florence had been like balm. Her soft voice with the slight catch in it, heard late at night over the telephone, was calming and comforting. Millie loved the respect Florence gave her, the respect of the young woman for the experienced older one. Florence loved telling her dirty stories and hearing her laughter, loved cooking for Millie and hearing her praise. These were the things that Florence would miss doing for Millie.

In all the years of their friendship they had been estranged only once, and then for such a short time, when Florence broke away to find her own place to live, when she felt too pressured, too embroiled, too wicked; and then all it took was Millie's phone call, her visit. Two weeks estranged, and they were never estranged again.

Florence poured the last of the wine into her glass. It was late in the afternoon now. There was a thunderstorm on the way. The sky was the colour of an old iron bath. Most of the cars in the street had their lights on. She finished her wine and picked up her bag. The barman looked at the second glass, still full. 'Looks as though your friend isn't coming,' he said.

'It looks that way,' said Florence. Then she went out into the dark street. The rain fell suddenly, crashing against the windows like birds.

After the audition Greg led the girls up to Tina's riverfront terrace for the press conference and photocall, which was well attended and chiefly notable for two incidents. The first was when Manon tried to be photographed with a plastic willie on her forehead. The second was when a young society journalist approached Joanna-Mary and introduced himself as Edmund Timpson. He had been asked by *Have a Nice Day*! to interview her. Joanna-Mary agreed. Presently his article appeared (AFTER THE TRAGIC DEATH OF HER FRIEND AND BUSINESS PARTNER MILLIE FISHER, JOANNA-MARY REED-HERBERT REBUILDS THEIR GROUP TO HONOUR HER MEMORY SURROUNDED BY THE LOVE OF HER FAMILY.) It was the start of a mutually fruitful alliance.

Later that night, Tina took Roger, Joanna-Mary and the new girls to dinner in Covent Garden. There were two others besides Manon. Annie was small, with freckles and red hair that she wore in a pony tail. She came from Glasgow and had tiny feet in pale blue shoes like sugar almonds. Cindy was from a village outside Hull and had a plump bottom and shiny brown hair cut in a bob.

Roger sat next to Manon. He said, 'That's a pretty name.'

'No it isn't,' she said. 'I hate it.'

'What would you like to be called?'

'Raelene,' she said. The people at the table behind him were looking over and laughing at him. Roger turned and gave them his standard Roger Reed-Herbert Acknowledges the Public smile.

Tina said, 'They're laughing at you because you have a plastic penis stuck to your back.'

Roger reached behind him and pulled it off. He looked at Manon. 'You little . . .' he said softly. Their eyes met and various invisible objects passed between them: stars, planets, Cupid's arrows, crashing waves. Tina recognized that look as one which, twenty years ago, had passed between Roger and her.

After that the evening wore on peacefully until the coffee came round, when Manon stood up. 'Must have a piss,' she said.

'I think I'll join you!' said Joanna-Mary merrily. She followed Manon to the lavatories and backed her against the washbasins. 'This is the last time I tell you this,' Joanna-Mary said, 'so I'll keep it short and simple. Stay away from my father.'

'What?'

'You aren't deaf.' Joanna-Mary turned and headed back into the restaurant. Manon stood by the basins for a while. When she returned to her seat, Joanna-Mary was all smiles. 'I thought we'd lost you!' she laughed.

Later when they were all leaving and Roger tried to get her on her own, Manon scowled and broke away. As she did, she saw Joanna-Mary glance at her, then nod, as though satisfied.

The next morning, Manon rang her mum at last. 'I got the job,' she said.

'Did you meet the old man?' said Fidelma. 'Did you meet Roger Reed-Herbert? What's he like now?'

'What d'you mean,' said Manon, '*now*?'

'Oh, there's a lot you don't know about me. What's your phone number, babe?'

'Haven't got one at the moment. I'll ring you soon's I know.'

'Great. Then I'll come down. I wouldn't mind seeing old Roger again.'

Chapter Twelve

One Day I'll Fly Away

IT WAS DARK when Janey got back from the audition. She walked along the wet street, side-stepping the glistening puddles. Her back ached from posing in a line with the new girls and her mouth ached from smiling when she didn't want to. She had been standing on one side of Joanna-Mary, who kept tossing her hair at the click of a camera shutter. It was like getting your face caught in a shrimping net.

From far away, police sirens sounded in discord. At the other end of the street two dogs were fighting, a small pale one and an Alsatian. A woman wearing an apron stood framed in a doorway, calling out, 'Eric, Eric!' The apron read, 'I may not always be right but I am never ever wrong'. Somewhere a phone rang. A child in a front garden sat on a toy car, blowing a harmonica.

Janey caught sight of someone moving on her doorstep. In the half-light she could make out the hardness of a leather jacket, and long legs in jeans. She would have known the legs anywhere, the way Florence leant against things, tucking one ankle behind the other. Running, Janey fished her doorkeys out of her bag.

'Hi, how are you?' said Florence. 'Mind if I stay the night?' then she collapsed.

Janey got her on to the sofa and went into the kitchen to make coffee. A chair was propped against the door of the fridge to keep it shut. She got out a bowl of stew and sniffed it but it seemed all right so she put it on the stove to heat. A small, neat earwig hurried across the lino and into the shadow of a cardboard box. Janey looked into the box and found a packet of custard creams. She took them back into the living room on a tray with the stew, but Florence had vanished. She looked into the bedroom, and found her sleeping.

Janey got some blankets out of the wardrobe and made a bed for herself on the sofa. Then she dimmed all the lights, knelt on the floor and set out the cards.

She used a five-card spread. The first she turned over was Death. Janey thought of the cards as her friends but Death never failed to shock her. A skeleton stooped against an empty horizon. He scythed away skulls and bones like litter: crowned heads, women who had just had their hair done, armless hands waving like the Queen. Death; unexpected change; destruction which is a blessing in disguise as it clears the way for something better; removal of the barrier so that you may move forward unto the future unhindered. Wilful destiny; loss without reason; the enforced removal of something that should have been dispensed with voluntarily, and is now taken.

Outside the window, thunder banged. The force of it blew the curtains inwards. In her sleep, Florence twitched and muttered.

Janey turned over the second card. This was Fortitude. The opportunity to put plans into action if one has the courage to take a risk; the defeat of base impulses; reconciliation with an enemy. Janey thought, This is my card. I must be strong and daring.

Card three was The Lovers. A young man stood between two females – a girl and a plump, middle-aged woman like a burgher's wife. A time of choice, a flash of insight that can resolve the insoluble; a moral choice which depends on maturity and integrity for its outcome. Janey thought, This is Tina's card. She has the power to save us all.

Card four was The Fool. The traveller, the journeywoman; the imminent start of a new cycle of destiny. Janey thought, This is Florence's card. She will go away, and after that I don't know.

The last card was Judgement. The resurrection, the healing, the rising from the tomb, the shedding of light, the promise of new life, angels, trumpets. Janey took it to mean revelation and healing contingent on Millie's death and funeral.

She gathered the cards together and as usual placed The World at the bottom of the pack so that when she picked it up her first sight would be of this fortunate card. She wrapped the cards in a blue silk scarf and put them in the top right-hand bureau drawer. Then she lay down on the mattress and fell asleep listening to the rain.

It was like any other summer day in London except that it was the day of Millie's funeral. Janey went out early and bought a copy of the *Pictorial*, a tabloid she regularly told herself she would never ever buy again.

Inside, taking up the centre spread, was a feature headlined THE TRAGEDY OF SWEET FANNY ADDAMS.

Janey and Florence sat on the mattress in the living room, reading it and eating toast and jam. There was a photograph of the wreckage of Millie's car, an inset photo of Florence, another of the old group dancing on Roger Reed-Herbert's show, a photo of Roger Reed-Herbert, one of the new group at yesterday's photocall. Across the top five photos were strung like knickers on a line. Millie, Ratty, Tina, Juliet, Collette. Under Millie's picture it said KILLED. 'Forgotten housewife dreaming of a come-back.'

There was an almost unrecognizable picture of a girl with dyed black hair and a safety pin in her nose. SACKED. 'Punk Ratty was dismissed from her teaching post at a select girl's seminary after revelations about a lesbian relationship.'

Collette's photo had been taken recently; she looked bloated and dazed. DRUNK. 'Prettiest of them all Collette has had three spells in a Los Angeles clinic in her fight against alcoholism. Collette is being divorced by husband Delaney Ward and sued for custody of their three children.'

Tina's picture was subtitled LONELY. 'Rich and successful in business, millionaire Tina Addams has never found a man to share her homes in London, St Tropez and Marbella and her collection of pop memorabilia.'

The picture of Juliet was recent, and captioned CALL GIRL. 'Actress Juliet Dexter is working on the continent where in her latest film she plays a call girl.'

Florence put the paper to one side and said, 'After today I

162

must make some arrangements. I think I shall have to go back to France. Make my father look after me.'

Janey took the dirty breakfast things out to the kitchen. She spoke with her back to Florence, from the sink. 'Pete came back,' she said. 'I threw him out and sold his guitar. I got £500 for it. I'd like you to have it, Florence.'

'I can't accept it. I've no way of paying you back.'

'I don't want paying back. This is something I owe you. Everything you've done, worked with me, taught me, stuck up for me against Joanna-Mary.' She came back into the living room. 'It'll tide you over till some work comes in, or your compensation for the accident. You can get a flat.' She plumped up the pillows on the mattress and straightened out the blankets. 'And you and I will take on Joanna-Mary.'

Florence found she had trouble speaking. 'Do you mind me saying I think you're a complete fool?'

'Say what you like. Makes no difference to me. I've already decided.'

'You can change your mind any time you want.'

'I won't,' she said. 'You're stuck with me now.'

The funeral was at twelve o'clock. Janey and Florence caught a bus to the crematorium and arrived there just as Juliet Dexter got out of a chauffeur-driven car. She was wearing a black dress by Bruce Oldfield and a very pretty veil. Tina saw her; both women hesitated, then walked towards each other and embraced. There was a certain amount of sniffing and rummaging around for hankies, then tremulous smiles and little compliments. More guests gathered around them. There was a tall, slim lady in her fifties who stood very erect and all in mourning clothes, giving the impression of a gentleman's furled umbrella. Florence recognized her as Greg's mother.

A London taxi drew up, and a skinny woman with spiky red hair, dark glasses and a wide-skirted floral dress climbed out. She was accompanied by a boy of around eight years old. He had a mass of brown curls, and coffee-coloured skin. On his shoulder he bore an enormous silver ghetto-blaster. Juliet said, tentatively, 'Ratty?'

Ratty said, 'Yeah – want to make something of it?' Hurriedly she added, 'Praise the Lord.'

'Oh no, but I,' said Juliet, 'I didn't expect – and who's this gorgeous, handsome young man?'

'Bram Nathaniel Sopwith Baptiste,' said Ratty, 'My son.'

'Good *God*,' murmured Tina, as the boy put the ghetto-blaster down carefully and shook hands.

Ratty swung round and glared at her. Juliet said hurriedly, 'I'm so glad you've come, Ratty. You don't look a day older.'

Ratty had not lost her tendency to address people as though they were at a public meeting. 'Yeah, well, Juliet,' she said, 'your prayers were answered. I know now that the Lord Jesus died for my sins.'

'Pardon?' said Juliet, panicking a bit. She was years away from the pious little prat of 1981. Since then she had worked in a dozen French films and was the favourite of a famous director, which had lightened her up a lot. Now she was married to her lighting man and had a two-year-old daughter.

'Hallelujah!' Ratty was attracting quite an audience.

'Yes, OK Ratty,' Juliet murmured. 'Let's go.'

The funeral was like any other funeral except it was Millie's. Hymns sung to the accompaniment of music on cassette, a speech by a cleric who had never met her, bits and bobs in Hebrew, stand up, sit down, more hymns. Everything went as expected till the rabbi was about to commit the coffin to the flames. At this point Ratty climbed out of her seat, followed by Bram with the ghetto-blaster. They walked up the aisle to stand in front of everybody.

'Before we take this thing any further,' said Ratty, 'I want to propose a tribute to Millie from her sisters at Sweet Fanny Addams. Bram?'

The boy placed the ghetto-blaster on the floor. Squatting, deliberate, he checked a tape that was inside. He put his finger to the Play button and looked up at his mother, waiting for her word.

'Oh no,' muttered Juliet. 'Don't let it be anything religious.'

Ratty said, 'Thirteen years ago when Millie, Tina, Juliet, Collette and I were dancers there was a favourite song of ours. One summer we seemed to be dancing to it everywhere we did a gig. Riding home down the motorway in the middle of the night we sang it. It's called "Young Hearts Run Free" and it's about being someone's old lady who's fed up with being stuck at home with her babies while her man's out drinking and whoring. She's telling all the young girls, Don't do it, have your fun, you're free! Now I don't want you to read too much into the words, but I want you to think back along with me to those times. We did have a lot of fun and freedom and we did ride along a lot of motorways. "Young Hearts Run Free", as sung by Candi Staton and danced by Sweet Fanny Addams in the summer of 1976. Tina and Juliet, if you would care to join me.'

She waited, one hand on hip. Juliet was the first alongside her. Tina, who was standing next to Curtis, squeezed his shoulder then walked out front with the other two. They looked round at each other, then placed their shoes neatly by the wall.

Bram pressed Play and they danced, and while they were dancing someone somewhere pressed another button, and the coffin began to slide behind a set of red velvet curtains.

'Chicken n'ham? Salmon mayonnaise?' Curtis's mother was holding out an oval metal plate piled with sandwiches. Florence took two, not knowing what else to do. She sat in a chair in the corner of Millie's dining room. Curtis was the other end of the room, talking to Tina. He was not looking Florence's way. He had not looked her way since the start of the funeral.

'To hell with this,' she said to Janey. She left the sandwiches on top of a floral tribute in the shape of a pair of ballet shoes and went up to Curtis. 'Why have you not spoken to me today?' When he didn't answer, she added, 'Why didn't you come and see me in hospital?'

Curtis said, 'Why didn't you tell me Millie was having an affair?'

Florence went white. 'I didn't know that,' she said shakily.

'C'mon,' said Curtis. 'You were her best friend. Best friends are meant to know each other's little secrets. Nice and cosy. Just between the two of you. Don't bother about me. I'm only the husband.' Anger and grief had given his voice a slightly gargling quality. 'Why else would she be leaving me?'

'That can't be true. You must have imagined it.'

'She wrote me a letter, missus. The day of the accident. She left a letter for me to find. She said she wanted to have time on her own to think and I could have a divorce if I wanted one.'

'But,' said Florence, 'why would she leave you? She was having a baby.'

'Oh wow,' said Tina softly. 'I think I've heard enough of this.' She took Florence's arm. She said to Curtis, 'Florence and I are going to have a talk. Come on, Florence.'

Tina, Florence and Janey shut themselves in the downstairs loo. A giant spider plant dangled from a white china bowl on the windowsill. Above the cistern was a framed picture of the Leeds United football team of '71-'72. Janey pulled the lid down over the loo and sat on it.

'Curtis,' whispered Tina, 'is infertile. He has a low sperm count.

Florence's face was stony. She said disbelievingly, 'Millie never told me this.'

'I don't suppose I was meant to know,' said Tina. 'She just kind of blurted it out.'

No one was ever meant to know, not Tina, not Florence, and certainly not Curtis. But you see how it could happen. An afternoon shopping in Covent Garden, a reviving bottle of champagne at the Pelican Café. These two women who once had shared so much. Unique experiences. Not having to explain to the person you were talking to – who X was, what happened when Y did that, where Z lived. Breaking the silence of years. Tina: 'So are you still planning to have kids?' Millie: 'Oh, Tina, if only it was that easy . . .' Tina: 'You *poor* thing.' (To waiter, in a low voice) 'Bring us another bottle of champagne.'

'Why didn't she tell me?' said Florence.

Tina said, 'Florence, you're only, what are you, twenty-three, Millie was nearer forty, a woman needs a friend of her own age for some things.'

Janey, perched on the lavatory, took a quick swig of wine. Tina said, 'They had all sorts of tests. She told Curtis that there was nothing wrong with him. She didn't want him to feel he wasn't a proper man. She thought it might ruin his sex drive.'

Somebody rattled on the door. Florence checked the bolt. Tina went on, 'When I saw her, she was talking about artificial insemination by donor.' She added drily, 'Perhaps she decided she preferred a more personal touch.'

Janey saw the warning glint of anger in Florence's eyes. She said hurriedly, 'And now we'll never know who it was, I suppose. Perhaps it's best that way.'

Florence said, 'I know who it might be.'

She wasn't completely sure but she had a very good idea. A message left, a phone call taken in another room, certain attitudes expressed for Curtis's consumption. It was something some women did. 'So-and-so?' they would say to their husbands. 'So-and-so, I can't stand him. Please, don't bring him to my house.' Millie . . . yes, Millie would do it that way. She would not want her lover in her house, she would not want to act out a lie in front of Curtis, she would protect him.

Florence looked at Tina, looked at her hard. This is bitchy, she thought. All right, I'm a bitch. 'Roger Reed-Herbert,' she said.

Tina dragged open the door of the loo and ran out of the house to her car. Janey and Florence followed. They flung themselves into the back seat, struggling to close the door as Tina started the engine and swung out into the road using at least 125 of its 130 horsepower. 'What the fuck are you doing in my car?' said Tina.

Janey said, 'We're worried in case you do anything stupid.'

'Stupid is where I've been for the last twenty years. Now I'm going to do something sensible.'

There was a scanner van and a limousine in the queue to get into the Associated British car park. Tina got under the checkpoint with a screech of burning rubber. By the time she reached the front entrance she must have been close to eighty. She jumped out and shut her Ralph Lauren mac in the door. She tugged at it, then let it drop off her back and fall to the ground on a little patch of oil. As she strode past the reception desk with her black hair streaming behind her like exhaust, the security guards were running up the drive, shouting. She went to ground like an expert in the maze of corridors. Janey and Florence tracked her past office after office where girls in little jackets and jean skirts were typing and talking on the phones, their specs perched on their noses. Ahead of them was a door with Roger's photo on the front. The Roger Reed-Herbert Show, it said, just in case he got any visitors who'd been on Mars for some time where they couldn't receive Associated British. Tina flung the door open. Janey and Florence, catching up with her, found themselves in an anteroom where a woman was barring their way. 'He's in a meeting,' she pronounced.

'Don't give me that crap,' said Tina, cutting a swathe through the gaping researchers. Janey and Florence scuttled after her, nodding this way and that, 'Scuse me. Scuse me. Sorry.' They went through another room where a smoothly barbered young man hanging on a phone tried to stop them, then another room where a secretary said severely, 'His Nibs is in conference.'

'Wrong, my darling,' said Tina in a voice that could have melted icebergs. 'His Nibs is in the shit.' She barged through the doorway at the end, put her engines into reverse thrust and stood there looking at Roger Reed-Herbert.

Half a dozen production staff were sitting round Roger's office, shooting-scripts on their knees. Their mouths were frozen in mid-smile as though Roger had just made a joke and they weren't sure whether or not Tina's arrival was all part of it. Roger was sure. He took one look at her face. He said to them, 'We're going to have to continue this meeting some other time, I'm afraid.' Tina just about gave him time to shut the door behind them. She said, 'Were you the father of Millie Fisher's baby?'

'Oh, was Millie going to have a baby?' said Roger in a cocktail party voice. 'I didn't – ' He caught Tina's eye. She was holding him in a steady gaze.

She shook her head said, 'Tch-tch.'

He put his head in his hands. 'How the fuck did you get hold of that?' he groaned.

'So it's true, then,' she said. She felt a great stone roll away from the door of her soul. For a long time she had known (and not cared to dwell on it) that much of her moral behaviour was equivocal. Choices she had made at twenty-four when she had the excuse of libido and unwisdom were less forgivable at forty-one. Now she was acknowledging that to herself, she would be able to walk free.

'It was over ages ago. Hadn't heard from her for six months. Anyway, it wasn't what you think. Nothing *happened* between us.'

'Oh, were you wearing wings and a halo at the time? What was your chat-up line – Behold, I bring you glad tidings?'

'She asked me if I'd be prepared to provide sperm with which she could inseminate herself and I said yes.'

'Why?'

Roger found something terribly arresting on the ceiling to look at. He said, 'Because I, um, had a proven track record, fertility-wise. Because I wouldn't require any, um, further involvement.'

'I mean,' said Tina, 'Why did you say yes? No, don't tell me – you've always been completely stupid where your prick's concerned.'

Roger said, 'If you must know, I was intrigued.' He began to pace around the room as though he was dictating a rather tricky memo. 'Flattered. What man wouldn't be? I found it very, yes, flattering . . . and I've always had a soft spot for Millie.'

'Hard,' said Tina. 'A hard spot, Roger.' She smiled encouragingly. 'And so every month . . .'

'Every month my – do I really have to go into all this detail?'

'All the detail I tell you to go into, horse-shit.'

'Every month my secretary would take a message – "The project is ready for your contribution". Sometimes she'd walk in in the middle of filming. I'd tell her to organize a motorbike messenger, then I'd make some excuse to the production team, shut myself in the executive john and, uh, come up with the goods, so to speak. It wasn't always easy and don't think I enjoyed it.'

'Did you,' said Tina, 'have to look at dirty pictures?'

'You tend not to find many of those in the Associated British house magazines.'

'Poor Roger. Life can be tough.' Tina settled into her chair.

Janey was impressed by her calm. It had an almost voluptuous quality. 'What did you place your contribution in?'

Roger opened a drawer in his desk and brought out an empty Marmite jar.

'A Marmite jar!' said Tina, almost cooing. 'Well, look at that. Janey? Florence?' She took it from Roger and showed it around. 'I, huh, I hope, huh – ' Tina's voice yo-yoed up and down – 'I, hope you respected its feelings, Roger, recognized it had a mind as well, and didn't just unscrew its lid and use it for your own selfish pleasure. Wham Bam Thank You Marm.'

'Tina,' said Roger, 'Tina, do you want me to finish this story?'

'Oh, please.'

'I put the top on the container. I put it in a Jiffy bag and sent it downstairs to be delivered to Millie by motorcycle messenger.

'Oh, Roger, how brave of you.' said Tina. 'What if the messenger had got his Jiffies in a twist and delivered your little offering to a press preview.'

'I wouldn't know,' Roger snapped. 'I did my bit and the rest was Millie's affair.'

'So that's what the turkey baster was for,' said Tina suddenly.

'What?'

'The miracle of creation,' said Tina. 'Poor old Roger. After all your efforts, given second place to a turkey baster.'

There was a silence. Roger sat back staring at the ceiling again.

'Thank you, Roger,' said Tina. 'Thank you very much indeed.' She turned to the others. 'I think it's time we went.'

Janey and Florence set off down the corridor in front of the other two. They stood at the lift and waited. They could glimpse Tina and Roger through the two glass panes in the swing doors, one face framed in each window like pictures on a wall, of a moment in time already past and gone.

Tina and Roger were standing close together, their heads nearly touching. This was the last time they would be so close. He said, 'Well. Where does that leave us?'

'Nowhere,' she said. 'There's nowhere we could ever go from here.'

'Do you want the money for New York?'

'If there are no strings attached.'

'OK,' he said. 'I'll get it organized.' He looked away from her and trod a bit of invisible dirt into the carpet with his foot and said, 'I'm sorry about the way things turned out. You deserved better.'

'Oh, it was nothing compared to open heart surgery.'

'I still love you, Tina. Always will. You're one hell of a woman.'

She said, 'And you're a prick but I won't hold it against you.'

Janey and Florence were looking the other way. Tina kissed him on the lips, then hugged him, blew a kiss at his cock for good luck, and walked towards the lift. She may even have said, 'Have a nice life. I'm going to.' She didn't look back at him in case he wasn't there.

Chapter Thirteen

Handbags at Dawn

THE LONDON AGE operated out of a newly completed sky-scraper in Docklands. The entrance doors were all glass and stretched the entire width of the façade. Downstairs was all the marble you could ever want and probably a little more besides. The place was built round an atrium which was covered over with a glass roof. Glass-walled lifts rose and sank either side.

Rory Cromarty got up from behind his desk and set off across the deep blue carpet to meet Florence at the door of his office.

'Florence,' he said. 'Dearie.' He had a handshake like a gym-shoe that had been left out in the rain. 'How lovely to see you. Sit down. Let me get you a drink.'

Florence sat on one of the soft leather chairs by a window. Rory Cromarty's windows were where ordinary people had walls. She could look down on London whichever way she turned.

'How do you like our new offices?' He handed her a cham-pagne kir, dearie-ing her a bit more on the way.

'Fabulous,' murmured Florence.

Cromarty sat himself on several thousands of pounds' worth of sofa and hunted around for his cigarettes. He looked a bit sofa-ish himself; one of those people who manage to be both tall and fat at the same time. He had thinning brown hair and pale eyes which bore an expression of benign spirituality: the sort of man who would hold up traffic on Hyde Park Corner so a family of ducklings could cross to the other side. There was so much of him that the cigarette hunt took an inordinate amount of time. 'You had a story I might be interested in.'

Florence sipped her kir. 'Yes,' she said, 'you might, though I don't feel very good about telling it to you.'

Florence had met Rory Cromarty through Millie, one night in August 1988. Florence had only recently stepped off the boat train with her bicycle. She had run out on Cal Johnson in such a hurry that she had no money and no clothes except two pairs of pants, one shoplifted flowered camisole and matching trousers, and her old grey cardigan.

Millie gave the dinner so that Florence could be seen by people who might further her interests, and also because Florence needed fattening up and because Millie wanted news to get around that Sweet Fanny Addams was back. As well as Rory Cromarty, she invited her neighbours Jeremy Bywater and Debbie Blake (producer husband/actress wife), Janine Round (worked for the sort of magazine that keeps closing and opening), the Reed-Herberts, Lord Duncannon and his wife Totty, Greg and his mother and, for crumpet, Fabian Hooper and Chrissie Snow (of a well-known London football club and England).

Millie spent a long time talking to Roger Reed-Herbert while Curtis sat looking rather cross and left out at the top of the table. Later Florence caught Millie and Roger doing the washing up together. 'Ah, there you are,' said Roger.

'We're talking over old times,' said Millie. Florence could see how Roger looked at her. She was wearing a black velvet jacket and jodhpurs. The jacket was nipped in at the waist and fastened all the way down the back with little links like paper clips. Underneath she had a white cotton shirt and round her neck hung a silver medallion as big as a church collection plate. Her hair was black and shiny with a fringe that parted slightly over her right eye. Her brows were thick and dark, her nose and chin uptilted, her neck hardly lined. She was bone-thin and pale and as mysterious as a young girl. 'Roger hasn't seen me for eight years. He was nice enough to say that I've grown into my looks.'

Florence said to her, 'Curtis wants to know if there's any likelihood of more coffee.'

Later on still, Millie took Florence to one side. 'Look after

Curtis, will you? Whisper to him, flirt with him, put the music on and dance, that's what I need you to do.'

'*Millie* – '

'I'll explain later.'

But every time Florence started to raise the matter, Millie seemed to take the conversation somewhere else.

Tall, fat Rory Cromarty was no smut-grubber even then. He was known to be the best gossip columnist there was. He was a kind man at heart, a sort of human *coeur à la crème*, who hardly ever said a mean word about anyone, who chatted to girls in Woolworth's with the same gentle deference as he spoke to princesses and Hollywood stars. There was also another quality about him for which the precise word did not exist: it was a species of silent power, a will, a look in his eye under which a catheterization process occurred in his subjects, so that with apparently no effort on his part everyone randomly spilled the beans to him: whether this actress had undergone a facelift, how many lovers that lady novelist had known, this writer's sexual prowess, why there was an atmosphere at that heir to the throne's christening.

Rory and Millie knew each other from the early days of Sweet Fanny Addams, when her little nuggets of information (suitably rewarded by teas at the Ritz and dinners at the Savoy) had found their way transmuted into Rory Cromarty's Diary, for Millie like Rory had a talent for knowing what was going on without necessarily giving much away about herself.

Rory took to Florence as Millie knew he would, and occasionally squired her round London to nightclubs and parties. He asked no favour in return, though was of course always grateful for any nuggets that Florence might provide for him.

Now Florence sat in his ritzy office and said, 'Rory, I'm going to tell you a story and I just hope you'll believe me.'

'I always believe you, ducks. In fact, you're far too honest for your own good. You wouldn't be out of work if you could bring yourself to kiss a few arses.'

'Who said I was out of work?'

'Come on, darling. We're not on blinking Saturn. News does get through.' Cromarty gave up the cigarette hunt as a bad job and brought out a wallet the size of a family bible. He counted out ten £50 notes and put them on the coffee table.

Florence said, 'For God's sake, Rory. That's not necessary.'

'You'll be doing me a great favour. Five hundred quid you take off me is five hundred quid less I have to spend on food and drink. Have it and you may save the arteries of my heart.'

Florence put it in her purse. It wasn't hard to find room for it.

'It's about Joanna-Mary Reed-Herbert.'

Cromarty lost his cool for a moment. 'Jesus Christ, that father of hers is a shit,' he said. 'Eighteen years ago he got me fired off the *Pictorial* Diary. Someone tipped the editor off that I was going to break the story about him and Tina Addams and the editor personally pulled the story.'

'He still likes young girls,' said Florence. 'Janey says he's after one of the new ones in the group.'

After Florence had told him her story, Cromarty sat back. He had found a cigar and was breastfeeding off it quietly. There was a long wait while he ruminated.

'I shall have to have proof, ducks,' he said. 'Documents, letters. A photo of you and Millie all chummy together would be a start. Not because I don't believe you. Legal department, they'll demand it.'

'I don't have proof. It's just the truth.'

'The truth's not enough. I need a picture.'

The street was filled with home-going pedestrians when Florence left the offices of the *London Age*. The shops were the kind which had one item of clothing displayed in each window. Florence stopped off at a café in a side street that was only half full of shrieking Henriettas and men with mobile phones.

She couldn't put off her next call any longer. She got on a bus which set off down the South Bank where the traffic was moving at the pace of asparagus growing. At Putney Bridge it had stopped altogether, as though caught in a photograph. The river shimmered in the heat. An optimist was sitting below Pryor's Bank, fishing against a backdrop of yellow flowers.

The front gate was just as she remembered it, hanging by one hinge, the black paintwork dulled by a greyish-brown film of dirt. The roses had died off but there were some hollyhocks growing.

'You took some pictures of me and Millie together,' she said.

Curtis hunted through the old map chest where Millie used to keep her ideas for routines and costumes. 'Here.' He brought out the drawer. 'I never do seem to get around to sorting these out. Take what you want.'

'I only want a photo.'

Curtis said, 'You always liked this, didn't you?' He patted the map chest. It was made of pitch pine and was worn light brown in colour. Millie liked to shop for small old bits of furniture. Florence recited Victor Hugo in her head so she didn't have to think of Millie out shopping. 'Why don't you have it?' said Curtis.

'I'm not interested in furniture these days, I don't need anything I can't fit in a carrier bag. Why don't you look at me when you talk to me? Are you afraid of me?'

'No, I'm not afraid of you but I don't know where we stand.'

'As Millie's husband and her friend, don't we? Both trying to do the best we can in a difficult situation.' Christ, when other people talked like that it made her want to vomit.

Curtis stood behind her, really close. She could feel his body warmth. He said, 'Forget Millie for a moment. What about us?'

She turned round so he could see her eyes. 'Look at me. There never was an "us". It was just something that happened in the house from time to time. Like weevils or the phone bill.'

'I'm sorry I gave you all that shit at the funeral. I know you're angry with me. But I think you should come and live here.'

'Jesus! Give me some of her knickers and earrings! I'll put them on for you as well!'

'There's no need to shout at me.'

'What should I do then? Cry?'

In Millie's office, he leant against the door and watched her with his arms crossed. She said, 'Did you ever hear of a footballer called Joe Daniel?'

'Yup.'

'Where has he gone?'

Curtis said, 'Back to France, I suppose. He left suddenly around the time, uh, the time, uh. Did you know him well?'

'Not well enough.'

'I liked him. Not that I saw that much of him. I just met him a few times through a couple of his team-mates that we handle at Plantagenet. Why are you asking?'

Florence shrugged. 'No reason.'

Curtis started to go down the stairs, then turned back to speak. He said, 'I can find out where Joe Daniel went to if you like. I know his agent.'

'That would be nice. Thank you.'

She blew the dust off the desk and sat down. She didn't put up the Amstrad; there was no point. The waste-paper basket was empty. There was a gap of six inches between the desk and the wall. Florence remembered Millie at work, running her hands through her hair and chewing her pencil, chucking things haphazardly away. She felt behind the desk and came up with a shrivelled apple core, a postcard from Mrs Fisher to 'My darlings' from the Costa Brava, and a few bits of screwed-up paper. There were some costume sketches roughed out on them, and notes and drawings for dance routines. The last one bore a draft of a letter.

Dear Florence, Enclosed please find (That was scratched out) Here is the copy of the contract you requested asked for, re your appointment as leader of SFA, please look it over and let me know if. May I I'm sorry that I want you to know that

Florence wondered what Millie had wanted her to know. Maybe it was in her mind already, it was just a question of knowing where to look.

It was time to leave. Curtis came out and stood by the garden gate with her. A gust of wind blew a few dead petals up the street. She kissed him slowly on the lips. His lovely plump face was lined with sadness. 'I'm sorry about everything,' she said.

'So am I.'

'Maybe you could take me upstairs next time I call round,' she said. 'I mean, not into the office.'

'Christ! I've got a terrible erection now.'

They looked each other in the eye and started to laugh. 'There you go,' she said. 'Exit laughing.'

There was a little post office at the top of the road. It sold sweets and wool, and the people behind the counter actually smiled. Florence bought two envelopes. She put the £500 in one and addressed it to Janey. The second envelope was for Rory Cromarty. She looked at the photo of her and Millie again before she sealed down the flap. It was one Curtis took when they drove out to Sussex one Saturday. The grass was dappled with light and shade and Millie had her head back, laughing. There was a castle in the background. One hand of Millie's was resting over Florence's arm, as though she was about to take her hand and show her something. Beauty, friendship and death – the readers of the *London Age* would love that. Real sobbing violins and teardrops on the pillow, it was.

She kept telling herself that this was her only recourse, that she was doing it for all the right reasons, but she still hated herself more than she would ever be able to say.

Four days later Florence was lying on the floor of her bedsit, trying to work out with her weights, when the doorbell rang. Joanna-Mary was standing there next to Greg and a tall, thin man with rimless glasses who looked as much fun as a Romanian night-spot.

'Oh, and this is Christopher Higgins, my lawyer.'

'Pleased to meet you,' said Higgins, in the way sharks might be pleased at the sight of a fresh amputated leg.

'Well!' said Joanna-Mary with a quick, meaningless smile. 'I think we all know why we're here.'

Florence's room was in a basement in Kilburn. Higgins looked round for somewhere to put his briefcase and settled for the floor. He brought out a tape recorder and balanced it on his knee. He switched it on.

Joanna-Mary said, 'How dare you. How dare you, how dare you, how dare you.'

'Are those the only words?' said Florence. 'If so, I'll join in.' She looked at Greg, who was fumbling in a packet for a cigarette.

He twiddled it around his fingers then peeled a loose bit of paper off the filter. He pulled out two individual strands of tobacco and stared at them on his finger.

Higgins said, 'My client is referring to your purveying of slanderous information to a Mr Rory Cromarty of the *London Age* with the intention of his publishing a Diary item insinuating quite incorrectly not to mention maliciously that my client gained control of the aforesaid Sweet Fanny Addams by dishonest means.'

'Does he always talk like that?' said Florence to Joanna-Mary.

'Luckily,' said Joanna-Mary, 'the owner of the *London Age* is a *nice* person who is getting your horrible Mr Cromarty to put an apology in his Diary tomorrow which will make him look very *small*.'

Higgins chimed in. They might have rehearsed it as a routine, they did it so smoothly. 'It need hardly be pointed out that your accusations are vexatious and should you further solicit Mr Cromarty or any other member of the press with the intention of gaining publicity for your malicious claims my client will be forced to stop you by legal means.'

Florence said, 'Go on, sue me. I can always sell my jewellery to pay for the damages. It'll fetch at least £35. In the mean time, a few more people will get to hear about you, Joanna-Mary.'

'As of course they will also hear,' said Higgins, 'about one or two other things. The late Mrs Fisher appears to have been somewhat casual in her morals. Leaving her husband? A mysterious affair?' (Joanna-Mary had overheard some, though not all, of Curtis's revelations at the funeral tea.)

'Golly.'

'Not everyone is sanguine about such behaviour these days.'

'I'm surprised you can bring yourself to be associated with Millie's group in that case,' Florence said to Joanna-Mary.

Joanna-Mary said, 'Let's not waste time.' She smiled and inclined her head. 'Greg?'

Greg looked up at Florence and down again. He said, 'I may not have mentioned this to you before. I discussed the situation with Millie before her death. I can confirm that she wished Joanna-Mary to succeed her.'

'As quoted in Edmund Timpson's write-up in the *Pictorial* tomorrow,' said Joanna-Mary. 'What do you think of that?'

Florence said, 'I think Greg must have a lot of trouble sleeping at nights. That's what I think.'

It was true. It was in the *Pictorial*, so it must be true. According to Greg, Millie had asked him to provide a legal contract that gave Joanna-Mary and Tina ownership of the group. Oh, of course, it was spoken in impeccable Greg-ese: the tensions in the group, the rivalries, Florence's foreign background, her Frenchness that may have led her to misunderstand Millie's words. Ever the diplomat, Greg.

It was a grey morning in late August. When Florence went up the road to the corner shop, Mr Ramesh tried to withhold the *Pictorial* from her. 'It is a very bad paper this morning. Why do you not buy the *London Age*? There is an article on the Prince of Wales which I am sure would interest you far more.'

'Thanks, Mr Ramesh, but I know what's in there.'

'It is disgusting that they can print these lies about you.'

'You know what they say. Any publicity is better than no publicity.'

He would not let her pay for the paper. She hurried away before he could see her face crumple. That was one thing she'd never been able to work out about life. When people were shitty to you, somehow you managed to tough it out. It was when people showed you decency and niceness that it broke you up.

She sat on the nylon-covered slab that passed for a sofa, flipping through the pages. It wasn't really so bad once you faced up to it, she thought. The person they were talking about, that wasn't her. It was an invention, like Mickey Mouse or Sooty.

Out of the corner of her eye she glimpsed some movement at the front gate. Through the grimy net curtain she could make out a pair of hefty female calves. Instinct told her that the calves were owned by the sort of person who would wear a uniform and might possibly call her Miss Johnson.

The doorbell rang. She sat very still. With luck, Rhino-legs would go away. The doorbell rang again.

A fist banged on the window.

'Come on, Miss Johnson, I know you're in there.'

Rhino-Legs was about twenty-five years old and had a haircut that the young Elizabeth Taylor might have had trouble carrying off. It made WPC Dawn Macdonald look like a bison wearing a nailbrush between its ears. 'You took a long time to come to the door, Miss Johnson.'

'You'll have to forgive me. I live a very quiet life. More than one visitor in a week and I have to go and lie down. Oh and it's Mrs Johnson, by the way.'

'Do you really think someone in as much trouble as you ought to try and be funny?'

The room at the police station was big and old-fashioned. There was a rectangular table with names and dates scored into the wood. The room had been visited by several people called Baz, or maybe just one Baz who came there often.

Florence was interviewed by WPC Macdonald and a middle-aged sergeant with a red sweating face, called Paisley.

Paisley said, 'We've got a sworn statement from Mr Casdon that Mrs Fisher wanted Miss Reed-Herbert to have her group.'

'Greg Casdon may believe that, but I doubt it. He knows as well as I do that Millie was my friend.'

WPC Macdonald leant forward, smiling thinly. 'Then why,' she said suddenly, 'were you and Mrs Fisher fighting just before the accident?'

'Fighting? I don't understand,' said Florence.

The policewoman said, 'Just before the accident, you and Mrs Fisher were fighting.'

'I didn't say I didn't hear,' said Florence, 'I said I didn't understand. What has got it into your head that Millie and I were fighting?'

The sergeant slid a piece of paper across the table towards her. Florence looked at it without much hope of making sense of it. It appeared to be another of those statements. This one was signed by a Mr B. L. Dring.

'I don't know anyone of that name.'

Paisley had a flat, unfriendly voice. He said, 'Mr Dring came forward as a result of seeing the photographs of you and Mrs

Fisher in the *London Age*. He recognized you as the woman he was driving behind on the afternoon of the 3rd of July.'

Macdonald read from the statement. 'The passenger was leaning over the driver. She appeared to be trying to pull the driver towards her. The driver was hitting out at her with her left hand. As I overtook, I looked through the driver's window. The passenger was shouting something. There was a struggle going on. It looked as though they were having a real ding-dong argument in there. The car was swerving dangerously and I increased my speed as I feared it would hit mine. I did not stop to report the incident to the police as I was already late for an appointment.'

Florence shook her head slowly. 'This isn't possible. Why will no one believe me? Millie and I were friends. Friends don't fight.' She swallowed hard, willing herself not to cry. 'I had just been to the antenatal clinic with her. She wanted me there. We were off to Hull for a three-week engagement. Why would we fight?'

'Come off it, Miss Johnson. What do you take us for?'

'I have always found,' said Florence, recovering herself slightly, 'that is the kind of question it's never advisable to answer honestly, in case one causes offence.'

Paisley said, 'What about your affair with her husband?'

'There was no affair.'

'We know all about it, Miss Johnson. Mr Fisher has told us everything. It appears that you and he enjoyed an incorrect relationship.'

Florence shrugged. 'Correct relationships are so unenjoyable.'

'What did your friend – ' she made *friend* sound as though it were something unpleasant, like *cancer* or *sputum* – 'think about your poaching?'

'She thought it was OK.'

Paisley said, 'Are you asking us to believe that she let you live in her house and sleep with her husband?'

'Yes,' said Florence. 'You never knew Millie, but she wasn't the possessive type. She was much more reluctant about letting me borrow her Jean-Paul Gaultier bra.' She watched a fly crawl slowly along the green window-ledge.

'So why did you move out of Mrs Fisher's house, then?'

'Because it was time. I'd relied on their hospitality long enough.'

'Obviously.'

Florence sighed. 'OK. Curtis is an attractive man. We were living in the same house, running into each other on the stairs, Millie wasn't always around, it just happened. I loved Millie and I loved him. But I was worried about where we'd go from there. So I said, No more. I told Millie, said I was moving out. She said, Why? I mean, Why? as in why are you moving out just because you're sleeping with my husband. But I moved out, anyway. She tried to stop me moving out, she was pissed off that I was leaving. That was the only time we ever didn't speak, and that was only for a couple of weeks.

The policewoman said, 'Miss Johnson, we've got enough to charge you with involuntary manslaughter, d'you know that?'

Florence said, 'Look, if you wanted to charge me with that, you'd have to believe I wanted to commit suicide, wouldn't you?'

After a short silence, the policewoman threw her pen on the desk. 'Some people choose a funny way to run their lives,' she said.

Florence wanted to say she thought taking people to a police station and bullying them was a funny kind of life, too, but she stayed silent.

'OK,' said the sergeant. 'Buzz off. We don't want to see you in here again, right?'

Florence nodded. She didn't want to see them again either. She belted along the high road till she found a phone. 'Curtis, why the fuck did you have to go and tell them all that?'

'Well,' he said, 'but they came round with that statement asking why you and Millie would have fallen out and I said no way would you two ever fall out, I'd even slept with you and there was no problem. You know how to say these things. I'm sorry.'

'Did you find out any more about Joe Daniel?' she said.

'One day he was on the team sheet for the game against Liverpool, the next he was sold to Paris St Germain. Maybe he had to get out fast. Betting, women, whatever.'

'Whatever,' said Florence.

A police car sped up the street, siren wailing. Afterwards came a moment of absolute silence before everything started up again.

'Florence? Are you there?'

'Uh-huh,' she said.

Curtis said, 'If you're in trouble, got no money, even just need someone to talk to, I want you round here.'

She looked down at the meter, ticking away. 'My time's up,' she said, though it wasn't really.

Some time later, after the coroner's inquest, Florence got a letter from the insurance company. It was full of clauses and sub-clauses which were hard to understand, but the gist was that they would be unable to offer compensation.

Well, at least she wasn't going to be charged with, what was it, involuntary manslaughter. Life was good.

On the same day there was a letter from Janey, postmarked Liverpool. Joanna-Mary had told her she didn't figure in Sweet Fanny Addams's plans for 1990 and she'd got a job at the Delphi. She was a Delphinium Girl. Florence thought of Janey wearing one of those bright blue Delphi leotards with fabric petals sewn on them, and over her round, flower-like face a little head-dress shaped like a bud.

She sat on the bed that doubled for her sofa and her dining table, and spread out her notebooks in front of her. She copied down some diagrams as neatly as she could, wrote a covering letter, and went up the road to the postbox.

Two weeks later, she was being shown into Betty Trout's office by Melvyn, the secretary.

There was a cheap rickety sofa, a hard chair and a stained desk. On the wall was a pinboard covered in postcards and snapshots. The snapshots were of Betty Trout's nephews and nieces. She herself had not married, nor given birth. She was wedded to Associated British, a bit like being a bride of Christ but you got an Associated British desk diary instead of a wimple.

The shelves were piled with old shooting scripts and plastic cups half full of cold brown liquid. A producer's life was not necessarily a good one at Associated British these days. Nor was it always long. Not getting the advertizing. Revenue down. Not the money to make programmes. Jobs going. Producers were only having their contracts renewed as long as they had something to produce. The same everywhere, of course.

Betty Trout sat at the desk, Melvyn had the sofa and Florence had the hard chair. They all had plastic cups containing more brown liquid, which was lukewarm and supposedly tea. Florence was not important enough for lunch.

Florence set out to explain the idea that had come to her as she lay in hospital, searching obsessively through the papers for information on Joe Daniel. What intrigued her was the leagues, the names, the teams, the personalities, the competition, the risings and sinkings of football. There was nothing like that in the world for women.

It would be a competition between dance groups. There would be elements of the old-style Sweet Fanny Addams, those erotic and virginal little routines to pop music, but a new approach as well – an expertise, rules, a formula, judges. Like Torville and Dean in the ice dance, the synchronized swimming and gymnastics in the Olympics. A competition for groups of young women which used dance in an original and compelling way. 'I've scouted around and there's this girl called Manon. She's beautiful and absolutely original, she can dance modern and ballet, turn cartwheels, she does somersaults. A cross between Madonna and Nadia Comaneci. She's going to rewrite all the rules.' As Florence spoke, she became more and more enthused. There could be different disciplines, each of which would have to be mastered: jazz dancing, a set routine, the execution of various standard manoeuvres, a freestyle display as the climax.

Betty Trout and Melvyn looked at each other. 'Shall I speak or shall you?' she said to him.

Melvyn arranged himself to speak. He had owlish, blinking eyes and his teeth protruded slightly.

'The thing is,' he said deferentially, 'it would be far too expensive – '

'And,' said Betty Trout, 'isn't dancing rather out of fashion?'

'No,' said Florence. 'People always want to dance.'

'Besides which, I don't think Gus Wycherley, our head of Light Entertainment, would like the idea of girls – women –

competing in that sort of way. Lovely to meet you for this natter, and if you do have any ideas which you think might work for Associated don't hesitate to give me or Melvyn a ring.'

The sun was cold. Summer was dying, leaving behind it a residue of dead leaves and empty fast food cartons on the grass. The air smelled of aeroplane fuel and dog-shit. Florence went running from her bedsit up to the Edgware Road and back to put condition on her legs. When she turned the corner into her street she slowed. There was a familiar figure sitting on the steps leading up to the rooming house.

'Greetings, Lily. Do you want to see me or have you just stopped to admire the colour of my front door?'

Lily was wearing a denim skirt that looked as though it had been torn off something else. 'Joanna-Mary wants to speak to you,' she said.

'That's a first.'

'I'm to make sure you bring the notes you and Millie made for the routine at the Scala.'

Florence stood in the street and just screamed with laughter. 'You're what?' she said. 'You're to do what? I'm to do what? Hah!' It sounded so good she said 'Hah!' again.

'Well,' said Lily, 'but are you coming?'

Florence hesitated but she knew she wouldn't be able to resist it because she was dying to see what kind of jam Joanna-Mary had got herself in, so she went and fetched her folder where she kept all the routines written out. A taxi was waiting just up the street. Lily climbed in behind Florence and gave the address to the driver. She was carrying Joanna-Mary's mobile phone, which she flung on to the worn black seat. The cab smelled of diesel fumes. They lurched off into the rush-hour traffic.

Lily said, 'The group are just about ready to bust up if you ask me, but we're trying to find someone as a mediator who we all rate, and we all said you. What we want you to do is come back and give us some ideas and basically run the show because Joanna-Mary doesn't know enough to manage it on her own, plus she needs a choreographer of your stature who knows what to do.'

'Bloody hell! Who wrote that speech for you? The Brothers Grimm?'

'No! No! I swear! Joanna-Mary is dead keen. Sees the error of her ways, wants to make it up to you, feels she's been a bit harsh, blah-de-blah.' Lily jabbed out a number on the phone. She listened to it ring and then shoved it at Florence. 'Here. Ask her if you don't believe me.'

'Hello, Florence!' trilled Joanna-Mary. 'Super to hear you. How is the taxi?'

'Why? Has it been unwell?'

'What? I want you to teach me everything you know about choreography. I want you to dance to "You're So Vain" the way you'd dance to it, and then I'm going to dance to it, and then I want you to dance to it with me.'

Florence said, 'You're joking. You expect me to do you favours?'

Lily whispered, 'Don't get mad. There's money in it. Ask her about Stoke-on-Trent.'

Florence would have preferred to say, 'After everything you've done I wouldn't bail you out for a million pounds,' but her poll tax needed paying. 'You said something about Stoke-on-Trent, Lily?' she asked, loud enough for Joanna-Mary to hear.

Joanna-Mary said, 'OK, yeah, we've got a gig there tomorrow night and we want you to come in on it.'

'Joanna-Mary,' said Florence, 'there's no way I can teach you everything about choreography in one afternoon.'

'Please,' said Joanna-Mary, 'please think about it.'

'A hundred quid cash up front, today, 25 per cent of the takings in Stoke, and my expenses paid.'

There was a pause, then Joanna-Mary said in a slightly tinny voice, 'Obviously I can't do it all in cash, but how about fifty and a cheque?'

Florence said, 'Well, OK, I'll come, but don't you try anything, Joanna-Mary, or I'll shit on you from a great height.'

'Oh, Florence, you really have got this weird idea of me as some sort of dragon. Let's not bring up the past. I'm so looking forward to seeing you and catching up on all your news.'

Lily said, switching off the phone for her, 'You know that

snot, she's like that, Florence. She doesn't want you to know how desperate she is.'

By this time they were going down Oxford Street. 'Stop the cab,' said Florence to the driver. She ran across the road and dived into Mark One. She picked up a top for £4.99 and a pair of leggings for £3.99, jumped back into the cab with them and started to change as they were going along. Some boys in a sports car applauded her so she waved her arse at them out of the window. Then Lily saw a shirt in the Gap marked down to £15.99 so she went in and snapped that up plus a pair of cream-coloured jeans. By the time they got to the Territorial Army hall it was so late that Joanna-Mary was fit to be tied, but she couldn't say anything because Florence would have walked out on her. She counted out Florence's money with a tight smile. The last fiver was in coins.

Florence looked around. On the table in the corner was a half-eaten loaf of bread, a nearly empty jar of pickled onions and a heel of cheese. The cassette player was blasting out Carly Simon's 'You're So Vain'. The paraffin heater stood in the middle of the floor, giving off heat with a little grinning blue flame. Annie Easterfield and Cindy Davies, the new girls, huddled by it in their worn-out leotards, smoking. Manon stood on her head by the wall. She lifted herself up on her hands and in time to the music performed three bounding somersaults across the boards. She smiled at Florence and waved, and somersaulted back where she came from.

Florence went dancing with them through the Scala routine. She was pleased with how her leg stood up to it. She was slower than before the accident but that wouldn't be for ever. She danced with them for four hours. She could tell that Annie and Cindy were good, reliable girls who only needed the right direction, and that she hadn't been wrong about Lily being a great dancer, and that Manon was potentially a sensation. But Joanna-Mary! She hadn't learned, and she probably never would. What Florence couldn't work out was how someone could be so pretty and still end up looking as if she were made of wood, like a toy on wheels or something. The girl just couldn't dance. She had rigid hands, and her bottom stuck out all over the place, and the only thing that really moved around was her mouth, though never in time to the music. Florence changed the line-up and stuck her second from the end, where people couldn't see what a prat she was. 'I need you there, Joanna-Mary,' she said. 'It's the most crucial position in the whole routine.'

At tea-time they went to Geronimo's, where Joanna-Mary followed her into the loo. 'Well?' she said. 'What do you think?'

'I think,' Florence said carefully, 'that we should take the show to Stoke and do it as it stands, and then when we get back we'll maybe . . . do a bit of tweaking here and there, you know?'

'Florence, you're so clever, you're so absolutely wonderful, you really are. I really insist you come back on some sort of contract.'

A cubicle door opened and Cindy scuttled away. Joanna-Mary said, 'Florence, those fucking girls are useless. They can't dance a thing. They never have been able to dance. I want to be with someone who can dance. They're hopeless.'

'Look,' said Florence, 'don't you go badmouthing anyone, Joanna-Mary, because that's where all the trouble started last time. These are your dancers, you've got to look after them and make them feel good so they'll go out and die for you.'

'Oh, absolutely, I see exactly what you mean.'

The next day, they set off for Stoke.

Greg had a new motor. It was a dented blue van with the name of a boy's school still legible on the side. 'Hello, Greg,' said Florence, jumping in beside him. 'You're looking a bit pale. Are you not sleeping well?'

Greg looked as though he'd been bitten in the arse by an alligator. He sprang out and opened up the bonnet and fiddled about with the distributor cap till everyone was ready to go. Then when they stopped off at the motorway service area for lunch, he wouldn't come in with them. Florence, who wasn't about to allow him to get away with it that easily, brought her coffee out and drank it noisily, leaning against the van.

'Well, Greg,' she said. 'Morning finds us in another strange place.'

'Leave me alone.'

'The hell I will. You let Joanna-Mary shaft me. Not just *let* –

helped her. Of all the all-time shitty things to do! Why? When did I ever hurt you? Florence tried to make Greg look at her but he wouldn't. He was staring across the car park at a fat woman's efforts to get out of a Ford Fiesta. She looked as if she were wearing it on her back. Florence said, 'Greg, I'm not going to let it go. What's that bitch got on you? Are you a secret child molester or the son of a Nazi war criminal or what? I'll find out, even if I have to drink coffee at you for ever.'

'I don't want to talk about it. I can't. I'm too ashamed.'

'Oh Jesus, I'm really moved. Let me regain control of myself.'

'Greg – ' Joanna-Mary was walking towards them. She spoke in a self-righteous, slightly whiny voice. 'I've been dashing around like a lemon for ten minutes getting this lunch thing organized. That's your job, or isn't it?'

'Sorry,' said Greg. 'I'll be right with you.'

'*Now*,' said Joanna-Mary. She put a restraining hand on Florence's arm as Greg scuttled towards the cafeteria. 'Oh, Florence,' she said, walking slowly. 'Huddles.'

Florence gave her an encouraging smile.

'I hope you don't mind my, um, um, mentioning it,' continued Joanna-Mary, 'but we have this unbreakable rule that we all eat together. Joanna-Mary's news-and-views sessions, Annie calls them. You know, it's just a chance to raise anything that's worrying anybody or even, well, just natter. Rather than this thing of one or two people going off into a huddle, and then everyone thinks, you know, what's she saying behind my back, all that sort of thing.' Joanna-Mary gave a little shrug then stared serenely into the distance.

'Thank you for telling me,' said Florence, 'I'm awfully grateful. I wouldn't want to rock the boat.'

The gig was at a club called Carizma, in a building of dark red brick. The paintwork was pale blue and the railway bridge ran over its roof. Across the road was a derelict site used as a car park. When they went in they found out they were expected to change in the Ladies, so they drove on half a mile to their guesthouse to get ready.

Mrs Guise, the landlady, was tall and scrawny and wore glasses with pearlized wings. Behind her desk in reception was a picture of Christ looming over someone in bed, a poster advertizing a jumble sale, and a notice saying GUESTS ARE RESPECTFULLY REMINDED THAT THIS IS A CHRISTIAN HOUSE, AND ARE ASKED TO BEHAVE IN A CONSIDERATE MANNER. Joanna-Mary and Lily had a big room with a washbasin and pink candlewick bedspreads, above the residents' lounge. Annie, Cindy and Manon were in a smaller room with three narrow beds in a row like cricket stumps, and Florence had the room that was meant for Greg. It measured seven foot by six and was mainly taken up by a small double bed with a cover of orange quilted nylon, and an imitation teak wardrobe which slanted forward menacingly. 'Don't worry about Greg,' said Joanna-Mary, 'he can sleep in the car.'

Getting ready took ages because Joanna-Mary commandeered the only bathroom for half an hour and Lily and Florence were so desperate they nipped out to pee in a pub up the end of the street. Lily was bored. She bought a bottle of Hirondelle with a screw top and started to work her way down it. The air was cold and smelt of northern cities in autumn, and the lights were just beginning to shine out of houses. As Florence walked back she was overcome by the strongest feeling of yearning and loneliness. She would give all she had to be back in a group, to belong again, to wait in Christmas dressing rooms with the back end of the pantomime cow and the dame in his jeans and check shirt, hearing faint snatches of dialogue from the stage – 'But I am only a poor shoemaker' – while perfect little snowflakes drifted past the windows.

The show was a disaster. Right at the last minute when they were waiting in the wings to go on, Joanna-Mary got wise to Florence's ploy and said no way was she going to dance second from the end. In the centre, that was where she always danced, and she was going to dance there now. 'You asked me to come in and sort out this group,' said Florence in a furious whisper, 'and now you're telling me you can't take it.'

'I realize,' said Joanna-Mary in a very starchy way, 'that there are a few things to be ironed out.'

Florence said, 'If you sorted out everything that needed sorting there wouldn't be anything left.'

The music blared and they ran on stage smiling. 'Such as what?' demanded Joanna-Mary through fixed lips.

Florence danced off across the floor and came back again. 'Such as you,' she said, 'wiggling around in the middle of the stage and making sure no one else gets a look in.'

At that moment, something went wrong with the sound system, and 'You're So Vain' came out in a series of splutters and jerks, so they had to go off again and wait half an hour for it to be fixed, by which time Florence and Joanna-Mary weren't talking and everybody in the audience had had six more lagers apiece. A bunch of men in the front started throwing chips at them when they came back on stage; Cindy trod on one and slipped over. They were meant to perform three more five-minute slots, but the sound system went funny again, and then some people at the back started breaking up the seats. Florence looked towards the wings and saw the manager waving his arms at them to come off, and that was that.

When they got back to the guesthouse it was eleven o'clock. Mrs Guise looked at Lily, who was swinging the half-empty Hirondelle bottle around by her knees, and declined to give them anything to eat. They set off into town again. Everything was closed except a very dimly lit Chinese restaurant. There were two lines of six tables, three of which were occupied. At the far end stood a waiter in a creased red jacket. Greg led the girls up to him and said, 'I want a table for seven, please.'

The waiter stared at them incredulously. He said, 'Oh *Christ.*'

Just then the head man came up and started to rattle off a bollocking to the waiter. He tore the jacket off Greg's back and shoved it at the waiter and gestured to him to take the girls' coats as well. The waiter took them and dropped them on the floor. By this time the head man was pushing two tables together and dancing round Greg and the girls and bringing them the Set Meal for Ten Persons without being asked, so they couldn't walk out, and then Lily ordered two bottles of foul white wine which nobody else wanted so she had the best part of them herself. Everyone was just starting on coffee when in the middle of saying something she gave a cough and did a sort of introductory barf on the tablecloth. 'Quick,' said Florence to Greg, 'get her out of here.'

Joanna-Mary was at her most charming to the waiter. 'Could we have our bill, please?' she said with a big smile. They could hear Lily burping and groaning outside. Joanna-Mary looked at the bill and said to Florence, 'I haven't got a bean on me. You'll have to lend me back that fifty pounds.'

'When am I going to get it back?'

'Oh, for God's sake, Florence, do you ever think about anything except money?'

'Not where you're concerned, no.'

Joanna-Mary said crossly, 'I'll let you have a cheque tomorrow. Is that all right? Will you trust me?'

They put Lily on the floor of the van with Manon's backpack to be sick into if she needed it, but she was all right till they got back to Mrs Guise's, when she went up the stairs as fast as anyone could go on all fours and threw up everywhere in the bathroom. Her catchment area included all the things it was really hard to get vomit off, like the toilet brush and a shag-pile bathmat. Florence and Annie followed her into the bathroom after a judicious interval. She was propped up against the bath with her eyes half open. While Annie and Cindy and Manon and Florence were trying to mop up, Joanna-Mary looked in. She said, 'Eucch! I'm not sleeping with her.'

Florence, who was slightly regretful that she'd mouthed off at Joanna-Mary at the show and in the restaurant, said, 'Lily can have my room – if you don't mind sharing with me.'

'Oh no,' said Joanna-Mary, 'great fun.'

It was past one o'clock when they finally turned in. Cindy popped her head round the door to say that the bathroom was more or less OK, so Florence used it, but Joanna-Mary absolutely wouldn't. Florence lay under the pink candlewick cover and listened to her tossing and turning uncomfortably in the other bed. How strange, she thought, after all this, sleeping in the same room as Joanna-Mary . . .

She was woken by a scream and a terrific crash. She jumped out of bed and switched on the light. Joanna-Mary was spread-eagled on the floor with her nightie around her waist and the washbasin in two chunks, one each side of her. Water was pumping everywhere.

'I was cleaning my teeth,' said Joanna-Mary.

Florence realized that Joanna-Mary must have sat on the washbasin to have a pee. She gave herself a terrible stitch trying not to laugh, because Joanna-Mary's bottom must be hurting like anything, not to mention her pride. Joanna-Mary saw all the water and opened her mouth to scream again and Florence said, 'Shut up. Don't wake the landlady.'

'But it's, but it's, oh my God. Do something, Florence.'

'I'm thinking about what to do.' She helped Joanna-Mary up and told her to get dressed. The carpet was already soaking. Florence crept downstairs. A low-wattage light on the reception desk gave the hall a yellow glow. She looked into the residents' lounge where a steady drip-drip, drip-drip from the ceiling below the washbasin was beginning to gain tempo. There was a pool of water on top of the television set and the plasterwork looked bulgy.

Greg was curled up under his overcoat across the front seats of the van. Florence tapped on the window and he opened his eyes with a look of bleary incomprehension. When she told him what had happened, he said 'What about the Yellow Pages? They usually have a list of plumbers,' and rolled over again.

'Don't go back to sleep,' Greg,' she said between her teeth. 'Start up the van now.'

She went and shook the others awake, and they all tiptoed down the stairs with their belongings and jumped into the van and set off back to London.

It was half-past five in the morning when the M1 became the North Circular and Greg steered the van towards the West End. Joanna-Mary, who had spent the whole journey silent and haughty, got out her mobile phone and had a short, elliptical conversation. Lily was asleep, and so was Manon. Annie and Cindy, who had been best friends since their first day at the Arts Educational, murmured and giggled in the back seat. Florence said to Joanna-Mary, 'Will you ring for a minicab for me?'

'One's on its way.' She shifted a little in her seat. 'Waiting for you outside the hall.'

Florence said, 'I hope you don't get a bruise.'

'What? Why should I get a bruise?'

'From your accident.'

'What are you talking about?'

'In the hotel.'

'No. No. You must be thinking of someone else.'

Greg dropped them off in front of the Territorial Army hall. A Mercedes was already waiting there, but Florence didn't take much notice of it. She and Manon unloaded the costumes from the van and then waved Greg goodbye and took them inside. The hall was cold and musty. Annie switched the lights on in the kitchen and put the kettle on, and Cindy got out some clean cups, whistling a little tune. Florence suddenly felt incredibly sleepy. She picked up her bag and went out into the street again. Her cab wasn't there yet.

While she was waiting the Mercedes whooshed past with Joanna-Mary in the passenger seat. She was lighting a cigarette, leaning back with it in the V of her fingers. The man driving her was a presence rather than a person with limbs and features and clothes. Florence was simply aware of bulk and shadow.

When Florence set off to look for her cab in the half-light two men blocked her way and asked for her bag. She said, 'If you want to take anything from me that's fine but you ought to know I've got a gun in here and I'm ready to die now. There's nothing to keep me hanging around.' Then she turned round and started walking slowly back towards the hall, waiting for them to jump her, but they never did.

She went back into the hall where Lily was stripwashing at the kitchen sink. The floor was covered in patterned vinyl which might have been turquoise once. Lily's small bare feet were positioned on a teacloth. 'I'm going to Yves St Laurent,' she said, 'to find the perfect shirt.'

'Joanna-Mary said there would be a cab to take me home,' said Florence. 'And where's my money?'

'Yeah, well,' said Lily. 'Joanna-Mary said to me you weren't to have any money.'

Florence had a sudden thought. She dived to pick up her bag

and rummaged in it. '*Fucking Hell*,' she shouted. 'Death isn't *bad* enough for her.'

Annie said diffidently, 'Did you say something, Florence?'

'The folder with all my routines in it has gone.' Florence wheeled round to interrogate Lily, but Lily had spied an opening and gone for it. Florence sat on the kitchen floor with her head in her hands, calling herself a wankpot several times over.

Annie, Cindy and Manon gathered round her saying how sorry they were and what a bitch Joanna-Mary was. 'Only say the word,' said Cindy. 'We'll ditch her right away and go with you.'

Florence said, 'Well, that's nice of you, Cindy, but you've got to think of yourselves. I can't give you any work right now.'

Anyway, nothing was going to make up for what had happened because Joanna-Mary had made her look a *fool*. Dammit, here was a girl who had everything in the world – work, a man, loving parents, fine clothes and more money than Florence would ever have. Six months ago she'd taken her group, and now she'd kebabbed her again.

Joanna-Mary on her mobile phone said to Edmund Timpson, 'I need to talk to you about another matter.'

'I shall be at Annabel's tomorrow night. Would you like me to collect you?'

'Perfect. Don't let anyone know we're seeing each other, will you?'

A broken tarpaulin flapped on the towpath. The river was a swirling torrent of brown. The view from Rory Cromarty's window was blocked off by several miles of curtains. 'The architect didn't think about what was going to happen when the weather turned nippy,' he complained. 'It was like living in an icebox. I suppose he just thought I'd sit here and die like a geranium.'

Florence broke in, 'Can you write something else about Joanna-Mary?'

'I can't do it, ducks. I've been nobbled. My proprietor's a personal friend of Daddy.'

'Bloody hell! Is there no one whose arm can't be twisted by Roger Reed-Herbert?'

'Looks like it, doesn't it? Come on, I'll take you to dinner.'

'No thanks.'

'Don't get upset about it, ducky. That's just the way life is, I'm afraid. You might just as well get upset about the Leaning Tower of Pisa not being straight.'

'Except the Leaning Tower of Pisa never told any lies.'

Florence tried taking her story to the *Pictorial*, the Daily Something-or-other, the Sunday Whoosit. The response was the same each time. They were not interested. People wanted to believe Joanna-Mary. It was convenient. To have believed Florence would have required too much emotional effort; too much acknowledgement of poor judgement, too much expenditure of sympathy and feeling. Florence, waiting at the reception desks of newspapers for journalists who declined to see her, had become a crank, a mad person in flapping black clothes in the lobby; a French nuisance, That Woman, a bore.

She wrote stylishly to Rory Cromarty, thanking him for all he'd done. She wrote to Janey enclosing some new ideas she'd had for dance routines, in case she could make any use of them. She wrote to Greg, enclosing a sleeping pill sellotaped on the paper.

One night, she opened the window of her room and leant out. Just her luck to get a basement flat so she couldn't even end it all by jumping out. Her anguished cry pierced the cold October air; 'All washed up and I'm only twenty-three!'

Then she disappeared off the face of the earth.

In the Territorial Army hall the windows were misted up. The girls were rehearsing in layers of jerseys, tights, socks, leg-warmers, gloves with cut-away fingers. They had another gig coming up in the Waterside Club.

After rehearsal, Joanna-Mary called Greg into the narrow kitchen.

'Some wonderful news,' she said. 'Edmund Timpson has agreed to handle our PR and um, um, suchlike.'

'I see,' said Greg. 'Would you like me to draw up a contract for him or do you intend this to be on an informal basis?'

She smiled on him warmly. 'Greg, you're so stuffy and sweet. Isn't he sweet, everybody?' She appealed to the girls as they filed through the double doors into the street. A blast of cold air swept in like a ghost who was in a hurry to get somewhere. 'Greg's the sweetest man. Isn't he?' She turned back to him. The doors flapped and were still. Greg had never found anything sadder than the emptiness of halls and theatres after the girls had gone. Joanna-Mary said, 'Regretfully, this means I'll have to lose you. The group's budget was badly overstretched by Millie and we've all got to make cutbacks. For this reason there can't be any question of compensation. You must see it's for the best. It would only upset you to have Edmund telling you what to do.' She held out her hand. 'Goodbye, Greg.'

Greg said, 'Goodbye.'

Chapter Fourteen

Footballing in Nantes

IN THE SPRING of 1991, Curtis Fisher sat in his warm office at
Plantagenet and Schwartz. He was in charge of putting
together a charity concert. It was an annual event, called Sweet
Charity as it had originally been the idea of a confectionery
manufacturer anxious to regain a few brownie points after some
nasty things had appeared in the press about what sugar did to
people's health.

Plantagenet and Schwartz inhabited a building in Bloomsbury.
There were two big plane trees outside. The brickwork had gone
grey over the years and the roof and pavements were covered
with pigeon shit in a surprisingly delicate pattern.

Inside the hall it was dark and cold, and without actually
featuring anything in that colour gave the impression of a lot of
maroon. At the end there was a dark wood revolving carousel
displaying postcards, of the kind once used in seaside tobacco-
nists'. The staircase got narrower and narrower as it climbed the
house, culminating in a rhombus-shaped landing where cardboard boxes full of things nobody could work out what to do
with were kept. Above it was a skylight leading on to a small
flat area of roof where Curtis and Millie made love most days
one far-off summer.

Curtis was expecting a visit from Janey Sears, whom he
vaguely remembered from the time before Millie was killed. It
was a wet day in April and the sky was a strange metallic colour.
The stubby cherry tree in the square had come out in a riot of
pink blossoms. All over London people glanced at office clocks
and saw it was ten to five.

Janey arrived out of the rain. She folded her umbrella and shook the drops out of her hair like some young but dignified blonde Labrador. She was wearing a calf-length skirt with white polka dots on brown silk, and a long brown jersey. 'Well, Curtis,' she said in her soft country girl's voice.

'Well, Janey.'

'I want you to put Sweet Fanny Addams on Sweet Charity.'

'That Reed-Herbert girl's group? I thought you and she hated each other.'

Janey said, 'The *real* Sweet Fanny Addams.'

Curtis thought of his dead wife. 'I don't think so,' he said churlishly. 'There's one missing, for a start. Anyway, that kind of thing is very old hat.'

'Oh . . .' She paused. 'I thought it would be rather nice if Florence danced for Millie. Matter of fact, it was Florence's idea.' She looked around his office. On the bookshelves were two photos of Millie in a silver frame next to a hyacinth in a bowl. The hyacinth was tall and had developed a slouch. Curtis said, 'You'll never get Tina and Collette to dance together again. You know what people say. If they were on the *Titanic* they wouldn't share the same lifeboat.'

'Tina's agreed already. Also, Curtis, you have to take the overview.' Janey was not quite sure what an overview might be but the phrase pleased her with its resonance. 'About Collette, I mean. The divorce from Delaney Ward has knocked her for six. She needs something to put her back on her feet again.'

'The drying-out clinic didn't work, then.'

'Think of it,' said Janey. 'The publicity, the newspapermen, the excitement.'

'Well, but there's everybody to find. The one who had the rude name.'

'I know where Ratty lives. I got her address from her at the funeral.'

'Well, but no one knows where Collette is.'

'Now Tina lives in New York she's been able to make enquiries.'

'But if there's a new Sweet Fanny Addams, that will make everything rather complicated,' said Curtis.

Janey's eyes took on a look of concern. 'How awkward. But surely no one in their right mind would make a fuss. It's in such a good cause.'

'I don't really think it would – ' Just then, the telephone rang. It was Juliet Dexter calling from Hollywood.

Juliet said, 'Hi, Curtis, how are you?' She liked to touch base with him every now and again, to see how he was getting on.

'I'm not doing so badly,' said Curtis.

Juliet said, 'I'll be filming in London soon. I'd love us to have some time together. Will you show me some interesting restaurants?'

She was in her trailer, having a bruise painted above her browbone for a scene containing domestic violence, though not too much. 'My twins are getting bigger by the hour,' she said. 'Eight months old now.'

'Well,' said Curtis, 'that's good to hear. And now I must – '

'Is that Juliet Dexter?' said Janey. 'Could I talk with her, please?' She took the phone off him before he could say no. 'Hello, Juliet? Janey Sears here. There's something Curtis and I would very much like you to do. You know Sweet Charity? Well – would you dance in it? Tina and Ratty have already said yes, and we're just waiting for Collette.'

'You mean, as Sweet Fanny Addams?'

Janey said, 'Mm.'

'Oh wow,' said Juliet, 'Is that Curtis's idea? I think it's wonderful. I would love to.'

After that, Janey said goodbye to Curtis and stepped softly out into the street. There was a phone box over the road, under a bright green sycamore tree. Janey balanced her umbrella against the side. 'Hello my lovey,' she said. 'How are you? It's very nice weather here. Are you enjoying some sun?'

Florence was using the phone in the Bar Tabac across the street from her apartment. That year she was in Passy, in a street close to the Place Chopin. The Métro went past in the distance, along a high grey bridge. Her apartment had no phone. Someone had to run across from the Bar Tabac to fetch her.

'Oh God!' shouted Florence, 'you can't do this to me! Get on with it!'

Janey cooed, 'It looks like we've got a show.'

Florence suddenly felt as though she'd been in prison for a hundred years and now someone had come along and left the door open. 'Tell me,' she breathed. 'Tell me everything.'

Janey said, 'Not till tomorrow. I'm catching the first boat over in the morning. Cheers ears.' She put the phone back and picked up her umbrella. Everyone in London had gone home. A plane sounded far away and a car door slammed. The evening was full of birdsong.

It was not strictly true to say that Florence had disappeared off the face of the earth.

There didn't seem anything to keep her in England. She made a few attempts to find dancing work but once they heard her name there was a strange unwillingness to employ her. Everybody's darling, that was her. Florence Johnson, the people's choice.

Eventually she decided to go back to Paris, where she still knew some people from her days at Au Pied de Vache. Her friend Roland knew a photographer with a Japanese girlfriend and an apartment in Passy. The photographer was working abroad for a couple of years. The apartment was reached through a courtyard lined with pebbles. On both sides of the courtyard were evergreens with low, heavy branches from the next-door gardens. A cat with a shiny tabby coat slept on the coalshed roof all day, its paws tucked under its chest.

The apartment was really a small one-and-a-half-storey building that might once have been a coach-house. It had a double entrance door with panes of dark blue glass. On the floor were cracked old tiles. Up a ladder was a platform just large enough for a double mattress and a row of lockers. Four feet above the bed was a skylight. She slept looking up at the silent stars, wrapped in a grey blanket.

Florence found work at the local school, teaching the children of well-to-do Parisians dancing to the sound of *ye-ye*. When she had saved enough money, she bought a train ticket to Nantes. It was a Saturday in February. She set off early, breaking her journey for coffee and bread in a café near the station in

Chartres. Rain was falling and the cars going past outside made a sizzling sound with their tyres. One wall of the café was entirely covered with a giant poster of Tahiti. The others were of unsealed tongue-and-groove wood cladding which stopped a few centimetres short of the top, revealing the soft blue peeling paint underneath.

Florence had never been to a football match before. Arriving at Nantes she looked around, but all she could see was miles and miles of city. On the train with her had been some supporters of Paris St Germain, and she followed them for a mile and a half through side streets, across parks, past the 'A nos morts' memorial. Every time she thought of what she was doing her heart gave a violent beat. The stadium rose in front of her, airy and echoing. There was a long time to go till kick-off, too much time, but she wanted to be sure of finding the place she wanted, behind the goal. Alone in her row, she sat on a red plastic seat, a small figure in black. She looked through L'Equipe, which had for some weeks been required reading for her. While walking to the ground she had brought a baguette filled with *jambon cru* but her throat muscles were too constricted to eat.

When the players came out on to the pitch from the tunnel, she saw him, Joe, wearing the Nantes colours. His hair was as beautiful and wild as ever, and his legs were long and milky-coffee brown against the pallid winter skin of the other players. He was two million pounds' worth of man. There was strapping on his ankle; Florence had learned from L'Equipe that he had been injured in the game at St Etienne in midweek and his fitness had been in question right up to the evening before the match. In the St Etienne game he had scored the first goal and assisted in the second. Florence had several more nuggets of football talk saved up should anyone question her right to be there. No one did. They were all so absorbed in the game that she could have been sitting next to them in a gondola.

All the first half the game stayed goalless. The crowd were first encouraging then restless and resentful. Then, in the seventy-eighth minute, Joe picked up the ball from deep inside his own half. He drifted across the pitch from left to right as though propelled by a wave. He glanced up briefly then found the Nantes striker with a long pass weighted so his team-mate could meet it running, but the number nine's shot was poor, ricocheting off the back of a Paris St Germain defender. Joe was not finished. He had moved in behind the defender as if the ricochet was exactly what he had predicted, even desired, and he met the ball on his head, chest, knee, then instep. He glanced up again to shoot. There was an open goal and the crowd was roaring him on. Behind the open goal was Florence. She stood motionless, and he stood too, as though they were statues in a park. Some player or other from Paris St Germain swiftly robbed Joe of the ball and booted it upfield. Two of Joe's team-mates came up to him, shouting and shoving. The crowd moaned. Joe walked away, a head-hanging diagonal progress to the tunnel. On his way he took off his shirt. After a while the game restarted with a substitute. Joe was suspended for the next two games and fined two weeks' wages, not that Florence could bring herself to find that out.

She carried on teaching and living in Paris. Lying awake one night, she became obsessed with thoughts of Cal, wondering if he was well and happy, wanting to drink and laugh with him again. The next afternoon she rode on the métro to St-Germain-des-Prés and walked from there up a wide avenue full of swirling leaves. The buildings on either side were bleak and grey. After a few minutes she came to Rue Jacob and stood looking down along the line of cars. The Renault 5 turbo was still there, parked on a crossing, one wheel on the kerb. Florence felt like someone newly dead, a lost soul rushing invisibly through her past haunts. She moved on, to the doors of the apartment building. The concierge let her pass through the foyer without comment. She entered the lift and climbed to the third floor. When she walked into the living room, the first person she saw was Godfrey.

He was standing by the fireplace with his arm resting on the mantelshelf and glass of brandy in his hand. His mouth dropped open slowly and stayed that way for some time. Cal was in the kitchen and had no idea. He chatted on easily to Godfrey, chopping mushrooms and parsley to go in a pan.

'Oh, don't stand on ceremony,' said Florence. 'It's only me.'

She dropped her jacket on a flimsy little chair that was probably worth about 30,000 francs.

Cal came out of the kitchen and took her in, standing there by the lift in her thin black jersey with buttons down the front and her shoulders hunched from the cold.

Godfrey started making sounds. There were a few seconds of him going 'Gwar, gwar, gwar,' and finally real words came out. 'You!'

'I'm really pleased to see you too, Godfrey. What a pity Lorna couldn't be here to make the reunion perfect. How is Lorna, by the way?'

'Mrs Snaleham and I have resolved our differences, if that's what you mean.' Godfrey slung her a look of extreme hatred. 'What are you doing here?'

Then Florence suddenly felt anger go whirling through her so fast it made her dizzy. How dare he? Just how dare he? Right then she didn't give a damn if Cal was well and happy. He and Godfrey were right at the head of a long line of people who had made a fool out of her and she wasn't going to be fooled by anyone any more. 'Hell! Why do you think I'm here? I want a divorce.'

Cal said, 'Well, sure, Florence, I'll – '

'Be quiet,' said Godfrey. 'I'll deal with this woman. What is it you want, money?'

Florence said, 'Don't you listen to anything anybody says to you? I want a divorce, dammit. D-I-V-O-R-C-E.' She turned to Cal. 'It's nothing complicated. We can get our marriage annulled on the grounds of non-consummation. All you have to do is swear an affidavit that you weren't prepared to consummate the marriage.'

'Cal will swear nothing,' said Godfrey. 'It's only your word against his. He hasn't walked out on your marriage. He isn't the guilty party.'

'Why shouldn't I let her divorce me?' said Cal. 'I don't mind. If you want to be free, Florence, that's fine by me. Have you found someone else?'

Florence said, 'No, but so what?'

'If you'll excuse us,' said Godfrey, full of sarcasm. He marched Cal back into the kitchen and shut the door on her.

Florence went to the door to listen. She could hear him expounding to Cal in his plummy legal voice about work permits and visas and residence laws and what would happen if he lost his rights as the spouse of a French national. She shoved the door open. 'Thank you, Godfrey,' she said. 'As a matter of fact, it hadn't occurred to me that Cal could get thrown out if I divorced him.'

Cal said, 'Well now, look here, Florence, if you haven't found someone else you want to marry, it would sure make it easier for me and Godfrey if you'd agree to keep things the way they are.'

'I wouldn't want to make Godfrey's *death* easy,' said Florence.

Godfrey said, 'If you embark on divorce proceedings, I promise you that Cal will have the best legal representation in Europe, I guarantee that he will contest your allegations most strenuously, and I will ensure that the case goes on so long that the cost of it will destroy you financially.'

Florence knew that he was talking absolute shit, but there was something about the way he was looking at her, like an alligator sizing her up for a light lunch, that made her just want to get out of there. She pressed the call button on the lift and of course the doors didn't open because it was stuck at the first floor, so she had to stand there with her back to him and count up to a hundred in her head so she didn't have to hear him droning on. In the street it was raining, and she realized her jacket was still in the apartment.

When she walked back into the living room Godfrey and Cal were standing in exactly the same positions as she'd left them, as though they were waiting for someone else to come along and animate them. She said, 'And I forgot to say, Cal, you ought to leave the poisonous bastard,' then picked up her jacket and left them to it.

She was just unlocking her front door when Vanessa from the Bar Tabac ran over to say someone was calling from England.

'Hello, my lovey,' said Janey. 'How are you?'

'I'm fine. Top of the world. Never better. In a limited kind of way.' She looked around the bar. It was before the early evening rush and the only sign of life was a large meat fly crawling sleepily along the Buvez Choky poster.

Janey said, 'I've seen a classified ad in the *Stage*. Associated British are looking for dance groups to take part in a competition. Shall I send off for details?'

There was a silence. Janey said, 'Are you there?'

'Yes,' said Florence.

'Well,' said Janey, 'are you interested?'

She could hear Florence's shrug down the wires. 'Janey,' she said, 'it's no good, I just don't have the capital for that kind of project. And I don't have something else, I don't know what the right word is but, you know, the Joanna-Mary thing, I got burned, I don't want to do it any more.'

'Don't *say* that,' said Janey. 'You can't go around saying things like that. There's a law about it. You've got to be strong.'

There was a pause and then Florence said in a little, tired voice, 'Ach, well.'

'Well, I'm going to write to Associated British anyway,' said Janey. 'Don't give up, Florence. Don't you give up hope. Something'll happen.'

The first thing that happened was that a month later Cal turned up at her apartment. 'I got your address from Roland,' he said, handing her a long, brown envelope.

She inspected it. He said, 'It's in there. The affidavit.'

She turned it over in her hand and said, 'What about Godfrey?'

'You don't have to worry about him. He says things and doesn't mean them.'

'Has he thought of going into politics?' said Florence.

'Pardon me? Anyway, he's got a case on in London at the moment, won't be back for three weeks. No, ah, you take that, Florence, and do what you want. It isn't right that you should tie yourself down for my sake. You don't owe me anything after what I got you into.'

She said, 'But I meant it, Cal, you aren't doing yourself any good staying with him. A married man is a married man. Look at you, on your own again, while he comes and goes as he pleases. The whole thing about loving someone is you want to hire an aeroplane and write their name in the sky and you're never going to be able to do that. How much longer are you going to go on being his sordid little secret? You're so sweet and good-looking, Cal, you could have any guy you want.'

'Well now, Florence, it's not as easy as that these days, as you know,' said Cal, 'playing the field, it can put you in danger of your life.'

Florence said, 'Bloody hell, I'd rather join a monastery than be stuck with Godfrey.' She put the affidavit away and studied him, her head on one side. He looked pale and thin. He was wearing faded dungarees and a shirt in black and blue checks with the sleeves rolled up in honour of the April sunshine. The apartment was always dark, but a clear spring light had managed to force its way through the coloured glass in the front door and was making purple diamond shapes on the floorboards. Florence thought of the motorway stretching all the way to the south, the sun beginning to burn her arms as she swung right at Montpellier and headed for the Spanish border. She said solicitously, 'You know what you need to do? Get out of the city for a while, drive around a bit in that nice car of yours, see the country, maybe the seaside.'

His face brightened, but then he said, 'Shit, they wouldn't give me the time off at work.'

'Tell them you're sick. You're going to make yourself sick, Cal, working all the hours you do, no holidays.'

They took off on the Route Nationale to Joigny, heading for Dijon and then Lyon where they slept in the Renault 5 and spent what they'd saved eating lunch at a restaurant with three stars. Then they drove down to Avignon which was crowded because of a fête and they had to queue outside the city walls to get in. After Avignon they passed through the Languedoc, Béziers and Narbonne, where Florence told Cal she didn't want to go to Spain after all. 'Turn off for Toulouse,' she ordered him.

'Florence,' he said, 'all this time I've been in Europe I never have seen Barcelona and I did think – '

'See Barcelona another time.'

'Well, I don't know that I want to see Toulouse.'

'Good, because we're not stopping there. We're going to the Atlantic coast.'

'Why are we going there?'

Florence said, 'It's where I had a formative experience.'

The road from Bordeaux to Cap Ferret was wet and sandy. Spring rain had turned the grass an unusually bright green. On either side of the road were low banks of sprouting earth that turned into flat fields and a horizon of bedraggled pines. The fields were empty except for one, which was occupied by a wooden caravan painted in red with gold letters bearing the name of a circus. There was no sign of human life, but a few yards beyond it a camel stood motionless with its bottom lip stuck out, staring into the distance.

Cal was looking more and more long-faced as well, because they'd been driving since seven o'clock that morning and it was now half-past one and his stomach was accusing Florence with blips and gurgles. She had promised him lunch at the Hôtel Kikinette, but when they got there it was shuttered and bolted.

She walked all around the outside, noticing the paint peeling off the window sills. When she pushed at the door leading to the courtyard it swung open to reveal cobbles overcome by weeds, and an old duster hanging stiffly from the washing line.

'Well,' she said, 'must be early-closing day or something.'

He followed her across the market square to a seafood restaurant with dark green paint and a couple of tables on the pavement. They sat outside because the sun was doing more shining than not. Florence ordered oysters and marinated tuna steak, then had to trade down to *crudités* and *andouillette* because they didn't take Barclaycard. After the waiter had gone Cal said, 'Some guy across the square waving at you, seems to know you.'

Florence turned to look. She thought she must be going mad. The man looked just like her father. He had very white skin and round blue eyes, and a beard that lacked conviction. He was tall and bony with a slightly shambling walk. He came up close and peered at Florence.

'Jesus wept,' she said. 'Papa?'

'This is unbelievable,' he said crossly. 'I've been looking for you everywhere. I was reduced to coming here and asking at La Poste if you had left a forwarding address. They weren't at all helpful.'

Florence said, 'Well, no need to worry now. Here I am.'

'You really should keep in touch better. Paulette would be devastated to know you were in France and hadn't even bothered to pick up a phone.'

'Why are you looking for me?'

'And another thing – you're married.'

'No I'm not.'

Gervaise Thomas turned to Cal. 'Well, who's this then?'

'He's my husband,' said Florence, 'but not really. We're getting a divorce.'

'Well, you shouldn't have married him without asking me.'

'How could I? You weren't there.'

'I don't know how you expect me to keep up with all this. The last address I have for you is in London. What are you doing in Cap Ferret?'

Florence said, urgently, 'Papa! Get on with it – what's happened?'

'Your Aunt Laurence has died. I heard from your Uncle Pierre. He's your mother's older brother, the one with the plumbing business in Menton, does very well for himself, I believe. Of course, he never married so he doesn't have the overheads I do.'

'Papa, for Christ's sake, you haven't come all this way to tell me about Uncle Pierre's sex life.'

'I wish people wouldn't always shout at me,' complained Gervaise. He took a piece of paper out of his pocket and consulted it. 'You see, Laurence was only your mother's cousin, but you, Pierre and Denis – your Uncle Denis, your mother's other brother – and his two children are her closest surviving relatives.' He turned and extended his arm towards the Hôtel Kikinette. 'In French law this gives you a claim on her property. So . . .'

'Go on,' breathed Florence.

'Pierre would like to know what you want. The Kikinette has been valued at 1,100,000 francs and the suggestion is that he and Denis buy you out, but just tell me what you want.' He frowned. 'What on earth are you doing?'

Florence's arms were waving wildly at the waiter. She put two fingers in her mouth and whistled for him to come quick. Gervaise said testily, 'Did you hear me? What do you want?'

Florence said, 'I want to change my order to lobster and champagne.'

A month later, Florence stood on the forecourt of the Gare du Nord and watched Janey get off the train and walk towards her. Janey was wearing a bottle green hip-length suede jacket, a flowered skirt and thick black tights. Her hair was cut in a fringed bob which was pulled back behind her ears and fastened with a black comb. The skirt was full and swirled round her knees. There was a kind of chic lusciousness about her. Florence remembered the mousy, submissive Janey of last year and felt proud. Janey had *grown*.

Florence said, 'I can't wait any longer. I want to know absolutely everything.'

Janey's description of the meeting with Curtis and the phone call from Juliet and the news of Tina and the hunt for Collette took her the whole of the Rue la Fayette and across the Boulevard Haussmann to Place Diaghilev where they ate lunch. The waitress served wine and bread to them over the heads of the other diners. There was a clatter of cutlery and clink of glasses in the background that was not at all disagreeable.

'And,' said Janey, 'I've brought you this.' She fished some papers out of her bag. 'I sent off to Associated British for the details. It's that competition I told you about. Dance Group of the Year.' Florence was leafing through the papers without much enthusiasm. Janey said, 'It's to take place over ten weeks. The first nine weeks are regional. On the tenth week there's a grand final between the nine regional winners.'

'Janey,' said Florence, 'so far it looks about as interesting as a pub crawl in Iran. It will all be the sort of stuff people did in 1975.'

Janey poured herself a glass of Badoit. 'I rang Associated British,' she said.

'Oh yes?'

'I got put through to the Dance Group of the Year office,' said Janey. 'I asked who the producer was.'

'And?'

'It's Betty Trout.'

Florence put the papers down carefully. She got a pack of Gitanes from her pocket and lit one. She put her elbows on the table and narrowed her eyes. 'Let's take 'em,' she said.

Betty Trout had spent most of the year staring out of her window at Associated British. The window looked on to a chimney stack that twice a day spewed forth brown smoke from the canteen incinerator. Betty was a Grade 3 producer. You had to be a Grade 2 producer to get a view of the car park.

One day, she was visited by a wonderful idea. Why not a competition for Dance Group of the Year? 'It's Choir of the Year meets Torvill and Dean with a bit of *Come Dancing* and Olympic Gymnastics thrown in,' she said to Gus Wycherley, her head of department. He was sitting in his leather armchair with his legs stretched out in front of him. His office had an all-wool carpet, the colour of deep rust, an antique oak desk with a Christopher Wray reading lamp, photographs of him receiving things from people, or perhaps giving people things, and bookshelves fitted into what had once been the fireplace. They were filled with videos.

'I don't know if I like the sound of girls – women – competing in that sort of way.'

'I believe Roger Reed-Herbert's daughter has her own dance group,' offered Betty diffidently.

'*Really*?' said Gus. He retracted his legs, sat forward and reached out for his plastic cup of coffee. There was a limit to everything, even for heads of department.

'Of course, he is very proud of her. Some might say ridiculously so, but . . .' Betty let her voice trail away.

'Leave it with me,' said Gus. 'I'll come back to you by tomorrow at the latest.'

Betty went back to her office, feeling violent vaultings of happiness and ambition. Roger Reed-Herbert had recently been made Controller of Associated British.

A week later, they were having lunch.

It was Roger's birthday. He was a Scorpio with the moon in

Aquarius and Venus in Libra. His Venus had been on Tina's Sun but his moon was opposite her Saturn which was why they had had such a tangled relationship. He had two secrets. The first was that in the New Year's Honours list he was to receive a knighthood for services to broadcasting. The second was that he had not learned: he was in love with another young girl, though 'in love' was a rather pale way of phrasing it. He felt that if he could not be with her he might die, there was none of the usual element of run-of-the-mill randiness and thrill of the hunt and the reassurance that he was still attractive; it was a compulsion, iron chains, an involuntary moan.

Vallie had absolutely no idea anything was going on, being completely taken over by the forthcoming wedding of Joanna-Mary to Nicholas Wenders, the tycoon's son. Every day she would take delivery of various packages through the postal system or from Peter Jones' vans. The wedding was due to take place the following October but already she was feeding off the drama and anguish of the electric can opener being the wrong model, the estate agent sending the details of unworthy properties. Vallie was much more interested in the wedding than Joanna-Mary, who sometimes had trouble identifying the church at which it was to take place, calling it St Andrew's when its name was St Alphege's. Sometimes she seemed like a toy, a still doll. 'You must speak to Joanna-Mary,' Vallie said to Roger while clearing away the breakfast things one day. She scraped breadcrumbs off the plates into the waste bin blindly, turning her head so he could catch her voice. They had the habit of addressing each other with their backs turned.

'Eh?'

'The sparkle has gone out of her.'

'I thought she was madly in love with Whatsit.'

'Nicholas, you silly old fart.' She tapped him cheerfully on the bottom with the egg whisk. 'It's the group. They aren't getting any bookings.'

'For Christ's sake. What am I meant to do about it?'

'Nicholas won't pander to her for ever. He can't want to marry such a wet blanket. I'm terrified he'll get browned off.'

Roger thought of how life with Vallie would be if she did not have the Wedding of the Decade to preoccupy her. He would have to take her on holiday to France, and there would be no more steamy little struggles on the floor behind his desk, and underground in the Associated British car park.

And so he had lunch with Gus Wycherley and Betty Trout.

'Betty!'

'Roger!'

Roger rose from his seat and kissed Betty first on one cheek, then the other, then the first cheek again. They had met twice before, the last occasion being in 1985. He tried to remember whether he had had her, but on the whole he thought not. The waiter sprang between them with an anxious entrechat.

'Well,' said Roger, beaming at Betty.

'Well, indeed,' she said, beaming back.

'I like it!'

Betty clapped her hands. 'Wonderful. Wonderful, wonderful.'

Gus leant forward. 'Roger has, uh, some suggestions which he very much hopes you might consider incorporating.'

'Oh,' said Betty, 'Of course, of course, wonderful.'

'Please don't feel duty bound to use them,' said Roger.

The waiter brought their first courses.

'I thought we might do it on the lines of the Eurovision Song Contest. On a national basis at first, of course, but widening it to Europe in the fullness of time.'

'Wonderful,' said Betty.

Gus wiped hollandaise sauce from his beard. 'I know you were very keen to have a sports element in it.'

Betty said, 'Yes, I thought a system of league tables might be a rather original starting point – '

Gus and Roger exchanged glances.

'But on second thoughts,' continued Betty seamlessly, 'it seems to me to be contradictory to the ethos of the project.'

'There is,' said Roger, 'one thing that does worry me. In fact I don't know that we really ought not to call a halt to the project right now.'

'Are you unscathed?' Gus said to Betty.

'Yes, fine. My hand slipped,' said Betty, mopping the spilt wine off the tablecloth.

'Are people,' said Roger, 'are people going to say, Sod this, he's only doing it as a cushy number for his daughter. Just supposing, for instance, and this is *only* a suggestion which you are completely free to accept or reject as the mood takes you, just supposing Joanna-Mary comes in on this as – well, your adviser, assistant, co-producer, you name it?'

Gus topped up his glass. 'How is Joanna-Mary? Busy with wedding plans at the moment, I suppose.'

'Bloody weddings!' said Roger. 'The house has been completely taken over by starry-eyed confetti fetishists purporting to be my wife and daughter.'

'Oh, but we must have Joanna-Mary,' said Betty. 'I'm counting on it.'

'Then would you mind too much,' said Roger, 'if it were on, let's say, an informal basis. By all means contract her as you wish, but not under her own name, I think. Let's say in the name of an independent company. Vallie thought Jonic Productions.'

'Good idea,' said Gus.

'That suit you, Betty?'

'Wonderful.'

The next day Roger took Joanna-Mary to lunch at a little restaurant behind Kensington Church Street. She wore a black leather shirt and a short tight skirt in some slightly furry fabric. There was a lot of darling-this and darling-that from Roger, and many daffy grins and smirked endearments from Joanna-Mary, and Joanna-Mary stealing tastes of food from his fork, and lighting two cigarettes at once and slowly placing one in his mouth. If you'd been sitting at the table next to them you would have thought nothing of it, because what really passed between them was quite unspoken. If it had been spoken, it would have sounded like this:

JOANNA-MARY: I'll do it.

ROGER: Good. It will be useful publicity for Sweet Fanny Addams. And of course Mummy will be very pleased.

JOANNA-MARY: We must be allowed to win.

(Here you would have seen him gape at her.)

ROGER: I don't really think, darling, that that's something you can stipulate.

(Here you would have seen her gape at him.)

ROGER: Stipulate. Uh, state beforehand, make a condition of an agreement –

JOANNA-MARY (breaking in): I'm not a fool. That Salmon creature knows shit about dancers and dancing. You mix with these people every day. They're bloodsuckers. None of them have any ideas of their own. I'm meant to tell her all I know so she can walk off with all the credit and all the money. We're talking hundreds of thousands in contracts, bookings, videos, endorsement. I want it. I want my nose in the trough.'

ROGER: Darling, you don't exactly need the money. Nicholas has all the money you could possibly need.

JOANNA-MARY: I want my own money. I'm not going to be like Mummy, forced to suck up to you and worse just to keep herself in clothes. I want my own money, and I want to be famous, as famous as you.

Afterwards, Joanna-Mary loitered outside on the pavement while Roger went for a pee. She was wearing a short shiny mackintosh. She leant against a lamp-post and was rewarded when a young man in a Ford Escort, gazing at her, drove into the back of a van.

Roger put money into a pay-phone. 'Hallo, it's me,' he murmured.

Manon said, 'I meant what I told you last night.'

'Come on, darling, we can't leave it like that.' The phone was at the bottom of some narrow stairs. Diners thumped down, brushing past him to get to the toilets.

'I don't want to be your girlfriend any more,' she said.

'I want to marry you.'

'You've already got a wife.'

He said, 'Let me just come and see you. I can't manage to go on without seeing you sometimes.'

'No.' She sounded as if she was crying. 'It's wrong.'

'It feels too good to be wrong.' He was crying now.

'Why d'you have to make it so hard for me?'

'I can't help it.'

And in her office at Associated British, Betty Trout was already getting to work on Dance Group of the Year: costings, timings, schedules, co-production money, locations. While she was about it, she also put in for some new office curtains.

Chapter Fifteen

I Say a Little Prayer

At the Carmen Sopwith Independent Day School (Head mistress: Mrs B. N. Weston. Prospectus from the Secretary by Request), the final bell had just rung. Girls streamed out of a large Victorian mansion of red brick faded to pink. It stood behind some stiff green pines on the main road into a northern town, and had once been a convalescent home.

Ratty slipped out of the staff quarters, a separate, modern building the shape of a matchbox, and set off at a brisk walk. She was wearing a black-and-white striped top and gored skirt in charcoal jersey which swung around her calves. Her hair was as ginger and vivid as it had been the afternoon of Millie's wedding nine years back. She was now thirty-five, and a widow. She taught drama, gym and dance to Mrs Weston's girls, and though she had given birth to Bram, her stomach was board-flat. There was a brown leather bucket bag hanging from her shoulder, and Reeboks on her feet. She moved with a distinctive upright bearing, her head high and tilted back slightly, her strange plume of hair wobbling above it so that she had the appearance of some mildly exotic bird, such as a hoopoe.

She caught up with Mrs B. N. Weston in the school drive. The headmistress was just finishing talking to a parent, a blonde woman who had a busy life that consisted of putting on an Yves St Laurent outfit and full make-up to collect her child from school every day plus, if she could find the time for it, complaining in a very loud voice about the standard of teaching. Mrs Weston had a wide smile on her face that said her favourite activity in the world was talking to this kind of person. There was the Appeal Fund for the new library to think of, and the main building needed a new roof.

'I wish to see you,' said Ratty, 'about Pollyanna Bear.'

Mrs Weston went red and glared at her. She was short and plump, and everything she wore was made of corduroy.

'I told you,' she said angrily, 'the matter has been investigated fully and nothing was found to substantiate Pollyanna's complaints against Amber Moloney.'

'The Lord forgive you, Barb.'

'Mrs Weston to you.'

'The Lord forgive you, Mrs Weston.'

'May the Lord close the subject, if you know what's good for you.'

Pollyanna 'Pola' Bear was in the fifth form, a sweet-faced girl who could sing like Bessie Smith and dance up a storm, and was also on for eight GCSEs, despite having spent her formative years inside a Sony Walkman. She had been at the school five years and was, for various reasons, special to Ratty. She was a black girl in a white school but nothing untoward came of that till Ratty decided to give her the lead in the end of term *My Fair Lady*. Then it turned out there were girls in the school who thought someone other than Pola Bear should be My Fair Lady, someone (1) older and (2) fairer. The main contender was a girl called Amber Moloney whose father owned a big factory somewhere in Manchester. Amber Moloney was pretty if you thought looking like a hamster with its mouth sewn up was pretty, and she was the kind of girl who had lots of other girls hanging round her, and also a load of brothers.

No matter how right you are, there has to be some evidence to show to the people who want you to be wrong, and Ratty knew Pola was suffering without being able to do anything about it. She knew Pola was getting teased and bullied, and having *coon* and *sooty* scrawled over her books and sprayed on her coat; and then Amber's brothers got involved – they put human shit in her schoolbag, and condoms that had been used, despite Pola being innocent and young for sixteen, and sheltered by her parents. Everyone knew it was going on, Mrs B. N. Weston knew it was going on, but there was nothing to pin it on Amber at all, nothing except that Ratty knew it was Amber.

Ratty said, 'At least you should tell Amber's parents what Pola's been saying and ask them to take it up with Amber.'

'I must ask you to stop persecuting a pupil whom the rest of us regard as an asset to the school.'

'Oh, you want her old man to pay for the library.'

Mrs Weston turned even redder. 'I'm not prepared to stand here and take this,' she said.

'In that case,' said Ratty, 'I'm going to go to the police.'

'Ha!' said Mrs Weston, 'They're very keen on your family, aren't they? I'm sure they'll bend over backwards to help.'

It was chilly in the northern summer afternoon and a long wait for the bus. Huge lorries rattled past Ratty, changing gear with a sighing bark as they started to climb the hill towards New Mills and Stockport. Salesmen with their suits hanging behind them in polythene bags drove up each other's arses at seventy. A few cars slowed as they saw her, and dingy little men suddenly found they couldn't remember the way to Manchester, and wound down windows to ask her. It gave Ratty great pleasure to send them off on the A6 where with any luck they'd be halfway to Sheffield before they noticed anything wrong.

There were no Carmen Sopwith girls waiting for the bus. Carmen Sopwith girls didn't go by bus. The younger ones were met by their mothers driving the company Mercedes and the older ones by boyfriends in soft-top Escorts. Ratty got on and went to the front behind the driver, where she sat near a woman a lot younger than her but with a craggy, hopeless face and three kids, one of which was in a dented pushchair. The other two wore shoes patched up with masking tape.

The bus took them uphill to the newly made roundabout, the construction of which had involved the pulling down of an old pub called the King Edward Hotel. Ratty had been quite fond of the King Edward. Eddie used to do his training there in the gymnasium above the lounge bar. She had also been quite fond of the Carmen Sopwith before Mrs Weston took over. The eponymous Mrs Sopwith had been a mad old former actress who ran the school as her own private fief. But it had a good reputation for dance and drama; several pupils were accepted for the National Youth Theatre and went on after that to the big London acting schools. Mrs Sopwith charged fees according to what she thought the parents could afford. She went round the community centres of the local housing estates, practically dragging little sassy black girls off to join her school. The filing cabinet in her study contained the entire works of Nat 'King' Cole and six different varieties of Scotch. Sometimes when she had been sampling the latter, Carmen Sopwith would sing 'Stardust' in her fluting tenor.

Carmen Sopwith liked to leave the impression that her acquaintance with the great man might have gone further than simple admiration for his body of work.

But now the school was run by Mrs Weston and a board of governors who talked of the product (education) and consumers (parents). There were no sassy black girls from the housing estates. Carmen Sopwith was dead, and so was Eddie Baptiste.

The bus turned left and roared along the old road past the Praise the Lord Tabernacle where Eddie Baptiste used to preach. For a long time after the shooting, they had kept the sky-blue board up that had his name on in gold lettering. Eddie 'Buster' Baptiste, the Punching Pastor. As part of his work, Eddie ran a club for young blacks in a mean estate full of dilapidated blocks. They might not have listened to a man of the cloth, but they respected the middleweight champion of Lancashire.

Carmen Sopwith met Eddie on her travels for sassy little black girls. She went to his church and heard him preach, and invited him back to drink whisky and sing 'Stardust' with her in the study. It was 1982. One afternoon she introduced him to a thin young woman with odd ginger hair and a terrible temper. 'This is Alexa Blows, known as Ratty,' she said. 'I am thinking of making her my gym and drama teacher.'

Eddie had the most beautiful smile. There was a small scar like an acute accent above his left eye, and a larger one above his right that bore the signs of fresh stitch marks. He had a broken nose and fine, close-cropped black hair. He took her twitchy hand in his huge paw and spoke her name. 'Haven't I heard that somewhere before?' he said.

'She is notorious,' said Carmen. 'She has been in the newspapers.' Carmen was referring to an article that had appeared some months previously in the *Pictorial*.

'ALEXA'S LIVE-IN LOVE IS A GIRL'

Alexa Blows of girlie dance group Sweet Fanny Addams is a LESBIAN.

Neighbours have complained constantly over all-night parties where women dressed in LEATHER cut away to reveal intimate parts of their BODIES have danced to non-stop loud music.

This is not the first time that wild girl Alexa has been in trouble.

Once she was nearly sacked from the group after claiming she had BONKED three men in ONE NIGHT.

Last night Millie Francis, a spokeswoman for the now-disbanded group, said Alexa had left 'by mutual consent'.

The article was months out of date. Ratty had not lived with Michaela for some time. However, she was called before the head of the school where she was teaching, and found herself relieved of her job.

Fate led her to buy a copy of the *Guardian* on the day that Carmen Sopwith's advertisement for a gym teacher with some responsibilities for drama and dance appeared.

There was no reason for Carmen to give her a job for she had inferior qualifications to some others who applied. For instance, at the time she could not tell a vaulting horse from a dancing bear. But Carmen Sopwith liked unusual people, especially those who had suffered for their unusualness. 'But if I were you,' said Carmen, 'I would change your surname and admit to nothing. You know how low and malicious some people can be.'

Inspired by the label on one of Carmen's whisky bottles, Ratty took the name Bell, though not for long. Within a few weeks she became Alexa Baptiste by marrying Eddie at the Praise the Lord Tabernacle. The ceremony was followed by a 24-hour party with lots of dancing and singing, particularly, on Carmen's part, of selections from Nat 'King' Cole.

Whereas Juliet had got God in a rather British and juiceless sort of way, Alexa was completely given over to the party spirit of the Praise the Lord movement. She had been looking for something for a long time. It had led her to man after man, 'ism after 'ism. Now the Holy Spirit had entered her, she became somewhat languid and boss-eyed, as though after a really good screw. Indeed, she became pregnant very quickly after her marriage and in the October of the year she was delivered of an eight-pound son, Bram Nathaniel Sopwith Baptiste.

At Eddie's club on the Bileborough estate there was a snooker table covered in threadbare green baize, some gym equipment that had to be bolted to the floor, and a stage where bands could play. Eddie knew that some of the rebellious unemployed boys who came to his club used drugs but it was not his policy to turn anybody away.

Probably no one would ever know the complete truth about the shooting. It happened on a sweltering August afternoon. The estate had echoed for days with the noise of windows breaking, metal buckling, the flat pop, pop of bullets. Caught in the crossfire when the police raided the centre and guns were pulled out on both sides, Eddie Baptiste the Punching Pastor fell dead. The grey flimsy building went up Whoosh and the flames consumed his body. The police claimed Eddie had been a drug peddler, and shot by one of his own kind. The boys on the estate said a police bullet killed him.

During the days following the death, Ratty received several letters written in green ink, calling her evil names. Later that year, Carmen Sopwith fell ill. One day she called Ratty to her hospital bed and said, 'I've had one too many whiskies. I'm dying, and don't say the Lord have mercy upon me.'

'Okeydoke.'

'I have made provision in my will to pay for the education of one child from the Bileborough estate. You choose her and look after her.'

This was Pola Bear.

The bus was at the estate now. Ratty got off and walked across the concreted-over waste ground where Eddie's club had been. They had taken away the burnt-out shell of the community centre and not rebuilt it. On the grass in front was a little plaque remembering him. The families who lived on the estate had had it put there. Next to it was a seat. Ratty sat down. Unseen people stood near windows, watching her.

It was four-thirty. Bram would be with the childminder who picked him up from primary school every day. Ratty imagined him, solemn and sturdy in his green trousers and yellow shirt.

Since Eddie died Ratty had rarely raised her voice with anybody. They knew that years ago she had been a dancer but she kept that period of her life private, as she did the shooting of Eddie Baptiste and her widowhood.

'I'm sorry,' she said, 'I really find it so very hard to talk about.'

She lived in a small terraced house in the shabby-smart part of town, sharing it with several overbearing cats as well as Bram. In the living room there was a television set, a picture of Eddie winning a fight, an old sofa and two armchairs in case the Princess of Wales was passing by with her husband. Her Jesus was the Lord of the widowed and fatherless. He came to her at odd moments, in the early morning when she lay alone in the double bed, watching the sky get lighter through the curtains. She would sense Him in the room and feel a mixture of grief and pain, love and joy, that she could not have put into words.

On the one hand, there was her job. She was already worrying that someone had matched her with the spindly, pouting girl dancing on the television news the day after Millie's death. These were not good times for ex-lesbian single-parent mothers of coffee-coloured sons to be looking for new employment.

Admit to nothing.

But Pola Bear needed to know that she had been heard, that someone was prepared to stand up and fight for her.

She had been cast out before and had come through it. Eddie wouldn't have walked away from anyone who needed him. She looked at the plaque again as if for inspiration but she knew already. She knew there was only one way her decision could go.

Pola Bear's people had moved from the Bileborough estate to a terraced house near Ratty's. There was a row of flowerpots in the front garden containing some untidy crocuses, and a poster in the front window which said Vote Charlene Bear Your Conservative Candidate.

Charlene Bear answered the door. She wore glasses and was dressed in a pair of black Crimplene slacks and a jade green blouse with a black cardigan over the top. 'Come on in, darling,' she said. Pola was in the hall. She shrank back to let Ratty and her mother go into the front room first. They sat down by the dining table where Pola's father was doing paperwork. He had broad cheekbones like Pola and the same gentle, slanting eyes, but his skin was as dark as hers was honey brown. He said, 'I got to tell you Pola ain't at all happy about this. She don't want no fuss. Not so sure I want it myself, now you mention it.' He reached over to Pola and dragged the Walkman off her ears.

'Julian,' said Charlene, 'these bullies counting on that, that Pola don't make no fuss, just lie down and let them walk all over her.'

Pola said, 'I'm afraid, if we do something against them, they're going to set fire to our house. I don't want to be Eliza Doolittle that badly. I'm pulling out, Mrs Baptiste. I got another two years at this school.'

'Look,' said Ratty, 'before you do any pulling out, let's have a go. Let's just for a couple of hours, say, get you people and Amber Moloney and her people together and talk about it, see if we can't sort it out that way.'

The next night, Ratty went round to see the Moloneys and fixed it up for them to meet the Bears in the school staff room the next night.

'I hope you know what you're doing,' said Mrs Weston.

The afternoon before the meeting, Pola caught Ratty up at the bus stop. 'Amber Moloney's brothers are back there,' she said.

Ratty looked round. There were two of them, walking towards the bus stop. One had the same rodentine face as Amber, but was darker-haired. Thin and not very tall, he could have been no more than sixteen and Ratty thought she could deal with him. The other was different altogether, being somewhere in his twenties, and big, on his way to plumpness. He had a mean look Ratty didn't like. The bus came past them and drew up. Ratty pushed Pola on and guided her to a seat beside the door that had just become vacant.

The brothers began running and the driver of the bus waited

for them. They got on board and made a point of staring all around the bus, their eyes coming to rest on Ratty and Pola before they sat down a few feet away. The big one rested his feet on the seat over the aisle from him.

Pola said, 'I'm scared. Where are we going?'

'Birtwhistles for tea,' said Ratty.

Birtwhistles was the best department store in town. The only department store in town. 'Let's go,' said Ratty, pushing her off the bus. 'Don't look round.' They went in through the swing doors and Ratty steered her left past scarves and gloves and on to the escalator. As it rose towards the tea room, she glanced back and saw the brothers walking up and down past the window, peering in.

They had egg and cucumber sandwiches, a selection of cakes from the trolley and a pot of tea. The table was covered with a white linen cloth, and the cutlery was silver plate. At one end of the tea room was a plate-glass window which looked on to Bridal. A young woman paraded in front of a mirror, walking up an invisible aisle in a white lace dress.

Pola was saying, 'I really want to do something with myself. Be a dancer, actor, someone. Get out of this town which is so *small*.'

Ratty reached for a rum baba and glimpsed the two brothers come past the cashier at the door. She turned her head away, though not before she'd seen them threading a path through the tables. Pola was saying, 'London, that's the place for me.'

'Hallo, darling.' The bigger of the brothers leant over Pola with his palms on the table. The younger brother was bringing two chairs over. 'What are you doing with that old dyke?'

Pola said, 'I don't believe we've been introduced.'

Ratty was impressed by her cool tone. She could see Pola's hands clasped together in her lap, shaking slightly. The younger boy lit a cigarette and blew smoke her way.

Big brother said, 'Nice girl like you doesn't want to hang around old dykes.'

'The lady isn't, what you say,' said Pola, 'and I'd like you to stop bothering us.' She offered Ratty a scone.

Little brother said, 'Aren't you going to offer us something to eat, then?'

'Take her for a ride in your car,' said the big one, 'and she'll let you eat something.'

Ratty said to Pola, 'Tea?' She raised the pot.

'Just a top-up, please.'

'Eee-oh,' said the big brother, 'Jee-ust a tee-op up, dahling.'

'Fine,' said Ratty, leaning over and pouring tea into his lap. He screamed and pushed his chair back. Pola helped it on its way so it deposited him on the floor. Ratty overturned the table on him. The little brother jumped out of his chair and started running. Pola and Ratty chased him. He was heading for the plate-glass window.

Ratty just had time to say, 'I do wish they'd have warning stickers put on those things – '

He went crashing through the window into Bridal. Ratty continued, ' – before someone has an accident.'

Mrs Weston said, 'I am pleased to say Mr Moloney has offered to pay for the damage. He has also agreed not to press charges for assault if we will agree to drop ours. It is obviously in the best interests of the school to avoid any more publicity than this unfortunate incident has already occasioned. Pola, of course, will leave. It is unfair to expect her to stay on in the circumstances. Besides, it is expressly forbidden in the rules to have tea in Birtwhistles while wearing uniform.'

'Well, shucks,' said Ratty, 'if I'd known that I'd have got her to take it off.'

'As for you,' said Mrs Weston, 'I'm afraid we have reached the parting of the ways. You will be suspended on full pay till the end of term, after which you will have to find alternative employment. I am sorry it has come to this, Alexa. If there is anything I can do for you and your little boy, just ask.'

Ratty said, 'There's something you can do, Mrs W. You can go shit in your hat.'

That very night, Janey called Ratty on the phone and asked her to come and dance again for Sweet Fanny Addams.

Chapter Sixteen

You're Having My Baby

IT WAS EARLY afternoon in New York. Tina stuffed the sheet into her mouth and bit hard on it, then drew her knees up towards her chest as far as she could and rocked from side to side in a hopeless attempt to dislodge the pain. The man kneeling behind her got her in an angry grip and jammed her body to the bed. 'Lie *still*.'

'You've been digging away at my back for gone half an hour. I asked for an epidural not a fucking gas main repair,' she said to him.

The nurse, rinsing something in the washbasin, said warningly, 'Sometimes, we don't know why, Mrs McCall, epidurals don't work.' She was a lanky middle-aged southern woman with glasses. She was the one who had rigged Tina up to a drip. Tina had a needle in her wrist, which was strapped to a narrow board. The needle was joined by several feet of transparent tube to a bag of saline solution hanging from a metal stand. Every time Tina wanted to move anywhere she had to take the metal stand with her.

'I know why this one isn't working. The anaesthetist is no fucking good. Jesus Christ. Even a smart bomb could have found the place better. I want Tom. Where is Tom?'

She knew where Tom was; in mid-air, on the way to London. He was due to be playing Le Palais in Hammersmith in a few hours' time. 'You don't need to do these things,' she had said to him. 'You can cut down on touring. You don't need the sales. I've got more than enough money for both of us.'

'Tina, I'm kind of old-fashioned. I like to support my wife.'

The delivery room was a large, white box without windows. There was a foetal monitoring machine on the right of the bed and a table on the left with a jug of water, a glass, an almost untouched lunch of Lobster Thermidor, and Tina's handbag. There was something pathetic about the handbag with its credit cards, wallet, house keys, purse, all completely irrelevant to her now. This is what being dead must be like, Tina thought. Except being dead probably didn't hurt so much.

The nurse said, 'Will he be singing "Sad Eyed Lady of the Lowlands" tonight? It's my favourite, after "You're Having My Baby". I met my boyfriend to it. We were on holiday in Europe. I didn't think much of Paris but Amsterdam was OK.'

Tom had recorded a cover version of the old Bob Dylan hit. It was slow and smoochy and made Tina weep with love every time she heard it. No man had never sung a song for her before. No man had ever been pleased that she'd been pregnant before, whispered to her in the darkness between the sheets, 'Wouldn't it be great if our baby was growing in there?', and day and night for three months torpedoed her quivering cunt with sperm till she got what she wanted. Tina, in her middle age, was having her first baby and Tom, in his middle age, was having his first number one hit.

The anaesthetist decided to move drilling operations about an inch further down her back. He said, 'Is your husband a rock singer?' He was a pale young man with all the interesting cragginess of an Edam cheese. He looked about sixteen.

'This is Mrs Tom McCall,' said the nurse.

'Uh-huh. A rock singer, right?'

Time was when you venerated the medical profession. Now she had the grey hairs and the medics didn't look old enough to get served a drink in Wes's bar.

'What are you looking for there?' she said to him. 'Fucking Australia?'

The nurse said to her in a low voice, 'Mrs McCall, would you please watch your language? You don't want to upset the other mothers, now.'

After Tina had pushed open the swing doors at Associated British

229

and walked away for ever, she went straight to her apartment and got all her clothes out and put them on her bed. She picked out a pair of jeans, two silk T-shirts, a linen jacket, her all-time favourite frock, a pack of spare tights, her toothbrush and toothpaste, make-up, a bottle of Magie Noire and one pair of shoes. She put them on top of the small suitcase that she always liked to fly with because she could pass it off as hand luggage. She rang Kit in reception and told him to come up.

'I'm going to New York,' she said. 'Get all these things packed. Sell my BMW and give the proceeds to whatever charity you want. As for the stuff on the bed, Janey Sears is to have the Jean Muirs and anything else she wants. The rest can go for jumble.'

'May I ask in that case how long you intend to be away?' said Kit.

'Possibly a lifetime,' said Tina.

Kit said, 'This might be the last time we see each other, then.'

'You can come out, visit me.'

'I, uh, don't know if I'll be able to leave Geordie.'

'He got the result of his tests then,' she said slowly.

'Yes.' Kit had a precise, friendly way of speaking, as though to an older child. 'It wasn't what he, we, hoped for, I'm afraid.'

'Oh Kit. I feel such a cow. How many times have I kept you from going home at nights, going on about my useless little problems?'

'Nothing you have ever said to me has been either useless or little.'

She hugged him hard and wept, then rang her lawyer and her accountant and told them to go ahead with the New York property. She cancelled a hair appointment she'd made for the next day, and took a taxi to Heathrow Airport where she managed to get on the late flight out of London.

Six and a half hours later she was flying over Albany and on her way down to JFK. It was half-past nine in the morning and New York State was topped by a pink and blue streaky sky. Her headphones were over her ears, the wires mingling with her hair. A song from long ago was playing – 'Loving You', by Minnie Riperton. She remembered making love to the sound of it with Roger, in a vast warm bedroom in a hotel in Lake Placid. The windows were protected by tall faded brown shutters. The bathroom door was ajar and beyond it had been the biggest bath she had ever seen. The taps were made of brass. The radiators looked like cinemas. It had been a snowy February night in 1975. She had no idea why they were there. It was the first time she had been to America. They rode on a light plane from Albany to Saranac Lake and touched down on ice. Above them the sky was stippled with cold stars. Their cab took them past quiet towns where the house lights glowed orange on hillsides like embers on a fire. When she arrived she was weary and she lay down on the huge soft bed while he padded around, putting his clothes away. Soon he left off doing that and, saying nothing, got on to the bed and lay on top of her. She was flooded with such desire for him that he did not even need to undress her. She came with a single kiss, twining her legs round him. Remembering this now she was filled with love for her younger self, the ardent and bold girl.

The plane touched down at JFK and she walked out with her suitcase and stood waiting for the bus to come. Why not? A cab driver would only ask her, Where to, lady? and at that moment she did not know where to. The bus came, empty, and she got on to it. Her soul was as light as a falling leaf. She sat behind the driver, a rugged man with a copy of *Sports Illustrated* on the shelf in front of him. Atop the windscreen was a slot which said: YOUR DRIVER (space). COURTEOUS, FRIENDLY, RELIABLE. The bus began to fill up, mainly with oddly shaped people carrying cardboard boxes held together with string. Between DRIVER and COURTEOUS the rugged one placed a metal sign saying Vic (Shaggy Bear) Lyle. He started the engine and moved the bus into the traffic stream.

When she walked into Wes's bar the back room looked exactly as it must have looked at two o'clock that morning. There was a customer curled up asleep, and Tom McCall's chair was lying on the floor where he must have knocked it over after getting up from the piano. There were three glasses on the piano top. One was empty, one was half-finished and the other was full of brown, flat beer. Tina hoped there hadn't been too many ladies in big-brimmed hats and fur-collared coats putting them on his piano. The regulars were already in their places by the bar; the Weasel and the two sportswriters. They all bought her Bloody Marys, after which she bought them Bloody Marys. 'I'll be right back,' she said. 'I just have to find out whether I'm in love or not.'

She phoned Tom from the cloakrooms. She had kept his number, the one he had scribbled for her on a torn-off cheque stub that last night in New York, a lifetime ago. He was a long while coming to the phone. She stood on the chair and smoothed her hair into shape in the Wilt Chamberlain Memorial Mirror. She was beginning to think he'd left town or she didn't have the right code, when he answered. 'Who is this?'

'It's the Yeti's daughter,' she said.

And here she was, twenty months later, on a trolley bed in a delivery suite where some teenager who'd got a medical qualification in his Christmas stocking was using her for darts practice.

She had felt angry when Tom said he was going to do London. She still had more than two weeks to go till the baby was due but it seemed to her it wouldn't be that long coming. When he went to kiss her goodbye before setting off for the airport, she turned her face away from him. Then the minute his cab had disappeared from view she thought, What if his plane goes down? I'll have sent him to his death with my unloving scowling face.

Their apartment was in Greenwich Village. Tom had lived there for almost all his bachelor years. There was a small bedroom, an even smaller bedroom, a bathroom the size of a dry cleaning ticket, and a living room with the kitchen leading off it and one wall completely covered in bookshelves. The living-room window looked out on to an inner court and a fire escape. The kitchen window was at right angles to it and had a huge old-fashioned air conditioner sticking out above the sill.

When Tom was composing, he'd shut himself in the bedroom. Tina would come in and find bits of paper covered in words, and staves, spread over the bed. They had a quilt in red, yellow, green, purple, blue, black and white patches that was a wedding present from Wes at the bar. Their bed was hand-carved out of golden wood, and had been given them by the band. When she was first there she'd suggested looking around for somewhere bigger. 'Anywhere bigger round here is too much money,' he said.

'You don't need to worry about money any more. Legwork New York is doing just great.'

'I have this weird need to support my wife.'

The second time Tom came out with this, Tina (schooled in twenty years of male bullshit) said, 'Rubbish. You just like to go on tour.'

After all the whirl of getting married, Tina sat down and did some thinking. What started her thinking was a letter from Janey Sears. Janey wasn't grinding any axes, but Tina couldn't but start thinking back, and what she thought was that Joanna-Mary had behaved very badly and she, Tina, had helped her get away with it. After giving it some more thought, Tina wrote to Joanna-Mary invoking her ownership of the name Sweet Fanny Addams and asking her to call her new group something else.

Joanna-Mary's response was tardy and insolent (as well as badly spelled). It was the sort of letter that had Tina ricocheting off the kitchen walls and screaming, 'Fucking cheek!' and 'Utter, utter wankpot!' It was a good moment for Janey to call with her suggestion about Sweet Charity. Tina sounded off and Janey called Florence and Florence called Tina and then Janey and so on. One result of all these calls was that Tina had to find Collette Sweet, no problem really, no worse than hunting for a sugar cube in a snowdrift.

All day after Tom left for London she kept getting these pains. She rang Juliet Dexter in her cabin as she filmed in Hollywood. Her children's nanny answered the phone. Besides the twins there was a daughter of four years. Juliet padded to the phone with her hair in curlers; the film was set in the early sixties when women wore such things in their hair. She took the receiver from the nanny and said, 'It could be Braxton Hicks contractions. But from what you say it sounds like the real thing.'

'Tom's gone to London,' wept Tina.

'Do you want me to fly over?' Since the day of Millie's funeral, Juliet's career had really taken off. Her last film in which she had played a call girl won an Oscar for Best Foreign Picture, and she was named Best Actress.

'I'll manage,' said Tina, pulling herself together, 'I don't think your director would be too pleased if he had to put back shooting on my account. But Juliet – thanks.'

She rang Ratty, who had moved down to London with Bram. 'I'm in labour,' she wailed, 'and Tom's on his way to play Le Palais.'

'Do your exercises,' exhorted Ratty. 'I'd pray for you, but exercising is a much better bet at times like these.'

'Exercise,' said Tina. 'Exercise is what brought me into labour two and a half weeks early. I drove must have been fifty miles and walked eight blocks yesterday, looking for Collette Sweet.'

'With Bram, I was out shopping. My waters broke in Marks and Spencer.'

'Ratty, I remember you were nineteen and I was twenty-six, sitting outside the Albany, Nottingham in a car, listening to Chicago on the radio,' Tina sobbed. 'We were doing Puss in Boots in panto. We had a part specially written for us. We were Puss's five naughty sisters. The snow was coming down like in a Hollywood movie. It's all gone now. I'll never be that girl again.'

At one o'clock she ordered a car to take her to the hospital. On the point of leaving, she remembered the note she had pushed through the door at the rooming house where finally she tracked Collette down. Asking Collette to drop by in Greenwich Village if she could. Tina stood in the foyer of her flat and quickly scribbled another note to Collette saying where she was going. She left it with the porter.

Some hours later a light-to-moderate hurricane blew into the delivery room. It swerved round the foetal monitoring machine but did not get quite the right angle on the corner, causing the screen by the bed to rock back and forward. The hurricane knelt beside Tina. It was Collette Sweet. She grasped Tina's left wrist, the one with a needle in the vein attached to the board and saline drip. 'It's all right, it's all right, I'm here, I'm here,' she said, banging Tina's wrist against the bed in repeated emphasis. 'You've got me now, I'm here, it's all right.'

She was followed in by a security guard. 'Have you seen a blonde broad who don't walk straight? Gatecrashed security and set off up the down escalator.'

There was a sort of jolt in the small of Tina's back, and then a wonderful numbness that stole all over her from the waist down. The epidural was working.

'Her name is Collette Sweet,' said Tina. 'She's a dancer.'

'Fantastic. She don't look to me like she's been doing a lot of dancing in the last few days. She don't look to me like she's washed herself in the last few days. She looks to me like she's a drunk and disorderly and it's my duty to turn her over to the cops.'

'We're in New York, for Christ's sake,' said Tina. 'Go and chase some muggers.'

Passing by the security guard, the midwife murmured, 'She's Mrs Tom McCall. You ever listen to his "Sad-Eyed Lady of the Lowlands?" She's *it*.'

'OK,' said the security guard. 'I'll let her get away with it this time. But get Ginger Rogers cleaned up.'

After he went, Tina turned back to Collette. Her hand was still clasped round Tina's wrist. She smiled at Tina encouragingly and gave it a squeeze.

'Collette,' said Tina, 'would you mind sitting over there?'

Collette obligingly headed for the seats, knocking a framed print of the Metropolitan Museum of Art off the wall on her way. She sat down and looked at the debris. 'Did I do that?' she said.

'Wash your face,' said Tina. 'You look like a hooker.'

'Here, let me do it.' The midwife sponged her face and hair and tidied her up, as brisk and thorough as a mother cat.

'What have you been doing?' said Tina.

'Party.'

'Oh yeah, I think I heard about it, the All-American Teetotallers' Association were having their annual get-together.'

'Met some people called, called, forget now, went to party, she was at school used to play lax against my cousin, rairly rairly nice.' Ten years in Los Angeles coupled with sixteen hours of solid drinking had failed to blunt Collette's Home Counties vowels.

'I meant, how have you spent the last eighteen months? It's been a real detective story tracking you down.' Tina studied her. Her hair was abundant and wavy still. The skin on her face was coarser and there were red veins on her cheeks. But at a distance she still looked like a beautiful creamy-yellow rose; past its best now, one you were afraid to pick because the slightest touch would start the petals falling.

Collette was absorbed in delving into the pockets of her coat. Five minutes went past. She brought out an envelope and stared at it in a puzzled way.

'Ah,' said Tina, recognizing the writing on it 'The porter gave my note to you, then.'

Collette summoned up all her clarity. 'Just then a yellow cab was coming past so I stepped out into the street in front of it to make it stop,' she said proudly. 'I said, "My best friend is having a baby and I must be with her! Take me to the hospital!"'

'Oh Collette.'

'Yes. I thought it was pretty good myself.' She picked at the remains of Tina's Lobster Thermidor. She tore the bread roll in half and stuffed it bit by bit in her mouth apart from one last piece which she kept in the palm of her hand. She studied it, absorbed. After a while, she said, 'Tina?'

'That's me.'

'Been meaning, been wanting, long long time. Soon's I got over here from Angleterre I knew I'd made a mistake 'bout Delaney.'

'Not worth it, eh?'

'Complete wanker.'

'Well, he was very good-looking.'

'Not him. Me. All those days, I was such a wanker.'

'I was a really stupid little prat. I can't forgive how I acted, towards you specially.'

'I missed you so much out here. Millie came but it wasn't the same thing.'

'I missed you. Life was terrible. Let's never be parted again.'

The midwife came and hooked Tina up to the foetal monitoring machine. Time passed. The consultant came in and out. He was wearing a green robe tied around the waist. Tina could see the black trousers of a dinner suit underneath. Above the waist he was bare chested. His forearms were sinewy and there was a spray of chest hair above the robe's green V. How mysteriously powerful he looks, thought Tina, he is like a shaman.

While the consultant was washing his hands, Collette said, 'Did I tell you how I got here?'

'You did. Clever girl.'

'There was a big yellow taxi going past and I made it stop.'

'Sweetie, enticing though it is to have another chance to hear how you got here, I think the baby's about to be born.'

'Tina!' Collette leapt to her side again and clutched at her waist. 'You're all right. I'll look after you. I won't leave you ever again.'

'Collette. Go and have a pee.'

'Oh yes. Where are the, where . . .'

As she pushed the baby out, Tina was extraordinarily aware of the room being without windows, aware of an extra-dimensional subterranean reality, undiluted by sky, a power that came from the earth, far, far down in the centre of the planet, a dark dot with rings that radiated out, rings of black, the contraction of muscle, the ripple of a whip cracked, a tail vanishing into an unknown grey-green light. So this was how life was given. The baby shot out into the consultant's hands and (though gently) he threw it between Tina's legs like a rugby ball. It rolled down the slope of her abdomen into her arms and she said, half-laughing, 'Oh!' Girl, little rosy thing, lots of black hair, my baby, my Ruby, my jewel from the sea, my baby, my baby.

Tina had a tiny cut in her vagina. She asked the midwife to sew it up for her. She wanted only other women to be there with her at that moment, no men. There was no pain. She lay back and rested with the baby in her arms. A sensation of peace and joy filled her, so profound that she was almost unable to class it as sensation, it was more like some essential unacknowledged mechanism of her body, the oxygenization of her blood.

Some time after this, Collette returned and sat down. 'Where am I?' she said.

'Hospital,' said Tina.

'I haven't been admitted here, have I?'

'No.'

'Oh, good.'

That night Tina felt she would never need sleep again. The baby in the crib did not want to sleep either. Her eyes were open. They were of a brilliant blue and gazed at Tina with a steady look of recognition. They were together at last, Tina thought, together again, the way they had been together, when was it, years, lives ago, once upon a, whenever, whatever.

In the morning, Tom walked in with a big bunch of flowers. Ratty had fetched him out of Le Palais. They had let her walk on stage and tap him on the shoulder just as he was singing his song, and here he was.

Chapter Seventeen

Florence's Game

IT WAS THE end of June and a near-gale was blowing. Pink and white blossom fell in the streets north-west of the river around which Florence was flinging her car. The houses she passed were wide and opulent. A scowling man in overalls pushed a wheelbarrow across a front lawn. The wind brought with it the sound of the motorway, the low constant roar of traffic heading out of the city.

Florence turned into a high street and scanned the shopfronts. Nicole Farhi, the Gap, Jigsaw, Warehouse. No, she told herself, she wasn't here to shop. She wedged her car between a messenger's bike and a big Ford which had overshot its meter space by a foot. The car was a Peugeot 205 GTI, bright red and with electronically operated windows and a Blaupunkt. She had spotted it signalling at her from the showroom at her local dealership some days after she arrived back in London. She was renting a place near Curtis's house, a top-floor flat with cream walls and a narrow kitchen which was lit by big sloping window-panes in the roof. She had bought the car with some of the proceeds of her share of the Hôtel Kikinette. A girl has only so much self-control.

The estate agent's shopfront was painted in tasteful white with its name picked out in navy. Above it was a sign saying W. Awty, Jeweller and Clockmaker in rusty lettering. It creaked as the wind caught it.

The estate agent was in his thirties, sallow-complexioned with straight abundant black hair. You could tell it was an upmarket agency because he wore a red carnation in the lapel of his charcoal suit. He was behind a desk at the back of the shop, talking into a phone, the receiver held between his chin and his shoulder. He looked round, saw Florence, then turned back to his conversation. Florence waited two minutes then said, 'Oh, please don't get up. I'm only here to kill some time.'

He put down the phone and motioned her to a seat. 'What can I do for you?' he asked in a tone that suggested that if you put in writing what he could do for her you might have trouble filling the back of a bus ticket.

'I run a dance group. I'm looking for somewhere, a hall, a room, where we can rehearse every day without interruption. I need it to have good security, a kitchen, a telephone and a changing room that doesn't double for a shoebox. In the short term I want it for a month but if everything works out how I hope I'll want to lease it on a long-term basis.' Florence gave him her card: Florence Johnson and Janey Sears, Choreographers and Dancers. He took it in one smooth-skinned hand and studied it dubiously.

'Halls are very highly sought after, Mrs Johnson. If you want one in a salubrious neighbourhood, as surely you do, you must expect to pay rather a high premium. I have a very nice property available at £2,000 a week – '

Florence said, 'I'm not after the Albert Hall. I picked this area because it's halfway between Wembley and Brown's Hotel, not because of the scenery. One of the people using the hall is a very public figure who's doing me a favour by being here. I don't want her to have far to travel, getting grabbed and gawped at. But I'm not prepared to stand the cost of the kind of place that you'd like to rent to me.'

'I'm not sure if – The neighbours may not be too happy. This is a wealthy area and the Residents' Association have to be kept happy. If you keep playing loud music, people are going to get very angry with you.'

'I don't keep playing loud music and people have got angry with me all my life. As for the neighbours, I'll introduce myself to them and if they don't like it they can refer it to Juliet Dexter and Sweet Charity.'

'You mean *the* Juliet Dexter? I heard she'd got involved in some hare-brained – some exciting project to do with an old pal. You're the old pal, are you? Well, I'm sure I can sort you out. But if you want my advice you'll steer clear of anything low rent. Juliet Dexter will surely expect the best.'

'Juliet's a pro. She doesn't expect special treatment. I'm not asking her to bankroll this project, she has enough claims on her time and charity as it is. Have you got anything or haven't you? Honestly, don't bother with any bullshit.'

As she was walking away from the estate agent's, a man began walking alongside her. He was faintly familiar but hard to put a name to, like a face unearthed in a school photo from long ago. He was wearing a red-and-white striped shirt, a small bow tie and a light-coloured jacket, and looked as though he had just been taken out of the packaging. Florence suddenly placed him – not a school photo, but the one which appeared above his byline in *Have a Nice Day*! and the *Pictorial*.

'Florence Johnson?'

'Don't I have to say something like, Who wants her?'

'Ha ha. I gather – '

'OK, who *does* want her?'

'Sorry! Edmund Timpson. I represent Sweet Fanny Addams – '

'What a coincidence. So do I.'

'Ah yes. It's that I wanted to talk to you about. Do you have time for a coffee?'

She followed him into a place with yellow walls and too-new Lloyd Loom furniture. Seamless Madonna music blared from speakers high on the walls. One of them was giving out a rustling noise, or maybe it was just the sound of Madonna fanning herself with dollar bills. Edmund Timpson leant back to his seat and said, 'I understand the original Sweet Fanny Addams will be dancing at the Sweet Charity concert.'

'That's the game plan.'

'And have you got anyone yet to dance in Millie Fisher's place? May I make a suggestion?'

'Let me guess. The Duchess of York? Arnold Schwarzenegger?'

'I don't think you've given enough thought to the implications. It's going to be exceptionally embarrassing for Joanna-Mary. It would look like a deliberate slight by the founder members of the group.'

'Life deals some cruel blows.'

'Besides which, there are legal complications involved regarding Associated British and their Dance Group of the Year competition.'

'Complicated for you, maybe. Not for us. Tina Addams and Collette Sweet are the surviving founder members of Sweet Fanny Addams. Not only do they own the rights to the name, they wish to dance as that group at the Sweet Charity concert and then in the competition. Sounds simple enough to me. No one's stopping Joanna-Mary having a dance group. She can call it anything she likes, too. Golden Girls, Gorilla Snot, Dead Ferret, Henry V. Anything except Sweet Fanny Addams.'

Timpson felt in the inside pocket of his jacket and brought out his wallet and chequebook. 'Naturally,' he said carefully, 'we would be prepared to make a substantial donation to Sweet Charity. Several thousand pounds. And we'd make the cheque out to you.'

'I think everyone's hoping you're going to donate to Sweet Charity anyway. And my mother told me never to take cheques from strange men.'

'Look here, sweetie, I don't think you get the point. You can either listen to me or do it the hard way. We've got some important people behind us. One way or another, we'll stop you.'

'Ooh. If I wasn't so brave I'd be halfway up the street already.' She drank up her coffee and dropped a fiver on the table. 'Nice meeting you, Mr Timpson. If you're ever close to our rehearsal hall, drop in. Bring Joanna-Mary. I'm sure she'd like to see some real dancing.'

She took the Peugeot to Janey's via a little section of the M40. The road was lined with lorries and motor coaches but she managed to get the car to ninety. Weaving it in and out of the lanes, she was pleased that she hadn't lost driving skills honed in her years of rush hours round the Arc de Triomphe. A middle-aged man in a Vauxhall, incensed at being overtaken by a woman in a fast car, blocked her lane. Poor dear, she thought, taking him on the inside.

Janey had dress fabric spread out all over the floor. They were going to open with 'You're So Vain'. Curtis had kept some of Millie's original drawings and Janey was making up the costumes on her sewing machine.

Florence said, 'I think I've just been threatened by Edmund Timpson.'

'Think?'

'Hard to say. It was like being menaced by a blancmange.'

Janey carefully cut a length of black-and-white check on the bias. She had pins in her mouth and her yellow hair fell at an angle over her eyes. 'Are we going to do anything about it?'

'I don't know. He could be doing a one man show, or he could just be the warm-up act. Probably is.'

'Who for?'

Florence was thinking. She said, 'I've heard some things about Joanna-Mary's boyfriend and his pals, they're high-class hard cases, and none of them's under six feet tall. Maybe I'm wrong. Maybe they drive around looking for old ladies to help over the road, and knit blanket squares for Romanian orphans in the evenings. But I wouldn't bet on it. And Nicholas Wenders's father didn't get his millions by running a soup kitchen.' Florence paused. 'Are you sure you want to go through with it?'

'It'll take more than being slapped on the wrist by Edmund Timpson to change my mind.'

'All right, but remember, it doesn't end at Wembley.'

'I do remember. I'm with you all the way.'

'I'm not very good at being sloppy,' said Florence, 'but when I lost Millie I thought I'd never have another friend like that again, and I was wrong.'

After Janey had tried the tacked-together costume on Florence, they walked the two blocks down to the Punch Tavern and drank white wine spritzers in the garden for an hour. Elton John was playing on the juke-box. They meandered back, in the metallic blue dusk, past old brick walls hung with wistaria and honeysuckle. 'You don't seriously think that there's any danger, do you?' said Janey.

'No,' said Florence. 'I was bored. I just frightened myself for something to do.'

Inside Janey's flat the phone was ringing. It was Curtis. He said, 'Someone's broken into my office and trashed it. All my photos of Millie are smashed.'

Florence said, 'My God, what on earth kind of people want to do a thing like that?'

'They left a note,' said Curtis. 'I've got to stop you dancing for Sweet Fanny Addams at the Sweet Charity concert or next time they'll come to my office while I'm there.'

'I've always thought my nose was too big,' said Florence. 'If I came over, do you think they could fix it while they're about it?'

Curtis said, 'I'm worried about you. Why can't you back down? Why do you have to put yourself at risk? Have you really got to put your head above the parapet all the time?'

'It's all I've got,' Florence said. 'I'm not blonde. I don't know anyone important. I don't have a mummy and daddy. All I've got is what I've made for myself. All I can go by is what I think is right.'

The next day, Betty Trout and Joanna-Mary had lunch in the Associated British executive restaurant. The tables were laid with white cloths and silver cutlery and there was a dark green carpet on the floor and chandeliers on the ceilings. The food was awful.

Betty said, 'I must announce the entries. There's only three months to go till the start of the competition and Gus is getting desperate.'

Joanna-Mary said, 'Wait.'

'Darling, I really think we ought to think seriously about this entry from Tina Addams.'

'We've already got a Sweet Fanny Addams.'

'Couldn't you call yourselves something else? When I look at you, I always think, Heavenly Bodies.' Betty took delivery of an omelette. It had a ruched appearance, like an evening glove. 'It would be a terrifice coup. Juliet Dexter dancing in our show.'

'It's a trick. We won't get Juliet Dexter. Or any of the other old biddies. Their places will be filled by my enemies, people who will make things difficult for me and spoil the show.'

'Darling, time is really getting very short.'

Joanna-Mary said, 'I'm Tina Addams's friend. I shall go and see her, and iron out any difficulties.'

Greg was still living in the gloomy Victorian house in Acton. Florence and Janey stood in the doorway, jackets over their heads against the early summer rain. The door was framed by a crumbling porch around which some creeper raged. There was a caravan in the front garden, standing on four piles of bricks. 'Are you sure this is a good idea?' whispered Janey. They could see a light go on at the top of the landing and hear someone descend the stairs.

'Yes,' said Florence. 'Besides, I want to know what Joanna-Mary had on him.'

Five minutes later they were sitting on a wrecked-looking sofa in Greg's bedsit, watching him make coffee from a jar of instant and carton of long-life milk. He carried it over to them on a tin tray bearing a picture of the Queen Mother at Balmoral. 'She raped me,' he said.

'Poor Greg,' said Florence, 'but can that be possible?'

'I don't really want to relive it in detail,' said Greg, 'but take it from me, it's possible.'

'And then?'

Greg shrugged. 'You may find this hard to believe, but she had power over me. I wanted to please her. I thought for a while that in order for her to do . . . what she did to me, I must mean something to her. It quickly became clear to me that I meant nothing to her except as a means to get what she wanted. But then I was just afraid. She seemed quite capable of anything. She might have had me arrested for assault, fraud, whatever she pleased.'

'So you helped her destroy me.' Florence flapped her hands in the air. 'Like that, la-la-la.'

'Yes.' He stared at his feet. 'Well. Anything I can do to make it up to you?'

'You could castrate yourself with a rusty breadknife,' said Florence. 'Alternatively, you could come and work for us again.'

'I don't know if I . . . My mother has organized me a job with a neighbour. He owns a chain of frozen-food outlets. I'm training to be a manager.'

'It sounds dead interesting. I suppose if the pace ever sags you can watch the ice melt.'

'Let's just say I've settled for a quiet life.'

Florence said, 'Greg, you can't turn this down, because I want you to look after Collette Sweet.'

Tina rang Janey and cried down the phone. For forty years she had not been a person who showed her emotions in case they were interpreted as weakness. Now she seemed to be unloading all the stored-up feelings in one go. She said, 'Tom doesn't want me to come to London. He says he only just got back from tour and he wants to see his wife and baby girl.'

'He should come with you,' said Janey.

'He can't. He's got to go to Japan. He wants me to fly out after him but I can't be away from the business that long.'

Janey said, 'Oh God.' She waited, the receiver feeling slippery in her hand. No Tina! She wondered how she would tell Florence.

Tina sniffed, 'No, wait, Janey, I said to him, "Too bad you don't want to come with me to London," I said, "too damn bad altogether because this means something to a lot of people besides me so I'm going," and he said, Seemed like there wasn't much point in being married then because it wasn't only this instance but hundreds of other instances when I wasn't there because I was away or out doing something on business, only because I'm opening up in LA. Oh and then I called him a shitbag. I'd better ring off now because I want to call Juliet and Tom can't believe the size of our phone bill.'

Florence found a rehearsal hall next to a United Reformed church off the North Circular. Curtis got the pictures of Millie reframed and a padlock for the door of his office. Tina Addams, Collette Sweet and Juliet Dexter flew into Heathrow one mid-

246

July morning. Juliet travelled with her children, Albertine and the twins, Percy and Elsie. The nanny had come with her but proved more useful guiding Collette through Arrivals. 'A nervous flyer,' everyone said. Tina carried Ruby in a sling. She had not hired a nanny yet, liking to do everything for Ruby herself. She was in good shape. She had lost an enormous amount of weight in the run-up to her marriage to Tom. She had a dancer's stomach muscles and they had snapped back into shape within weeks of giving birth. She looked joyous, more beautiful than she had ever looked at twenty-five.

Florence, Janey and Ratty were there to meet them, and Greg and Curtis organized a press conference in the arrivals lounge. The four old girls posed with children and without. They sat splay-legged and fawn-like on sofas, on the floor, the way they used to do. They called Florence over so she could be photographed too. After a quarter-hour was up, Ruby started to wail and the press conference ended. The evening paper photographer knelt on the marble floor, operating the wire machine which would get his picture into the early edition.

As they drove from the airport into London there was bright sky and then grey. Coming towards them on the Talgarth Road the cars had their headlamps on. The rain showered down suddenly and with violence as though someone had punched a hole through the clouds. A building in construction just where the overpass turned a corner loomed up at them like an approaching ship. There was a rainbow across the city, and a rainbow under that.

Chapter Eighteen

Alive from Wembley

A WEEK WENT by. They appeared in three chat shows, were in every newspaper except the *Morning Star*, gave interviews on morning television and the early evening news. They started rehearsals in the hall by the United Reformed church. Trailers appeared around Wembley, the cables thick and intertwined like a river in flux. One afternoon they went through their routine on the stage, to an audience of two men with earphones, a dismantled goalpost and a heavy-duty mower. Afterwards Florence, Ratty and Janey went back to the rehearsal room and discussed this and that over Gruyère sandwiches.

'This and that' was actually the new team they had to build for the Dance Group of the Year.

They drove north up the motorway in the evening, after the London rush hour had died down. Ratty sat in the front, wearing dark glasses and a yellow headband, and a pair of very tight black leggings. In the back, Janey cradled Bram's head in her lap as he slept, stroking the side of his face with her little slim hand. Florence drove wordlessly, listlessly to the low throb of the engine nearing 110 m.p.h. The motorway was as flat and hypnotic as a bore at a party. Under a bridge, past a lorry, round a curve, under a bridge, past a lorry, round a curve.

Just after nine o'clock they turned off and headed for the mill towns on the high winding road across the peaks. Ratty spread the map across her lap and read it by the light of a torch. It was nearing eleven when they drew up outside the terraced house where Pola Bear lived. Ratty and Janey rang the doorbell while Florence locked the car. All the light there was in the house came from upstairs. There was a long wait and Ratty rang again. Bram stirred once in Janey's arms. Mrs Bear came down in her dressing gown. When she saw Ratty she held out her arms and lifted her off her feet. Mr Bear followed his wife down the stairs. He gave Ratty and the other two an icy stare. 'What the hell do you want?' he said.

Mrs Bear said, 'Whatever kind of a welcome is that to give Alexa and her friends.'

'You gone and forgot the trouble she brought us?'

'It wasn't Alexa who brought us trouble. It was that Moloney girl and the school. And Pola brought some of the trouble on herself, letting them get away with it.'

'However you tell it, Pola ain't home.'

'Then we'll wait for her,' said Florence, following Ratty into the sitting room.

Mrs Bear set about making them something to eat and drink. 'She got herself a part-time job,' she said. 'Selling rowing machines on commission at the sports shop. She have to sit herself on them and demonstrate. Brings all kinds of people in the shop but they don't seem to buy no rowing machines out of it.'

Pola came home around midnight. She was warm and bright-eyed from working out at the gym, and smelt of fresh sweat and Blue Grass perfume. She took one look at them and said, 'I'm going to bed.'

'Wait and see what these people are offering you,' said Mr Bear, who by this time had warmed to them, as they had gone into the kitchen and done all the washing up.

Florence said, 'Ratty's told me a lot about you. We want you to come in on Sweet Fanny Addams with us. We've got all the founder members with us including Juliet Dexter and after the Sweet Charity concert the group is staying together for Dance Group of the Year. You'll be working with some of the best dancers the country's ever produced, you can stay at Janey's flat and she'll look after you till you know your way around. It'll be instant exposure for you and I'm offering six months' contract.' She got the contract out of her bag and gave it to Mr

Bear. There was a cheque for £200 fixed to it by a paper clip. 'That's an advance against Pola's week's wages.'

'I don't need your job,' said Pola. 'I don't like dancing. I'm happy where I am – without Mrs Baptiste stirring things up.'

'Pardon me, I hear you get your names mixed up,' said Mrs Bear. 'It was that Amber Moloney you meant, wasn't it.'

'It's all right for her. I've got to live here, see these people in the street.'

'Keep your head down, then,' said Ratty. 'Keep on with the job in the sports shop and marry the owner's son and have three kids in five years and bawl them out in the supermarket. Watch *Neighbours* twice a day and fight with hubby about his nights out with the boys. Why, you and he might even make it big. A detached house with a garage, a second car, lunch with the in-laws every Sunday, you dressed to kill and hubby falling asleep in the armchair all afternoon 'cos his brain's turned to vegetable soup from working all hours. You stay right where you are, girl. We're heading back to the big, bright, noisy, dangerous city.'

Florence said, 'Think about it. Take as long as you want. We're not leaving till you say yes.'

Mrs Bear said, 'If they want you in their group that badly, Pola, I think you should go along with them.'

Pola said, 'I don't want to miss a chance to get somewhere. If it really is a chance and not just Mrs Baptiste causing trouble.'

Ratty prayed inside her head for the Lord's strength and said sweetly, 'It's the best chance you'll get, Pola. You, me and any of us.' She went to the front door and held it open.

All the way back down the motorway, Pola slept, curled up with Janey and Bram. The sky was getting light as they crossed into North London. The street lamps started to go out like popping balloons. Pola woke up and burst into tears. 'I've made the biggest mistake of my life,' she said. 'I can't believe I've been such a moron. You're all mad and I don't want to be a dancer. I was going to be promoted to selling leisurewear this morning. They were going to let me model the outfits and keep them. One more night and I'd never have had to set eyes on you again.'

Florence stopped at a 24-hour transport café where someone recognized them from their chat show appearance. They scribbled autographs and took addresses so they could send on signed pictures of Tina, Juliet and Collette. 'How's Pola now?' Florence said to Ratty.

'Better,' said Ratty. 'She's resigned herself to the idea of being rich and celebrated.'

Florence left them at Janey's flat. Her travels weren't over. She turned the Peugeot round and took it south-west on the M3 to the Pier Gardens, Bournemouth, where Annie Easterfield and Cindy Davies were wowing the blue-rinse brigade in the back line of *Les Mis*. She talked them into joining when they came off stage and after the matinée. The dressing room was all Formica and wire coat hangers. There were six seats between twenty girls. Annie and Cindy had to share a peg with someone who kept dropping their clothes on the floor to make room for hers.

Annie wanted to sign straight off, but Cindy wasn't so keen. 'After Joanna-Mary, I said I wasn't going to have any more to do with any more dance groups,' she said. 'We turned up for rehearsal and there were these two other girls there and Joanna-Mary got us to work out with them, and at the end she said, "These girls are much better than you, so you can go." She didn't even let us shower and change. We had to go out in our leotards, and it was fucking cold outside. So I'm staying with the chorus, thank you. Give myself a break.'

'You don't need a job in the chorus to get a break,' said Florence. 'You need a miracle. Where the hell's *Les Mis* in Bournemouth going to get you? Next month you'll be laid off, the month after that you'll be in the back row in *Starlight Express* in Newcastle on Tyne. Next year maybe they'll ask you back here and put you in the front row. The year after that you'll be doing *Fame* in Coventry and probably the next ten years after that as well, and when you're forty-five you'll be first on after the interval at the Alhambra with Band-Aid, hitching up your dewlaps. You might just get a West End producer here this afternoon, who might just spot you in the chorus if he just happened to have a telescope on him and the stars of the show stood aside and pointed at you as you did your routine. But he'd have to *be* in Bournemouth. It's not exactly even money, is it? You know that.'

Cindy sighed. 'OK,' she said, I'll come.'

Florence had one more dancer in mind. The next day she paid a visit to Geronimo's. She ordered a red wine from the normal Scot behind the bar and sat on a high chair making it last with the help of a book. 'Does a tall fair-headed girl come in here a lot?' she asked. 'One of the dancers who rehearses over the road. Her name's Manon.'

'Funny you should say that,' said the barman. 'A guy came in here a few days ago asking after Manon. Big, heavy-set young guy. Wore one of those shiny mauve and red and green striped track suits. You and he in any way connected?'

'Not as far as I know,' said Florence. 'I want to offer her a job.' She wrote her name and number down on a beer mat. 'If you see her, would you give her that? It needs to be done discreetly.' She paid for her drink and left. The Peugeot had the sickly smell of all cars left too long in the sun. She set off home through the stiffly moving traffic. It was too late to go up to the church hall and watch rehearsals. Janey would see to all that as well as she always did. Florence felt a stab of guilt about Janey. She'd put herself on the line all the way, and what did she ask for in return? Not much. Enough money to stop the building society repossessing the flat. Pickled onions with lunch. And sometimes if Janey were really lucky Florence might stop moving long enough to say thank you.

The phone rang about halfway through the evening. It was Manon from a call-box.

'Where are you?' said Florence.

'Standing under a portrait of Margaret Thatcher,' said Manon. 'We're in Trimmingham. I haven't got long. I've come out in the interval and the Joanna-Mary police will come after me in one minute flat. She's fit to be tied these days. We're billed as the *Real* Sweet Fanny Addams.'

Florence said, 'Well, how'd you like to dance in *my* group, the Unreal Sweet Fanny Addams?'

'What? Now?' Manon looked round, hearing a car draw up outside the club, and the buzz as the automatic glass doors slowly opened to let someone in. Her heartbeat slowed when she saw a bunch of strangers. Not Ray. Ray finding her and making a song and dance and getting himself gawked at, that was all she needed. As if she didn't have enough to worry about as things were.

She shook her head, impatient at her own fear. Maybe she'd been imagining things. There were millions of tosspots in England who wore tinsel track suits and rode around in Ford Escorts, Why be surprised if one of them was parked in the street outside your flat one night? That didn't mean it was Ray come to threaten her and drag her back to Eastleigh. 'Now?' she said again.

'As soon as you can. I've never seen anyone dance like you before. I want to build the group round you.'

'Funny thing,' said Manon. 'I liked you when you came over to rehearsal that day. I hoped we'd work together then.'

'Is that a Yes?' Florence waited. It sounded as if Manon had dropped the phone.

'Christ,' said Manon, who'd just seen Roger Reed-Herbert walk past, looking around. 'I'm not up to this.'

'What's wrong?'

'Better not say, if you don't mind.'

'Shit!' yelled Florence, 'if you're in trouble, don't minnie about, just tell me and I'll sort it out for you!'

'I can't,' said Manon. 'It, like, puts me in a bad light.' She dropped her voice. 'Joanna-Mary's coming. Got to go.'

Florence said quickly, 'Come and rehearse with us next week.' She gave Manon the address of the hall. 'There's one more thing. Don't say anything at all to anyone, not even to your old teddybear, specially not to Joanna-Mary, till I say it's time.'

'Hello, Teens.' Joanna-Mary stood in the doorway of Holly Tree Cottage. She was head to foot in Nicole Farhi. Vallie was beside her, carrying a large pink-wrapped present tied up with ribbon. Her chin rested on the top as though it was something she'd picked up at the last minute and had nowhere else to put it.

Tina led them into the kitchen, which was also the dining and sitting room. It was floored with huge cold flagstones over which was a faded brown rug with pink and turquoise flowers. Though old, the rug shone as the sunlight caught it. There was a great yawning fireplace in one wall. Behind the kitchen a door led to a small bathroom with lots of underwear and baby clothes hanging out to dry. Up some stairs were two bedrooms with bare floorboards and old wooden cupboards. The staircase was behind another door. It was uncarpeted and had a dramatic crick at the top. The windows looked out on to a field containing a piebald horse. Collette had one room and Tina and Ruby had the other. The cottage was in Buckinghamshire, but on a route convenient for the north-west of London. Greg had rented it for them for the summer.

'Well,' said Tina.

Joanna-Mary leant over the baby. Ruby was sleeping in her carrycot on the kitchen table. All you could see were some spikes of black hair. Joanna-Mary's expression was a screwed-up simper, as though she were advertizing vaginal deodorant. She poked at Ruby beneath the blanket. 'Hello,' she cooed.

For some reason, Tina felt the urge to pull the carrycot near her protectively. 'You shouldn't have travelled out all this way,' she said. 'We could have met up in town.' She would have preferred not to see Joanna-Mary at all, but could not say so because Vallie had wanted to come. She felt too guilty about Vallie to deny her.

'Oh, but it's no trouble,' said Vallie, 'such a beautiful day for a drive. I won't be having many more drives with Joanna-Mary so I intend to make the best of what's left. After she's married I'll only see her one Sunday in every four.'

Joanna-Mary was intended to reply. 'Oh, Mummy,' at which Vallie would cross her arms and say, 'No, I am not going to be one of those mothers-in-law so beloved of comedians, thank you very much.' Instead, Joanna-Mary got up and started wandering about the cottage. She peeked into the bathroom and opened the door to the stairs.

Tina called out sharply, 'Don't go up there. Collette's asleep.'

'Tell me which her room is and I won't go in.'

Tina and Vallie exchanged childbirth stories. They could hear Joanna-Mary clunking about on the floor above. As she came down, Vallie was saying, 'When you have children you really need your women friends.'

'I say, Mummy,' said Joanna-Mary. 'Any chance of a cup of tea?'

'I'll make it,' said Tina, getting up.

'I want you to show me the beautiful fields,' said Joanna-Mary.

They walked up the rutted track that led to the main road. There was an old-fashioned signpost at the top that pointed, askew, to the heavens. 'So quiet,' breathed Joanna-Mary. 'I don't suppose you get any cars coming past at all.'

'Very few.'

'No one else at all for miles. You're brave.'

'Oh, there's a farmhouse behind the copse. If we need help or anything we can go up there.'

Joanna-Mary leant on a gate. She jerked back her head and put up a hand to smooth her hair. 'Tina, what is this I hear about you entering Dance Group of the Year?'

'Sounds like fun, don't you think?' said Tina.

'You can't have thought it through,' said Joanna-Mary. 'What about me?'

'Oh, are you entering too?' said Tina jovially. 'Terrific. What are you going to call yourselves?'

Joanna-Mary said, as if to an imbecile, 'Sweet Fanny Addams, of course.'

'I'm afraid you can't,' said Tina. 'That name is the legal property of Collette and me, and we want it for ourselves.'

'You can't seriously tell me that you're going to take up dancing again.'

'Why ever not?'

'Because,' said Joanna-Mary, 'you are fat and Collette is a drunk, and both of you are too old.' She stroked her hair again. 'And if you don't let me have Sweet Fanny Addams, Daddy will um, um, take all his money out of Legwork and you'll go bust. Well? I haven't got long. I've already wasted time looking at your baby. So move it. You know I didn't come here for the country air.'

Tina said thoughtfully, 'Joanna-Mary, I've taken shit from you all your life, everywhere from the rehearsal room at Legwork

255

to the changing room at Joseph but do you know, I always thought you liked me.'

'Well, you were wrong, you fat slag.'

Tina followed her back to the house. Funny, she quite liked the sound of what Joanna-Mary had said about Roger taking all his money out of Legwork. She wouldn't be torn between her business and her family if there wasn't a business for her to feel torn about. She sighed. No, things weren't ever as simple as that. She needed both. She would have to find her own way through. 'Anyway,' she said, 'It's too late. We can't turn back now.'

'Of course you can. You don't think anyone actually wants to watch you, do you? They'll all be embarrassed at the sight of you. None of them will know who you are. Most of them weren't born when you were dancing. It will be horrible for them, like watching their parents fucking. If you pull out there'll be relief all round.'

'You probably didn't mean to have this effect,' murmured Tina, 'but I'm really glad you said all this. It's sorted everything out in my mind. No woman wants to turn her back on a friend, but I wouldn't turn my back on my worst enemy if she were in your hands. You can't run a dance group, you can't spell and to say you've got the ethical standards of Lucretia Borgia is to slander Borgia. You've bent me to your will for years by playing the friendship card. And now here you are looking at me as though I mean no more to you than something you've got on your shoe. If you told me the sky was blue I'd go and check with someone else to make sure. Before I came to London, I was still unsure whether I was doing the right thing. A bit of humaneness and affection from you and I could have changed my mind even then. But you had to insult me, and threaten me, and show your hatred and disrespect. I tell you, Joanna-Mary, from this day forward if you were bleeding to death I wouldn't throw you an elastoplast.'

After that it was a quiet week. There was no sinister phone calls, or invitations to tea from Edmund Timpson. Nobody broke into the cottage and smashed it up, or followed her car, or tried to snatch the baby from her arms. Every afternoon Tina drove Collette up to London for rehearsals and back again in the evening. There was a time during the twenty-four hours of each day when Collette was wonderful – between her second drink and her sixth. The trick was to get her dancing around the third, fourth and fifth. Then she moved to the music as though she'd never stopped, she was the old Collette, erotic and maidenly at the same time, prim and wicked, classy and a whore. Tina got her to sleep during most of the day so that she was primed to hit drink two at lunchtime and step on stage directly after; the Sweet Charity concert began mid-morning and Sweet Fanny Addams were a quarter of the way down the bill.

In the evenings Tina and Collette came home to Holly Tree Cottage and Tina gave baby Ruby her eight o'clock feed. Greg would drive over from Acton to spend the night. At first he slept outside the house, in the car, alert like a guard dog to every snap of a twig, but after two nights of that the women insisted he come in. They made him a bed on the sofa. They had dinner together. Greg liked to see that Collette ate well; left to herself her dinner was entirely liquid. After eating they sat around the yawning fireplace and fell asleep over the television. They all felt at ease. Joanna-Mary had come and gone without getting her own way, and they were still there. There was nothing for them to worry about beyond the concert on Saturday.

On the evening before the concert Curtis booked a table at Orso in Covent Garden. 'I can't go,' said Tina. 'Ruby will wail, and spoil the meal for everyone else, and I don't want to leave her with an unknown babysitter.'

'If you leave her feed in the fridge,' said Greg, 'I can look after her.'

Juliet said, 'You must go out without Ruby some time. It's only for a few hours. You are other people besides Ruby's mother. You owe it to yourself and Tom.'

Tina went to dinner at Orso with Curtis, Florence, Janey, Ratty and Juliet. Collette stayed with Greg at the cottage. It was the ninth birthday of her oldest son Aaron, and she was waiting till he got out of school to phone him, Los Angeles time. She had stayed off the booze for the call. After they'd spoken, it was gone ten o'clock. She felt an aching sadness at the loss of her sons' daily presence. The divorce judge had awarded custody to Delaney. She couldn't blame anyone but herself, she thought. What a Godawful mother she had been in those last two years. Probably too late to change things now. And yet, and yet . . . She was more sober each one of these days than she had ever been in Los Angeles. Somehow with all the dancing and the company . . . But when you didn't drink, you ached. She went to pour herself a drink, realized it was just automatic and she didn't really want one, reached in her bag for a cigarette instead and saw she was out of them. 'Greg?'she said, flapping the empty box at him.

Greg had none.

'There's a pub in the village,' she said. 'They'll have some.'

'Will you be all right?'

'Oh Greg, *do* give over. A six-mile round trip to a pub, can I bear it?'

After Greg had gone she started to feel drowsy. She left the downstairs lights on for him and went up. Wandering into the smallest bedroom, she watched Ruby asleep on her side, thumb in mouth, making odd snuffly sounds. A moth blundered noisily around the dim bedside lamp. Collette gently took out Ruby's thumb. It wasn't good for the teeth, whatever anyone said. Then she stepped softly out and along the corridor to her own room. She lay on the bed with her hands over her head and closed her eyes. Waiting for Greg to come back, she fell into the sleep of the physically exhausted.

One of Nicholas Wender's friends rang Nicholas from his mobile phone. He was stationed with it behind an oak tree in the field containing the piebald horse. He said, 'Little Smoothie-chops has gone out. It's all clear.' He thought that because he had already seen Tina's car drive away. He had no grounds for thinking Collette was still in there because Collette always went everywhere with Tina and anyway it would never have occurred to him to check. He was a handsome young man with rich parents, but completely stupid.

Nicholas took the call in his Mercedes. There were five other young men with him. One was a financial consultant, another a mortgage broker, the rest doing something which involved moving notional amounts of money around linked computers. They were all members of the same rugby team. Nicholas was their captain. They would do anything he asked of them. They had about them a kind of free-floating violence and materialism which enabled them to act without the disadvantage of soul-searching.

They moved off in the Mercedes, drinking whisky out of a bottle, apart from Nicholas who had his driving licence to protect. As they turned into the rutted track that led to the cottage, the young man reached into bags that contained milk bottles filled with petrol. They acted interdependently, as the game of rugby had taught them. In later life they would give each other's sons jobs in their companies, and meet annually in large picnic parties in Twickenham car park.

The Mercedes stopped by the front gate of Holly Tree Cottage and out they ran. Nicholas turned the car round. Who knows what was really meant to happen, whether they intended such a wicked act or had in mind some sort of smoking out, a scare, that got out of hand? The front-row forward had a crowbar with which he forced open the door. The others ran in with their heads down and their shoulders hunched, milk bottles in bunched fists, dripping, shaking, pouring and soaking; carpet, curtains, sofa and armchairs. When the last of the petrol had been discharged, the full-back lit a match with a rather showy gesture and threw it towards the furthest point of the room.

Joanna-Mary stuck the votive candle in a holder, having lit it with another that was already burning alongside. She had now ignited a whole row and was becoming mesmerized. The church was in near-darkness and the candles flickered with a weak yellow light. There was a smell of musty kneelers and days-old incense. It was a London church, rebuilt after the last war. She heard footsteps behind her and turned. 'Good evening, vicar. I was just passing St Andrew's, um, St Alphege, and thought I would remember my friend who died. It's two years ago almost to the day. Such a waste.' She lowered her eyes. There was a tactful pause, after which the vicar said, 'Apart from that, every-thing is well with you and Nicholas, I hope?'

'Oh yes. He would be with me, but he's playing rugby tonight.'

'Jolly good. A Harrow man isn't he? I'm an Old Carthusian.' The vicar caught her eye and looked away again. Illuminated by the flickering candles, there was something alarming in her expression. 'Honoured to turn out for the veterans' team when I can. Not great rugby, but it keeps us fit, wa-ha-har.'

'Nicholas and I will make an appointment with you soon,' said Joanna-Mary, 'so you can talk to us about the meaning of marriage.'

The flames burst into being. It was then that Ruby started to wail, disturbed by the young men's urgent crepitations. They said, all of them, just about all at once, 'Fuck me, there's a baby up there.' They had not been told about a baby. Two of the young men chased up the stairs towards the open door of Ruby's room. One lifted her out of the carrycot and ran with her tucked under his arm. When he came to the flames beginning to lick at the door to the stairs he passed her back to his team-mate, the front-row forward, and smothered them with the old brown rug. The hooker of the team was waiting at the door with his arms out. He caught the baby from the front-row forward and ran with her to the safety of the field. It was a forward pass, but who's carping? He dropped her down on some couch grass among the bushes and sprinted to the car where the rest were waiting. They were moving away as he jumped in.

Returning from the pub in the village. Greg was nearly forced off the road by a car driving straight at him. Blinded by its headlights, he could not tell what make it was or who drove it, but a torpedo of fear hit his heart. He tried to tell himself that this was merely hysteria, but then he saw the glow behind the copse. There was a mile to go to the cottage and he covered the distance in ten seconds; to this day he does not know how. The ground floor was burning, but the stairway was still passable thanks to the rugby team's work in extinguishing the flames by the door. First Greg went to Tina's room and took the carrycot. He hung it over his arm by the handles. He ran to Collette's room. She was still asleep, not drunk but exhausted. He tipped her over his shoulder: she was so light it was almost like putting on a stole.

All the way down the stairs the carrycot banged and stuck between the walls. All the time he could hear a noise and he recognized it as the sound of himself sobbing. He stumbled out into the sweet night air, dropped the carrycot and laid Collette on the grass. 'Collette,' he said hoarsely, 'Collette.'

She stirred and opened her eyes.

Greg said, 'I'll look after you. I'll make sure you're always safe. I won't let anyone near you who could harm you ever again.'

She smiled and closed her eyes.

The fire brigade arrived, called by the farmer and his wife. Seconds later, Tina came back from her evening out. She began to scream, so they told her Ruby was safe and indeed she could see the carrycot. She hurried towards it, some of her mind taking in Greg half collapsed with Collette in his arms in a puddle of foamy water. When she reached it there was no baby. She looked at the flames raging through the cottage and howled out great shrill hoots of panic, grief and desolation.

The firemen held her back. She would otherwise have run into the cottage. If she could not have found her baby, she would have thrown herself on the fire. It was just as well they did hold her back, or Ruby would have woken up to a world without her mother. As it was the commotion and shouting brought a sudden indignant cry from Ruby in her little nest in the couch grass.

Tina stopped screaming and stood absolutely still, listening, even though the noise was no more than a squawk. She was Ruby's mother, she could have heard her breathe in the mouth of an erupting volcano. She pushed the firemen aside and ran through the bushes, her hands and feet beating and tearing a path to where Ruby lay.

She seized her and hugged her, weeping, laughing, rocking, stroking the downy back of her head. 'My baby,' she said, over and over, 'my baby, my baby.' Then she fell silent and thoughtful. Holding Ruby to her heart, she stood up and looked around at the cottage, skeletal, wet, smouldering.

Tina breathed in deeply. Her legs were shaking now, but she was going to do what she had to do. She carried Ruby up to the hissing ruins and showed her them. 'Someone has done this to us,' she whispered to her. 'Someone who doesn't care if we die or live.'

One of the firemen was shaking her arm, trying to coax her back. 'Come away from there if I was you, love.' 'Fuck off,' she said. Then she filled her lungs with air and shouted, 'Evil, evil bitch, I'll have you for this!'

Greg drove them into town and they spent the rest of the night in Juliet Dexter's suite at the best hotel in north-west London. 'The show will go on,' announced Tina in a resonating voice, then fell asleep with Ruby encased in her arms. It was half-past six in the morning. Florence, Janey, Ratty and Juliet held a council of war over strawberries and champagne.

'I'm going to go round Joanna-Mary's house,' said Ratty, 'and set fire to *it*.'

'Are you stark raving mad?' said Florence. 'You'll get arrested.'

'Don't anyone stop me.' Ratty jumped up out of her chair. 'That girl's got to be sorted out once and for all.' Florence tried to push her down again. It was like trying to get a cork back in a wine bottle. 'Ratty,' she said with her teeth clenched, 'if you don't sit down you're out of a job.'

'Think that'll stop me?'

Juliet said, 'Quieten down, Ratty, Florence is right. What's the point of lowering yourself to her level?'

'All right,' said Ratty, 'if you know so much better than everyone else, what's your solution?'

'I think we should all enjoy the delicious strawberries and champagne,' said Juliet, buffing her nails delicately, 'and remember what we're here for – a charity concert.'

'Oh,' said Collette, peeking through from the bedroom, 'did I hear champagne?' She was wearing a white satin dressing gown of Juliet's and her lemony yellow hair was thick and rumpled. She looked as thin and fragile as a rose in cellophane.

'Now then, Collette,' said Janey, 'you must go and lie down. You've had a shock.'

'Oh, have I?' said Collette, smiling benignly. 'Rairly?' She felt too amazed to lie down. She got dressed and paced around the sitting room with its gold-painted mirrors and reproduction French chairs, clutching a livener in her pale narrow hand. Greg took her out into the early morning, walking her past silent shops and car parks. He held on to her as he had gripped the strings of balloons as a boy. When they returned it was eleven o'clock and Tina was awake, calmly feeding the baby with a blanket wrapped round her shoulders. They were watching the television, which was showing the entire Sweet Charity concert live. The stadium had no ground as far as anyone could see, it was entirely obliterated by people. The opening act had just arrived on stage. 'Who are they?' said Juliet.

'The Red Helicopters,' said Florence.

'Oh,' said Juliet, 'well, of course, I wouldn't know them because I've been in the States.'

Janey said, 'They're an American group.'

'But,' said Juliet, 'aren't they terribly young, no more than sixteen?'

'Oh no,' said Janey, 'quite old.'

'Who else is going to play at this concert?' said Juliet.

Florence said, 'Obituary, Steel Magnolias, Testing Testing, Killer Chrysanthemum – '

'I haven't heard of any of them,' said Juliet faintly. 'Isn't there anyone who was around when we were? The Bay City Rollers? Gary Glitter? The Sweet? Minnie Riperton?'

'Yes, plenty, plenty,' said Tina soothingly. She handed the sleeping Ruby to Juliet's nanny, who was going to stay at the hotel and look after all the children.

'Minnie Riperton's dead,' said Janey.

'Vodka Frenzy,' said Florence hurriedly, 'you must have heard of them, they're huge in the States.'

Tina looked at Juliet who was hanging on to her nail file as if it were stuck to her hand. 'Florence,' she said sharply, 'that's enough groups.'

Greg watched Tina as she sat there, thinking that there was something magnificent and terrible about her that morning, like a great natural disaster that was about to wreak itself on the unsuspecting. He cleared his throat and said, 'May I remind you that two limousines are arriving at half-past eleven to transport us to the stadium?'

Juliet suddenly started screaming with laughter, her head back over her shoulders, tears forming in her eyes. 'Transport,' she spluttered. 'Transport.' After a while she stopped and gave a little smile and a couple of hiccups.

Florence said, getting her coat on, 'Greg always talks like that. You get used to it.'

'I don't see anything funny about the way Greg talks,' said Collette with her sudden lucidity, 'so stuff it, Florence.'

Juliet nodded. Her face had gone as white as milk. Tina said, 'Come on, Juliet. Pull yourself together.'

Juliet said, 'I can't do it.'

'Juliet,' said Ratty, 'every day of your life you go out before a camera, what is this "I can't do it"?'

'I haven't been live on stage for eight years,' whispered Juliet.

Collette sat down next to her and hugged her tight. 'Darling,' she said, 'I promise you'll be fine, you've just got a touch of stage fright.'

'I can't do it,' Juliet repeated. 'I'm going to die out there. We're all going to die out there.'

Collette shot an arm out and snapped her fingers and gestured for a drink. Greg came rushing up with a glass of champagne. 'Thank you,' said Collette, and drank it herself. Then she helped Juliet to her feet and she and Tina bundled her into the limo. They were only half a mile out of Wembley but the drive took twenty minutes because of the crowd. Some of them banged on the window when they saw Juliet, and waved autograph books at her, which perked her up a bit so that by the time they got to their dressing room she was too busy dimpling and signing and waving to have time to be scared. Their dressing room was in one of a line of Portakabins behind the stage. It was grey and smelt of disinfectant but someone had prettied it up with a bunch of gladioli that were red and orange and pink like a firestorm in the vase. The time for their performance grew near. There was a tap on the door and a voice that said, 'Sweet Fanny Addams, five minutes, please,' and then a year after that another tap and the voice again, 'Two minutes.' They sat in their costumes in absolute silence, listening to the final notes of the last song before them. The tap on the door. They filed out through the corridor of canvas that led to the stage. They saw sky and sun and heard a blast of noise that they realized was people shouting and cheering for them. The opening guitar notes of 'You're So Vain' began to twang and they jumped on stage one by one in the time it took for Dom-diddle-om-diddle-om. Dom-diddle-om-diddle-om. Tina looked around her. The intensity of her recent experiences drove her momentarily into a different time dimension, in which music played but it was no song that she had ever heard on this earth: floating, sweet, strange, haunting. She saw not the crowded stadium but a succession of green hills and oceans over which she was flying at a low height. She was filled with wonder and thankfulness for the life she had been allowed to live. Why, she thought, how marvellous, how marvellous that I should have been a dancer. Then the music inside her head faded and time returned to its ordinary pace, and she joined the dance.

Joanna-Mary and Vallie went to Peter Jones to shop for washing machines and toasters. They were in the electrical goods department, assessing compact disc players, when Sweet Fanny Addams took the stage. All fifty televisions in the department were on, so Joanna-Mary was able to watch Sweet Fanny Addams's performance wherever she looked, and see the ecstasy and triumph on their faces, and listen to the acclaim that followed it whichever way she turned.

The microphones were out for them as they came off stage. There were presenters and comedians and newsmen. Tina leant forward smiling, her lips slightly apart and almost nudging the mike as though about to take a little bite out of it. It was hard to describe her, she was alight, alive, a little breathless, without chronological age. 'Thank you, thank you. Sweet Fanny Addams,' she said, 'are back. We are going to be doing a lot of dancing from now on, a lot.'

'We hear you had a nasty scare in the night. What happened?'

'Oh, that,' she said, '*that*. Let's just say, somebody played with fire.' There was a look in her eyes as she spoke which made the interviewer draw back slightly and hold the microphone at Florence. 'Is it true that you've entered for Dance Group of the Year?'

Florence was game for a long speech but she could see the cameras about to be turned elsewhere. So she said, 'Yes.'

'Well, we wish you luck. Tina Addams and Florence Johnson of Sweet Fanny Addams, thank you.'

They went back to the Portakabin to change out of their costumes. Ratty and Juliet were ready quickly because they wanted to get back to the children. Florence and Janey wanted to see the replay of their performance that Juliet's nanny had videoed for them, and Collette was very tired. When they left for the hotel Tina sat in the cabin and cried and cried because she'd been out there in front of a hundred thousand people, and now she was alone.

Betty Trout saw Tina being interviewed on the television. She turned to Gus Wycherley and said, 'I don't think we can wait any longer, do you?'

'What will you do?'

'Oh, a compromise. But I don't see what else we can do.'

The entries for the competition were announced early the next week. Joanna-Mary's group were included in the London and the South-East regional final, under the name Heavenly Bodies. There was nothing there about Sweet Fanny Addams at all.

Florence rang and asked to be put through to Betty Trout.

'Betty is in a meeting,' said a man's voice. Florence recognized it as Melvyn's.

'I've seen her office,' said Florence. 'It's about the size of my driving licence. There's nowhere for her to be holding meetings in unless she likes having conferences behind the filing cabinet.'

'Leave your name and she'll get back to you.'

'Of course she will, And I'm Raisa Gorbachev. You tell me –
did she receive an entry for Sweet Fanny Addams?'

'I'm afraid I can't say.'

'Maybe you'd like to look it up in your files. Don't worry –
you're not keeping me from doing anything important. I can
wait. Nothing I like better than to hang on telephones. Watching
the damp race up the walls of my flat. Listening to the relaxing
sound of my own breathing.'

'I know who you are. You're Florence Johnson and you don't
bother me in the slightest.'

'Oh hell. I was hoping you'd want to go through a form of
marriage with me.'

Florence heard a female voice in the background. Its owner
took hold of the phone. 'Florence,' said Betty Trout, 'How nice
to hear from you. When are we going to have that natter?'

'Whenever you like. But I'm sure you're very pushed for time.'

'Not half. This bloody *Dance Group* programme. Have you
heard about it?'

'I have. I was just asking young Melvyn what had happened
to our entry.'

'Your entry?'

Florence, realizing they could go on flinging 'entry' around
indefinitely, said, 'Sweet Fanny Addams applied for the London
heat on the 16th of July, a week before closing date. Since then,
nothing. I'd like to know what's happened.'

Betty said sharply, away from the phone, 'Melvyn, have you
any record of Florence's entry?' She turned back to the receiver.
'Sweetie, Melvyn's gone away to look. Can we get back to you?'

'Sure,' said Florence. 'I'll wait in.'

Melvyn called back five minutes later. 'I'm awfully sorry,' he
said, 'but we have absolutely no record of your entry, and the
heats are now full. All we can do is put you down for next year.'

It was a beautiful midsummer day. The hedgerows were full of
wild roses and Canterbury bells, and honeysuckle flowered on
the walls of old village houses. Tina drove past the ruin of Holly
Tree Cottage and five miles along the winding B road to the
nearby market town.

She visited the police station first. 'I'm surprised,' she said, 'that no one's asked me for a statement yet.'

The sergeant on duty made a big thing of getting out a buff folder and shuffling through the papers inside. 'Holly Tree Cottage, Holly Tree Cottage,' he said. 'Oh, that's right, love. No problem. Enquiry's closed to our satisfaction.'

Tina said, 'What does that mean?'

'It means the police will be taking no further action.'

'What about my satisfaction?'

'Well, that's what it says here,' said the sergeant. 'We can only go on the fire officer's report.'

Tina went to the fire station. It was a high, cool building, sticky with dust. There was a front office where a man in a white shirt and dark trousers sat drinking coffee from a cracked beige mug. The station officer had a room upstairs. It was small, painted regulation magnolia, with a chipped metal cupboard where he kept his boots and helmet. The window looked down on to a car park paved with hot black tarmac. In the distance an ice-cream van moved slowly along, chiming 'Greensleeves'.

'I'm surprised,' said Tina, 'that the police are taking no further action.'

The station officer shrugged. He was a big man with greasy, charcoal-coloured hair. There was a pencil in his hand. He kept tapping on the desk with it. 'It's a dry summer, love,' he said.

'I didn't come for a weather report,' said Tina, 'I came for justice for my baby and my friend.'

'Your friend,' said the station officer. 'Hear she likes a drink. Happen all the time, these fires. Falls asleep with a lighted cigarette – in an old property like the cottage, what can you expect?'

Tina said, 'Quite. I'm just a silly little woman. Anyone could pull my nose off and I wouldn't notice.' She leant forward and plucked the pencil from his hand. 'My baby and my friend could have been killed,' she said. 'I want to see your chief.'

'Suit yourself. I think you'll find the order came from him.' He reached forward and reclaimed the pencil with a grin. 'If I were you, love, I'd give it a rest. No one was harmed. Wasn't your cottage.'

'Why,' said Tina, 'would your chief bother himself with the

kind of fire that happens all the time? Is he close to a man called Wenders, by any chance? No, don't bother to answer. Why waste oxygen.'

Juliet was due to fly back to the States the day after that. Her children had already left for Los Angeles with the nanny, but she was going via New York to discuss a Broadway play with her agent and a producer. Tina, Ruby and Collette were booked to go out on Juliet's flight. They piled into Greg's car with Ratty and drove to the airport. They were travelling on the nine o'clock.

Their last night in England, Ratty was meant to be Collette's minder, but Collette took her out on the town instead. Ratty woke at dawn to find Collette taking the precaution of drinking the contents of her hotel mini bar in case she couldn't get anything at Heathrow. 'I'm a nervous flyer,' Collette protested. Ratty went to restrain her then thought better of it. Bram was staying at Janey's and it was the first night she'd had him off her hands since he was born. She loved the boy to bits but she was going to make the most of her one night of freedom 'A nervous flyer? So am I,' said Ratty, helping herself to a couple of miniatures.

'You aren't flying with us,' said Collette.

'Just the thought of it,' said Ratty, 'makes my heart beat like a hammer. Skol.'

Greg drove them out to Heathrow. When they reached the airport, Collette inclined sharply towards Tina all the way to the baggage check-in and then fell into a party of Japanese.

Juliet and Tina helped her up. 'A nervous flyer,' said Juliet to the Japanese with her sweetest smile. Juliet said, 'Come on, Collette, you're an Italia Conti girl. Pull yourself together.'

Collette swayed backwards into the check-in desk and then forward again like a tenpin that the bowl hadn't managed to knock down cleanly. She thrust out her hand to the Japanese, who shrank away, thinking she was about to hit someone.

'Get a wheelchair,' hissed Juliet at Greg. Tina turned to Ratty and started bollocking her for letting Collette go on the piss. Ratty suddenly lost her rag and grabbed Collette. She pushed her against the check-in counter and tried to throttle her. Tina pulled them apart. 'It's all right, Ratty, it's all right, don't worry about it.' Collette tried to shake hands with the Japanese again. Juliet held her back, saying, 'She's a nervous flyer.' Tina was revolving like a radar scanner. 'Greg! Greg!' she bawled.

Ruby in her sling woke up with a bellow. 'Oh, baby, baby, sorry, sorry,' said Tina, 'I didn't mean to wake you. Sorry, sorry, sweetie, mm, mm, sorry.' Juliet said discreetly, 'Everything's under control. He's gone to fetch a wheelchair.' At that moment there was a commotion by the ticket desk. Greg was waving his wallet and shouting at the clerk. 'What d'you want? American Express? Visa? Access? Debenham's? I'll pay £2,000.' Credit cards snowed to the floor. Collette went up and twined herself round him. The clerk said, 'The flight is *closed*, sir.'

Greg said, 'I don't care. I'm not leaving my fiancée. She's a nervous flyer.'

'Am I your fiancée?' asked Collette. 'When did that happen? Sorry, I don't, absolutely frightful memory.'

Greg said, 'I told them that because I thought it might help me get a ticket, but if you'd like to marry me, that would be very nice.'

'Tina,' called Collette, 'Ledbury, Delaware, you know, the divorce, me, is that all through?'

'Yes, my darling,' said Tina, 'your divorce from Delaney became absolute last month, if you remember.'

'There you are, then,' said Greg, 'Will you be my wife?'

'Oh yes,' breathed Collette. 'Absolutely.'

'Oh no,' said Tina, 'no Collette, there you go again.'

'What?'

'Doing silly things, marrying silly men.' She turned to Greg. 'Collette will think about it.'

'Greg isn't silly, and you're the last person to accuse anyone of silly men.'

'What?' said Tina. 'Tom? Silly?'

'No, no, not him, the other one, married one, you went around with him years and years, whoever, Roddy Handjob.'

'Greg is 23 years old,' shouted Tina. 'Eighteen years younger than you. I bet when he was seven he was playing pocket billiards watching us on Tuesday nights.'

Juliet looked at the audience who had gathered round, recognizing them despite their dark glasses and chiffon scarves, and said hurriedly, 'There's Tina for you, plenty of bawdy northern humour.'

'Pocket billiards,' said Collette, 'well, now he can have the real thing.'

Ratty said, 'Don't like to break up such a happy scene, but that was the last call for your flight.'

'Jesus!' said Tina. She grabbed Collette's left wrist, Juliet grabbed her right wrist and they pulled her along the walkway. Greg called, 'I'll come out as soon as I've got enough money.'

Collette had reached the departure gate. She turned. 'Darling,' she called back, 'darling, what's your surname?'

'Casdon,' he shouted.

'Mrs Casdon,' she said. 'I will be Mrs Gregory Casdon.' Electronic glass doors opened as they went through, and closed behind them.

Chapter Nineteen

Manchester Night Out

THE FIRST THING Pola did when she saw the TV studio in Manchester was cry, because she'd imagined a big white skyscraper full of indoor fountains and marble, and all it was was a dowdy aircraft hangar of a thing. To get to the dance floor the girls had to walk across yards of rucked-up dirty tarpaulins past flimsy partitions and discoloured scaffolding which hadn't been dusted thoroughly and Pola was wearing her Walkman so she didn't know how loud she was crying, and a young woman wearing a tight skirt and carrying a clipboard asked them please not to make a noise in the corridor.

They were in Manchester to record the North-West regional heat of Associated British TV's Dance Group of the Year contest. They were dancing as Bees Knees. Florence had entered them under this name as well as that of Sweet Fanny Addams, having suspected from the outset that deception would be necessary. Bees Knees were allegedly managed by a Mrs Charlene Bear of Macclesfield.

It was early August when they went up to Manchester. Janey was in charge. Florence was staying home, keeping out of the way of Betty Trout till after the heat. She said to Janey, 'If we win the heat I'll come out of hiding because by then we'll be in the final and there's nothing any of them can do about it.'

Janey knew they would win because she had done a nine-card spread and the final card was The World. Another aspect of the spread was rather unsettling – the Choice card which appeared to relate to her stewardship of the group – but she didn't want to think about that now. She stood outside the studio cafeteria and called Florence in London from the pay-phone. She said, 'This show is a fiasco. We've only just got into a dressing room because the maintenance man went home with the keys overnight. And inside it's not clean at all, full of dirty cups and bits of cotton wool left on the make-up table, and nobody seems to know what we're meant to do next, it just seems to be a lot of sitting and waiting while Betty Trout runs about bitching.' She lowered her voice. 'And as soon as she saw Ratty, Betty got such a *look* on her face, as though to say, "I've seen you somewhere before" and wouldn't stop staring, so Ratty's shut herself in the toilet.'

The competition took most of the day: there were six groups who each had to dance to three different tunes, and the programme was what Betty Trout called a new concept and she was flying it by the seat of her black Lycra pants. Late in the afternoon, Janey went to the cafeteria to pick up some food for the girls. As she stood watching the show on the monitor, a small bald man moved alongside. He helped himself to three chicken legs and said, 'Might as well get our money's worth.' Then he nodded at the monitor. 'What do you think of Fallen Angels?'

'Oh,' said Janey, 'are they anything to do with you?' There wasn't much she could say because Fallen Angels were probably going to finish bottom.

'I'm supposed to be taking them on tour in Australia,' he said. 'You look a bright girl. How am I going to get them sorted out?'

'Oh, excuse me,' said Janey, 'I think I see my friend waving to me.' She found Ratty at the phone, ringing the childminder to find out if Bram was all right. 'Cheeky bugger,' Janey said indignantly, 'wanting me to do his job for him free of charge.'

Ratty put three cocktail sausages in her mouth at once and looked over Janey's head. 'I'll say one thing for him,' she said, 'He's persistent.'

The man tapped Janey on the shoulder. 'Care to join me for dinner?' he said, giving her his card which said, Louis Winter, Artistes Management, Manchester.

Janey said, 'Going back to London tonight, sorry.'

'What time's your train? I'll book an early table.'

'Let me think about it,' said Janey.

Annie and Cindy said she ought to go, persuade him to take Sweet Fanny Addams to Australia instead of Fallen Angels. Ratty said she had to go in case the man was suicidally depressed and asking her to dinner had been a cry for help that if it went unheeded would end with him jumping out of a window at the Piccadilly Hotel. Pola said she shouldn't go because he might be a pervert. Manon said that they'd all follow her around like bodyguards and if he tried anything pervy they'd jump on him.

Janey decided to go because Bees Knees had won the heat and she felt like celebrating.

He took her to a really posh restaurant just behind the Britannia Hotel. The waiter came up and recited Today's Specials to them, which freaked Janey out because she couldn't remember what he'd said. She said, 'I'll have the fish, please,' because these places always had something fishy.

'*Meunière* or *bonne femme*?' said the waiter.

'The first one,' said Janey.

Louis Winter ordered a T-bone steak. 'What would you like to drink?' he said, handing her the wine list. Janey ran her finger down it. 'Have they got any Hirondelle?' she said.

Louis took the wine list back and said, 'They don't seem to, but I think you'll enjoy the '89 Mercurey.'

'Oh yes,' said Janey, 'I'm sure I will.' She wondered what he was after. She hoped it wasn't her body because he was nearly sixty probably, and his head was only one of the things about him which was shiny. He was wearing a black satin jacket embroidered in gold, and in his ear was a diamond stud, and then there were his nose and his horse's teeth.

'To the Bees Knees.' He raised his glass and Janey glimpsed the Bees Knees outside the restaurant, their noses pressed to the window.

After that he fell very quiet. About halfway through the main course he put his knife and fork down and said, 'Have you got a card?' As she hunted around in her bag, Janey noticed he'd gone completely white. He said, 'I'm having one of my migraines. I'll have to leave you to it, sorry,' and put £80 on the table. Then he walked out, knocking into the reception desk on his way. Janey shrieked after him, 'Where shall I send the change?' but he didn't seem to hear.

The girls rushed in and ate his steak and chips and then the bread rolls from the empty table alongside. 'But what did he say?' said Ratty when Janey couldn't tell them any more than they knew already. 'What did he *say*? But didn't he say anything before he went?' 'No, nothing,' said Janey helplessly.

They travelled back to London on the milk train. Janey had a double seat to herself, but she couldn't rest. She stared out of the window into the blackness. Her face looked back at her, the eyes that slanted upwards, her big snub nose, brown eyebrows and yellow fringe. A half-lit station whizzed by, some distant motorway beacons, a brilliantly lit garage with hard red petrol pumps. She thought of the strange meal with Louis Winter. She looked at his card, turning it over and over in her hand and rubbing it between her thumb and forefinger. She felt the stir and flutter of a feeling she couldn't identify, she didn't have a word for it, she hadn't seen it acted out on TV.

The train drew into Euston at ten to six in the morning. They walked in silence up the slope from the platform. Ratty, Manon and Pola set off home by taxi. Annie and Cindy were meant to be going flat-hunting, but they'd had a tiff about areas on the train and were standing three feet apart on the forecourt, not talking; not moving either. Janey didn't want to go home. She wandered up Euston Road till she got to Warren Street tube and took the Northern Line south to Florence's. The train was dirty and a quarter full and there were random lines of spray paint along the inside. By the time she turned into Florence's street, a weak sun was shining. Janey saw Florence jogging up the road towards her. She was wearing a grey hooded parka and black shorts, and kicking an empty crisp packet away from her. Her legs were brown. She hugged Janey and called her her clever, clever girl.

Janey had a shower and Florence made coffee.

'Go on,' said Florence, 'Describe it!'

'Well,' said Janey, 'it was . . . Don't know what it was, really.'

'Tell me about the lights, the set.'

Janey didn't respond. Florence listened to the sound of rushing water. 'What was the audience like?' she said. More water. 'When is it going out?'

Janey turned off the shower. 'Two weeks from today,' she said.

'But what else?'

'Oh, I don't know.'

'Well, there must be something,' said Florence, crestfallen. She crammed toast into her mouth. 'What did the other groups look like? Were there any girls from the Pepita Vasquez there?'

Janey said, 'It was nice being the boss.'

Florence paused, mug of coffee in her hand.

'Could I have more responsibility?' said Janey, emerging with a towel wrapped around her.

'Like how?'

'An idea I had, I could run Bees Knees for you as an offshoot of Sweet Fanny Addams. What do you think?'

'What?' screamed Florence. 'No, I think it's a terrible idea, how could you?'

'Oh,' said Janey. 'Well, I'm a bit tired of doing things for other people, really.'

Florence was so stunned she boiled the kettle again for no reason. 'Don't, don't – hold me to *ransom*, Janey.'

'I wouldn't do that.'

'Christ, I mean, I had no, no idea you – Aren't you happy?'

'Oh, yes,' Janey said. 'Probably.'

There was a silence, then Florence said, 'Greg's got Sweet Fanny Addams on the *Seven O'Clock Show*.'

'Oh, lovely. When does that start, then?'

Florence eyed Janey. She seemed perfectly serene but there was something about her, as though a door had been banged shut. 'December,' she said. 'Plus we're going to do the *Testing Testing* video.'

'Just fancy,' said Janey, 'Famous already. We don't really need to win Dance Group of the Year at all.'

'Yes we do,' snapped Florence.

Gus Wycherley took his feet off his desk as Betty Trout came in, but did not stand up. 'Ah, Betty,' he said. It was tea-time of the same day. Gus clasped a plastic cup as though trying to nurse its contents back to life. The curtains were drawn halfway across his window, shutting out the building work that was taking place underneath. Further off, the railway bridge was a black shape. Homegoing trains crossed over it, rattling tinnily. People with one-person suppers in string bags set off for the station out of the metal gates.

Betty was smoking a cigarette in a holder. 'Someone told me you wanted me to come in. What is it about? I'm working all the hours God made as it is, with the final coming up.'

'Sit down.'

'Oh. Well, if I must.'

'Great news!' Gus Wycherley said. 'Roger's given us the OK to do a second series.'

'Wonderful!' said Betty, clasping her hands. 'I've got some really exciting ideas already.'

Gus said, 'Ah. Yes. As you know, the budget has been one of our problems.' He got up and peered out of the window, through the gap in the curtains. They were made of some khaki-coloured fabric which sloughed off little bits of itself. 'But now that Hot Shots International has come in on it – '

'Who are Hot Shots International? I never negotiated with them.'

'Hot Shots, a New York-based film and TV company, now they have agreed to put up co-production money – '

'This is quite outrageous. I am the series producer. I am the one who arranges co-production. How do I know Hot Shots is suitable? I may not think so.'

'Betty, I know that you and I and Roger are all working for one thing, and that is the future of Dance Group of the Year.'

'Well, of course,' said Betty, 'and I'm very excited about getting co-production, but there must be no more lack of consultation.' She leant back in her chair slightly, crossed her left leg over her right, clasped her hands around her knee, and executed a short series of kicks. 'So. When do I get to meet Hot Shots?' She added roguishly, 'I expect at least a trip to New York out of all this, you know.'

Gus raised his hands above his head and advanced towards

her on tiptoe, lowering his voice. 'Look, I know you're going to bite my head off for this, but it's bad news, I'm afraid. We need a change of producer.'

'What?'

'We need a – '

'I *heard*.'

There was silence between them. Outside, the tea trolley rattled past the office and towards the lifts. Betty was completely motionless. Gus said, 'There was a feeling – '

'Why? Why change the producer?'

'Betty, you and I have been in this business long enough to know that a fresh face is, many, many, er, common practice – '

'Don't talk crap.'

Gus shouted, 'It didn't help that you let Florence Johnson in through the back door!'

'That Reed-Herbert bint,' said Betty calmly. 'I knew she'd be behind it.'

The 18th of August was Greg and Collette's wedding day in New York.

They were staying in a flat on Columbus Avenue which had been lent to them rent-free by Juliet, and were going to honeymoon in Tina's house in Sag Harbor. Tina stood behind Collette and looked at her reflection in the dressing-table mirror and said, 'I'm sorry I was mean about you getting married, because you look so beautiful and happy.' She was doing Collette's make-up for her and gently dusted cream powder across her browbone with a tortoiseshell-stemmed brush. 'Your skin is so perfect,' she said, 'what have you been using on it?'

'Oh,' said Collette, 'well, I've been cutting down.' She lowered her eyes. 'We thought we might have a baby.'

Greg from the door said, 'May I remind you ladies that our car is arriving in twenty minutes?'

Collette said, as though she wasn't conscious of Tina being there, 'Oh darling, whenever I look at you I'm looking at the father of my child.'

'Don't close your eyes,' said Tina, 'I can't draw a proper line.'

'Hundreds and hundreds of babies,' said Collette. 'Oceans and oceans of them.'

They were married in a room over Wes's bar, by a priest of the First Church of the Third Coming.

'Who is giving this lady away in marriage?'

Tina handed Ruby to Tom and stepped forward. She was wearing a white silk shirt, a tail coat and tight black trousers. There was an ebony Victorian pin fixing her neck tie. Collette was in a sheath dress of creamy yellow. She wore a pillbox hat with a little veil and carried a spray of mimosa. She had on something old in the form of the shoes Juliet had worn in *Only My Heart*, something new (her underwear), something borrowed (Tina's pearls), and something blue which was the antique engagement ring that had belonged to Greg's grandmother and had a sapphire set in silver that was almost as big as an airmail stamp. Rory, Aaron and Jason, Collette's children from her marriage to Delaney, wore velvet and tartan. Juliet was in something quiet though special from Ralph Lauren.

'You saved me,' Collette whispered to Greg. 'I would have died if it hadn't been for you. Not only the fire. You saved me from my life.'

The reception was downstairs in Wes's bar, and a big crowd had gathered to see them emerge into the sunlight afterwards. Juliet hung back. She did not want to hijack their wedding morning. By then, Tina had already slipped away in a yellow cab to visit her accountant. Now Legwork was established in New York, she was looking to diversify. She thought it was time she got into the film and television industry.

Chapter Twenty

Fallen Angel

JANEY AND MANON were coming out of the rehearsal room together when a man's voice shouted, 'Hoy!' behind them.

It was three o'clock on an afternoon in early October. There was a suggestion of mist in the air. These days the street lamps came on early, splashing the pavements with little circles of light the colour of goldfish. On the wall of the corner shop, a peeling notice left over from July asked whoever was looking to give a day's chocolate money to Sweet Charity.

There were only days left till the final of Dance Group of the Year, live from the Albert Hall. Rehearsal had just finished. Annie, Ratty, Cindy and Pola were still inside, getting showered. Florence was sitting at the trestle table, hands clasped in front of her, being interviewed by a young woman from a local newspaper. A photographer prowled around them with his camera raised away from him and his head at a funny angle, as though the camera were frightening, a bomb or something.

Florence recalled afterwards that the man and woman had very similar names, like Doris and Boris or something.

Janey and Manon were talking and when the man shouted 'Hoy!' they did not hear him at first. Only when he chased after them up the street did they respond to the noise of his pounding footsteps. Manon and Janey turned and found themselves face to face with Sir Roger Reed-Herbert.

Manon went white. 'Don't you ever listen to people?' she said. 'I told you, I don't want anything more to do with you. I came here to get away from you.'

Roger grabbed her wrist. 'Excuse us,' he said to Janey, 'this is a private matter.'

'It isn't private, it isn't anything at all,' said Manon. She stood her ground, in the street. There was something Joan of Arc-ish about her, hair burnished by the glow of the lamp: Joan of Arc defending her honour against a background of a dusty sweet-shop and a builder's skip.

'Darling, let's sit in my car down the road and we can talk about it there. Please. I've so much I want to say to you.'

'Fuck off,' said Manon.

Janey said to Roger, 'If you don't go away I'll call the police.'

Roger let go of Manon's wrist long enough to flick an imaginary speck of dust off his cuff. 'Do you know who I am?'

Janey said, 'I know what you are.'

Roger made a sort of spitting sound rather like, 'Tuh!', tossed his head in best Joanna-Mary style, and took hold of Manon's wrist again. 'Don't tell me to fuck off, darling,' he said to her. 'We've been through so much together.'

Florence, Ratty, Annie, Cindy and Pola came out of the rehearsal room with the local newspaper photographer, in time to hear Roger say, 'I love you, darling. I love you so very much.' He got down on his knees and put his arms round her legs. 'Don't make me go away. I can't go on without you. I've tried but it's impossible. I think about you all the time. I'm not ashamed of my love for you, darling. I'll shout it from the rooftops if you want. *I love you!*'

'Blimey,' said the photographer, raising his camera. 'There is a God.'

Janey said pleadingly, 'Oh, please don't – think of his wife.'

'That's his business, not mine.' The photographer kept snapping. You couldn't blame him, the tabloids would pay £50,000 for pictures like these.

'You walked out on me,' said Roger to Manon.

'I did not,' said Manon. 'Nothing to walk out on. You spun me a line when I was first in London and I was just sixteen and didn't know too much about anything, and I fell for it because you were famous on the telly.'

Roger said, 'How can you be so cold about it?' By this time

a number of passers-by had gathered. There was a pensioner carrying a bag of cat litter, and a woman with two young children who glared at Roger, side by side in their pushchair. 'Bite her leg,' one of the crowd shouted. 'That's Roger Reed-Herbert,' another said. Then one by one they all showed their diplomatic sympathy by launching into a chorus of 'Dirty old man.'

Manon sidefooted Roger gently in the chin as he knelt there. 'Get up, tosspot,' she said. 'This is one audience you don't want.'

Roger scrambled up and slapped her face. She put her hand to her cheek and stared at him for a long time. 'I'm sorry, darling,' he said in a contrite voice. 'I shouldn't have done that.'

'Too fucking right you shouldn't,' said Manon. She punched him between the eyes with a well-coordinated right hook. Roger Reed-Herbert staggered back against the skip. It was filled with bricks, chairs and an old television set which the photographer tried to get framing his face but couldn't. You can't have everything.

A light was glowing above the doors of St Alphege's. It was the back-street entrance, opposite a shop where you could buy men's shirts hand made in striped silk, and one that sold Persian carpets. The doors were painted black and beginning to peel after the hot summer. On the left was the St Alphege Drop-In and Cafe. There were still people in there, pushing heavy cake around plates with a fork, though it was five o'clock, close to closing time. As Roger pushed open the church doors, some looked round. He gave them a warm smile, though not a long one.

Voices rose from the main body of the church, bouncing off the white walls. Roger stepped across the cold flagstones of the foyer and stood in the wide arched entrance that led into the church, looking in. There was a pair of double doors, made of glass. Beyond them the altar was covered in cloth of gold. Above it were some bits and bobs of carved wood and then a large embroidery of the sun in a somewhat stylized design, like an airline logo. Standing at the altar were Joanna-Mary and Nicholas. It was their wedding rehearsal. They were to be married on Friday. Vallie was sitting on a front pew, her arm over the back.

The best man was one of Nicholas's rugby team. There were four bridesmaids and two pages, the children of some women Joanna-Mary had once been to school with. Joanna-Mary was wearing a blurred cream coat of long fake fur.

Roger's breath misted up the glass of the doors. He touched his nose where Manon had punched it. It wasn't bleeding any more but it felt tender and a raw bruise was forming on the bridge. He brushed the mist off the glass. Vallie thought he was waving. 'Here we are, darling,' she called, walking towards him on low safe heels. 'About blinking time, too.'

Roger said, 'Sorry, darling. I got away as fast as I could.'

'Huh,' said Vallie to the vicar. 'Don't you believe him. Wedded to the job.' She held her arm out to Roger. 'Come on, stinker,' she said affectionately. Roger took her arm and followed her up the aisle. The rehearsal of Joanna-Mary's wedding continued.

Florence took Manon to the Victorian pub down the road. It had just opened for the evening and the floor was clean. Florence loved Victorian pubs in England, at this time of day especially. A wood fire began to spring up in the grate under the grey marble surround. It was so quiet you could hear the twigs crackle. The bar-top was glossy and dry, with six neat rows of shining glasses in one corner. The pub was across the road from the station and the glasses clinked softly every time a train rumbled in. Behind the bar, a girl with a Russian face sat on a high stool, waiting to pour the first drink of the evening from a big green bottle of red wine, the kind that showed purple if you held it up to the light, and was guaranteed lead-free. Everything was warm and quiet, and solid and dark with wood. An English pub with a fire burning in an empty room while outside cars hooted and people shouted at each other as if what they were doing mattered – it was the best feeling.

Manon asked for a double vodka.

'That photographer – will he sell the photos?'

Florence said, 'Unless he's very stupid or some kind of saint.'

There was a silence. Florence sipped her drink. The fire was sending off showers of sparks from a damp hissing piece of wood. Manon said, 'I was crazy about him at first. After the audition, when he took us all out to dinner. I'd never been anywhere like that.'

'Maybe it was just the dinner and the Savoy you were crazy about.'

'No. I can't explain it, but there was something much more. Not just ordinary getting the hots for someone. It was, well, like I had to have him, like water or food, something you die if you can't have. All my life I'd felt kind of . . . not completed. And being with him would make me complete.'

'Did it?'

'Yeah, for a bit. Then I just saw sense, I suppose. The age thing, and him being married and Joanna-Mary's dad, and always, always wanting me to have sex with him. You don't end up complete in that kind of relationship, you end up in a nuthouse.'

Florence didn't say anything. She listened to the sound of the fire. It was peaceful in there. No mobile phones. No one picking cricket teams. And the quiet desperation of a young woman whose life was in the process of being ruined.

'I didn't do it with him.' Manon thought about it for a bit. 'I'm a liar. I did it once.' She stared into her glass. 'I'm a worse liar than I thought. Three times. Three times and they were all horrible. No bells ringing or waves crashing or anything. He went on and on about it for so long, and I was feeling really down and lonely and wishing I'd never come to London, and he sort of pounced. Here, Florence – ' Manon looked round and then she whispered. 'It was disgusting. I mean, he knew all the buttons to twiddle and press. That seemed to make him even more disgusting in a way. Doing it with someone who'd had all the girls in the world and probably had his own face in the mirror every morning too. Then he started going round the twist over it all. Saying he was going to leave his wife and marry me, and he couldn't live without me, and all the crap he came out with today. I just wish men like that could be stopped.' She paused, pushing her glass away. 'I don't know what to say to you. You've worked so hard for us, you've put everything into the group and been a real mate to me, and I've gone and got into this. Plastered all over the papers. Roger Reed-Herbert's bit of skirt.'

'Look, stop hating yourself. You didn't ask him to be such a prize fool. Stop hating, stop blaming, stop thinking of it.'

'Do yourself a favour, Florence. Stop being so bloody supportive. You don't want me dancing in the group on Saturday. And afterwards, when we've got all those – '

'I don't know where you got that impression. Not from me. If you can face it, if you can bring yourself to go out there in front of the cameras, in front of a live audience, I want you to go out there.' She picked up her things. Then she put her hand on Manon's arm. 'Don't tell anyone else he screwed you,' she said. 'It never happened. Not even once. You looked on him as a father figure and anything else he says is simply the raving of a mad old lech.'

As they left, the pub was beginning to fill up. No one watched Manon go out. She was just an ordinary young woman in jeans and a fake fur coat, if someone that pretty could be called ordinary. Florence ached for her. It would be the last chance she had to walk anywhere unrecognized for a long time.

Janey let herself into her flat. It smelt of damp and talcum powder. She lit the gas fire in the living room. There was a film of talc on the hearthrug where she dried herself in the warm after a bath.

The phone rang. It was Louis Winter from his office in Manchester. She had been expecting him to call. 'Have you come to a decision yet?' he asked.

'This is the worst time in the world I could tell her,' said Janey. She saw him in her mind's eye, in his little cluttered office with the photos of rock stars and pictures to do with winter on the walls. There would be phones ringing and faxes buzzing, and noisy blonde girls bringing him coffee. She said, 'We've got so much on at the moment. She depends on me.'

'We don't go to Australia till the end of next month. But I need to know, so I could look for someone else if necessary.' He paused. 'I want you to make Fallen Angels a class act like Sweet

Fanny Addams. When I saw you with Bees Knees in Manchester I knew you were the girl to do it.'

'I owe Florence everything,' said Janey, 'that's the problem.'

Louis Winter said curtly, 'OK. Well. Have a nice life, as the saying goes.'

'Ooh,' said Janey. 'No, don't ring off.'

Roger took the wedding party to dinner at the little restaurant off Kensington Church Street. 'Must have a pee,' he said, darting downstairs to the phone. 'Hello,' he said. 'I must see you.'

Edmund Timpson was at a preview in an art gallery. He was using his mobile phone. 'I have to go to Annabel's after this,' he said.

'A malicious hatchet job is about to break,' Roger said. 'I want to give my side of the story. It must go in the paper tomorrow.'

'There are too many spies around here,' said Timpson. 'I'll be at the *Pictorial* in half an hour. Meet me there.'

Roger returned to the wedding party. 'Something's cropped up at the studio,' he said. 'I'll have to go round and sort it out. Carry on and do excuse me.'

Vallie said, 'Oh darling, when are you going to stop running around for these flipping people? It's terribly stressful.'

He stood behind her seat, resting his hands briefly on her shoulders. She was wearing a dress of some kind of synthetic material. It felt slimy underneath his hands. 'Sorry, darling,' he said.

'Oh, go on, have a heart attack. See if I care.'

The next morning, Janey went to see Florence at her flat. The attic rooms were full of angles and shadows. There was coconut matting on the floor. 'Coffee?' said Florence. She reached for the cigarettes, looked at her watch, thought better of it and put the packet back. 'Well. What's brought you round?'

Janey said, 'Florence, I've come to a decision. I'm leaving.'

'Oh,' said Florence, slowly. She put her coffee on the table and looked at Janey. 'When?'

'End of next month.' Janey paused, then said, 'Don't kill me,

Florence. It's the chance of a lifetime. I've got to take it. Louis Winter wants me to lead a group. He's going to put us on the Killer Chrysanthemum video and we'll be dancing with them on their Australian tour. We're going to open in Sydney.' She could hear music playing softly in the flat below. The St Matthew Passion rose through the old floorboards. All the blood seemed to have gone from Florence's face. It was the colour of rope. Janey said, 'Florence, don't hate me, I've been waiting so long for something like this to come along, to prove to everyone I'm worth something, not just dopey old Janey.'

Florence got the cigarettes out after all. 'Been quite a twenty-four hours, what with Manon.' She lit one and drew on it. 'Ah. A slight improvement. The world's stopped pretending to imitate the inside of a washing machine. So. How long's this been going on?'

'Louis Winter approached me in Manchester,' said Janey. 'He'd put together Fallen Angels for the competition.'

'The terrible group who finished last,' said Florence.

'I can make them into something.'

Florence was still very pale. She said, 'It's going to be difficult without you, Janey. It's going to take a long time to get used to you not being there.'

Janey said, 'Hard for me too.'

Florence said, 'Always easier for the one who's leaving.'

'Well,' said Janey, 'but it isn't yet. We've got some time left together.'

Florence said, 'No we haven't.'

'Pardon?'

'Go on, Janey. Go now.'

'*Florence –* '

'I don't want you dancing for us any more. You've committed yourself to Fallen Angels. You're with them now.'

'You don't think I'd do anything but my best for you, do you?'

'I don't think anything. Except if you're going, it's best you go now, so you don't have to worry about what we're doing, and worry about what they're doing, and go for bookings with us that you'd rather go for with them, and wonder if you should say this and that in front of us or in front of them, and all that shit.' Florence stubbed her cigarette out halfway through and stood up. 'Go *on*, Janey. That's it. Off you go.'

She came down the stairs with Janey and opened the front door for her. Janey stood, looking out. She said, 'When I came here this morning it looked like the sun was trying to shine.'

Florence said, 'Still is.'

'Yeah, but when something's happened to change your life for ever, you expect it to be different. Great craters in the street, the sun turning black, that kind of thing.' She stood for a moment longer, her back to Florence, and then she was gone.

Chapter Twenty-one

A Misrepresentation

THE NEXT DAY the *Pictorial* published Edmund Timpson's interview with Sir Roger and Lady Vallie Reed-Herbert, and the *London Age* came out with Boris's pictures of Roger and Manon, and Doris's recording of the proceedings, which had been beefed up by staff writers at the newspaper, though heaven knows they were beefy enough without that. The *London Age* had been intending to hold them over till Sunday but had been alerted to the *Pictorial*'s plans by a small, dark-haired young woman in their personnel department who was the *London Age*'s spy.

Vallie did not quite understand what was happening. When Roger told her what was required of her it was rather late at night. She remembered receiving the news in the bedroom, Roger telling her to get dressed and come downstairs where Edmund Timpson was waiting with a photographer. The outfit she was to wear at Joanna-Mary's wedding was hanging on the outside of the wardrobe, billowing every now and then. 'Nothing happened,' Roger said to her. 'I have been misrepresented.'

'Whatever shall we do?' said Vallie. 'We'll have to cancel the wedding.'

'Of course not. No one will believe the *London Age* story. Our guests are all people like us, potential victims of the gutter press. We are going to carry on as if nothing had happened. Nothing *has* happened.'

Edmund Timpson's article said: "WE LOVE EACH OTHER AND THAT'S ALL THAT MATTERS. A defiant Vallie Reed-Herbert fought back her tears last night and said, 'We have been through worse times than this and each time our marriage has come out stronger than ever.' "

'Nothing happened,' said Roger to Joanna-Mary. To the father and mother of Nicholas Wenders, he said, 'I've been the victim of a smear, Billy. Can I count on you not to spoil the young people's day?' He felt a sudden stab of terror. Billy Wenders was worth a million pounds times ten. Roger had only a vague idea how he made it but Wenders's house was staffed by some odd-looking buggers. They had broken noses and bulges one side of their jackets. There was no reason to expect violence but these were strange times. There were people with cameras and note-books outside his house, fighting with other people with cameras and notebooks. Beyond them, in the lane outside the driveway, a young man waited in a flash car which had pink furry dice dangling from the rear-view mirror. The young man looked up as Roger's face appeared in the window. Roger moved back hurriedly but not before he had seen the young man take a pair of scissors and snip the furry dice off.

At eleven-thirty, two white Rolls-Royces arrived and the wed-ding party set off for St Alphege's, followed by the cars of the reporters and photographers and the young man. 'Nothing happened,' repeated Roger to Joanna-Mary in the back of the leading Rolls. She was looking at her veiled face in the rear-view mirror. Her wedding dress was of cream shantung with a train of embroidered and beaded voile. Over the bodice was a black leather harness.

'Are you nervous, Daddy?' said Joanna-Mary.

'Petrified.'

'Your speech isn't to go on and on,' said Joanna-Mary. 'Every-one will be much more interested in getting drunk than listening to you boring on.'

'How nicely you put it,' said Roger. He thought of her lov-ingly, luxuriatingly, how she restored his soul.

'And you're not to tell any dirty jokes,' said Joanna-Mary waggishly. 'They only embarrass the guests.'

The white Rolls-Royce circled the one-way system and drew up outside the entrance to the church of St Alphege. The vicar was waiting to greet them. Joanna-Mary got out of the car in a swirl of rustling cream, and went in on the arm of her father to be married.

It was lunchtime. Over the other side of the river, Annie and Cindy, who lived together in the badlands of North London, were fooling around putting up pictures when Cindy fell off the stepladder and broke one of the small bones in her foot.

Around the same time, Rory Cromarty took a call from a woman identifying herself as Fidelma Cole.

Her voice had a whispering, rasping quality. She was ringing from seaside Essex. Cromarty heard her out. Her story had already been heard by his acolytes and he knew enough about what she had to tell to make him order the office Bentley. It was waiting for him outside the front entrance next to the statue, an abstract representation of Truth. The driver opened the door for him, and he sat down and helped himself to peanuts from a cabinet behind the front seat. He switched on the television for the lunchtime news, then sat back with his shoulders resting against the hide upholstery, in his pocket a £50,000 cheque made out to Fidelma Cole.

Annie phoned up Florence's flat to tell Florence about Cindy, and Florence put the phone down and spent the next two minutes running around and slamming doors and shouting every variation on damnation and the devil she could imagine.

'Something wrong?' said Ratty. She was sitting on a big cream cushion on the coconut matting floor. Pola had taken Manon home to her place to hide out from the press. Florence said, 'Oh, it's nothing, just the end of the world.'

'You'll have to dance in Cindy's place,' Ratty said when she had finished telling.

'I can't! How can I do that with my leg? So many routines, so much dancing, give me a new leg, I'll dance!'

'Your trouble,' said Ratty, 'your trouble, if you'll forgive me, is you give up too easily. If you had a faith – '

Florence made a fist and said, 'Ratty, if you dare say anything with Jesus in it I'll put this in your face.'

'Jesus is – '

'If you want the truth, Ratty, you and Jesus give me the willies.'

Ratty uncoiled herself from the cushion. 'Right,' she said. 'If that's your attitude.'

Florence said, 'Sit down, Ratty. It's been a long week.'

'No way am I going to sit down. If you got on your hands and knees and begged me I wouldn't sit down.'

'Oh, away you go then,' said Florence, who was beginning to feel awfully weary. 'The show's off anyway.'

'I could dance you off the floor any time I wanted to.'

'I never said you couldn't, Ratty. Away you go.'

'Right.'

Ratty went out down the stairs and slammed the front door. Florence grabbed a bottle of Juliénas and crossed over into the kitchen for the biggest tumbler she could find. She filled it to the top.

There was a bang on the door. Florence went downstairs and opened it. Ratty was standing in the porch. 'Bollocks,' she said and walked away again.

Florence went back upstairs and drank the tumbler of Juliénas as fast as she could and stood to attention against the wall while the wine set fire to her insides and did various things to her brain. This time last week everything had seemed reasonably simple. She was a successful choreographer employing six happy dancers. It hadn't been long since this time last week – only about a quarter of a century.

She went back into the sitting room. Somebody else seemed to be in charge of her legs, somebody who insisted on moving them out of time with the rest of her body. She swigged down some more Juliénas, direct from the bottle this time. There didn't seem much point going to all the bother of pouring it into the tumbler. She flopped on to the sofa, but had to sit up again because the room had started to rotate and the windows were on the ceiling. She must have gone on to finish the bottle because the next time she looked it was empty. She let it topple on to the coconut matting. Nothing else happened after that, or if it did, her mind wasn't around to register it.

*

Joanna-Mary stood next to Nicholas at the top of the staircase, greeting the wedding guests. She held a glass of champagne in one hand. Her wedding band was of platinum. Nicholas had one to match, though larger. Behind them lilies fountained out of a white vase. They were on the first floor of a large London hotel. The ballroom floor stretched out shinily. At the far end, a 22-piece orchestra was playing selections from *Aspects of Love*. 'Lovely to see you,' Joanna-Mary was telling a fat woman known for some reason to Vallie. She was wearing magenta and a hat like a Big Mac.

'What a dreadful thing for your father on today of all days,' said the fat woman, who prided herself on speaking her mind.

'What thing?' said Joanna-Mary mystified. Her face cleared. 'Oh, that — we didn't see it.'

Vallie was talking to a large sandy-haired man who had become rich through selling carpets. '. . . honeymoon at the end of the month,' she was saying. 'Couldn't miss the Dance Group of the Year final on Saturday. She's strongly tipped to win. Critics raved about her first appearance. The camera loves her. Just like the flipping old man.'

The man with sandy hair leant forward to take a salted almond and lowered his voice. 'Heard about it. Terrible for Roger. Do something about these people.'

'Oh, you get used to it,' said Vallie. 'In our position. We never read these things.'

Roger stepped on to the balcony. It had been glassed over, like a conservatory. The floor was tiled in white and black. Everywhere were vases of lilies, and empty wicker chairs. Beyond the glass, London was going about its business, unaware that a man in his fifties watched it from a first-floor room, in morning dress. For a few seconds a shift took place in Roger's perception of the world. He saw a city out of control, a place of insane, frantic, meaningless energy, men digging holes in roads, pavements cracking, people trying to drive cars up narrow alleyways.

He was brought back to normal consciousness by the noise of someone moving around behind him. A young man in the white coat and black trousers of a waiter stood with a silver salver. The man's face was slightly familiar. With a quick smile Roger reached out for a drink. He realized there were no drinks there. At that moment, the man raised the salver above his head rather in the manner of the Wimbledon Ladies' Champion, and brought it down on Roger who, stepping backwards to protect himself, fell over one of the wicker chairs. Ray leapt on him. 'You old bastard,' he shouted, his arms windmilling. 'You dirty old bastard.' He had been following Manon for some weeks, but had lately switched to Roger. Hotel staff and male guests ran on to the balcony and rescued Roger, though not before Ray managed to kick him several times in the balls.

Florence dreamed she was lying on the pale brown sand of the Gironde beaches. She was fourteen again and wearing a silky bikini with a pattern of red fish, and Joe was walking towards her from the sea, smoking a cigarette from a blue packet. The clock on the church tower was chiming the hour, except that when it came to twelve it did not stop. Thirteen o'clock. Fourteen o'clock. Twenty. Forty-one. Over the ringing, Florence heard herself groan. The sun was glaring directly into her eyes. She woke up. It was not the sun, but the street lamp outside her living-room window. The doorbell was ringing.

She got herself into a standing position and that was not an easy thing to do. She walked down the stairs towards the front door, wondering if her visitor would notice the automatic hammer drill going flat out on top of her head.

It was Curtis. 'Help yourself to a drink,' she said.

'You already have, by the look of you.'

She shoved her head under the shower, not bothering to take her shirt off. 'It's finished,' she said. 'I'm done in. No more dancing. I'm going to take an interior design course. I think I'll head for the Lake District and open a shop selling stencilling kits and amusing knick-knacks.'

He sat back in the armchair. 'Lily Smith was ringing for you,' he said.

'When?'

'Most of the day, by the sound of my answer machine. The phone was going when I got home from the office.'

Florence checked the number he gave her. She remembered it

from whenever it was. A couple of years back when she was young and untroubled and Lily was the best dancer in the country. Or something.

He held his arm out. 'Come over here,' he said.

She sat next to him on the sofa. He'd been walking in the rain. His hair was damp. It was always fluffy. He smelt of man, that indescribable smell of jackets and shoes and whisky and a warm male body. Something inside her lurched like a ship in a big wave. He murmured something, a little noise of need and desire in the back of his throat, and pulled her face round to his and kissed her. They made love slowly and gently, though not too gently.

Afterwards, he went and found a blanket from her bed and wrapped her in it. Her clothes were lying on the floor by her feet. She didn't even remember taking them off.

'You'll have to marry me now,' he said. But when she laughed, he said, 'Well, I suppose I meant it.'

'I don't know if I feel like being serious right now.'

'Think about it.'

'Well, I can't marry you,' she said solemnly. 'You're Jewish.'

'I'll have a foreskin transplant.' He tucked the blanket under her shoulder where it had slipped off. She remembered how he'd do that in the days when she lived with him and Millie. Tucking her into bed like a child.

'You're not joking, are you,' she said. She felt odd, shaky. There was a reality to what was going on between the two of them right there. Something might stem from this, her life might change again. She looked into his eyes. 'Curtis, I don't know, I mean I do know, there's a lot between us but I don't think it'd work.'

'How do you know?' he said angrily. 'How come you're so up on what does and doesn't work?'

Florence said, 'Sorry. I was just being smart.' She got up with the blanket still wrapped round her and crossed the room for her cigarettes. She leant on the desk and slowly got one out of the pack and lit it, studying him. He was sitting on the edge of the seat, elbows rested on his knees. She thought a lot of him. He was probably the best man she'd ever know. He was decent and kind and tough and unafraid and honest and generous. A real man. He would provide for her and protect her if she needed it, but he would also let her be what she wanted. He would play no games. They could have good dinners at Mon Plaisir on weekday nights, and a circle of arty friends. In July and August they'd go to their *gîte* in the Dordogne and throw pebbles into the cool rushing rivers round Mussidan. Her life would be very easy.

'We could give it a try.' His arm out to her again.

'Mm.' As she looked across at him, she felt an overwhelming need to join him, almost as if someone were shoving her between the shoulder blades. Maybe Millie was doing it. She forced herself to turn and pick up the phone. 'Hello, Lily. This is Florence. I hear you were looking for me.'

Lily Smith said, 'Florence, I just wanted you to know first, I'm thinking of leaving Joanna-Mary.'

Florence said, 'Well, hell.'

'If I'd known when I was starting out with her,' said Lily, 'what I was going to have to go through I'd have quit along with Manon. The group's just desperate. It's just totally phoney and silly and it's going to fuck my career up if I don't go somewhere else soon.'

Florence imagined her in the tiny council flat bedroom, discarded clothes spread over the bed. In the background, a man coughed. Probably a doctor. She always went for doctors, tired young doctors with their handy little prescription pads. She thought of Lily with a gin glass in her hand, popping another amphetamine into her mouth and washing it down. Lily. Radio Lily.

Lily said, 'So . . .'

'I might be interested,' said Florence, 'and then again I might not.'

'Great,' said Lily. 'I'll trot round and talk to you at the show.'

'You can't. We won't be there.'

Lily made a sort of O-*ho* noise.

'Is that why you're ringing?' said Florence. 'Does Joanna-Mary want you to find out what's going on? Because I don't give a damn about the final. We're pulling out. She can be Dance Group of the Year, Miss Beautiful Eyes, whatever she wants.'

Lily said, 'No need to lose your rag.' She giggled. 'You would have wasted your time anyway, turning up.'

'Oh,' said Florence slowly. 'I'm not quite sure of your meaning, Lily.'

'Oh, come on, Florence. You're not dumb.'

'I must be, because all I can think you mean is, well, it isn't thinkable.'

'Honestly, Florence, you are a romantic. Your group could never win.' When Florence didn't speak, she said, 'Joanna-Mary's more or less the exec. producer of Dance Group of the Year. Her old man green-lit the whole project for her. I can't believe you never guessed that.'

Florence would never be able to decide afterwards why Lily told her. Spite, maybe. A need to appear in the know. Maybe she might even be trying to please. She'd given up long ago trying to fathom out what was in Lily's head. A torn copy of *The Complete Works of Shakespeare*. A list of all-night chemists in the Central London area. Some of those cocktail sticks in the shape of coloured parasols.

Curtis must have seen her face as she put the phone down. 'I'm just going round to Ratty's,' she said.

He said, 'You never give in, do you? It's not finished, is it? I know you. Whatever's happened, whatever's been said, it's enough to make you drag yourself and everyone else off the floor. The show must go on. Three cheers for the show. A V-sign for everyone else.'

'Curtis, don't give up on me.'

'I'll wait around and you'll come back, and then there will be something else, and away you'll go again. Who are you? What are you looking for? Why can't you rest, why won't you settle for being happy and having someone love you?'

Florence said, 'I suppose I'm not the happy endings type. There's nothing else to do afterwards. The ending's been and gone and that's it. The rest is just small talk. Shall I take your coat? Would you like cream in your coffee?' She was putting her clothes on, putting her make-up on at the mirror as she spoke, putting it on like warpaint.

'Anyway,' she said, 'It's hard work being happy all the time. I don't want to go off into the sunset with a film star. Collette's done that. Wasn't much of a happy ending for her. I never dreamed of being shut in the chocolate factory, either. I like being on my own and wandering round the city getting lost and lost till I'm not lost any more. I like bomb sites and ugly buildings and bars that haven't been cleaned for thirty years. I like London when it's raining in the afternoon and all the lights go on in the office blocks. I like wondering where I'm going to be this time next year and who I'm going to know. I hope one of them's going to be you, Curtis, though I'll understand if you want to take your name off the list.'

Then she kissed him and headed off to Ratty's to tell her to come back. They weren't pulling out of the show after all. They were turning up. She didn't know what they were going to do when they did turn up, but that was what they were going to do.

Chapter Twenty-two

Girls Just Want To . . .

THERE WAS A man sitting in a silver Ford Fiesta on the far side of the street in Acton where Pola lived. He had a brown suede bomber jacket, a pack of tuna sandwiches and a mobile phone. He watched as the door of Pola's house opened. Manon came out in a hurry. The man punched out a number. 'She's coming down the street,' he said as Manon turned up the collar of her linen jacket and stepped out in the fog and dark.

Rory Cromarty's driver threw his phone on to Rory Cromarty's lap and swung the Bentley into Pola's street. 'Open your window,' he ordered Fidelma, who was in the back seat in her newest stonewashed denim and white stilettos.

'*Please*,' said Fidelma. 'Whatever happened to Please?' She hunted around. 'You haven't got a fucking handle.'

Rory said from the front passenger seat, 'I think you'll find there is a button in the arm-rest.'

'Oh,' said Fidelma, fascinated. 'I've never seen anything like that before.'

Rory said, 'When the car stops, call out to her and we'll do the rest.'

'Now, Rory,' said Fidelma, 'you're not going to be rough with my baby, are you?' She leant out of the open window and said, 'Pst, Manon.'

Manor turned and her face went white. 'Mum? What are you doing here? Has something happened to Dad?'

'Something, yes,' said Fidelma, 'but I don't want to speak about it in the street, Manon.' She swung the door open.

Manon took in the Bentley, the driver, and the fat man sitting next to him. The driver got out. She said to him, 'I'm not getting in there.' He shoved her and Fidelma pulled her into the back and sat on her. The car moved off. It turned on to the dual carriageway and started heading out of town.

'Here,' spluttered Manon disbelievingly, 'I've got to get back. What about the final?'

Fidelma said, 'There are some things more important than the final, Manon. Your reputation.' Manon started to yell, so Fidelma put her hand over her mouth. 'I have reason to believe,' said Fidelma, 'that you are in moral danger. These kind people are removing you for your own safety.'

Manon found the button that operated the window and pressed it with her foot because both her arms were in use trying to push her mother off her. 'Close that window,' Rory muttered to the driver. Manon shouted, 'Air! I got to have air or I'm going to throw up.'

Rory looked round. 'Let her sit up,' he said.

'Who's that?' Manon said to Fidelma.

'Oh, just a friend of mine,'

'How much are they paying you?' said Manon.

'Money doesn't come into things like this,' said Fidelma. She reached into her bag and brought out a 20-pack of Benson and Hedges. 'Go on, baby, have a fag.'

'No thanks,' said Manon.

Fidelma lit one and waved her hand to blow away the smoke. Rory leant forward and turned on the air conditioning. Manon sat miserably in silence for a while, wondering what her best bet was. She looked out of the window for landmarks. The fog was getting worse, swirling in wisps along the carriageway. Rear lights of other vehicles appeared suddenly in front of them out of the blackness. The car sped on. Manon craned her neck to see the dashboard. They were doing ninety miles an hour. 'Dad,' said Manon. 'You said something about Dad.'

'Not as such.'

'Is he all right or isn't he?'

'You've no need to worry yourself about that.' Fidelma glanced at her and took her hand. 'Manon, tell your mum,' whispered Fidelma, 'have you *been* with him?'

'Who?'

'You know. Roger Reed-Herbert. Have you romped with him and that?'

Manon said, 'Mind your own business, Mum.'

'I have to know. Cos if you have . . .'

'Shit!' The driver banged his foot on the brakes. The back of a lorry loomed out of the fog in front of them. Swerving, the Bentley clipped the lorry's wing then ploughed across two lanes and up a bank where it came to a jolting halt.

Rory said, 'Reverse it and get going.'

The driver opened the door and looked out. 'Offside tyre's gone,' he said. 'Have to change the wheel.'

'I absolutely forbid you to do anything of the sort in this fog. Drive on slowly to the nearest service station.'

'Tyre isn't flat. It's completely torn off.' The driver went round the back to open up the boot.

Cromarty sighed and opened a picnic hamper. 'Quiche, anyone?' he said, rustling and unwrapping.

'Ta,' said Manon. She leant forward, took the plate out of his hand and shoved it in his face. While he was spitting out bits of parma ham and asparagus, she back-kicked Fidelma in the chin and was out of the driver's door and running before the driver had a chance to see where she had gone.

'Manon! Stop!' shouted Fidelma, jumping out. She gathered breath and bellowed, 'Roger Reed-Herbert is your *father*!' There was a silence, except for the muffled sound of traffic in the fog.

Florence was sleeping when the doorbell rang again. She pushed the bedclothes back and looked at her watch. Just past three o'clock. What was going on? Had she slept through nearly twenty hours? She went to the window. Outside it was dark and nothing in the street, no cars going past, nobody walking. Down below her window, in the doorway, she caught the movement of a shoulder, a sleeve, the top of heads, Ratty and Pola.

Florence opened the door in her dressing gown. 'What's the matter with me, sleeping such a lovely morning away?' she said. 'Tch-tch, three-fifteen.'

Ratty pushed Pola in and slammed the door behind the two of them. 'Never mind that,' she said. 'Where's she hiding?'

'Who?'

'Who do you think?' Ratty was opening all the cupboards. Pola said, 'She's a big girl, Ratty, you're not going to find her in the bathroom cabinet.'

'You've lost Manon,' said Florence.

Ratty flung herself on to the sofa and threw her shoe at the wall. 'Bastorial cocksuckers!' she shouted.

'She said she was mad all day in one room,' Pola explained to Florence, 'and she was going for a walk. That's the last we saw of her.'

Florence sat down with her forearms resting on her thighs. None of them said anything. Ratty curled up on the sofa and shut her eyes, then Pola went into the bedroom and flopped on the bed and after a while Florence lay down next to her and went to sleep.

At half-past six, Pola woke her up.

'The phone,' said Pola. 'Ringing.'

Florence said, 'That'll be Annie, calling to say she's broken her back.'

Ratty answered the phone. She listened and called to Florence. 'It's the operator,' she said. 'Will you accept a call from a Watford call-box?'

Florence snatched the receiver. 'Yes,' she almost yelled, 'I will, I do.'

It was close to eight-thirty when she and Ratty drove into Watford. Manon was sitting on a bollard outside a multi-storey car park on the ring road. Ratty leant over from the back seat and opened the passenger door. 'How'd you get here?' she said, 'if it isn't a crime to ask.'

'Hitched,' said Manon. She got in and said, 'Christ, I'm knackered,' then burst into tears.

Florence crawled round Watford till she saw the lights of a parade in front of them. She parked at a Happy Shopper and came out with a packet of Jaffa cakes and some cans of Irn-Bru to wash them down. They sat in a lay-by. The air smelt of wet leaves. Florence looked at the time. In less than thirty-four hours the final was going to begin. She hoped Annie was remembering to pick up the costumes from the dry cleaner. Her eyes strayed to Manon next to her and she gave a little moan. 'Oh God,' she said, 'I can't stand it any longer, you've got to tell us what happened.'

Manon opened an Irn-Bru and told them while Florence drove along the motorway murmuring 'Bloody hell' from time to time. When she had finished, she started crying again and said, 'I can't believe that bastard's my father. He's not, he's not. He didn't walk me to school and work overtime so I could have the right things. My dad did that.'

Ratty said, 'You always said your dad was a stupid old tosspot.'

'I never,' wept Manon, 'He's the best dad in the world.'

'For Christ's sake, Ratty,' said Florence, 'you've set her off again.'

Ratty said, 'As far as I am concerned, there is too much joking with the name of Jesus around here.'

'Joking?' said Florence. 'I'm *crying*, all because Roger Reed-Herbert can't keep his trousers on.'

The road ahead was beige with fog. Ratty said, 'Plenty of other ways you can say, For you-know's sake. Pete. Goodness. Heaven if you must.'

'Shut up,' said Florence. 'I've got to think.' Something was beginning to form in her mind. She wasn't going to dignify it by calling it an idea, but it was better than nothing.

Florence was glad she had lived to be twenty-five just to see the look on Rory Cromarty's face when she brought Manon into his office.

Halfway back to London, Manon had fallen asleep in the car. Florence said to Ratty, 'That scene outside the rehearsal room, Roger and Manon, the pictures, what was going on. It could all be passed off.'

'Tell me some more,' said Ratty.

'There's this man, OK? Rich and powerful now, but he's got a tragic secret, a daughter living in poverty somewhere.'

'I can't bear it,' said Ratty, 'it's making me so sad I can't speak.'

Florence said, 'So he tries to come back into the girl's life. But she's hurt and shocked and doesn't want to know. So he runs around after her, begging her to accept and acknowledge him. Still means Roger's had a bit of unsanctioned nookie along the line, but so long ago, and didn't everybody in those days? Well, that's pretty rough, but you get the general picture.'

'You couldn't have him dying of cancer too, could you?' said Ratty. 'That always goes down well.'

'It would,' said Florence, 'save Manon's reputation, as Greg might put it.'

Ratty said, 'It would also save Roger Reed-Herbert's reputation, that's no plus.'

'Isn't that a price worth paying, though?' Florence said. 'For Manon to be able to walk down a street and not be pointed at, and not dread the ringing of the phone, and not be sniggered at, and not have people say, "You know what she did, don't you?" '

While she and Ratty had been talking, Manon had opened her eyes and had been sitting there, silently listening. Florence glanced at her and broke off.

Ratty said to her, 'Did you hear what Florence said?'

'Yeah.' Her expression was blank.

Florence said, 'Is that all right? It's all a lot of fuss about nothing? There's no scandal? Well, a bit of scandal, maybe. But nothing to harm you.'

'Or Roger,' said Ratty.

Florence tightened her grip on the steering wheel and said, 'That's enough, Ratty, you've got to bear in mind Roger *is* her father.'

'Yeah,' said Manon. 'Too true.'

An hour later they were walking into Rory Cromarty's office and seeing the look on his face. It was like an inflatable fun castle in which someone had just detonated a bomb. Florence said, 'Good morning, Rory. Are you able to claim whitewash on expenses?'

He didn't seem to be able to speak, so Manon said, 'Sorry about the quiche.'

'Sit down,' Florence said to her. 'Make yourself comfortable.' She moved around Rory's office, opening a window, emptying crisps and nuts into bowls and putting them down in front of Manon. There was some nice fresh fruit in the fridge so she gave her that as well. All the time she was doing that, she talked over her shoulder to Rory, and when she had finished she said to him, 'Manon will have to be photographed with Roger, Vallie and Joanna-Mary as soon as we can arrange it. You'd better send him a fax telling him everything, because all his telephones will be off the hook.'

'Florence,' he said, 'dearie, I've waited years for my revenge on Roger Reed-Herbert and now to be told I can't have it – no, no, it's quite unbearable.'

'Please,' said Florence. 'You've still got an exclusive.'

'If you don't mind my saying so, it's not quite the same.'

'All right,' said Florence, 'I'll give you my *car*.'

He cranked himself up out of the chair and went to stare out of the window. 'Buzz off, dearie,' he said. 'I've refrained from saying this to you before, but you're a very tiresome girl who can't bear to be thwarted. I won't rewrite my copy to suit you, let alone that mini-harridan over there.' Florence watched as he glanced at Manon and actually flicked an imaginary piece of fluff off his sleeve, or perhaps it was a crumb of quiche.

Florence said, 'You kidnapped Manon. You and your newspaper and Manon's mother. That's a really shitty way to go about things. Millie always told me you were a nice person.'

'Don't bring Millie into this, for God's sake.'

'Everything I've done, I've done for Millie, and now you're going to wreck it all, just because you're in a snit. Jesus, if only all I'd had thrown over me in life was a bit of food.'

She didn't know what it was she'd said that got to Rory, but something had, because suddenly he started talking in a silly falsetto soap opera voice and she knew it was going to be all right. 'That,' he fluted, 'is emotional blackmail.'

'I know,' said Florence. 'Tomorrow I'm really going to sit down and work hard to rid myself of the tendency.'

Vallie shuffled into the bedroom. Her slippers made a rubbing sound on the carpet. She hadn't bothered to take her make-up off since the wedding and grey eyeshadow had lodged in various ruts and hollows. 'Fax for you,' she muttered.

Roger Reed-Herbert stared at the document from Rory Cromarty. Fidelma? He'd shagged so many girls in those days that it seemed entirely likely. Felicity, Daniella, Gloria, Ann, Anne, Suzy, Dympna, yes, he did seem to remember a Fidelma in some shape or form. The dates tallied. He recalled some sort of fuss in 1973, and having to take Vallie on a camping holiday afterwards.

He picked up the phone and got through to Rory Cromarty on his direct line.

It was the day of the final.

The plane from New York was beginning its descent over London. Greg looked out of the window, but all he could see was cloud. The plane gave a little jolt and there was a Ting! sound as the FASTEN SEAT BELTS sign came on. 'Are you all buckled in?' he said to Collette. Tina and the baby were riding in first class. Tina had wanted to pay for Collette and Greg to be upgraded, but Greg was on his dignity. They were sitting in the tail end behind a scrawny, restless woman who for the whole journey had had her hands clenched on the arm-rests. Collette had tried to comfort her. 'I'm a nervous flyer, too,' she volunteered. 'Try not to drink, it'll only make you feel worse.' She caught Greg looking at her with pride. She had said nothing about it but giving up drink had taken all her will. She was doing it for their baby who, who knew, might have been conceived on any of the seven nights of the past week. Collette thought of those nights, with his fingers tracing over her flesh as though reading her by Braille. He was so beautiful, such a pretty young man, so slim. When she put her long hands either side of his waist she was for some reason reminded of her mother arranging long-stemmed flowers in a vase. Her own waist and belly were marred, or so she thought, by little pearly stretch marks. She was self-conscious about them at first, trying to hide herself under the sheet till Greg realized and told her over and over that he loved every single line. Greg, oh Greg, she thought. So much ruder as a lover than old Delaney, who did it as though in front of a camera and lighting man. Then, as if in response to a command of 'Cut!' he would jump off her and start primping. Whereas Greg, Greg, well, if he got his pleasure before she did, he would . . . Collette gave an involuntary moan which she disguised as a throat-clearing session. Misinterpreting her, Greg held tight to her hand. 'It's all right, it's all right, I'm here, you've got me.' 'I have, haven't I,' Collette murmured low, and the plane went on its way into the London rain.

Manon spoke to Fidelma over the phone from Rory Cromarty's Kensington flat where she was hiding out. 'Hello, Mum,' she said in a hard little voice.

Fidelma was being put up in a London hotel at the *London Age*'s expense. She had a minder, the man who had staked out Pola's house in the Ford Fiesta. She sent him out of the room and whispered indignantly down the phone, 'He could have been your father. I was very popular at the time. At one time I was never home any night of the week.'

Manon told Rory to go out of the room as well, and said, 'But was he?'

'Oh, I don't know,' said Fidelma. 'It was all so long ago. I just thought it might make us a few bob towards a house of our own. Your dad's never going to get anywhere at the biscuit factory.'

'But did you . . .'

'Might have done. He was one of the regulars at the bar where I worked. Although . . . Here, not that I'm denying anything, but the dates never seemed quite right.'

'Mum,' said Manon, 'I've got to know.'

'All right, babe.' Fidelma sighed. 'No, it was most likely Brendan who ran the bar. He didn't want to know and I was in a bit of a spot. But your dad always liked me and he was very decent about it.' She paused. 'You going to say anything to them?'

'Bit late now,' said Manon bitterly. 'It's in the papers.'

'I'd go along with it if I was you, babe. Can't do your career any harm, people thinking you're his kid. Look how well he's done by that Joanna-Mary. You want to keep him sweet.'

Florence drove round the Albert Hall to see what was happening. The Associated British TV scanners were already parked outside. Men with headphones on their ears and reindeer on their woollies moved around the dark auditorium like the duller forms of marine life. A couple of young guys and a woman were leaning against the wall by the stage door. The woman was in her late twenties, a thin glossy blonde. They looked up as she drove by, recognized her and started to give chase. Press, thought Florence. She accelerated away and swung the car down through Fulham towards Wandsworth Bridge, then edged home in the Saturday shopping traffic. The post was lying on the mat inside her front door. She inspected a long white envelope. It looked official. She boiled the kettle for coffee, put bread in to toast, poured herself orange juice, closed the fridge door with her bottom and tore the letter open. It was from a firm of solicitors, informing her that her divorce from Cal Johnson was now absolute. She reread it. For a moment she had to remember who this Cal Johnson was, that she had had cause to divorce him in the first place.

The doorbell rang. Florence shoved the letter in a drawer and went to answer it. Janey was standing there in a pair of pink leggings and a big woollen jersey with green hearts and yellow crosses and grape zig-zags and ochre strips on an old rose background. Her eyes were round and anxious. She didn't seem to know how to begin, so Florence said, 'Fabulous. It must be a French Connection.'

Janey got her wits about her and said, 'Florence, you aren't to say anything. I've read the papers and I've been on the phone to Annie. I'm going to dance for Bees Knees tonight and if Louis doesn't like it and if you don't like it, that's too bad.'

Florence flung herself out of the door, put her arms round Janey and almost hugged her to death. 'Janey,' she said, 'the times in the last two days I've wanted to pick up a phone and say I was sorry and beg you to come back.'

They climbed up the stairs to Florence's flat. 'Annie's on her way round,' said Janey, 'and I phoned up Ratty. She's had a call from Manon and she's going to pick Manon up at the *London Age* then go round for Pola and they'll be here soon after lunch. Oh,' Janey added, 'you were right. It *is* a French Connection.'

They put some music on and Florence took Janey through the last-minute change she'd made in their third routine, which they were doing to Tina Turner's 'Private Dancer'. Annie arrived with the costumes, then Ratty, Pola and Manon, and Manon's two minders from the *London Age*. Ratty made them wait in the street. They had tea and played some music. Near half-past four, a taxi drew up outside and Florence went to the window to see Greg get out and open the door for Collette, Tina and Ruby.

'We have come,' said Tina gravely, 'to see justice done.'

They travelled to the Albert Hall in a convoy. 'I always like this time best of all, ' said Ratty, 'just before you're going to go out there.'

'You all right?' said Janey to Manon.

Manon said, 'All I want to do is sleep.'

'How many other groups are in the final?' asked Pola.

'If you'd listened,' said Ratty, 'instead of keeping your head inside that Walkman, you'd have known that.'

'Eight,' said Janey.

The driver took them round to the back of the Albert Hall, to the stage door. A whole crowd of reporters and photographers was waiting now, but Manon was out of the cab and running so fast she bumped into the two uniformed doormen.

The dressing rooms were warm and smelt of talcum powder. There was a group from Birmingham, wearing floppy hats and shrieking at each other with the door ajar. The group from Belfast hurried past, chattering and giggling. The West Country girls were sitting in a little huddle, hands around their knees. Someone had a radio on. Music floated down the corridor, a rasping female voice belting out a heavy ballad.

Annie was too small for the mirror. She got her suitcase and stood on it and frizzed out her red hair. Ratty hung her costumes on a wall hook and stood beside them with her arms folded, upright like an ironing board. Manon stretched out on a line of hard chairs and went to sleep with her minders at the door. Collette, Greg and Tina had to squeeze past them to get in.

'Have you seen the set?' asked Florence. 'What's it like?' She had pins in her mouth and was kneeling on the floor, making last minute adjustments to Pola's costume for the first routine, which according to the rules of the contest had to be 'nostalgic'. They were dancing to an early eighties number by the Human League, 'Don't You Want Me,' which had a good thumping beat and lines about being a waitress in a cocktail bar which lent themselves very well to costumes.

Collette flapped her hands. 'Hundreds and hundreds of yards of curtains at the back, ghastly loo-roll pink, and a big bunch of balls hanging down over the stage. Turn purple every so often, frightful sight.' She sat on the edge of one of the chairs occupied by Manon and patted her back. 'Speaking of purple balls,' she said, 'Is this the poor bunny who's got Roddy Handjob for her father as well as her lover?'

'Collette,' said Tina sharply.

'What?'

Tina made a little opening and closing gesture with her hand. Collette said, 'Oh, sorry. Always talking too much these days. Terrible problem knowing what to do with my mouth now I don't drink.' She caught Greg's eye, went bright red and emitted a series of low mirthful honks and snorts.

'Ten minutes,' said the call-boy from the door.

Florence went outside and stood in the corridor leading to the stage. She listened to the buzz of the audience for a while and hoped in a rather detached way that they would not go home disappointed. When she turned away, Joanna-Mary was coming towards her. Joanna-Mary waved and smiled at someone beyond her. The waving and smiling almost took her past, then at the last moment she glanced at Florence and gave a quick nod of her head, as though Florence was someone she'd come across at some time or another, maybe at a party or an audition or something, but it wasn't an encounter that had lingered in her memory.

Florence went to the big ante-room backstage where tables had been set out for the groups to view the show on TV monitors. A young waiter with tight trousers brought her a coffee which she was too keyed up to drink. Bees Knees were fifth down the order of dancing. She knew she ought to go back to them, but lingered first to watch the compère introduce the judges. There was a comedian who was currently starring in an Associated British sitcom and also advertized instant coffee and insurance; a senior international footballer who had his own sports quiz on Associated British; a rock star whose show went out on Associated British on Friday evenings. As each judge was introduced, a fashion designer, a hairdresser, a businesswoman, a ballad singer, Florence's eyebrows began to knit together and by the end she was almost shaking with anger and disillusionment for almost all of these people had some connection with Associated British, and she knew, she absolutely *knew*.

Oh, she thought to herself, they wouldn't be bent, exactly. No one would actually have told them what to do. A lunch here, a little squeeze of the arm from Roger there, a wink and a smile from Joanna-Mary, tickets for Wimbledon, days at Royal Ascot, contracts, guarantees of work and patronage, kickbacks, kickbacks, kickbacks, so when it came to awarding the points (ten for their favourite down to two for their least favourite) they would Um and Er and consider everyone impartially and award their points and Heavenly Bodies would creep ahead, but not too far ahead, just enough, by the time the last judge gave her score, to make Heavenly Bodies the winners.

Florence went back to the dressing room and said nothing. Pola was in a panic about her lip brush. Florence took it from the shelf behind the washbasin and said, 'Is this it?' Ratty looked at her and said, 'What's got into you?'

'Nothing.'

'You seen who the judges are?'

'Yep.'

'Think they've been told about us?'

'Oh,' said Florence, 'I couldn't say.' She opened the door. 'Janey,' she said, 'you take charge for now. I'm going to look at the opposition.'

She returned to the ante-room and watched the first act, Step Out Sister from Birmingham. She felt dazed. Girls went on stage and danced, the music stopped, they went off stage. Another act went on. The Big Why from Southampton. The music started, they danced.

Florence felt movement behind her. Tina and the baby were at her shoulder. Ruby was chomping on a large pink dummy which almost concealed her cheeks and chin. She had Tina's knowing brown eyes and was already developing a certain grandeur of hairdo. Tina murmured, 'None of these groups can get near us. Under normal circumstances, we'd walk it.'

'These aren't normal circumstances,' said Florence.

Tina said, 'Don't get too pissed off. This isn't where it ends.'

'No,' said Florence, 'it isn't. All my life, that girl is going to go on making a fool out of me.'

'We need to meet,' said Tina, 'and talk. After tonight.'

Florence, only half listening, put her hand on Tina's wrist and said, 'This is us.'

Janey, Annie and Ratty were lined up as if at the counter of a cocktail bar. Janey was wearing her Marilyn Monroe look, Annie was a football supporter and Ratty was a Sloane Ranger. They were all dressed in black and white so the tiniest touch of colour was like a firework going off – Janey's red shoes, Annie's green hat, Ratty's blue jewels. The opening notes of the song started and Pola danced on dressed as a waitress and carrying an invisible tray. Manon in pin-striped trousers and bow tie sprang on from the other end. They were meant to be a girl and a boy who had once been lovers, but Pola had gone on to find fame and fortune and left Manon behind. Florence knew every single movement of the dance, every single breath the girls had to take. Her fists clenched at the smallest misalignment, the least hesitation, things that only she could see. As they danced, she tried to convince herself that winning didn't matter, what counted was what they were doing out there on stage, that everyone could see that Bees Knees were far and away the best.

She turned away and went back to the dressing room to be there waiting for them.

The evening wore on. When it was time for the judging, the groups sat in the ante-room. Every so often a camera would be turned on them so the judges, the presenter, the commentator, the viewers could watch the dancers watching them. It was during one of these moments that Joanna-Mary came across to the table where Bees Knees listened to the scoring and knelt down by Manon's seat.

Joanna-Mary was all smiles and her hair was falling over her forehead. Manon was, perhaps, less effusive, but she grinned back. On televisions across the country, the commentator's voice was emollient and respectful. 'Rather a touching scene here. Joanna-Mary Reed-Herbert and Manon Cole, chatting together and very much enjoying it. Half-sisters united after all these years thanks to the efforts of their families.'

Joanna-Mary said to Manon, 'Could you um, um, possibly bear to do some sort of interview with the presenter when all this is finished? Frightful drag, I know, but the viewers would love it and it wouldn't take long.'

Manon looked at her. They weren't really alike, and yet they were. Their hair was the same. It was long and it fell over their faces in the same way. Their cheekbones, their tallness. Yes, they could pass for sisters. 'All right,' she said. 'I'll do it.'

Joanna bunched her fists and screwed up her eyes. 'Good,' she said, with pleasure. She grasped Manon's upper arm, gave her a click of encouragement and went back to her seat. She was not there for long; Heavenly Bodies were announced as the winner and she had to get up with the rest of the group to receive her award.

Bees Knees were placed sixth.

Ratty was all set to sort the judges out then and there but Florence grabbed her and sat her down again. She comforted Annie, who was crying her eyes out, and removed Pola's earphones. The music sounded out on the Formica-topped table. It was only playing softly but to Florence it was as loud as having a concert orchestra play in your living room.

'What's happened?' said Pola.

Florence didn't answer. She was putting the Walkman over her ears.

'The Cocteau Twins,' said Pola. 'Head over Heels.'

Ratty was saying, 'Come on, come on, let's jump on them.'

The Cocteau Twins. The Cocteau Twins. Where – ? The –

Florence put the Walkman down again and they walked out

to stand in the wings, and from there they walked on stage with the rest of the losers.

'And now,' said the compère, 'ladies and gentlemen, a very special moment.' He was an elderly man with a toupee and teeth like an armadillo's. The band began playing a tune appropriately sentimental in nature. Two leering blondes with big busts guided Manon and Joanna-Mary towards him. He probably wasn't intelligent enough to find them by himself. The balls turned purple, then the lights dimmed except for one spotlight.

'Once upon a time,' intoned the compère, 'there was a little girl called Joanna-Mary who lived in a great big house with her mummy and daddy. Her daddy wasn't quite a king, but he was doing very nicely for himself, thank you. Roger was his name and Roger was what he did, by the sound of it, ha-ha. No, seriously, ladies and gentleman. Far away by the sea, there was another little girl called Manon . . .' He went on in this vein for some minutes longer than was humane. Eventually, he turned to Joanna-Mary.

'And so,' he said. 'Sisters.'

'I'm – ' Joanna-Mary tossed back her hair. 'Flabbergasted,' she said, 'but it's wonderful. Exciting. I can't put it into words.'

'And how did you feel when your father told you about your little sister?'

'It was very brave of him,' said Joanna-Mary. 'He could have swept it all under the carpet, being a well-known public figure. But he thought he was doing the right thing and that carried him through, even when he was terribly, terribly misunderstood.'

'There was some rather naughty gossip in the papers.'

'He knew there would be. He was unable to deny it until he had the consent of everyone involved, of course.' She gave a little flashing smile and said, 'He thought he was doing the right thing and that carried him through, even when he was terribly misunderstood.'

The compère turned to Manon and said, 'Manon. That's an unusual name, isn't it?'

Manon said to Joanna-Mary, 'You mean he knew all along he was my father?'

'Yes, yes, of course,' said Joanna-Mary. 'All right?'

'Wait a minute,' said Manon. 'You mean when he first met me and he spent the next six months trying to get me into bed, he knew he was my father?'

'Of course he did not try to get you into bed,' said Joanna-Mary. 'You must have misunderstood him.'

'He took off all his clothes and got his dong out and tried to stick it up my fanny,' said Manon. 'There's not much room for misunderstanding there, I wouldn't have thought.'

Here Associated British should, perhaps, have replaced the broadcast with a picture of the fjords at sunrise, followed by an old Burt Reynolds movie, but they did not. Across the nation, Joanna-Mary was observed losing control of herself. She jumped so high her legs were round Manon's waist and she got hold of Manon's ears and tried to wrestle her head off her neck. Ratty paused on the sidelines, then launched a pincer movement with her elbows although there was no need; Manon was well able to take care of herself. She put the palm of her hand under Joanna-Mary's chin and pushed it back as far as she could. Other people on the stage joined in, to stop the fight, or enter it, the leering blondes screaming, the compère pedalling backwards, fearing for his toupee. At last Associated British pulled the plugs and the screen went dead. Soon there was music playing, and a picture of lobster-pots on a Cornish beach.

Long before that happened, Florence was gone. Quietly she returned backstage and wandered through the deserted ante-room with uneaten food on the tables. No one was there, not even a tight-trousered waiter sweeping up.

She took one last look at the TV monitor. It was just before they put the lobster-pots on. She saw Manon's face. She had never seen anyone who was having so much fun in her life.

The lights were off at Millie's house. Florence stood in the shelter of the porch, looking out over the city. The moon was high and it was a clear late autumn night. The centre of London lay in shadow across the river, lights winking. She could make out dark dramatic shapes that in daylight would be buildings merely, places where London people worked, laughed, hated, drank, cried, worshipped. She loved this city where Millie had brought her to live and make her mark. The drone of a late plane heading for a runway, a train drawing up at a station, full of people going home, two girls with their arms linked, shrieking at private jokes. A man sleeping where he sat, with a notice round his neck that says WAKE ME UP WHEN WE GET TO BRIGHTON.

She loved these streets of Victorian houses with their faded stonework round the front doors, and gardens full of may trees and bluebells and cats. At nights the darkness and quietness closed round them and lights would shine from hallways through coloured glass, on to white front doors hung round with bushy creepers and rambling roses.

Florence walked up the road. She found Curtis at the pub overlooking the common. The Last Orders man had long since shut up. She felt a sort of energy building up in her, like a car with the accelerator pushed to the floor. There was no time for Hello, What will you have, You'll like this joke. She said, 'What did Millie think about Joe Daniel?'

Curtis had long since given up trying to work her out in his mind. He said, 'Millie thought about Joe Daniel that she didn't like him. She didn't want him in our house. I brought him to the house once on account of he was a potential client of Plantagenet's and they seemed to get on right enough. Couple of weeks later, she said, Joe Daniel – ugh! Well,' said Curtis, 'maybe not in those words, but you get the picture.'

'Thank you, Curtis,' said Florence. 'You've solved a mystery for me.' She patted his arm and turned away.

'Where are you going?' he said.

'I'll be travelling for a while.'

'Are you coming back?'

'Expect so. Some time.' She was struggling to put on a pair of black wool gloves. She crossed the quiet room without looking back. A man held open the door for her.

Chapter Twenty-three

The Fool

AFTER FLORENCE WALKED out of the pub, she went back to her flat, posted letters to Curtis, Tina and Janey, then got into the Peugeot and drove through the night to Folkestone.

There was a ferry leaving at eight o'clock. She hung about on the quayside, watching the winter sun come up. The marina was full of little ships banging against each other as the wind moved the water. Over the road was a high-sided hotel the colour of unwashed sheets.

The ferryboat took her over the green heaving water. It was mid-morning in Boulogne. The air smelled of Boulogne; nowhere else had that combination of fish and diesel. She drove the car up the main street past shops selling carpets faded by the long-departed summer sun, and restaurants even the English didn't like to eat at. The cobbled square was quiet, a few cars parked round the church, a narrow grey van with the doors open and an aproned man backing out of it with four crabs in a wooden crate.

She'd been on the road a short time when she remembered she hadn't eaten. She stopped at a small place the other side of Abbeville and a tall old man in navy served her a baton spread with brie. She asked him for two glasses of red wine and he brought them to her table, which had a real marble top with a metal rim. She ate the bread and drank one glass of wine and left the other for Millie.

Rouen, Brionne, Bernay, Gacé, Sées, Alençon. Florence knew that Roger Reed-Herbert was never the father of Millie's baby, the timing was all wrong, she had known that since the day of

317

Millie's funeral, worked it out, took a few seconds. She'd probably known the father was Joe all along. Just didn't want to acknowledge it to herself. But when she heard that music again, the Cocteau Twins. That had been the music playing in Millie's car the day they drove up to Hull, Millie in such a strange mood, not saying much, and her so excited and wanting to tell Millie everything and not knowing where to begin, how to.

She could imagine how it all started. Millie wanting a baby for so long, wanting not to injure Curtis or make him feel small, wanting an adventure maybe. Wouldn't be the first adventure she'd had; Millie and Curtis had been together for eighteen years, bound to get a bit restless. Look at Curtis with her.

Millie thinks she could maybe get something going with Roger, old times, a secret to be enjoyed with him for ever after, but it doesn't happen. Then one day she's in Geronimo's where the footballers come and she sees Joe with his golden-brown skin and dark eyes. Probably goes up to him; when it comes to sex, she's not shy. Probably says, 'I suppose a fuck's out of the question.'

Starts casually, a baby's what she wants, not a love affair. But you know what these things are like, you can't control them like a space invaders' game. He makes her pregnant, she falls in love with this golden man who's given her what she wanted. She plans to run away with him, her plans run away with her. She's out of her mind with love and pregnancy; and him, he's just kind of swept along, by this beautiful passionate older woman who's carrying his child, he who's without any flesh and blood in the world.

One afternoon he's waiting for her in Geronimo's and the past comes up and hits him between the eyes. Florence. He can't help himself, and now he's committed on both sides. And the next day one of them's dead and the other's in hospital, turns out they're friends; he can't handle it, he runs. Well. Something like that. That'll do to be going along with.

Beaumont, Le Mans, La Flèche, Angers. Florence thought back to it now, the day they set off to drive to Hull. Leaving London behind them, the sun out, the road brown and flat as you come out of the north-west side of the city. 'Millie,' she said, 'Millie, are you listening.' You know I told you about that boy when I was fourteen, she said. You know, Yusuf. Well. You'll never believe this, but. I've found him again, Millie. I've found Yusuf. His name's Joe Daniel.'

Something was happening, Millie white as though she was frozen over, then starting to try to turn the car round. In the middle of the road. Three-lane motorway and she was setting out to turn the car round, drive back down it to London, from what Florence could see. That's what the driver behind them saw, the one who told police there were these two women fighting. He saw Millie trying to turn the car round, and Florence in desperation trying to stop her. What the fuck are you doing, getting us both killed?

Florence would never be completely sure what it was made Millie do it, except there was that letter Curtis said she had left for him. Saying she was going, propped up where he'd find it in the hall. Millie was going back for the letter, Florence was sure of it. She was going to go back and get that letter, tear it up. Live the rest of her life with Curtis and the baby, no one any the wiser. Say nothing to Florence. Let Florence have Joe. Didn't know what she was doing, except she was going to turn the car around and save everyone, and instead she sent herself to wherever it was you go to. Oblivion, an eternity of something or other, a lasting peace.

It was early evening when Florence drove into Nantes. She took the car in a circle round the football club a couple of times. It was shut for the night. She booked in at the Hôtel Terminus, thin and old and nine floors high, on the edge of a whole terrace of thin, old, tall hotels. The flyover was 25 yards distant, and in the lift was a metal sign in English which said, 'Please Don't Press the Red Buttom!' She took a walk into the town centre and ate steak *frîtes* at a restaurant with plate-glass windows and a sign advertizing Jupiler beer.

The next morning there was a motor coach parked outside the club doors. By the front wheel was a pile of kitbags. Young men with heavy thighs walking around in blazers looked formal and old-fashioned. Florence asked the coach driver. He said they were going to the airport, then Lazio, Italy, a European game, they were playing in the European Cup-winners' Cup.

Just then Joe came along. He stopped when he saw Florence, not sure whether to run or hold his ground. She said, 'It's OK, I know about Millie, it's all right, it doesn't matter.'

He walked with her away from the coach so they could talk. They had five minutes together. She said, 'I'm going to go back to Paris now. Here's my address. I'll wait there for you for four weeks. After that, the offer's closed.'

'I'll see you in Paris,' he said, and then he walked back to the motor coach to go to the airport.

When Janey reached the hospital, Tina was already there. She was sitting outside reading *The Times* in a great black limousine. There was a man in the back seat. He wore a dark grey suit and emerald silk tie.

The hospital was a private one in St John's Wood, far away from the road behind a high wall and bare trees. As Janey walked up the drive, Tina lowered the newspaper to her lap and slowly lifted her head. For a moment Janey saw a vision of the Death card, the skull in the hood, the grim carriage drawing up on the rocks. Then Tina got out of the car, quite lazily, letting the door swing closed behind her. The man in the grey suit got out too. 'This is Richard,' said Tina, 'my lawyer.' Richard carried a documents case in soft black leather. He followed Tina and Janey into the hospital.

'I've got a copy of Betty Trout's signed statement,' said Tina. 'I thought Joanna-Mary ought to see it.'

'She won't,' said Janey. 'She'll refuse.'

'Then,' said Tina, 'one of us will read it out to her.'

It was the Wednesday after the final of Dance Group of the Year.

Joanna-Mary's mistake was to rush out of the Albert Hall alone. She had not even bothered to change out of her costume. She had screamed at everyone who looked her way for twenty minutes, thrown the cut-glass prize against the wall and gone. She left by a fire door at the back. It was dark as hell out there. She hurried through the dimmest parts of the car park where no one could see who she was and then veered away when she saw the press waiting to catch her by her Mercedes. There was a gateway in a far wall, left open for the television scanners. She passed through it at a run. Soon she realized someone was running behind her. A voice said in phoney Italian, 'I told you Paolo would get you.' She turned and saw a small man with a knife in each hand, one of which he fumbled and dropped. With the other he tore her face to shreds in a windmilling adrenalin rush that took him beyond the moment of realization that though this girl was tall with white-blonde hair, she was not Manon.

When Tina heard about it, she was almost deflected from her course out of pity, but not quite. Now she and Janey filed into the hospital room and stood there quietly while the lawyer settled discreetly in a chair by the door. 'Hello, Joanna-Mary,' Janey said. She had wondered whether to bring flowers, but decided it might seem facetious.

Joanna-Mary turned her face towards them. It was a crazy blotched patchwork of swellings and darning. She said, 'Go away. I'm tired.'

'We'll be as quick as we can,' said Tina. She reminded herself that this woman had all but murdered Ruby, and her body began to hum and throb with anger. Janey said, 'Betty Trout has told us all about Dance Group of the Year, how it was fixed for you to win and so forth.'

'She's a liar. She's just sore because she was pulled off the production.'

'There are also a number of documents and letters,' murmured Tina, 'which Betty took the precaution of photocopying before she left the programme. They go right back to the beginning of Jonic Productions. My lawyer has them here if you'd like to validate them.'

Joanna-Mary said, 'If Betty's so pissed off, let her go public. Let's see what happens to her then.'

Even to the end, Tina could not help marvelling at Joanna-Mary's ruthlessness and cheek. She said, 'Betty doesn't want this to be made public because she's still working for Associated British and she doesn't want to make trouble, either for herself or for the company.'

'Well, that's you finished then, isn't it? As for Betty, I'll see she isn't working for Associated British any longer, as of today's date.'

'Joanna-Mary,' said Tina, 'I have *bought* Associated British.'

Janey wondered if Joanna-Mary had understood, because there was absolutely no reaction from her at all.

'As you may know,' said Tina, 'I have been looking to diversify into film and television for some time, and when I heard that Hot Shots was co-producing various Associated British ventures, of which Dance Group of the Year was soon to be one, I thought, "This is the company for me!" ' She smiled. Her eyes bored into Joanna-Mary's face. 'Following which, in for a penny, in for a pound, who dares wins and all that – I went for a majority shareholding in Associated British and got it.' She paused. 'A piece of luck for us. The price of shares had dropped very steeply owing to those embarrassing revelations about, er, the Controller's private life, so we picked the company up at quite a fair price. What fun it was to walk through those doors at the Centre and not be stopped by anybody's secretary.' She paused again, then looked down at her hands for a moment. 'I . . . think of your parents as old friends, Joanna-Mary, and I hope I can arrange something that means your father's career isn't entirely destroyed, even if his professional, er, standing will never be the same.'

Janey saw Joanna-Mary's eyes beginning to close and said quickly, 'All we want you to do is sign a statement saying that you *did* cheat Florence out of Sweet Fanny Addams and that Heavenly Bodies are forfeiting the title of Dance Group of the Year.'

Joanna-Mary whispered, 'For God's sake, I'm never going to be able to appear in front of a camera again, isn't that enough for you?'

'No,' said Tina. 'You will also give us your letter of resignation from the production team of Dance Group of the Year.'

'But nobody knows I was *on* the production – '

Tina said, 'I will keep that confidential, as a condition of your future good behaviour.'

Afterwards Janey shuddered as she recalled Joanna-Mary's

closing outburst, her rucked skin red with fury, her eyes slits of pain and humiliation. 'What have I done to deserve this?' she wept, 'What have I ever done to you? *Ever?*' and then, in a last pleading whisper, 'How can you be so unkind to me . . . after all I've been through . . . so *unkind?*'

Janey left Tina with her lawyer, sorting out the papers in the back of the great black limousine, and went home to Shepherd's Bush to pack for her trip to Australia.

Tina met Florence for Sunday lunch in Paris, at the Brasserie Flo.

Florence arrived there early to get a table. She found one for four behind the waiters' station. Plates clattered, trays banged on marble tops, corks popped. There was a babbling queue stretching all the way from the waiters' station to the doors and out into the street. Florence wore a long brown coat with fur round the neck and wrists. She had dark brown lace-up ankle boots and a velvet hat with a narrow brim and wide grosgrain band. Underneath was a brown and cream flowered frock. She watched Tina and Tom push their way past the queue carrying Ruby in her carrycot above their heads. An elderly woman in musquash stuck her face into Tina's, wagged her finger and said, 'Pas de bébés,' to which Tina replied, 'Pas de arseholes.' Tom sat down next to her with the baby in his arms and Tina sat opposite with the carrycot. Tina turned her dark majestic gaze on Florence and placed her palms on the table. She said, 'It is finished.'

It was the first time Florence had met Tom in person. He was a slow-talking, long-legged man with curly hair beginning to turn grey. His forearms were hairy and tattooed. He chewed gum and looked around the place a lot, smiling but not doing much talking. Tina said his band was touring the Benelux countries, but she had persuaded him to meet her here for the weekend. There was something about the way she said 'persuaded', something crisp yet defiant, which made Florence decide not to ask them how they were enjoying married life.

Tina noticed that Florence was pushing her food around the plate and said, 'Did Joe turn up?'

'No,' said Florence. 'Nantes have a very crowded fixture list at the moment. It's probably been difficult for him to get away.'

'Florence,' said Tina briskly, 'you have to give some thought to your career. What are you going to do?'

Florence shrugged and said, 'Go back to England, I suppose.'

She thought despairingly of England in winter; England without Millie, without Janey, without Joe; the pantos, the clubs, the dressing rooms, the same old songs.

Ruby started to bawl. Tina filled up her bottle with Badoit, handed it to Tom, and said, 'Of course, as an Associated British production, Dance Group of the Year is now my property.' She lit a cigarette. 'I want to dispose of it.'

'Oh,' said Florence, 'but . . .'

'To you. Betty Trout pinched your idea. Now I'm bringing it back to you.' She beckoned the waiter over and told him to bring a bottle of wine. 'I'll commission the 1992 series from you, if you want. I think you should join the programme team with a view to becoming a producer eventually.'

Tom said, 'Tina, for Christ's sake, let the girl make her own decisions.'

'She has to think of her future,' said Tina. 'She won't be a dancer for ever.'

'She's probably worked that out for herself.'

'It's a very short career. It's not like being an accountant.'

'Maybe she wants a short career. Maybe she wants to meet a nice guy, settle down and raise her kids.'

'What is that meant to mean?'

Florence said hurriedly, 'You know, Tina, what you ought to do is launch the competition in the States.'

'Don't go giving her more ideas,' said Tom. 'She's never home as it is. That baby thinks an aeroplane is home. Tina, you said you weren't going to drink.'

'In the States,' continued Tina. She topped up her wine and said, 'Why didn't I think of that?' She leant forward. 'But Florence,' she said, 'I couldn't do that on my own. It's no end of a job. Start completely from scratch, get all the dancers – it would take a year at least of one person working on it full time. I'd need someone to develop it for me.' She looked at Florence. 'Why not you?'

Florence thought of America, the bigness and movement and limitlessness of it, and suddenly she knew that she would die if she didn't go there and launch Dance Group of the Year. She said, tentatively, 'Janey. Janey could look after the British side of things.'

Suddenly Tina said, 'No, of course. It wouldn't be possible. You in the States. Couldn't swing it.'

'No?' said Florence.

'Darling, you're an alien. You wouldn't get a work permit, a green card. The authorities would say that it was work that could be done by a US national.'

For a few moments there was silence between them. The noises of the restaurant filled it, the waiter bawling to the *sous-chef*, the plangent creak of the entrance doors opening and closing, letting in gusts of November air.

Florence said, 'If I could legally work in the States, would you let me do it?'

'My God,' said Tina, 'that's what I've been saying, but I don't see – '

Florence jumped up from the table. 'Don't say anything about it to anyone,' she said, 'till I get back to you.'

After Florence had gone, Tom and Tina said nothing to each other for a bit and then Tina burst out, 'I'm embarrassed, you coming out with all that patronizing shit in front of her.'

'Ah,' said Tom, 'well then, you think it was shit, do you?'

'Talking about her as if she was a complete doozy, nothing more on her mind than hooking a man.'

Tom said nothing. He paid the bill, tucked Ruby in her carrycot and got up. Tina's eyes filled with tears. She said, 'You don't know what I think is shit. You're never there to know what I think.' She picked up the carrycot and followed him out. The winter cold hit them after the warmth of the restaurant. Tina, who had consumed much more wine than she realized, said, 'I'm fucking sorry I married you.'

'Well' said Tom, 'well, I've managed on my own before and

I'll manage again.' He stepped off the pavement and started threading his way through the cars.

Tina called, 'Where are you going?'

He got to the other side of the road and yelled back at her, 'I'm on tour, remember? I got a living to earn.'

'Tom!' shouted Tina.

Florence jumped out of the taxicab. The shops in Rue Jacob were already bright and glittering with presents for Christmas. As she rushed towards the apartment building, the display lights dappled her skin red and green. The concierge jumped up when she went in but his challenge was lost beneath the clang of the lift doors, and up she sailed to the third floor, where the lift did not open.

Florence pressed the button again and again, then remembered that the doors would not function when the apartment was empty. She was just starting to force them when there was a jerk and she travelled down again to the ground floor. The doors opened to reveal Cal and Godfrey.

They had obviously had a good lunch somewhere; Godfrey's face was all pink. His mouth dropped open and stayed there as though someone had shoved a newspaper through it. Florence barged out of the lift, grabbed Cal's arm, and dragged him into the street. 'I've got to talk to you about the divorce,' she said.

'Why, ah, Florence,' said Cal, 'it's all gone through, you should have heard from your lawyers weeks back.'

Florence said, 'I made a mistake. I didn't want a divorce.'

'Well, I don't know what you're going to be able to do about that,' said Cal. 'I believe once a divorce has gone through, every-thing's kind of over. But I'll ask Godfrey, if you like, see if there's anything can be done.'

Godfrey appeared at Cal's shoulder. 'What does this woman want?' he said.

'The name's Florence,' she said, 'and I want Cal to marry me again.'

Cal said, 'Lord deliver us.'

'Why?' Godfrey managed to spit out.

Florence said, 'Well, Godfrey, correct me if I'm wrong but if

326

I'm the wife of an American national I can work in the United States. Would I be right?'

'Oh,' said Cal, 'have you got a job in the States?'

'Yes,' Florence shouted, 'yes, yes, all there waiting for me, if I can get in.'

'Well, Florence,' said Cal, 'what you have to do is apply for a green – '

'I can't wait for a green card! It'll take weeks and weeks, months and months, then they'll probably say no! I need to go now, Cal! Now!'

Godfrey said, 'If Cal were to marry you, would you absolutely and unequivocally guarantee that neither of us would ever have to set eyes on you again?'

'I do,' said Florence.

'Then,' said Godfrey, 'Cal will marry you.'

Florence waited outside the Air France departure lounge. She had arrived early at Charles de Gaulle but had not yet checked in for the New York flight. Two brown leather suitcases stood at her feet like Dobermanns. There was an umbrella strapped to one, moss green with a wooden handle in the shape of a duck's head. She was carrying a paperback book and a copy of *L'Equipe*. Rain stippled the windows of the terminal. From where she stood she could watch the taxicabs draw up with their wipers going, and see who got out, but it was no one she knew.

She realized with a small jolt of despair that it was time to go. Dragging the suitcases, she joined the queue at the check-in desk. In front of her was an American family with a young boy, and an elderly French couple, the woman with a lavender rinse, the man small and portly with a silver-topped walking cane and a carnation drooping in his lapel. Suddenly Florence heard her name called and her heart did a somersault. She looked round. Cal was running towards her, waving a ticket.

He was grinning all over his big bony face and stood before her, clutching his suitcase and a string bag full of newspapers and pyjamas. 'I got your letter,' he said.

Florence felt a great surge of delight and a terrible rush of disappointment, both at the same time, and hugged him. 'Oh,

Cal,' she said, 'Have you really done it? Have you really, really left Godfrey?'

'Well,' he said, 'I told him I haven't been home in a long time, which is the truth, plus I also said to him all the things you said to me in your letter – how our relationship wasn't fair on me and I owed it to myself to look for someone who could commit himself to me and me alone.'

'Oh, Cal,' Florence said again. 'How did he take it?'

'Well, to be fair to Godfrey, he has his good points, Florence. But he also has a real mean streak, I discover, because do you know what he went and did? He went and closed our joint bank account so I wouldn't be able to buy myself a ticket.'

'That's typical of the shit,' said Florence. 'It's as well I thought to send you that ticket myself.' She put her hand on his arm. 'I think I hear them calling our flight,' she said.

The plane was a long time filling up. It seemed not many people wanted to go to New York that morning. Cal put his string bag on the seat next to him and stretched out. His great feet jutted into the aisle. He stared all around the plane and grinned toothily at the handsome blond steward by the exit door. Then he turned back to Florence and put his hand over hers. 'Florence,' he said, 'Mrs Calvin Johnson, you don't look all that happy to me. Are you regretting you're doing this now?'

'Oh,' she said, 'no, no, I want to work for Tina in New York, more than anything in the world. If she asked me again this minute I'd still say yes. It's just . . .'

'Someone you're leaving behind?' said Cal.

'I had hoped I wouldn't be leaving him,' confessed Florence. 'You weren't the only person I left a note and a ticket for.'

There was a clunk as the blond steward closed the door. Florence sat back and waited for the low thrum of the engines to start. There was a hiatus, and then the steward opened the door up again. Someone, a late arrival, was running towards it. Florence craned her head to see over the headrest of the seat in front. Bending over to check the new arrival's ticket, the steward obscured her view. Florence told herself not to be ridiculous, but then the steward turned and seemed to be pointing in her direction . . .

Not long after that, Tina was lying on the big double bed in the Greenwich Village flat, watching a video Ratty had sent her of the Wembley concert. She flicked through and pressed the pause button and flicked backwards, lazily, like a cat playing with a catnip mouse. Tom was the other side of the land, playing Las Vegas. Ruby lay beside her, sleeping. Stealthily Tina wiped a dribble of apricot purée off her chin. They were making real progress on solid food. Ruby wore an all-in-one that was white with a pattern of big pink flowers, and over the top was a dark pink and cream waistcoat knitted in a chevron pattern. She had a sort of collapsed bonnet on. As the two of them lay there, Tina started to feel pain in the centre of her chest. Outwards it radiated, like radio waves. If you could see a picture of that pain, it would be a hard glowing thing, an appliance, a yellow glaring lamp surrounded by rings, on the ceiling somewhere, you had to look up at it, forced to, someone behind you pulling the back of your head down.

Tina knew she was having a heart attack. Just when her life looked as if it was going to be all right this had to go and happen. She reached for her baby and took her in her arms. The pain was immense. She kissed Ruby and cried in case it was kissing her goodbye. Her desire was to keep Ruby there but she knew she had to put her safe in her crib, in case. She laid Ruby down, under the red, blue, purple, pink knitted blanket. Then she called the ambulance. She unlatched the security door so she could be reached, and returned to bed to wait. She remembered a life of little and big indulgences and emergencies. Cigarettes smoked, meals scoffed, heartbreaks, turbulent flights, amphetamines, butter. As the spasms went ripping through the muscle, great sounds from the depths of her being forced themselves out of her mouth. She buried her face in the pillow so that Ruby wouldn't hear her and be frightened.

The ambulance took her to the hospital. A paramedic with a gentle face sat by her head, carrying Ruby in his big arms. The pain was less now. She was put in a room like a white dungeon, all metal and wheeled devices. Ruby was next to her, a little patch of life and colour. Over the next few hours and the next few days Tina began to survive, regroup. The heart attack was mild. She would not die from it, but return to a normal life in which most things would not have to change. A little less business, not so many planes taken in a week, a day.

Tom came back from Las Vegas. He stayed with her all day and had to be persuaded to go back to the flat sometimes. As Tina regained strength he came to a decision which he stuck to all the years that remained to them: no more tours. Well, there were one or two, but that was much, much later, when Ruby was almost a grown·woman, and Tina had cut down on her business interests and would travel with him. So Tina's heart attack was not the catastrophe it might have seemed. In fact you might wonder if somehow she had not arranged it for herself, this mild fleeting affliction that required such a little sacrifice of habit and activity on her part, and brought her husband to her side for ever. Or you might think all that just a lot of nonsense. Whatever. Their married life was long and happy and their daughter grew tall and beautiful.

WINE JOURNAL

FOR THOSE WHO LOVE WINE
OR JUST NEED A DRINK

KNOCK
KNOCK®
VENICE, CALIFORNIA

Created and published by Knock Knock
1635-B Electric Avenue
Venice, CA 90291
knockknockstuff.com

© 2014 Who's There Inc.
All rights reserved
Knock Knock is a trademark of Who's There Inc.
Made in China

Illustrations by Kelly Thompson

ISBN: 978-160106584-1
UPC: 825703-50068-4

10 9 8 7 6 5 4 3 2 1

THIS JOURNAL BELONGS TO

_____

(If found, please give it back.)

HOW I FEEL ABOUT WINE:

☐ O, for a draught of vintage! that hath been
  Cooled a long age in the deep-delvèd earth . . .
      —John Keats

☐ Wine is the most healthful and most hygienic
  of beverages.
      —Louis Pasteur

☐ What wine goes with Cap'n Crunch?
      —George Carlin

If you're over the age of twenty-one, chances are you've had the occasion to drink a glass of wine. And while most people drink a lot less than they do in Vatican City (where they drink over six cases a year per capita), wine consumption is growing—and why wouldn't it? It's delicious, pairs well with nearly any food, is packed with healthy antioxidants, and comes in an astonishing variety of blends, styles, and prices. If wine's your thing, and even if it isn't (we're talking to you, beer fanatics), it stands to reason you're going to be drinking more of it.

Wine is now produced commercially in nearly eighty countries. With so much great wine out there to enjoy, it's easy to find something new to try. What's not so easy is keeping track of what you've already consumed. Whether the wine is red or white, good or bad, even the most casual imbibers will want to recall what they liked or didn't like. After all, choosing the right wine with confidence is one of the surest ways to impress the boss, please parents, or wow a date. As much as wine is about immediate gratification, it is also about creating fond memories. While some may drink to forget, with this journal on hand you're sure to be the one who remembers.

Day and night my thoughts incline
To the blandishments of wine:
Jars were made to drain, I think,
Wine, I know, was made to drink.

—Richard Henry Stoddard

HOW TO TASTE WINE
(So You'll Look Like a Pro)

You can read as much as you'd like about wine, but the only way to really know wine is to taste it (and to taste more of it).

Even if you haven't taken a course in the oenophilic arts, wine tasting doesn't have to be complicated. Much can actually be covered in three simple steps: looking, smelling, and tasting.

Hold the glass by the stem. Hands on the bowl will create smudges and warm the wine.

STEP ONE: LOOKING

When pouring wine, remember that at least half the glass should be empty to capture the aroma. So don't fill your glass to the top—you can always refill.

The first step is perhaps the most contemplative: pure observation. Hold your glass up against a white background, such as a tablecloth or blank wall. What's the clarity of the wine? Is it crystal clear (good), cloudy (bad), or something in between?

Next, take note of the wine's color. Color often leaves clues as to the varietal, age, and the region of the wine. For instance, if you tilt the glass slightly you may notice the wine is lighter at the edges compared to the center—typically a sign of aging in red wine. In contrast, white wine often deepens in color over time.

DOES THE WINE HAVE "LEGS"?

You've probably seen a so-called wine aficionado hold up a glass and admiringly say, "great legs!" But what does it mean? A gentle roll of the glass will reveal elegant streaks, or legs, as the wine flows down the sides. Caused by evaporation, legs are theoretically longer in wines with more sugar or alcohol, but they are not necessarily an indication of a better wine.

Place your glass on a table and swirl gently—exposing the wine to air and releasing its aroma. Try not to spill.

STEP TWO: SMELLING

Since much of what we consider our sense of taste actually comes from what we smell, taking the time to savor a wine's bouquet is key to getting the most out of it.

So go ahead and stick your nose in the glass. Inhale slowly, taking note of any dominant aromas (aka initial scents). Then, take a moment and smell again. Do you smell any secondary notes? Like a good perfume, a complex wine should reveal many levels of fragrance over time. Let your mind wander . . . Do you smell apples? Tobacco? Grandpa Larry's basement? No image or memory is forbidden. It's all up to you.

Many wine experts pride themselves on detecting as many different aromas in a wine as they can. For the budding oenophile, start with the following general scent groups:

- Floral: honeysuckle, lavender, orange blossom
- Fruity: citrus, berry, tropical fruit, dried fruit
- Vegetal: herbal, dried hay, tea, tobacco
- Earthy: mushroom, mildew, dusty
- Spicy: licorice, black pepper, cloves
- Woody: vanilla, oak, smoke, coffee
- Nutty: walnuts, almonds
- Chemical: tar, cabbage, wet dog, wet cardboard, vinegar
- Caramelized: honey, chocolate, butterscotch

WHAT DO YOU DO WHEN HANDED A CORK?

The tradition of presenting the cork dates from the time when wines were known by the markings on the cork. Contrary to popular (mis)conception, don't feel as though you need to do anything with it.

A wine that's been ruined by a tainted cork is rare, occurring in about 1% of all bottles. (And if, by chance, the wine is indeed "corked," you'll know it right away—it'll have the odor of a wet dog.) So just politely take the cork and set it on the table.

Proper technique

Improper technique

STEP THREE: TASTING

After you've swirled and observed, sniffed and sniffed again, it's time to get to the part you've been waiting for: tasting. Take a small sip of wine—or better yet, an aerating slurp—and swish it around your mouth, allowing all of your taste buds to be washed in the wine. Some describe it as "chewing" on the wine. Do this for at least fifteen to twenty seconds. (Professional tasters will swish for a full minute, taking flavor notes at each fifteen-second mark.)

As with the smelling stage, you'll want to take note of the impressions you have while you're swishing. Put simply, what flavors do you detect in the wine? Does the flavor change over time?

Beyond flavor, you'll want to notice a few additional characteristics. First, what is the wine's acidity? Like a spritz of lemon on fish, a certain degree of acidity is needed in most wines to give it a brightness or freshness or else it becomes dull and flabby. Next, what is the wine's sweetness? The less sugar you detect, the drier it is. Third, does the wine have a lot of body (a heaviness or velvety feeling on your tongue) or does it feel as light as water?

Finally, there is the finish to consider: the lasting sensation the wine leaves after you've tasted it. Generally speaking, the longer the aftertaste—provided it is pleasant—the finer the wine. On the other hand, too many harsh tannins in the wine (particularly in young red wines) can leave your mouth feeling rough and dried out.

WHICH WINE GOES WITH WHICH FOOD?

A lot of fuss is made over the proper pairing of wine to a meal. Don't feel hemmed in by rules like "red with beef" and "white with fish"—just know that in essence, you'll want to pair lighter food with lighter, fresher wines, and heartier food with heavier, big-flavored wines.

Remember, this is a pairing. You're looking for a balance in which one thing doesn't overpower the other. For instance, a robust meat stew would most likely drown out the crisp, delicate flavors of a white Pinot Grigio—so why not switch to a bold, spicy glass of red Zinfandel instead? In the end, it's most important to eat what you like and drink what you like. The only (and most enjoyable) way to know what combinations work best is to keep experimenting.

NAME: _____ VINTAGE (aka year): _____

GRAPE VARIETY/BLEND: _____ ALCOHOL %: _____

PRICE: _____ ☐ Cork ☐ Fake cork ☐ Screw top ☐ Box

I DRANK THIS:

When: _____ Where: _____

With: _____ Because: _____

COLOR:

Greenish · Yellowish · Golden · Pinkish · Light red · Medium red · Dark red · Nearly midnight

AROMA

First impression:

_____

Second thoughts:

_____

☐ Short legs

☐ Long legs

SWEETNESS

| ☐ Bone dry | ☐ Dry | ☐ Not so dry | ☐ Sweet | ☐ Like candy |

ACIDITY

| ☐ Tart | ☐ Crisp | ☐ Fresh | ☐ Soft | ☐ Flabby |

FLAVOR INTENSITY

| ☐ DOA | ☐ Subtle | ☐ Bold | ☐ Ferocious |

BODY

| ☐ Watery | ☐ Silky | ☐ Velvety | ☐ Syrupy |

FINISH

| ☐ Flash in the pan | ☐ Pleasantly lingering | ☐ Won't go away |

THIS WINE WILL PAIR WELL WITH:

☐ Fish   ☐ Chicken   ☐ Meat

☐ A cheese plate ☐ Dessert   ☐ Brussels sprouts

OVERALL RATING:

PURE   PURE
VINEGAR   DELIGHT

SWEET SPOT MATRIX

Considering price and taste,
indicate wine's position on
the graph.

$$$$

• Jet fuel   • 1869
                     Château
                     Lafite

Swill   Nectar

                    • Two-buck
                      Chuck

¢

DRINK IT AGAIN?

☐ Not even if you paid me.   ☐ Maybe, if very drunk.   ☐ Sure, why not?

☐ Yes, please.   ☐ And again, and again.   ☐ If only I could afford it!

NOTES:

NAME: _____ VINTAGE (aka year): _____

GRAPE VARIETY/BLEND: _____ ALCOHOL %: _____

PRICE: _____ ☐ Cork ☐ Fake cork ☐ Screw top ☐ Box

I DRANK THIS:

When: _____ Where: _____

With: _____ Because: _____

COLOR:
Greenish · Yellowish · Golden · Pinkish · Light red · Medium red · Dark red · Nearly midnight

AROMA
First impression:

_____

☐ Short legs

☐ Long legs

Second thoughts:

_____

SWEETNESS
☐ Bone dry   ☐ Dry   ☐ Not so dry   ☐ Sweet   ☐ Like candy

ACIDITY
☐ Tart   ☐ Crisp   ☐ Fresh   ☐ Soft   ☐ Flabby

FLAVOR INTENSITY
☐ DOA   ☐ Subtle   ☐ Bold   ☐ Ferocious

BODY
☐ Watery   ☐ Silky   ☐ Velvety   ☐ Syrupy

FINISH
☐ Flash in the pan   ☐ Pleasantly lingering   ☐ Won't go away

THIS WINE WILL PAIR WELL WITH:

☐ Fish   ☐ Chicken   ☐ Meat

☐ A cheese plate   ☐ Dessert   ☐ Plaids or stripes

OVERALL RATING:

PURE
VINEGAR

PURE
DELIGHT

SWEET SPOT MATRIX

Considering price and taste,
indicate wine's position on
the graph.

$$$$

• Jet fuel

• 1869
Château
Lafite

Swill

Nectar

• Two-buck
Chuck

¢

DRINK IT AGAIN?

☐ Not even if you paid me.   ☐ Maybe, if very drunk.   ☐ Sure, why not?

☐ Yes, please.   ☐ And again, and again.   ☐ If only I could afford it!

NOTES: _____

_____

_____

_____

_____

_____

_____

_____

_____

_____

_____

_____

NAME: _____ VINTAGE (aka year): _____

GRAPE VARIETY/BLEND: _____ ALCOHOL %: _____

PRICE: _____ □ Cork □ Fake cork □ Screw top □ Box

I DRANK THIS:

When: _____ Where: _____

With: _____ Because: _____

COLOR:
Greenish · Yellowish · Golden · Pinkish · Light red · Medium red · Dark red · Nearly midnight

AROMA

First impression:

_____

Second thoughts:

_____

□ Short legs

□ Long legs

SWEETNESS
□ Bone dry   □ Dry   □ Not so dry   □ Sweet   □ Like candy

ACIDITY
□ Tart   □ Crisp   □ Fresh   □ Soft   □ Flabby

FLAVOR INTENSITY
□ DOA   □ Subtle   □ Bold   □ Ferocious

BODY
□ Watery   □ Silky   □ Velvety   □ Syrupy

FINISH
□ Flash in the pan   □ Pleasantly lingering   □ Won't go away

THIS WINE WILL PAIR WELL WITH:

☐ Fish ☐ Chicken ☐ Meat

☐ A cheese plate ☐ Dessert ☐ Shrimp cocktail

OVERALL RATING:

PURE
VINEGAR

PURE
DELIGHT

SWEET SPOT MATRIX

Considering price and taste, indicate wine's position on the graph.

$$$$

Swill

• Jet fuel

• 1869
Château
Lafite

Nectar

• Two-buck
Chuck

¢

DRINK IT AGAIN?

☐ Not even if you paid me.　☐ Maybe, if very drunk.　☐ Sure, why not?

☐ Yes, please.　☐ And again, and again.　☐ If only I could afford it!

NOTES:

NAME: _____ VINTAGE (aka year): _____

GRAPE VARIETY/BLEND: _____ ALCOHOL %: _____

PRICE: _____ □ Cork   □ Fake cork   □ Screw top   □ Box

I DRANK THIS:

When: _____ Where: _____

With: _____ Because: _____

COLOR:
Greenish · Yellowish · Golden · Pinkish · Light red · Medium red · Dark red · Nearly midnight

AROMA
First impression:

_____

Second thoughts:

_____

□ Short legs

□ Long legs

SWEETNESS
□ Bone dry   □ Dry   □ Not so dry   □ Sweet   □ Like candy

ACIDITY
□ Tart   □ Crisp   □ Fresh   □ Soft   □ Flabby

FLAVOR INTENSITY
□ DOA   □ Subtle   □ Bold   □ Ferocious

BODY
□ Watery   □ Silky   □ Velvety   □ Syrupy

FINISH
□ Flash in the pan   □ Pleasantly lingering   □ Won't go away

THIS WINE WILL PAIR WELL WITH:

☐ Fish   ☐ Chicken   ☐ Meat

☐ A cheese plate ☐ Dessert   ☐ Pickled beets

OVERALL RATING:

PURE
VINEGAR   PURE
                                 DELIGHT

SWEET SPOT MATRIX

Considering price and taste,
indicate wine's position on
the graph.

$$$$

• Jet fuel   • 1869
                                Château
                                Lafite

Swill   Nectar

                              • Two-buck
                                Chuck

¢

DRINK IT AGAIN?

☐ Not even if you paid me.   ☐ Maybe, if very drunk.   ☐ Sure, why not?

☐ Yes, please.   ☐ And again, and again.   ☐ If only I could afford it!

NOTES: _____

_____

_____

_____

_____

_____

_____

_____

_____

_____

_____

_____

NAME: _____ VINTAGE (aka year): _____

GRAPE VARIETY/BLEND: _____ ALCOHOL %: _____

PRICE: _____ ☐ Cork   ☐ Fake cork   ☐ Screw top   ☐ Box

I DRANK THIS:

When: _____ Where: _____

With: _____ Because: _____

COLOR:

Greenish · Yellowish · Golden · Pinkish · Light red · Medium red · Dark red · Nearly midnight

AROMA

First impression:

_____

Second thoughts:

_____

☐ Short legs

☐ Long legs

SWEETNESS

| ☐ Bone dry | ☐ Dry | ☐ Not so dry | ☐ Sweet | ☐ Like candy |

ACIDITY

| ☐ Tart | ☐ Crisp | ☐ Fresh | ☐ Soft | ☐ Flabby |

FLAVOR INTENSITY

| ☐ DOA | ☐ Subtle | ☐ Bold | ☐ Ferocious |

BODY

| ☐ Watery | ☐ Silky | ☐ Velvety | ☐ Syrupy |

FINISH

| ☐ Flash in the pan | ☐ Pleasantly lingering | ☐ Won't go away |

THIS WINE WILL PAIR WELL WITH:

☐ Fish   ☐ Chicken   ☐ Meat

☐ A cheese plate   ☐ Dessert   ☐ "Fantasia No. 3 in D Minor"

OVERALL RATING:

PURE VINEGAR   PURE DELIGHT

SWEET SPOT MATRIX

Considering price and taste, indicate wine's position on the graph.

$$$$

• Jet fuel   • 1869 Château Lafite

Swill   Nectar

• Two-buck Chuck

¢

DRINK IT AGAIN?

☐ Not even if you paid me.   ☐ Maybe, if very drunk.   ☐ Sure, why not?

☐ Yes, please.   ☐ And again, and again.   ☐ If only I could afford it!

NOTES: _____

_____

_____

_____

_____

_____

_____

_____

_____

_____

_____

NAME: _____ VINTAGE (aka year): _____

GRAPE VARIETY/BLEND: _____ ALCOHOL %: _____

PRICE: _____ ☐ Cork   ☐ Fake cork   ☐ Screw top   ☐ Box

I DRANK THIS:

When: _____ Where: _____

With: _____ Because: _____

COLOR:

Greenish · Yellowish · Golden · Pinkish · Light red · Medium red · Dark red · Nearly midnight

AROMA

First impression:

_____

Second thoughts:

_____

☐ Short legs

☐ Long legs

SWEETNESS

☐ Bone dry   ☐ Dry   ☐ Not so dry   ☐ Sweet   ☐ Like candy

ACIDITY

☐ Tart   ☐ Crisp   ☐ Fresh   ☐ Soft   ☐ Flabby

FLAVOR INTENSITY

☐ DOA   ☐ Subtle   ☐ Bold   ☐ Ferocious

BODY

☐ Watery   ☐ Silky   ☐ Velvety   ☐ Syrupy

FINISH

☐ Flash in the pan   ☐ Pleasantly lingering   ☐ Won't go away

THIS WINE WILL PAIR WELL WITH:

☐ Fish   ☐ Chicken   ☐ Meat

☐ A cheese plate ☐ Dessert   ☐ Ceviche

OVERALL RATING:

PURE
VINEGAR

PURE
DELIGHT

SWEET SPOT MATRIX

Considering price and taste,
indicate wine's position on
the graph.

$$$$

• Jet fuel

• 1869
Château
Lafite

Swill

Nectar

• Two-buck
Chuck

¢

DRINK IT AGAIN?

☐ Not even if you paid me.   ☐ Maybe, if very drunk.   ☐ Sure, why not?

☐ Yes, please.   ☐ And again, and again.   ☐ If only I could afford it!

NOTES:

NAME: _____ VINTAGE (aka year): _____

GRAPE VARIETY/BLEND: _____ ALCOHOL %: _____

PRICE: _____ ☐ Cork ☐ Fake cork ☐ Screw top ☐ Box

I DRANK THIS:

When: _____ Where: _____

With: _____ Because: _____

COLOR:

Greenish · Yellowish · Golden · Pinkish · Light red · Medium red · Dark red · Nearly midnight

AROMA

First impression:

_____

Second thoughts:

_____

☐ Short legs

☐ Long legs

SWEETNESS

☐ Bone dry   ☐ Dry   ☐ Not so dry   ☐ Sweet   ☐ Like candy

ACIDITY

☐ Tart   ☐ Crisp   ☐ Fresh   ☐ Soft   ☐ Flabby

FLAVOR INTENSITY

☐ DOA   ☐ Subtle   ☐ Bold   ☐ Ferocious

BODY

☐ Watery   ☐ Silky   ☐ Velvety   ☐ Syrupy

FINISH

☐ Flash in the pan   ☐ Pleasantly lingering   ☐ Won't go away

THIS WINE WILL PAIR WELL WITH:

☐ Fish   ☐ Chicken   ☐ Meat

☐ A cheese plate   ☐ Dessert   ☐ Canned chili

OVERALL RATING:

PURE
VINEGAR

PURE
DELIGHT

SWEET SPOT MATRIX

Considering price and taste, indicate wine's position on the graph.

$$$$

• Jet fuel

• 1869
Château
Lafite

Swill

Nectar

• Two-buck
Chuck

¢

DRINK IT AGAIN?

☐ Not even if you paid me.   ☐ Maybe, if very drunk.   ☐ Sure, why not?

☐ Yes, please.   ☐ And again, and again.   ☐ If only I could afford it!

NOTES:

NAME: _____ VINTAGE (aka year): _____

GRAPE VARIETY/BLEND: _____ ALCOHOL %: _____

PRICE: _____ ☐ Cork ☐ Fake cork ☐ Screw top ☐ Box

I DRANK THIS:

When: _____ Where: _____

With: _____ Because: _____

COLOR:

Greenish · Yellowish · Golden · Pinkish · Light red · Medium red · Dark red · Nearly midnight

AROMA

First impression:

_____

☐ Short legs

☐ Long legs

Second thoughts:

_____

SWEETNESS

☐ Bone dry   ☐ Dry   ☐ Not so dry   ☐ Sweet   ☐ Like candy

ACIDITY

☐ Tart   ☐ Crisp   ☐ Fresh   ☐ Soft   ☐ Flabby

FLAVOR INTENSITY

☐ DOA   ☐ Subtle   ☐ Bold   ☐ Ferocious

BODY

☐ Watery   ☐ Silky   ☐ Velvety   ☐ Syrupy

FINISH

☐ Flash in the pan   ☐ Pleasantly lingering   ☐ Won't go away

THIS WINE WILL PAIR WELL WITH:

☐ Fish ☐ Chicken ☐ Meat

☐ A cheese plate ☐ Dessert ☐ A book of quotations

OVERALL RATING:

PURE
VINEGAR

PURE
DELIGHT

SWEET SPOT MATRIX

Considering price and taste,
indicate wine's position on
the graph.

$$$$

• Jet fuel

• 1869
Château
Lafite

Swill

Nectar

• Two-buck
Chuck

¢

DRINK IT AGAIN?

☐ Not even if you paid me. ☐ Maybe, if very drunk. ☐ Sure, why not?

☐ Yes, please. ☐ And again, and again. ☐ If only I could afford it!

NOTES: _____

_____

_____

_____

_____

_____

_____

_____

_____

_____

_____

_____

NAME: _____ VINTAGE (aka year): _____

GRAPE VARIETY/BLEND: _____ ALCOHOL %: _____

PRICE: _____ ☐ Cork   ☐ Fake cork   ☐ Screw top   ☐ Box

I DRANK THIS:

When: _____ Where: _____

With: _____ Because: _____

COLOR:

Greenish · Yellowish · Golden · Pinkish · Light red · Medium red · Dark red · Nearly midnight

AROMA

First impression:

_____

Second thoughts:

_____

☐ Short legs

☐ Long legs

SWEETNESS

☐ Bone dry   ☐ Dry   ☐ Not so dry   ☐ Sweet   ☐ Like candy

ACIDITY

☐ Tart   ☐ Crisp   ☐ Fresh   ☐ Soft   ☐ Flabby

FLAVOR INTENSITY

☐ DOA   ☐ Subtle   ☐ Bold   ☐ Ferocious

BODY

☐ Watery   ☐ Silky   ☐ Velvety   ☐ Syrupy

FINISH

☐ Flash in the pan   ☐ Pleasantly lingering   ☐ Won't go away

THIS WINE WILL PAIR WELL WITH:

☐ Fish   ☐ Chicken   ☐ Meat

☐ A cheese plate   ☐ Dessert   ☐ Chinese takeout

OVERALL RATING:

PURE
VINEGAR

PURE
DELIGHT

SWEET SPOT MATRIX

Considering price and taste, indicate wine's position on the graph.

$$$$

• Jet fuel

• 1869
Château
Lafite

Swill

Nectar

• Two-buck
Chuck

¢

DRINK IT AGAIN?

☐ Not even if you paid me.   ☐ Maybe, if very drunk.   ☐ Sure, why not?

☐ Yes, please.   ☐ And again, and again.   ☐ If only I could afford it!

NOTES:

_____

_____

_____

_____

_____

_____

_____

_____

_____

_____

_____

NAME: _____ VINTAGE (aka year): _____

GRAPE VARIETY/BLEND: _____ ALCOHOL %: _____

PRICE: _____ ☐ Cork ☐ Fake cork ☐ Screw top ☐ Box

I DRANK THIS:

When: _____ Where: _____

With: _____ Because: _____

COLOR:
Greenish · Yellowish · Golden · Pinkish · Light red · Medium red · Dark red · Nearly midnight

AROMA

First impression:

_____

Second thoughts:

_____

☐ Short legs

☐ Long legs

SWEETNESS

☐ Bone dry   ☐ Dry   ☐ Not so dry   ☐ Sweet   ☐ Like candy

ACIDITY

☐ Tart   ☐ Crisp   ☐ Fresh   ☐ Soft   ☐ Flabby

FLAVOR INTENSITY

☐ DOA   ☐ Subtle   ☐ Bold   ☐ Ferocious

BODY

☐ Watery   ☐ Silky   ☐ Velvety   ☐ Syrupy

FINISH

☐ Flash in the pan   ☐ Pleasantly lingering   ☐ Won't go away

THIS WINE WILL PAIR WELL WITH:

☐ Fish ☐ Chicken ☐ Meat

☐ A cheese plate ☐ Dessert ☐ Schnitzel

OVERALL RATING:

PURE
VINEGAR   PURE
                           DELIGHT

SWEET SPOT MATRIX

Considering price and taste, indicate wine's position on the graph.

$$$$

• Jet fuel   • 1869
                      Château
                      Lafite

Swill   Nectar

              • Two-buck
                Chuck

¢

DRINK IT AGAIN?

☐ Not even if you paid me. ☐ Maybe, if very drunk. ☐ Sure, why not?

☐ Yes, please. ☐ And again, and again. ☐ If only I could afford it!

NOTES:

NAME: _____ VINTAGE (aka year): _____

GRAPE VARIETY/BLEND: _____ ALCOHOL %: _____

PRICE: _____ ☐ Cork ☐ Fake cork ☐ Screw top ☐ Box

I DRANK THIS:

When: _____ Where: _____

With: _____ Because: _____

COLOR:

Greenish · Yellowish · Golden · Pinkish · Light red · Medium red · Dark red · Nearly midnight

AROMA

First impression:

_____

Second thoughts:

_____

☐ Short legs

☐ Long legs

SWEETNESS

☐ Bone dry   ☐ Dry   ☐ Not so dry   ☐ Sweet   ☐ Like candy

ACIDITY

☐ Tart   ☐ Crisp   ☐ Fresh   ☐ Soft   ☐ Flabby

FLAVOR INTENSITY

☐ DOA   ☐ Subtle   ☐ Bold   ☐ Ferocious

BODY

☐ Watery   ☐ Silky   ☐ Velvety   ☐ Syrupy

FINISH

☐ Flash in the pan   ☐ Pleasantly lingering   ☐ Won't go away

THIS WINE WILL PAIR WELL WITH:

☐ Fish   ☐ Chicken   ☐ Meat

☐ A cheese plate   ☐ Dessert   ☐ Hot buttered popcorn

OVERALL RATING:

PURE
VINEGAR   PURE
                                 DELIGHT

SWEET SPOT MATRIX

Considering price and taste,
indicate wine's position on
the graph.

$$$$

• Jet fuel   • 1869
                               Château
                               Lafite

Swill   Nectar

                              • Two-buck
                                Chuck

¢

DRINK IT AGAIN?

☐ Not even if you paid me.   ☐ Maybe, if very drunk.   ☐ Sure, why not?

☐ Yes, please.   ☐ And again, and again.   ☐ If only I could afford it!

NOTES:

NAME: _____ VINTAGE (aka year): _____

GRAPE VARIETY/BLEND: _____ ALCOHOL %: _____

PRICE: _____ □ Cork □ Fake cork □ Screw top □ Box

I DRANK THIS:

When: _____ Where: _____

With: _____ Because: _____

COLOR:
Greenish · Yellowish · Golden · Pinkish · Light red · Medium red · Dark red · Nearly midnight

AROMA

First impression:

_____

Second thoughts:

_____

□ Short legs

□ Long legs

SWEETNESS
□ Bone dry   □ Dry   □ Not so dry   □ Sweet   □ Like candy

ACIDITY
□ Tart   □ Crisp   □ Fresh   □ Soft   □ Flabby

FLAVOR INTENSITY
□ DOA   □ Subtle   □ Bold   □ Ferocious

BODY
□ Watery   □ Silky   □ Velvety   □ Syrupy

FINISH
□ Flash in the pan   □ Pleasantly lingering   □ Won't go away

THIS WINE WILL PAIR WELL WITH:

☐ Fish ☐ Chicken ☐ Meat

☐ A cheese plate ☐ Dessert ☐ A passionate squeeze

OVERALL RATING:

PURE VINEGAR
PURE DELIGHT

SWEET SPOT MATRIX

Considering price and taste, indicate wine's position on the graph.

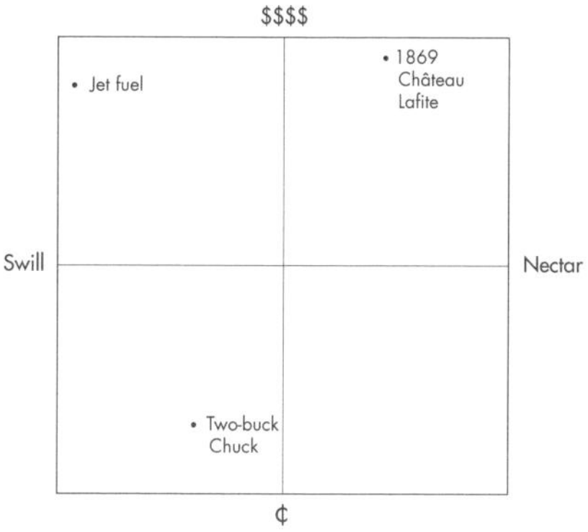
$$$$
Swill
Nectar
¢
• Jet fuel
• 1869 Château Lafite
• Two-buck Chuck

DRINK IT AGAIN?

☐ Not even if you paid me. ☐ Maybe, if very drunk. ☐ Sure, why not?

☐ Yes, please. ☐ And again, and again. ☐ If only I could afford it!

NOTES:

NAME: _____ VINTAGE (aka year): _____

GRAPE VARIETY/BLEND: _____ ALCOHOL %: _____

PRICE: _____ ☐ Cork ☐ Fake cork ☐ Screw top ☐ Box

I DRANK THIS:

When: _____ Where: _____

With: _____ Because: _____

COLOR:
Greenish · Yellowish · Golden · Pinkish · Light red · Medium red · Dark red · Nearly midnight

AROMA

First impression:

_____

Second thoughts:

_____

☐ Short legs

☐ Long legs

SWEETNESS
| ☐ Bone dry | ☐ Dry | ☐ Not so dry | ☐ Sweet | ☐ Like candy |

ACIDITY
| ☐ Tart | ☐ Crisp | ☐ Fresh | ☐ Soft | ☐ Flabby |

FLAVOR INTENSITY
| ☐ DOA | ☐ Subtle | ☐ Bold | ☐ Ferocious |

BODY
| ☐ Watery | ☐ Silky | ☐ Velvety | ☐ Syrupy |

FINISH
| ☐ Flash in the pan | ☐ Pleasantly lingering | ☐ Won't go away |

THIS WINE WILL PAIR WELL WITH:

☐ Fish   ☐ Chicken   ☐ Meat

☐ A cheese plate   ☐ Dessert   ☐ Beer nuts

OVERALL RATING:

PURE
VINEGAR   PURE
DELIGHT

SWEET SPOT MATRIX

Considering price and taste,
indicate wine's position on
the graph.

$$$$

• Jet fuel   • 1869
Château
Lafite

Swill   Nectar

• Two-buck
Chuck

¢

DRINK IT AGAIN?

☐ Not even if you paid me.   ☐ Maybe, if very drunk.   ☐ Sure, why not?

☐ Yes, please.   ☐ And again, and again.   ☐ If only I could afford it!

NOTES:

NAME: _____ VINTAGE (aka year): _____

GRAPE VARIETY/BLEND: _____ ALCOHOL %: _____

PRICE: _____ ☐ Cork   ☐ Fake cork   ☐ Screw top   ☐ Box

I DRANK THIS:

When: _____ Where: _____

With: _____ Because: _____

COLOR:

Greenish · Yellowish · Golden · Pinkish · Light red · Medium red · Dark red · Nearly midnight

AROMA

First impression:

_____

Second thoughts:

_____

☐ Short legs

☐ Long legs

SWEETNESS

☐ Bone dry   ☐ Dry   ☐ Not so dry   ☐ Sweet   ☐ Like candy

ACIDITY

☐ Tart   ☐ Crisp   ☐ Fresh   ☐ Soft   ☐ Flabby

FLAVOR INTENSITY

☐ DOA   ☐ Subtle   ☐ Bold   ☐ Ferocious

BODY

☐ Watery   ☐ Silky   ☐ Velvety   ☐ Syrupy

FINISH

☐ Flash in the pan   ☐ Pleasantly lingering   ☐ Won't go away

THIS WINE WILL PAIR WELL WITH:

☐ Fish　　☐ Chicken　　☐ Meat

☐ A cheese plate　☐ Dessert　☐ Moonlight

OVERALL RATING:

PURE
VINEGAR

PURE
DELIGHT

SWEET SPOT MATRIX

Considering price and taste,
indicate wine's position on
the graph.

$$$$

• Jet fuel

• 1869
Château
Lafite

Swill

Nectar

• Two-buck
Chuck

¢

DRINK IT AGAIN?

☐ Not even if you paid me.　　☐ Maybe, if very drunk.　　☐ Sure, why not?

☐ Yes, please.　　☐ And again, and again.　　☐ If only I could afford it!

NOTES: _____

_____

_____

_____

_____

_____

_____

_____

_____

_____

_____

_____

NAME: _____ VINTAGE (aka year): _____

GRAPE VARIETY/BLEND: _____ ALCOHOL %: _____

PRICE: _____ ☐ Cork   ☐ Fake cork   ☐ Screw top   ☐ Box

I DRANK THIS:

When: _____ Where: _____

With: _____ Because: _____

COLOR:

Greenish · Yellowish · Golden · Pinkish · Light red · Medium red · Dark red · Nearly midnight

AROMA

First impression:

_____

Second thoughts:

_____

☐ Short legs

☐ Long legs

SWEETNESS

☐ Bone dry   ☐ Dry   ☐ Not so dry   ☐ Sweet   ☐ Like candy

ACIDITY

☐ Tart   ☐ Crisp   ☐ Fresh   ☐ Soft   ☐ Flabby

FLAVOR INTENSITY

☐ DOA   ☐ Subtle   ☐ Bold   ☐ Ferocious

BODY

☐ Watery   ☐ Silky   ☐ Velvety   ☐ Syrupy

FINISH

☐ Flash in the pan   ☐ Pleasantly lingering   ☐ Won't go away

THIS WINE WILL PAIR WELL WITH:

☐ Fish   ☐ Chicken   ☐ Meat

☐ A cheese plate   ☐ Dessert   ☐ Grits

OVERALL RATING:

PURE
VINEGAR
                 PURE
DELIGHT

SWEET SPOT MATRIX

Considering price and taste,
indicate wine's position on
the graph.

$$$$

• Jet fuel   • 1869
Château
Lafite

Swill   Nectar

• Two-buck
Chuck

¢

DRINK IT AGAIN?

☐ Not even if you paid me.   ☐ Maybe, if very drunk.   ☐ Sure, why not?

☐ Yes, please.   ☐ And again, and again.   ☐ If only I could afford it!

NOTES:

NAME: _____ VINTAGE (aka year): _____

GRAPE VARIETY/BLEND: _____ ALCOHOL %: _____

PRICE: _____ ☐ Cork   ☐ Fake cork   ☐ Screw top   ☐ Box

I DRANK THIS:

When: _____ Where: _____

With: _____ Because: _____

COLOR:
Greenish · Yellowish · Golden · Pinkish · Light red · Medium red · Dark red · Nearly midnight

AROMA

First impression:

_____

Second thoughts:

_____

☐ Short legs

☐ Long legs

SWEETNESS
☐ Bone dry   ☐ Dry   ☐ Not so dry   ☐ Sweet   ☐ Like candy

ACIDITY
☐ Tart   ☐ Crisp   ☐ Fresh   ☐ Soft   ☐ Flabby

FLAVOR INTENSITY
☐ DOA   ☐ Subtle   ☐ Bold   ☐ Ferocious

BODY
☐ Watery   ☐ Silky   ☐ Velvety   ☐ Syrupy

FINISH
☐ Flash in the pan   ☐ Pleasantly lingering   ☐ Won't go away

THIS WINE WILL PAIR WELL WITH:

☐ Fish   ☐ Chicken   ☐ Meat

☐ A cheese plate   ☐ Dessert   ☐ Summer in Provence

OVERALL RATING:

PURE
VINEGAR   PURE
DELIGHT

SWEET SPOT MATRIX

Considering price and taste, indicate wine's position on the graph.

$$$$

• Jet fuel

• 1869
Château
Lafite

Swill

Nectar

• Two-buck
Chuck

¢

DRINK IT AGAIN?

☐ Not even if you paid me.   ☐ Maybe, if very drunk.   ☐ Sure, why not?

☐ Yes, please.   ☐ And again, and again.   ☐ If only I could afford it!

NOTES:

_____

_____

_____

_____

_____

_____

_____

_____

_____

_____

_____

NAME: _____ VINTAGE (aka year): _____

GRAPE VARIETY/BLEND: _____ ALCOHOL %: _____

PRICE: _____ □ Cork   □ Fake cork   □ Screw top   □ Box

I DRANK THIS:

When: _____ Where: _____

With: _____ Because: _____

COLOR:
Greenish · Yellowish · Golden · Pinkish · Light red · Medium red · Dark red · Nearly midnight

AROMA
First impression:

_____

Second thoughts:

_____

□ Short legs

□ Long legs

SWEETNESS
□ Bone dry   □ Dry   □ Not so dry   □ Sweet   □ Like candy

ACIDITY
□ Tart   □ Crisp   □ Fresh   □ Soft   □ Flabby

FLAVOR INTENSITY
□ DOA   □ Subtle   □ Bold   □ Ferocious

BODY
□ Watery   □ Silky   □ Velvety   □ Syrupy

FINISH
□ Flash in the pan   □ Pleasantly lingering   □ Won't go away

THIS WINE WILL PAIR WELL WITH:

☐ Fish ☐ Chicken ☐ Meat

☐ A cheese plate ☐ Dessert ☐ Sushi

OVERALL RATING:

PURE
VINEGAR

PURE
DELIGHT

SWEET SPOT MATRIX

Considering price and taste, indicate wine's position on the graph.

$$$$

• Jet fuel

• 1869 Château Lafite

Swill

Nectar

• Two-buck Chuck

¢

DRINK IT AGAIN?

☐ Not even if you paid me. ☐ Maybe, if very drunk. ☐ Sure, why not?

☐ Yes, please. ☐ And again, and again. ☐ If only I could afford it!

NOTES:

NAME: _____ VINTAGE (aka year): _____

GRAPE VARIETY/BLEND: _____ ALCOHOL %: _____

PRICE: _____ ☐ Cork   ☐ Fake cork   ☐ Screw top   ☐ Box

I DRANK THIS:

When: _____ Where: _____

With: _____ Because: _____

COLOR:
Greenish · Yellowish · Golden · Pinkish · Light red · Medium red · Dark red · Nearly midnight

AROMA
First impression:

_____

Second thoughts:

_____

☐ Short legs

☐ Long legs

SWEETNESS
☐ Bone dry   ☐ Dry   ☐ Not so dry   ☐ Sweet   ☐ Like candy

ACIDITY
☐ Tart   ☐ Crisp   ☐ Fresh   ☐ Soft   ☐ Flabby

FLAVOR INTENSITY
☐ DOA   ☐ Subtle   ☐ Bold   ☐ Ferocious

BODY
☐ Watery   ☐ Silky   ☐ Velvety   ☐ Syrupy

FINISH
☐ Flash in the pan   ☐ Pleasantly lingering   ☐ Won't go away

THIS WINE WILL PAIR WELL WITH:

☐ Fish ☐ Chicken ☐ Meat

☐ A cheese plate ☐ Dessert ☐ *Sunday in the Park with George*

OVERALL RATING:

PURE
VINEGAR

PURE
DELIGHT

SWEET SPOT MATRIX

Considering price and taste, indicate wine's position on the graph.

$$$$

• Jet fuel

• 1869
Château
Lafite

Swill

Nectar

• Two-buck
Chuck

¢

DRINK IT AGAIN?

☐ Not even if you paid me. ☐ Maybe, if very drunk. ☐ Sure, why not?

☐ Yes, please. ☐ And again, and again. ☐ If only I could afford it!

NOTES:

NAME: _____ VINTAGE (aka year): _____

GRAPE VARIETY/BLEND: _____ ALCOHOL %: _____

PRICE: _____ ☐ Cork   ☐ Fake cork   ☐ Screw top   ☐ Box

I DRANK THIS:

When: _____ Where: _____

With: _____ Because: _____

COLOR:
Greenish · Yellowish · Golden · Pinkish · Light red · Medium red · Dark red · Nearly midnight

AROMA
First impression:

_____

Second thoughts:

_____

☐ Short legs

☐ Long legs

SWEETNESS
☐ Bone dry   ☐ Dry   ☐ Not so dry   ☐ Sweet   ☐ Like candy

ACIDITY
☐ Tart   ☐ Crisp   ☐ Fresh   ☐ Soft   ☐ Flabby

FLAVOR INTENSITY
☐ DOA   ☐ Subtle   ☐ Bold   ☐ Ferocious

BODY
☐ Watery   ☐ Silky   ☐ Velvety   ☐ Syrupy

FINISH
☐ Flash in the pan   ☐ Pleasantly lingering   ☐ Won't go away

THIS WINE WILL PAIR WELL WITH:

☐ Fish ☐ Chicken ☐ Meat

☐ A cheese plate ☐ Dessert ☐ A tailgate party

OVERALL RATING:

PURE
VINEGAR

PURE
DELIGHT

SWEET SPOT MATRIX

Considering price and taste,
indicate wine's position on
the graph.

$$$$

• Jet fuel

• 1869
Château
Lafite

Swill

Nectar

• Two-buck
Chuck

¢

DRINK IT AGAIN?

☐ Not even if you paid me. ☐ Maybe, if very drunk. ☐ Sure, why not?

☐ Yes, please. ☐ And again, and again. ☐ If only I could afford it!

NOTES:

NAME: _____ VINTAGE (aka year): _____

GRAPE VARIETY/BLEND: _____ ALCOHOL %: _____

PRICE: _____ ☐ Cork   ☐ Fake cork   ☐ Screw top   ☐ Box

I DRANK THIS:

When: _____ Where: _____

With: _____ Because: _____

COLOR:

Greenish · Yellowish · Golden · Pinkish · Light red · Medium red · Dark red · Nearly midnight

AROMA

First impression:

_____

Second thoughts:

_____

☐ Short legs

☐ Long legs

SWEETNESS

☐ Bone dry   ☐ Dry   ☐ Not so dry   ☐ Sweet   ☐ Like candy

ACIDITY

☐ Tart   ☐ Crisp   ☐ Fresh   ☐ Soft   ☐ Flabby

FLAVOR INTENSITY

☐ DOA   ☐ Subtle   ☐ Bold   ☐ Ferocious

BODY

☐ Watery   ☐ Silky   ☐ Velvety   ☐ Syrupy

FINISH

☐ Flash in the pan   ☐ Pleasantly lingering   ☐ Won't go away

THIS WINE WILL PAIR WELL WITH:

☐ Fish   ☐ Chicken   ☐ Meat

☐ A cheese plate   ☐ Dessert   ☐ Caviar

OVERALL RATING:

PURE
VINEGAR

PURE
DELIGHT

SWEET SPOT MATRIX

Considering price and taste, indicate wine's position on the graph.

$$$$

• Jet fuel

• 1869
Château
Lafite

Swill

Nectar

• Two-buck
Chuck

¢

DRINK IT AGAIN?

☐ Not even if you paid me.   ☐ Maybe, if very drunk.   ☐ Sure, why not?

☐ Yes, please.   ☐ And again, and again.   ☐ If only I could afford it!

NOTES:

_____

_____

_____

_____

_____

_____

_____

_____

_____

_____

_____

_____

NAME: _____ VINTAGE (aka year): _____

GRAPE VARIETY/BLEND: _____ ALCOHOL %: _____

PRICE: _____ ☐ Cork   ☐ Fake cork   ☐ Screw top   ☐ Box

I DRANK THIS:

When: _____ Where: _____

With: _____ Because: _____

COLOR:

Greenish · Yellowish · Golden · Pinkish · Light red · Medium red · Dark red · Nearly midnight

AROMA

First impression:

_____

Second thoughts:

_____

☐ Short legs

☐ Long legs

SWEETNESS
☐ Bone dry   ☐ Dry   ☐ Not so dry   ☐ Sweet   ☐ Like candy

ACIDITY
☐ Tart   ☐ Crisp   ☐ Fresh   ☐ Soft   ☐ Flabby

FLAVOR INTENSITY
☐ DOA   ☐ Subtle   ☐ Bold   ☐ Ferocious

BODY
☐ Watery   ☐ Silky   ☐ Velvety   ☐ Syrupy

FINISH
☐ Flash in the pan   ☐ Pleasantly lingering   ☐ Won't go away

THIS WINE WILL PAIR WELL WITH:

☐ Fish ☐ Chicken ☐ Meat

☐ A cheese plate ☐ Dessert ☐ Tater tots

OVERALL RATING:

PURE
VINEGAR   PURE
DELIGHT

SWEET SPOT MATRIX

Considering price and taste,
indicate wine's position on
the graph.

$$$$

• Jet fuel   • 1869
                               Château
                               Lafite

Swill   Nectar

• Two-buck
  Chuck

¢

DRINK IT AGAIN?

☐ Not even if you paid me.   ☐ Maybe, if very drunk.   ☐ Sure, why not?

☐ Yes, please.   ☐ And again, and again.   ☐ If only I could afford it!

NOTES:

NAME: _____ VINTAGE (aka year): _____

GRAPE VARIETY/BLEND: _____ ALCOHOL %: _____

PRICE: _____ ☐ Cork ☐ Fake cork ☐ Screw top ☐ Box

I DRANK THIS:

When: _____ Where: _____

With: _____ Because: _____

COLOR:

Greenish · Yellowish · Golden · Pinkish · Light red · Medium red · Dark red · Nearly midnight

AROMA

First impression:

_____

Second thoughts:

_____

☐ Short legs

☐ Long legs

SWEETNESS
☐ Bone dry   ☐ Dry   ☐ Not so dry   ☐ Sweet   ☐ Like candy

ACIDITY
☐ Tart   ☐ Crisp   ☐ Fresh   ☐ Soft   ☐ Flabby

FLAVOR INTENSITY
☐ DOA   ☐ Subtle   ☐ Bold   ☐ Ferocious

BODY
☐ Watery   ☐ Silky   ☐ Velvety   ☐ Syrupy

FINISH
☐ Flash in the pan   ☐ Pleasantly lingering   ☐ Won't go away

THIS WINE WILL PAIR WELL WITH:

☐ Fish   ☐ Chicken   ☐ Meat

☐ A cheese plate   ☐ Dessert   ☐ Duck a l'orange

OVERALL RATING:

PURE VINEGAR   PURE DELIGHT

SWEET SPOT MATRIX

Considering price and taste, indicate wine's position on the graph.

$$$$

• Jet fuel   • 1869 Château Lafite

Swill   Nectar

• Two-buck Chuck

¢

DRINK IT AGAIN?

☐ Not even if you paid me.   ☐ Maybe, if very drunk.   ☐ Sure, why not?

☐ Yes, please.   ☐ And again, and again.   ☐ If only I could afford it!

NOTES: _____

NAME: _____ VINTAGE (aka year): _____

GRAPE VARIETY/BLEND: _____ ALCOHOL %: _____

PRICE: _____ ☐ Cork ☐ Fake cork ☐ Screw top ☐ Box

I DRANK THIS:

When: _____ Where: _____

With: _____ Because: _____

COLOR:

Greenish · Yellowish · Golden · Pinkish · Light red · Medium red · Dark red · Nearly midnight

AROMA

First impression:

_____

Second thoughts:

_____

☐ Short legs

☐ Long legs

SWEETNESS

☐ Bone dry ☐ Dry ☐ Not so dry ☐ Sweet ☐ Like candy

ACIDITY

☐ Tart ☐ Crisp ☐ Fresh ☐ Soft ☐ Flabby

FLAVOR INTENSITY

☐ DOA ☐ Subtle ☐ Bold ☐ Ferocious

BODY

☐ Watery ☐ Silky ☐ Velvety ☐ Syrupy

FINISH

☐ Flash in the pan ☐ Pleasantly lingering ☐ Won't go away

THIS WINE WILL PAIR WELL WITH:

☐ Fish   ☐ Chicken   ☐ Meat

☐ A cheese plate ☐ Dessert   ☐ A complete breakfast

OVERALL RATING:

PURE
VINEGAR

PURE
DELIGHT

SWEET SPOT MATRIX

Considering price and taste,
indicate wine's position on
the graph.

$$$$

• Jet fuel

• 1869
Château
Lafite

Swill

Nectar

• Two-buck
Chuck

¢

DRINK IT AGAIN?

☐ Not even if you paid me.   ☐ Maybe, if very drunk.   ☐ Sure, why not?

☐ Yes, please.   ☐ And again, and again.   ☐ If only I could afford it!

NOTES:

NAME: _____ VINTAGE (aka year): _____

GRAPE VARIETY/BLEND: _____ ALCOHOL %: _____

PRICE: _____ ☐ Cork   ☐ Fake cork   ☐ Screw top   ☐ Box

I DRANK THIS:

When: _____ Where: _____

With: _____ Because: _____

COLOR:

Greenish · Yellowish · Golden · Pinkish · Light red · Medium red · Dark red · Nearly midnight

AROMA

First impression:
_____

_____

Second thoughts:

_____

☐ Short legs

☐ Long legs

SWEETNESS
☐ Bone dry   ☐ Dry   ☐ Not so dry   ☐ Sweet   ☐ Like candy

ACIDITY
☐ Tart   ☐ Crisp   ☐ Fresh   ☐ Soft   ☐ Flabby

FLAVOR INTENSITY
☐ DOA   ☐ Subtle   ☐ Bold   ☐ Ferocious

BODY
☐ Watery   ☐ Silky   ☐ Velvety   ☐ Syrupy

FINISH
☐ Flash in the pan   ☐ Pleasantly lingering   ☐ Won't go away

THIS WINE WILL PAIR WELL WITH:

☐ Fish   ☐ Chicken   ☐ Meat

☐ A cheese plate   ☐ Dessert   ☐ A three-pound lobster

OVERALL RATING:

PURE
VINEGAR   PURE
DELIGHT

SWEET SPOT MATRIX

Considering price and taste,
indicate wine's position on
the graph.

$$$$

• Jet fuel

• 1869
Château
Lafite

Swill   Nectar

• Two-buck
Chuck

¢

DRINK IT AGAIN?

☐ Not even if you paid me.   ☐ Maybe, if very drunk.   ☐ Sure, why not?

☐ Yes, please.   ☐ And again, and again.   ☐ If only I could afford it!

NOTES:

NAME: _____ VINTAGE (aka year): _____

GRAPE VARIETY/BLEND: _____ ALCOHOL %: _____

PRICE: _____ ☐ Cork ☐ Fake cork ☐ Screw top ☐ Box

I DRANK THIS:

When: _____ Where: _____

With: _____ Because: _____

COLOR:
Greenish · Yellowish · Golden · Pinkish · Light red · Medium red · Dark red · Nearly midnight

AROMA

First impression:

_____

☐ Short legs

☐ Long legs

Second thoughts:

_____

SWEETNESS
☐ Bone dry   ☐ Dry   ☐ Not so dry   ☐ Sweet   ☐ Like candy

ACIDITY
☐ Tart   ☐ Crisp   ☐ Fresh   ☐ Soft   ☐ Flabby

FLAVOR INTENSITY
☐ DOA   ☐ Subtle   ☐ Bold   ☐ Ferocious

BODY
☐ Watery   ☐ Silky   ☐ Velvety   ☐ Syrupy

FINISH
☐ Flash in the pan   ☐ Pleasantly lingering   ☐ Won't go away

THIS WINE WILL PAIR WELL WITH:

☐ Fish ☐ Chicken ☐ Meat

☐ A cheese plate ☐ Dessert ☐ Rock and roll

OVERALL RATING:

PURE
VINEGAR

PURE
DELIGHT

SWEET SPOT MATRIX

Considering price and taste, indicate wine's position on the graph.

$$$$

• Jet fuel

• 1869
Château
Lafite

Swill

Nectar

• Two-buck
Chuck

¢

DRINK IT AGAIN?

☐ Not even if you paid me. ☐ Maybe, if very drunk. ☐ Sure, why not?

☐ Yes, please. ☐ And again, and again. ☐ If only I could afford it!

NOTES:

NAME: _____ VINTAGE (aka year): _____

GRAPE VARIETY/BLEND: _____ ALCOHOL %: _____

PRICE: _____ ☐ Cork ☐ Fake cork ☐ Screw top ☐ Box

I DRANK THIS:

When: _____ Where: _____

With: _____ Because: _____

COLOR:

Greenish · Yellowish · Golden · Pinkish · Light red · Medium red · Dark red · Nearly midnight

AROMA

First impression:

_____

Second thoughts:

_____

☐ Short legs

☐ Long legs

SWEETNESS

☐ Bone dry ☐ Dry ☐ Not so dry ☐ Sweet ☐ Like candy

ACIDITY

☐ Tart ☐ Crisp ☐ Fresh ☐ Soft ☐ Flabby

FLAVOR INTENSITY

☐ DOA ☐ Subtle ☐ Bold ☐ Ferocious

BODY

☐ Watery ☐ Silky ☐ Velvety ☐ Syrupy

FINISH

☐ Flash in the pan ☐ Pleasantly lingering ☐ Won't go away

THIS WINE WILL PAIR WELL WITH:

☐ Fish   ☐ Chicken   ☐ Meat

☐ A cheese plate   ☐ Dessert   ☐ Street tacos

OVERALL RATING:

PURE
VINEGAR

PURE
DELIGHT

SWEET SPOT MATRIX

Considering price and taste,
indicate wine's position on
the graph.

$$$$

• Jet fuel

• 1869
Château
Lafite

Swill

Nectar

• Two-buck
Chuck

¢

DRINK IT AGAIN?

☐ Not even if you paid me.   ☐ Maybe, if very drunk.   ☐ Sure, why not?

☐ Yes, please.   ☐ And again, and again.   ☐ If only I could afford it!

NOTES:

_____

_____

_____

_____

_____

_____

_____

_____

_____

_____

_____

_____

NAME: _____ VINTAGE (aka year): _____

GRAPE VARIETY/BLEND: _____ ALCOHOL %: _____

PRICE: _____ ☐ Cork ☐ Fake cork ☐ Screw top ☐ Box

I DRANK THIS:

When: _____ Where: _____

With: _____ Because: _____

COLOR:

Greenish · Yellowish · Golden · Pinkish · Light red · Medium red · Dark red · Nearly midnight

AROMA

First impression:

_____

Second thoughts:

_____

☐ Short legs

☐ Long legs

SWEETNESS

☐ Bone dry   ☐ Dry   ☐ Not so dry   ☐ Sweet   ☐ Like candy

ACIDITY

☐ Tart   ☐ Crisp   ☐ Fresh   ☐ Soft   ☐ Flabby

FLAVOR INTENSITY

☐ DOA   ☐ Subtle   ☐ Bold   ☐ Ferocious

BODY

☐ Watery   ☐ Silky   ☐ Velvety   ☐ Syrupy

FINISH

☐ Flash in the pan   ☐ Pleasantly lingering   ☐ Won't go away

THIS WINE WILL PAIR WELL WITH:

☐ Fish   ☐ Chicken   ☐ Meat

☐ A cheese plate   ☐ Dessert   ☐ Hemingway

OVERALL RATING:

PURE VINEGAR   PURE DELIGHT

SWEET SPOT MATRIX

Considering price and taste, indicate wine's position on the graph.

$$$$

- Jet fuel

- 1869 Château Lafite

Swill   Nectar

- Two-buck Chuck

¢

DRINK IT AGAIN?

☐ Not even if you paid me.   ☐ Maybe, if very drunk.   ☐ Sure, why not?

☐ Yes, please.   ☐ And again, and again.   ☐ If only I could afford it!

NOTES:

NAME: _____ VINTAGE (aka year): _____

GRAPE VARIETY/BLEND: _____ ALCOHOL %: _____

PRICE: _____ ☐ Cork   ☐ Fake cork   ☐ Screw top   ☐ Box

I DRANK THIS:

When: _____ Where: _____

With: _____ Because: _____

COLOR:

Greenish · Yellowish · Golden · Pinkish · Light red · Medium red · Dark red · Nearly midnight

AROMA

First impression:

_____

Second thoughts:

_____

☐ Short legs

☐ Long legs

SWEETNESS

☐ Bone dry   ☐ Dry   ☐ Not so dry   ☐ Sweet   ☐ Like candy

ACIDITY

☐ Tart   ☐ Crisp   ☐ Fresh   ☐ Soft   ☐ Flabby

FLAVOR INTENSITY

☐ DOA   ☐ Subtle   ☐ Bold   ☐ Ferocious

BODY

☐ Watery   ☐ Silky   ☐ Velvety   ☐ Syrupy

FINISH

☐ Flash in the pan   ☐ Pleasantly lingering   ☐ Won't go away

THIS WINE WILL PAIR WELL WITH:

☐ Fish ☐ Chicken ☐ Meat

☐ A cheese plate ☐ Dessert ☐ Pupusas

OVERALL RATING:

PURE
VINEGAR

PURE
DELIGHT

SWEET SPOT MATRIX

Considering price and taste,
indicate wine's position on
the graph.

$$$$

Swill

Nectar

• Jet fuel

• 1869
Château
Lafite

• Two-buck
Chuck

¢

DRINK IT AGAIN?

☐ Not even if you paid me. ☐ Maybe, if very drunk. ☐ Sure, why not?

☐ Yes, please. ☐ And again, and again. ☐ If only I could afford it!

NOTES:

NAME: _____ VINTAGE (aka year): _____

GRAPE VARIETY/BLEND: _____ ALCOHOL %: _____

PRICE: _____ ☐ Cork   ☐ Fake cork   ☐ Screw top   ☐ Box

I DRANK THIS:

When: _____ Where: _____

With: _____ Because: _____

COLOR:

Greenish · Yellowish · Golden · Pinkish · Light red · Medium red · Dark red · Nearly midnight

AROMA

First impression:

_____

Second thoughts:

_____

☐ Short legs

☐ Long legs

SWEETNESS

☐ Bone dry   ☐ Dry   ☐ Not so dry   ☐ Sweet   ☐ Like candy

ACIDITY

☐ Tart   ☐ Crisp   ☐ Fresh   ☐ Soft   ☐ Flabby

FLAVOR INTENSITY

☐ DOA   ☐ Subtle   ☐ Bold   ☐ Ferocious

BODY

☐ Watery   ☐ Silky   ☐ Velvety   ☐ Syrupy

FINISH

☐ Flash in the pan   ☐ Pleasantly lingering   ☐ Won't go away

THIS WINE WILL PAIR WELL WITH:

☐ Fish ☐ Chicken ☐ Meat

☐ A cheese plate ☐ Dessert ☐ Macaroni and cheese

OVERALL RATING:

PURE
VINEGAR

PURE
DELIGHT

SWEET SPOT MATRIX

Considering price and taste,
indicate wine's position on
the graph.

$$$$

• Jet fuel

• 1869
Château
Lafite

Swill

Nectar

• Two-buck
Chuck

¢

DRINK IT AGAIN?

☐ Not even if you paid me. ☐ Maybe, if very drunk. ☐ Sure, why not?

☐ Yes, please. ☐ And again, and again. ☐ If only I could afford it!

NOTES: _____

_____

_____

_____

_____

_____

_____

_____

_____

_____

NAME: _____ VINTAGE (aka year): _____

GRAPE VARIETY/BLEND: _____ ALCOHOL %: _____

PRICE: _____ ☐ Cork   ☐ Fake cork   ☐ Screw top   ☐ Box

I DRANK THIS:

When: _____ Where: _____

With: _____ Because: _____

COLOR:

Greenish · Yellowish · Golden · Pinkish · Light red · Medium red · Dark red · Nearly midnight

AROMA

First impression:

_____

Second thoughts:

_____

☐ Short legs

☐ Long legs

SWEETNESS
☐ Bone dry   ☐ Dry   ☐ Not so dry   ☐ Sweet   ☐ Like candy

ACIDITY
☐ Tart   ☐ Crisp   ☐ Fresh   ☐ Soft   ☐ Flabby

FLAVOR INTENSITY
☐ DOA   ☐ Subtle   ☐ Bold   ☐ Ferocious

BODY
☐ Watery   ☐ Silky   ☐ Velvety   ☐ Syrupy

FINISH
☐ Flash in the pan   ☐ Pleasantly lingering   ☐ Won't go away

THIS WINE WILL PAIR WELL WITH:

☐ Fish   ☐ Chicken   ☐ Meat

☐ A cheese plate   ☐ Dessert   ☐ A midnight tryst

OVERALL RATING:

PURE
VINEGAR   PURE
                                 DELIGHT

SWEET SPOT MATRIX

Considering price and taste,
indicate wine's position on
the graph.

$$$$

• Jet fuel

• 1869
  Château
  Lafite

Swill   Nectar

• Two-buck
  Chuck

¢

DRINK IT AGAIN?

☐ Not even if you paid me.   ☐ Maybe, if very drunk.   ☐ Sure, why not?

☐ Yes, please.   ☐ And again, and again.   ☐ If only I could afford it!

NOTES:

_____

_____

_____

_____

_____

_____

_____

_____

_____

_____

_____

_____

NAME: _____ VINTAGE (aka year): _____

GRAPE VARIETY/BLEND: _____ ALCOHOL %: _____

PRICE: _____ ☐ Cork   ☐ Fake cork   ☐ Screw top   ☐ Box

I DRANK THIS:

When: _____ Where: _____

With: _____ Because: _____

COLOR:

Greenish · Yellowish · Golden · Pinkish · Light red · Medium red · Dark red · Nearly midnight

AROMA

First impression:

_____

Second thoughts:

_____

☐ Short legs

☐ Long legs

SWEETNESS

☐ Bone dry   ☐ Dry   ☐ Not so dry   ☐ Sweet   ☐ Like candy

ACIDITY

☐ Tart   ☐ Crisp   ☐ Fresh   ☐ Soft   ☐ Flabby

FLAVOR INTENSITY

☐ DOA   ☐ Subtle   ☐ Bold   ☐ Ferocious

BODY

☐ Watery   ☐ Silky   ☐ Velvety   ☐ Syrupy

FINISH

☐ Flash in the pan   ☐ Pleasantly lingering   ☐ Won't go away

THIS WINE WILL PAIR WELL WITH:

☐ Fish   ☐ Chicken   ☐ Meat

☐ A cheese plate ☐ Dessert   ☐ Leftovers

OVERALL RATING:

PURE
VINEGAR   PURE
DELIGHT

SWEET SPOT MATRIX

Considering price and taste,
indicate wine's position on
the graph.

$$$$

• Jet fuel

• 1869
Château
Lafite

Swill ——————————— Nectar

• Two-buck
Chuck

¢

DRINK IT AGAIN?

☐ Not even if you paid me.   ☐ Maybe, if very drunk.   ☐ Sure, why not?

☐ Yes, please.   ☐ And again, and again.   ☐ If only I could afford it!

NOTES: _____

_____

_____

_____

_____

_____

_____

_____

_____

_____

_____

_____

_____

NAME: _____ VINTAGE (aka year): _____

GRAPE VARIETY/BLEND: _____ ALCOHOL %: _____

PRICE: _____ ☐ Cork   ☐ Fake cork   ☐ Screw top   ☐ Box

I DRANK THIS:

When: _____ Where: _____

With: _____ Because: _____

COLOR:

Greenish · Yellowish · Golden · Pinkish · Light red · Medium red · Dark red · Nearly midnight

AROMA

First impression:

_____

Second thoughts:

_____

☐ Short legs

☐ Long legs

SWEETNESS

☐ Bone dry   ☐ Dry   ☐ Not so dry   ☐ Sweet   ☐ Like candy

ACIDITY

☐ Tart   ☐ Crisp   ☐ Fresh   ☐ Soft   ☐ Flabby

FLAVOR INTENSITY

☐ DOA   ☐ Subtle   ☐ Bold   ☐ Ferocious

BODY

☐ Watery   ☐ Silky   ☐ Velvety   ☐ Syrupy

FINISH

☐ Flash in the pan   ☐ Pleasantly lingering   ☐ Won't go away

THIS WINE WILL PAIR WELL WITH:

☐ Fish ☐ Chicken ☐ Meat

☐ A cheese plate ☐ Dessert ☐ Oysters Rockefeller

OVERALL RATING:

PURE
VINEGAR

PURE
DELIGHT

SWEET SPOT MATRIX

Considering price and taste,
indicate wine's position on
the graph.

$$$$

• Jet fuel

• 1869
Château
Lafite

Swill

Nectar

• Two-buck
Chuck

¢

DRINK IT AGAIN?

☐ Not even if you paid me. ☐ Maybe, if very drunk. ☐ Sure, why not?

☐ Yes, please. ☐ And again, and again. ☐ If only I could afford it!

NOTES:

_____

_____

_____

_____

_____

_____

_____

_____

_____

_____

_____

_____

NAME: _____ VINTAGE (aka year): _____

GRAPE VARIETY/BLEND: _____ ALCOHOL %: _____

PRICE: _____ ☐ Cork   ☐ Fake cork   ☐ Screw top   ☐ Box

I DRANK THIS:

When: _____ Where: _____

With: _____ Because: _____

COLOR:
Greenish · Yellowish · Golden · Pinkish · Light red · Medium red · Dark red · Nearly midnight

AROMA

First impression:

_____

Second thoughts:

_____

☐ Short legs

☐ Long legs

SWEETNESS
☐ Bone dry   ☐ Dry   ☐ Not so dry   ☐ Sweet   ☐ Like candy

ACIDITY
☐ Tart   ☐ Crisp   ☐ Fresh   ☐ Soft   ☐ Flabby

FLAVOR INTENSITY
☐ DOA   ☐ Subtle   ☐ Bold   ☐ Ferocious

BODY
☐ Watery   ☐ Silky   ☐ Velvety   ☐ Syrupy

FINISH
☐ Flash in the pan   ☐ Pleasantly lingering   ☐ Won't go away

THIS WINE WILL PAIR WELL WITH:

☐ Fish   ☐ Chicken   ☐ Meat

☐ A cheese plate   ☐ Dessert   ☐ Barbequed ribs

OVERALL RATING:

PURE
VINEGAR

PURE
DELIGHT

SWEET SPOT MATRIX

Considering price and taste, indicate wine's position on the graph.

$$$$

• Jet fuel

• 1869
Château
Lafite

Swill

Nectar

• Two-buck
Chuck

¢

DRINK IT AGAIN?

☐ Not even if you paid me.   ☐ Maybe, if very drunk.   ☐ Sure, why not?

☐ Yes, please.   ☐ And again, and again.   ☐ If only I could afford it!

NOTES: _____

_____

_____

_____

_____

_____

_____

_____

_____

_____

_____

_____

_____

NAME: _____ VINTAGE (aka year): _____

GRAPE VARIETY/BLEND: _____ ALCOHOL %: _____

PRICE: _____ ☐ Cork ☐ Fake cork ☐ Screw top ☐ Box

I DRANK THIS:

When: _____ Where: _____

With: _____ Because: _____

COLOR:

Greenish · Yellowish · Golden · Pinkish · Light red · Medium red · Dark red · Nearly midnight

AROMA

First impression:

_____

Second thoughts:

_____

☐ Short legs

☐ Long legs

SWEETNESS

☐ Bone dry ☐ Dry ☐ Not so dry ☐ Sweet ☐ Like candy

ACIDITY

☐ Tart ☐ Crisp ☐ Fresh ☐ Soft ☐ Flabby

FLAVOR INTENSITY

☐ DOA ☐ Subtle ☐ Bold ☐ Ferocious

BODY

☐ Watery ☐ Silky ☐ Velvety ☐ Syrupy

FINISH

☐ Flash in the pan ☐ Pleasantly lingering ☐ Won't go away

THIS WINE WILL PAIR WELL WITH:

☐ Fish   ☐ Chicken   ☐ Meat

☐ A cheese plate   ☐ Dessert   ☐ Tuna noodle casserole

OVERALL RATING:

PURE
VINEGAR   PURE
DELIGHT

SWEET SPOT MATRIX

Considering price and taste,
indicate wine's position on
the graph.

$$$$

• Jet fuel   • 1869
                     Château
                     Lafite

Swill   Nectar

                    • Two-buck
                      Chuck

¢

DRINK IT AGAIN?

☐ Not even if you paid me.   ☐ Maybe, if very drunk.   ☐ Sure, why not?

☐ Yes, please.   ☐ And again, and again.   ☐ If only I could afford it!

NOTES:

NAME: _____ VINTAGE (aka year): _____

GRAPE VARIETY/BLEND: _____ ALCOHOL %: _____

PRICE: _____ ☐ Cork   ☐ Fake cork   ☐ Screw top   ☐ Box

I DRANK THIS:

When: _____ Where: _____

With: _____ Because: _____

COLOR:

Greenish · Yellowish · Golden · Pinkish · Light red · Medium red · Dark red · Nearly midnight

AROMA

First impression:

_____

Second thoughts:

_____

☐ Short legs

☐ Long legs

SWEETNESS

| ☐ Bone dry | ☐ Dry | ☐ Not so dry | ☐ Sweet | ☐ Like candy |

ACIDITY

| ☐ Tart | ☐ Crisp | ☐ Fresh | ☐ Soft | ☐ Flabby |

FLAVOR INTENSITY

| ☐ DOA | ☐ Subtle | ☐ Bold | ☐ Ferocious |

BODY

| ☐ Watery | ☐ Silky | ☐ Velvety | ☐ Syrupy |

FINISH

| ☐ Flash in the pan | ☐ Pleasantly lingering | ☐ Won't go away |

THIS WINE WILL PAIR WELL WITH:

☐ Fish   ☐ Chicken   ☐ Meat

☐ A cheese plate   ☐ Dessert   ☐ Truffles

OVERALL RATING:

PURE
VINEGAR   PURE
DELIGHT

SWEET SPOT MATRIX

Considering price and taste,
indicate wine's position on
the graph.

$$$$

• Jet fuel   • 1869
Château
Lafite

Swill   Nectar

• Two-buck
Chuck

¢

DRINK IT AGAIN?

☐ Not even if you paid me.   ☐ Maybe, if very drunk.   ☐ Sure, why not?

☐ Yes, please.   ☐ And again, and again.   ☐ If only I could afford it!

NOTES: _____

NAME: _____ VINTAGE (aka year): _____

GRAPE VARIETY/BLEND: _____ ALCOHOL %: _____

PRICE: _____ ☐ Cork   ☐ Fake cork   ☐ Screw top   ☐ Box

I DRANK THIS:

When: _____ Where: _____

With: _____ Because: _____

COLOR:

Greenish · Yellowish · Golden · Pinkish · Light red · Medium red · Dark red · Nearly midnight

AROMA

First impression:

_____

Second thoughts:

_____

☐ Short legs

☐ Long legs

SWEETNESS

| ☐ Bone dry | ☐ Dry | ☐ Not so dry | ☐ Sweet | ☐ Like candy |

ACIDITY

| ☐ Tart | ☐ Crisp | ☐ Fresh | ☐ Soft | ☐ Flabby |

FLAVOR INTENSITY

| ☐ DOA | ☐ Subtle | ☐ Bold | ☐ Ferocious |

BODY

| ☐ Watery | ☐ Silky | ☐ Velvety | ☐ Syrupy |

FINISH

| ☐ Flash in the pan | ☐ Pleasantly lingering | ☐ Won't go away |

THIS WINE WILL PAIR WELL WITH:

☐ Fish   ☐ Chicken   ☐ Meat

☐ A cheese plate   ☐ Dessert   ☐ 1980s flashbacks

OVERALL RATING:

PURE
VINEGAR

PURE
DELIGHT

SWEET SPOT MATRIX

Considering price and taste, indicate wine's position on the graph.

$$$$

• Jet fuel

• 1869
Château
Lafite

Swill

Nectar

• Two-buck
Chuck

¢

DRINK IT AGAIN?

☐ Not even if you paid me.   ☐ Maybe, if very drunk.   ☐ Sure, why not?

☐ Yes, please.   ☐ And again, and again.   ☐ If only I could afford it!

NOTES:

_____

_____

_____

_____

_____

_____

_____

_____

_____

_____

_____

_____

_____

NAME: _____ VINTAGE (aka year): _____

GRAPE VARIETY/BLEND: _____ ALCOHOL %: _____

PRICE: _____ ☐ Cork   ☐ Fake cork   ☐ Screw top   ☐ Box

I DRANK THIS:

When: _____ Where: _____

With: _____ Because: _____

COLOR:

Greenish · Yellowish · Golden · Pinkish · Light red · Medium red · Dark red · Nearly midnight

AROMA

First impression:

_____

Second thoughts:

_____

☐ Short legs

☐ Long legs

SWEETNESS
☐ Bone dry   ☐ Dry   ☐ Not so dry   ☐ Sweet   ☐ Like candy

ACIDITY
☐ Tart   ☐ Crisp   ☐ Fresh   ☐ Soft   ☐ Flabby

FLAVOR INTENSITY
☐ DOA   ☐ Subtle   ☐ Bold   ☐ Ferocious

BODY
☐ Watery   ☐ Silky   ☐ Velvety   ☐ Syrupy

FINISH
☐ Flash in the pan   ☐ Pleasantly lingering   ☐ Won't go away

THIS WINE WILL PAIR WELL WITH:

☐ Fish   ☐ Chicken   ☐ Meat

☐ A cheese plate   ☐ Dessert   ☐ The Argentine tango

OVERALL RATING:

PURE
VINEGAR   PURE
                          DELIGHT

SWEET SPOT MATRIX

Considering price and taste, indicate wine's position on the graph.

$$$$

• Jet fuel   • 1869
                              Château
                              Lafite

Swill   Nectar

                    • Two-buck
                      Chuck

¢

DRINK IT AGAIN?

☐ Not even if you paid me.   ☐ Maybe, if very drunk.   ☐ Sure, why not?

☐ Yes, please.   ☐ And again, and again.   ☐ If only I could afford it!

NOTES: _____

NAME: _____ VINTAGE (aka year): _____

GRAPE VARIETY/BLEND: _____ ALCOHOL %: _____

PRICE: _____ ☐ Cork ☐ Fake cork ☐ Screw top ☐ Box

I DRANK THIS:

When: _____ Where: _____

With: _____ Because: _____

COLOR:

Greenish · Yellowish · Golden · Pinkish · Light red · Medium red · Dark red · Nearly midnight

AROMA

First impression:

_____

☐ Short legs

☐ Long legs

Second thoughts:

_____

SWEETNESS

☐ Bone dry   ☐ Dry   ☐ Not so dry   ☐ Sweet   ☐ Like candy

ACIDITY

☐ Tart   ☐ Crisp   ☐ Fresh   ☐ Soft   ☐ Flabby

FLAVOR INTENSITY

☐ DOA   ☐ Subtle   ☐ Bold   ☐ Ferocious

BODY

☐ Watery   ☐ Silky   ☐ Velvety   ☐ Syrupy

FINISH

☐ Flash in the pan   ☐ Pleasantly lingering   ☐ Won't go away

THIS WINE WILL PAIR WELL WITH:

☐ Fish ☐ Chicken ☐ Meat

☐ A cheese plate ☐ Dessert ☐ Salami

OVERALL RATING:

PURE
VINEGAR

PURE
DELIGHT

SWEET SPOT MATRIX

Considering price and taste,
indicate wine's position on
the graph.

$$$$

• Jet fuel

• 1869
Château
Lafite

Swill

Nectar

• Two-buck
Chuck

¢

DRINK IT AGAIN?

☐ Not even if you paid me. ☐ Maybe, if very drunk. ☐ Sure, why not?

☐ Yes, please. ☐ And again, and again. ☐ If only I could afford it!

NOTES:

NAME: _____ VINTAGE (aka year): _____

GRAPE VARIETY/BLEND: _____ ALCOHOL %: _____

PRICE: _____ ☐ Cork   ☐ Fake cork   ☐ Screw top   ☐ Box

I DRANK THIS:

When: _____ Where: _____

With: _____ Because: _____

COLOR:

Greenish · Yellowish · Golden · Pinkish · Light red · Medium red · Dark red · Nearly midnight

AROMA

First impression:

_____

Second thoughts:

_____

☐ Short legs

☐ Long legs

SWEETNESS

☐ Bone dry   ☐ Dry   ☐ Not so dry   ☐ Sweet   ☐ Like candy

ACIDITY

☐ Tart   ☐ Crisp   ☐ Fresh   ☐ Soft   ☐ Flabby

FLAVOR INTENSITY

☐ DOA   ☐ Subtle   ☐ Bold   ☐ Ferocious

BODY

☐ Watery   ☐ Silky   ☐ Velvety   ☐ Syrupy

FINISH

☐ Flash in the pan   ☐ Pleasantly lingering   ☐ Won't go away

THIS WINE WILL PAIR WELL WITH:

☐ Fish   ☐ Chicken   ☐ Meat

☐ A cheese plate   ☐ Dessert   ☐ Fried calamari

OVERALL RATING:

PURE
VINEGAR   PURE
DELIGHT

SWEET SPOT MATRIX

Considering price and taste, indicate wine's position on the graph.

$$$$

• Jet fuel   • 1869
Château
Lafite

Swill   Nectar

• Two-buck
Chuck

¢

DRINK IT AGAIN?

☐ Not even if you paid me.   ☐ Maybe, if very drunk.   ☐ Sure, why not?

☐ Yes, please.   ☐ And again, and again.   ☐ If only I could afford it!

NOTES: _____

_____

_____

_____

_____

_____

_____

_____

_____

_____

_____

_____

NAME: _____ VINTAGE (aka year): _____

GRAPE VARIETY/BLEND: _____ ALCOHOL %: _____

PRICE: _____ ☐ Cork ☐ Fake cork ☐ Screw top ☐ Box

I DRANK THIS:

When: _____ Where: _____

With: _____ Because: _____

COLOR:

Greenish · Yellowish · Golden · Pinkish · Light red · Medium red · Dark red · Nearly midnight

AROMA

First impression:

_____

Second thoughts:

_____

☐ Short legs

☐ Long legs

SWEETNESS

☐ Bone dry   ☐ Dry   ☐ Not so dry   ☐ Sweet   ☐ Like candy

ACIDITY

☐ Tart   ☐ Crisp   ☐ Fresh   ☐ Soft   ☐ Flabby

FLAVOR INTENSITY

☐ DOA   ☐ Subtle   ☐ Bold   ☐ Ferocious

BODY

☐ Watery   ☐ Silky   ☐ Velvety   ☐ Syrupy

FINISH

☐ Flash in the pan   ☐ Pleasantly lingering   ☐ Won't go away

THIS WINE WILL PAIR WELL WITH:

☐ Fish   ☐ Chicken   ☐ Meat

☐ A cheese plate   ☐ Dessert   ☐ The blue plate special

OVERALL RATING:

PURE
VINEGAR   PURE
DELIGHT

SWEET SPOT MATRIX

Considering price and taste,
indicate wine's position on
the graph.

$$$$

Swill   Nectar

• Jet fuel

• 1869
Château
Lafite

• Two-buck
Chuck

¢

DRINK IT AGAIN?

☐ Not even if you paid me.   ☐ Maybe, if very drunk.   ☐ Sure, why not?

☐ Yes, please.   ☐ And again, and again.   ☐ If only I could afford it!

NOTES:

_____

_____

_____

_____

_____

_____

_____

_____

_____

_____

_____

_____

NAME: _____ VINTAGE (aka year): _____

GRAPE VARIETY/BLEND: _____ ALCOHOL %: _____

PRICE: _____ ☐ Cork   ☐ Fake cork   ☐ Screw top   ☐ Box

I DRANK THIS:

When: _____ Where: _____

With: _____ Because: _____

COLOR:

Greenish · Yellowish · Golden · Pinkish · Light red · Medium red · Dark red · Nearly midnight

AROMA

First impression:

_____

Second thoughts:

_____

☐ Short legs

☐ Long legs

SWEETNESS

☐ Bone dry   ☐ Dry   ☐ Not so dry   ☐ Sweet   ☐ Like candy

ACIDITY

☐ Tart   ☐ Crisp   ☐ Fresh   ☐ Soft   ☐ Flabby

FLAVOR INTENSITY

☐ DOA   ☐ Subtle   ☐ Bold   ☐ Ferocious

BODY

☐ Watery   ☐ Silky   ☐ Velvety   ☐ Syrupy

FINISH

☐ Flash in the pan   ☐ Pleasantly lingering   ☐ Won't go away

THIS WINE WILL PAIR WELL WITH:

☐ Fish ☐ Chicken ☐ Meat

☐ A cheese plate ☐ Dessert ☐ Carne asada

OVERALL RATING:

PURE
VINEGAR

PURE
DELIGHT

SWEET SPOT MATRIX

Considering price and taste, indicate wine's position on the graph.

$$$$

Swill

• Jet fuel

• 1869
Château
Lafite

Nectar

• Two-buck
Chuck

¢

DRINK IT AGAIN?

☐ Not even if you paid me. ☐ Maybe, if very drunk. ☐ Sure, why not?

☐ Yes, please. ☐ And again, and again. ☐ If only I could afford it!

NOTES: _____

NAME: _____ VINTAGE (aka year): _____

GRAPE VARIETY/BLEND: _____ ALCOHOL %: _____

PRICE: _____ ☐ Cork   ☐ Fake cork   ☐ Screw top   ☐ Box

I DRANK THIS:

When: _____ Where: _____

With: _____ Because: _____

COLOR:

Greenish · Yellowish · Golden · Pinkish · Light red · Medium red · Dark red · Nearly midnight

AROMA

First impression:

_____

Second thoughts:

_____

☐ Short legs

☐ Long legs

SWEETNESS

☐ Bone dry   ☐ Dry   ☐ Not so dry   ☐ Sweet   ☐ Like candy

ACIDITY

☐ Tart   ☐ Crisp   ☐ Fresh   ☐ Soft   ☐ Flabby

FLAVOR INTENSITY

☐ DOA   ☐ Subtle   ☐ Bold   ☐ Ferocious

BODY

☐ Watery   ☐ Silky   ☐ Velvety   ☐ Syrupy

FINISH

☐ Flash in the pan   ☐ Pleasantly lingering   ☐ Won't go away

THIS WINE WILL PAIR WELL WITH:

☐ Fish   ☐ Chicken   ☐ Meat

☐ A cheese plate   ☐ Dessert   ☐ Franks and beans

OVERALL RATING:

PURE
VINEGAR

PURE
DELIGHT

SWEET SPOT MATRIX

Considering price and taste,
indicate wine's position on
the graph.

$$$$

• Jet fuel

• 1869
Château
Lafite

Swill

Nectar

• Two-buck
Chuck

¢

DRINK IT AGAIN?

☐ Not even if you paid me.   ☐ Maybe, if very drunk.   ☐ Sure, why not?

☐ Yes, please.   ☐ And again, and again.   ☐ If only I could afford it!

NOTES: _____

NAME: _____ VINTAGE (aka year): _____

GRAPE VARIETY/BLEND: _____ ALCOHOL %: _____

PRICE: _____ ☐ Cork ☐ Fake cork ☐ Screw top ☐ Box

I DRANK THIS:

When: _____ Where: _____

With: _____ Because: _____

COLOR:

Greenish · Yellowish · Golden · Pinkish · Light red · Medium red · Dark red · Nearly midnight

AROMA

First impression:

_____

☐ Short legs

☐ Long legs

Second thoughts:

_____

SWEETNESS

☐ Bone dry　　　☐ Dry　　　☐ Not so dry　　　☐ Sweet　　　☐ Like candy

ACIDITY

☐ Tart　　　☐ Crisp　　　☐ Fresh　　　☐ Soft　　　☐ Flabby

FLAVOR INTENSITY

☐ DOA　　　☐ Subtle　　　☐ Bold　　　☐ Ferocious

BODY

☐ Watery　　　☐ Silky　　　☐ Velvety　　　☐ Syrupy

FINISH

☐ Flash in the pan　　　☐ Pleasantly lingering　　　☐ Won't go away

THIS WINE WILL PAIR WELL WITH:

☐ Fish   ☐ Chicken   ☐ Meat

☐ A cheese plate ☐ Dessert   ☐ Dark chocolate

OVERALL RATING:

PURE
VINEGAR

PURE
DELIGHT

SWEET SPOT MATRIX

Considering price and taste,
indicate wine's position on
the graph.

$$$$

Swill

Nectar

• Jet fuel

• 1869
Château
Lafite

• Two-buck
Chuck

¢

DRINK IT AGAIN?

☐ Not even if you paid me.   ☐ Maybe, if very drunk.   ☐ Sure, why not?

☐ Yes, please.   ☐ And again, and again.   ☐ If only I could afford it!

NOTES:

NAME: _____ VINTAGE (aka year): _____

GRAPE VARIETY/BLEND: _____ ALCOHOL %: _____

PRICE: _____ ☐ Cork ☐ Fake cork ☐ Screw top ☐ Box

I DRANK THIS:

When: _____ Where: _____

With: _____ Because: _____

COLOR:

Greenish · Yellowish · Golden · Pinkish · Light red · Medium red · Dark red · Nearly midnight

AROMA

First impression:

_____

Second thoughts:

_____

☐ Short legs

☐ Long legs

SWEETNESS

☐ Bone dry ☐ Dry ☐ Not so dry ☐ Sweet ☐ Like candy

ACIDITY

☐ Tart ☐ Crisp ☐ Fresh ☐ Soft ☐ Flabby

FLAVOR INTENSITY

☐ DOA ☐ Subtle ☐ Bold ☐ Ferocious

BODY

☐ Watery ☐ Silky ☐ Velvety ☐ Syrupy

FINISH

☐ Flash in the pan ☐ Pleasantly lingering ☐ Won't go away

THIS WINE WILL PAIR WELL WITH:

☐ Fish   ☐ Chicken   ☐ Meat

☐ A cheese plate   ☐ Dessert   ☐ Wintry nights
by the fire

OVERALL RATING:

PURE
VINEGAR

PURE
DELIGHT

SWEET SPOT MATRIX

Considering price and taste,
indicate wine's position on
the graph.

$$$$

• Jet fuel

• 1869
Château
Lafite

Swill

Nectar

• Two-buck
Chuck

¢

DRINK IT AGAIN?

☐ Not even if you paid me.   ☐ Maybe, if very drunk.   ☐ Sure, why not?

☐ Yes, please.   ☐ And again, and again.   ☐ If only I could afford it!

NOTES: _____

NAME: _____ VINTAGE (aka year): _____

GRAPE VARIETY/BLEND: _____ ALCOHOL %: _____

PRICE: _____ ☐ Cork   ☐ Fake cork   ☐ Screw top   ☐ Box

I DRANK THIS:

When: _____ Where: _____

With: _____ Because: _____

COLOR:

Greenish · Yellowish · Golden · Pinkish · Light red · Medium red · Dark red · Nearly midnight

AROMA

First impression:

_____

Second thoughts:

_____

☐ Short legs

☐ Long legs

SWEETNESS

☐ Bone dry   ☐ Dry   ☐ Not so dry   ☐ Sweet   ☐ Like candy

ACIDITY

☐ Tart   ☐ Crisp   ☐ Fresh   ☐ Soft   ☐ Flabby

FLAVOR INTENSITY

☐ DOA   ☐ Subtle   ☐ Bold   ☐ Ferocious

BODY

☐ Watery   ☐ Silky   ☐ Velvety   ☐ Syrupy

FINISH

☐ Flash in the pan   ☐ Pleasantly lingering   ☐ Won't go away

THIS WINE WILL PAIR WELL WITH:

☐ Fish ☐ Chicken ☐ Meat

☐ A cheese plate ☐ Dessert ☐ Caesar salad

OVERALL RATING:

PURE VINEGAR — PURE DELIGHT

SWEET SPOT MATRIX

Considering price and taste, indicate wine's position on the graph.

$$$$

Swill — Nectar

¢

• Jet fuel

• 1869 Château Lafite

• Two-buck Chuck

DRINK IT AGAIN?

☐ Not even if you paid me.   ☐ Maybe, if very drunk.   ☐ Sure, why not?

☐ Yes, please.   ☐ And again, and again.   ☐ If only I could afford it!

NOTES:

NAME: _____ VINTAGE (aka year): _____

GRAPE VARIETY/BLEND: _____ ALCOHOL %: _____

PRICE: _____ ☐ Cork ☐ Fake cork ☐ Screw top ☐ Box

I DRANK THIS:

When: _____ Where: _____

With: _____ Because: _____

COLOR:

Greenish · Yellowish · Golden · Pinkish · Light red · Medium red · Dark red · Nearly midnight

AROMA

First impression:

_____

Second thoughts:

_____

☐ Short legs

☐ Long legs

SWEETNESS

☐ Bone dry ☐ Dry ☐ Not so dry ☐ Sweet ☐ Like candy

ACIDITY

☐ Tart ☐ Crisp ☐ Fresh ☐ Soft ☐ Flabby

FLAVOR INTENSITY

☐ DOA ☐ Subtle ☐ Bold ☐ Ferocious

BODY

☐ Watery ☐ Silky ☐ Velvety ☐ Syrupy

FINISH

☐ Flash in the pan ☐ Pleasantly lingering ☐ Won't go away

THIS WINE WILL PAIR WELL WITH:

☐ Fish ☐ Chicken ☐ Meat

☐ A cheese plate ☐ Dessert ☐ Quiche

OVERALL RATING:

PURE
VINEGAR

PURE
DELIGHT

SWEET SPOT MATRIX

Considering price and taste,
indicate wine's position on
the graph.

$$$$

• Jet fuel

• 1869
Château
Lafite

Swill

Nectar

• Two-buck
Chuck

¢

DRINK IT AGAIN?

☐ Not even if you paid me. ☐ Maybe, if very drunk. ☐ Sure, why not?

☐ Yes, please. ☐ And again, and again. ☐ If only I could afford it!

NOTES: _____

_____

_____

_____

_____

_____

_____

_____

_____

_____

_____

_____

NAME: _____ VINTAGE (aka year): _____

GRAPE VARIETY/BLEND: _____ ALCOHOL %: _____

PRICE: _____ ☐ Cork   ☐ Fake cork   ☐ Screw top   ☐ Box

I DRANK THIS:

When: _____ Where: _____

With: _____ Because: _____

COLOR:

Greenish · Yellowish · Golden · Pinkish · Light red · Medium red · Dark red · Nearly midnight

AROMA

First impression:

_____

Second thoughts:

_____

☐ Short legs

☐ Long legs

SWEETNESS

☐ Bone dry   ☐ Dry   ☐ Not so dry   ☐ Sweet   ☐ Like candy

ACIDITY

☐ Tart   ☐ Crisp   ☐ Fresh   ☐ Soft   ☐ Flabby

FLAVOR INTENSITY

☐ DOA   ☐ Subtle   ☐ Bold   ☐ Ferocious

BODY

☐ Watery   ☐ Silky   ☐ Velvety   ☐ Syrupy

FINISH

☐ Flash in the pan   ☐ Pleasantly lingering   ☐ Won't go away

THIS WINE WILL PAIR WELL WITH:

☐ Fish ☐ Chicken ☐ Meat

☐ A cheese plate ☐ Dessert ☐ A three-piece suit

OVERALL RATING:

PURE
VINEGAR

PURE
DELIGHT

SWEET SPOT MATRIX

Considering price and taste,
indicate wine's position on
the graph.

$$$$

• Jet fuel

• 1869
Château
Lafite

Swill

Nectar

• Two-buck
Chuck

¢

DRINK IT AGAIN?

☐ Not even if you paid me. ☐ Maybe, if very drunk. ☐ Sure, why not?

☐ Yes, please. ☐ And again, and again. ☐ If only I could afford it!

NOTES: _____

_____

_____

_____

_____

_____

_____

_____

_____

_____

_____

_____

NAME: _____ VINTAGE (aka year): _____

GRAPE VARIETY/BLEND: _____ ALCOHOL %: _____

PRICE: _____ ☐ Cork   ☐ Fake cork   ☐ Screw top   ☐ Box

I DRANK THIS:

When: _____ Where: _____

With: _____ Because: _____

COLOR:

Greenish · Yellowish · Golden · Pinkish · Light red · Medium red · Dark red · Nearly midnight

AROMA

First impression:

_____

Second thoughts:

_____

☐ Short legs

☐ Long legs

SWEETNESS

☐ Bone dry   ☐ Dry   ☐ Not so dry   ☐ Sweet   ☐ Like candy

ACIDITY

☐ Tart   ☐ Crisp   ☐ Fresh   ☐ Soft   ☐ Flabby

FLAVOR INTENSITY

☐ DOA   ☐ Subtle   ☐ Bold   ☐ Ferocious

BODY

☐ Watery   ☐ Silky   ☐ Velvety   ☐ Syrupy

FINISH

☐ Flash in the pan   ☐ Pleasantly lingering   ☐ Won't go away

THIS WINE WILL PAIR WELL WITH:

☐ Fish ☐ Chicken ☐ Meat

☐ A cheese plate ☐ Dessert ☐ Jalapeño poppers

OVERALL RATING:

PURE
VINEGAR

PURE
DELIGHT

SWEET SPOT MATRIX

Considering price and taste, indicate wine's position on the graph.

$$$$

Swill

Nectar

• Jet fuel

• 1869
Château
Lafite

• Two-buck
Chuck

¢

DRINK IT AGAIN?

☐ Not even if you paid me.   ☐ Maybe, if very drunk.   ☐ Sure, why not?

☐ Yes, please.   ☐ And again, and again.   ☐ If only I could afford it!

NOTES: _____

_____

_____

_____

_____

_____

_____

_____

_____

_____

_____

_____

_____

NAME: _____ VINTAGE (aka year): _____

GRAPE VARIETY/BLEND: _____ ALCOHOL %: _____

PRICE: _____ ☐ Cork ☐ Fake cork ☐ Screw top ☐ Box

I DRANK THIS:

When: _____ Where: _____

With: _____ Because: _____

COLOR:

Greenish · Yellowish · Golden · Pinkish · Light red · Medium red · Dark red · Nearly midnight

AROMA

First impression:

_____

☐ Short legs

☐ Long legs

Second thoughts:

_____

SWEETNESS

☐ Bone dry   ☐ Dry   ☐ Not so dry   ☐ Sweet   ☐ Like candy

ACIDITY

☐ Tart   ☐ Crisp   ☐ Fresh   ☐ Soft   ☐ Flabby

FLAVOR INTENSITY

☐ DOA   ☐ Subtle   ☐ Bold   ☐ Ferocious

BODY

☐ Watery   ☐ Silky   ☐ Velvety   ☐ Syrupy

FINISH

☐ Flash in the pan   ☐ Pleasantly lingering   ☐ Won't go away

THIS WINE WILL PAIR WELL WITH:

☐ Fish ☐ Chicken ☐ Meat

☐ A cheese plate ☐ Dessert ☐ Anything your
heart desires

OVERALL RATING:

PURE
VINEGAR

PURE
DELIGHT

SWEET SPOT MATRIX

Considering price and taste,
indicate wine's position on
the graph.

$$$$

• Jet fuel

• 1869
Château
Lafite

Swill

Nectar

• Two-buck
Chuck

¢

DRINK IT AGAIN?

☐ Not even if you paid me.

☐ Maybe, if very drunk.

☐ Sure, why not?

☐ Yes, please.

☐ And again, and again.

☐ If only I could afford it!

NOTES:

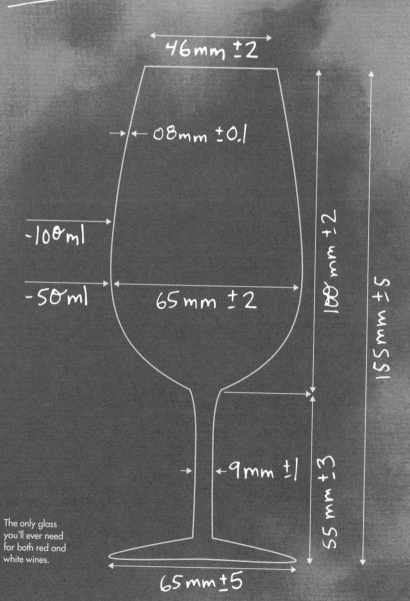

The ISO TASTING GLASS

46mm ±2

08mm ±0.1

-100ml

-50ml

65mm ±2

100 mm ±2

155mm ±5

9mm ±1

55mm ±3

65mm ±5

The only glass you'll ever need for both red and white wines.

HOW TO SERVE WINE
(So You'll Pour Like a Pro)

GLASSES

Wine glasses come in all shapes and sizes—and these days, many glassware brands promote uniquely designed glasses optimized for each individual varietal. In truth, you only need one glass for both red and white: a clear glass with a stem, a wide base, and a narrower opening to allow swirling without spilling. It should also hold at least four ounces (120 ml). To make matters easier, the International Organization for Standardization (ISO) has stipulated a standard design.

Beyond the standard glass for red and white wines, there are two additional styles worth purchasing. For sparkling wines like Champagne and prosecco, a tall, narrow flute helps to retain the effervescence. This design also provides the optimal way to appreciate a bubble's graceful rise.

A sherry or port glass is essentially a smaller version of a wine glass, perfect for sipping sweet dessert wines that are higher in alcohol, and thus served in smaller quantities.

CHAMPAGNE
flute

SHERRY
or
PORT
glass

Champagne flute—much better than a flat champagne saucer for maintaining fizz and showing off bubbles.

Sherry or port glass (aka copita)—six-inch high wine glass for high-alcohol aperitif or dessert wine sipping.

TEMPERATURES

Perhaps the most overlooked aspect of wine drinking is serving it
at the right temperature. As noted wine expert Jancis Robinson
explains: "Serving a wine at the most flattering temperature may
seem absurdly high-falutin' and precious as an activity, but it
really can transform ink into velvet and, conversely, zest into flab."
Assuming you're not going to go to the trouble of carrying a
pocket thermometer around, it may help to know that most white
wines are commonly served too cold, while many reds are served
too warm.

When it comes to white wine, don't leave it too long in an ice bucket
or serve it right out of the fridge, where it's typically kept in the low
forties. You won't taste very much when it's that cold. Instead,
a good rule of thumb is to take a bottle out of the fridge about
a half hour before drinking, allowing the wine to warm up just
enough to bring out its delicate bouquet.

Conversely, you'll want to chill your red wines just a bit before
serving. Many guides will say to drink red wines at room
temperature, neglecting to mention that the "room" they're
referring to is a wine cellar (or the standard temperature of a

cozy European castle). Wine cellars are typically kept in the autumn-like low sixties. Most homes today hover around seventy. A sensible solution is to pop that bottle of Cabernet in the fridge for a half hour before serving—allowing it to warm up in the glass as you drink.

TEMPERATURE GUIDE

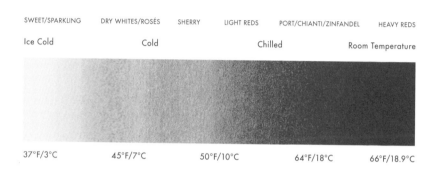

SWEET/SPARKLING	DRY WHITES/ROSÉS	SHERRY	LIGHT REDS	PORT/CHIANTI/ZINFANDEL	HEAVY REDS
Ice Cold	Cold		Chilled		Room Temperature

| 37°F/3°C | 45°F/7°C | 50°F/10°C | 64°F/18°C | 66°F/18.9°C |

COMMON GRAPE VARIETALS
(So You'll Order Like a Pro)

RED	DETAILS	COMMON FLAVOR NOTES
Cabernet Franc	Lighter, softer, and less intense ancestor of Cabernet Sauvignon.	tobacco, raspberry, freshly-mown grass
Cabernet Sauvignon	Best grown in Bordeaux and Napa Valley; high in tannins and intense in flavor; ages well.	black currant, cedar, chocolate
Gamay	Most common in Beaujolais wines; thin, tart, light red; low alcohol and tannins; often drunk young.	pomegranate, strawberry
Grenache	Commonly blended grape often used in rose wines; also known as Garnacha in Spain.	smoke, pepper, berries
Malbec	Most popular grape in Argentina; spicy, concentrated; high in alcohol.	violets, plums, red fruit, earth
Merlot	Soft; low in tannins; easy to grow and drink; made to be drunk with food; velvety.	black cherry, plums
Nebbiolo	Northern Italian grape similar to Pinot Noir; found in Barolo and Barbaresco; difficult to grow; ages well.	tar, roses, smoke, violets
Pinot Noir	Famous red grape of Burgundy; complex flavors; difficult to grow.	raspberry, cherry, violets, gaminess, farmyard
Sangiovese	Most common Italian grape; featured in Chianti, Brunello, and Montepulciano.	herbs, black cherry, leather, earth
Syrah	Most planted grape in Australia (known as Shiraz); high in tannins.	black/white pepper, dark chocolate, blackberry, smoke
Tempranillo	Famous grape of Spanish Rioja; yields deep savory flavors.	vanilla, spices, leather, tobacco
Zinfandel	High alcohol grape grown commonly in California; also known as Primitivo in Italy.	black cherry, pepper, spice, mint

WHITE	DETAILS	COMMON FLAVOR NOTES
Chardonnay	Perhaps the world's most popular and versatile grape; key ingredient in Champagne.	butter, melon, apple, pineapple, vanilla
Chenin Blanc	Versatile and widely planted; often medium-sweet.	honey, almond, wet wool, damp straw
Gewürztraminer	Unique, powerful aroma; copper color; full-bodied.	rose petals, tropical fruits, lychee, spice
Grüner Veltliner	Signature grape of Austria; refreshing and tangy; often sold in extra large bottles.	pepper, green apple, dill
Marsanne	Frequently blended; full-bodied; deep golden color; high in alcohol.	almond, marzipan
Pinot Gris	Known as Pinot Grigio in Italy; derived from Pinot Noir; powerful, soft.	smoke, white peach, pear, apricot
Riesling	German grape low in alcohol yet highly aromatic; high in acidity; ages well.	floral, citrus, nuts, honey, minerals
Sauvignon Blanc	Aromatic; fresh; best drunk young; pairs with seafood.	asparagus, cut grass, green fruits, cat pee
Sémillon	Produces superior, long-lasting, velvety-textured, sweet dessert wines such as Sauternes.	figs, honey, orange, lime
Viognier	Full-bodied and frequently high in alcohol; best drunk young.	honeysuckle, nutmeg, apricot

PINOT Gris
Chardonnay
CHENIN BLANC

COMMON WINE TERMS
(So You'll Sound Like a Pro)

ACID: A key component in every wine. In the right proportion, provides liveliness and refreshment.

AERATION: The process of exposing wine to air, allowing its flavor and aroma to fully develop, usually through decanting.

AFTERTASTE: The lingering taste left in the mouth after swallowing, also known as the *finish*.

ASTRINGENT: Having a mouth-puckering and/or harsh taste, usually caused by tannins.

BALANCE: A condition in which the fruit flavors, acidity, and tannins of a wine are in harmony.

BIG: Having intense flavors and a full body. See also *chewy* and *fleshy*.

BODY: The sensation of weight a wine has as it washes over the palate—often referred to as *mouthfeel*. Light-bodied wines feel watery, medium-bodied wines are like milk, while full- or heavy-bodied wines are compared to cream, with a silky or velvety feel.

BOUQUET: All the aromas of a wine.

CORKED: Exhibiting the off-putting flavor and aroma of moldy socks that result from a tainted cork.

CHEWY: Possessing high density of body and a thick, mouth-filling texture. See also *big* and *fleshy*.

DECANT: To gradually pour from one container into another without disturbing sediment. Also allows for aeration.

DRY: Lacking sweetness.

FINISH: The lasting sensory impression left in the mouth after swallowing. See also *aftertaste* and *long*.

FLABBY: Lacking sufficient acidity. See also *flat*.

FLAT: Similar to *flabby*. When used to describe sparkling wines, flat refers to a loss of effervescence.

FLESHY: See *chewy* and *big*. Also referred to as meaty or beefy.

FRESH: Lively and cleanly made. Does not necessarily refer to the age of a wine.

FRUITY: Having the aroma and/or taste of fruit(s). Not necessarily sweet.

HARSH: Astringent, with an unpleasant taste that may linger in the back of the throat. Found in wines that are high in tannins or alcohol.

HERBACEOUS: Having the aroma and/or taste of fresh herbs such as thyme, lavender, rosemary, oregano, fennel, or basil.

HOT: Too high in alcohol, creating a burning sensation in the back of the throat. Unrelated to temperature.

JAMMY: Possessing ripe fruit intensity.

LEAN: Lacking in strong fruit flavors.

LONG: Exhibiting a long-lasting aftertaste.

MOUTHFEEL: The overall sensation of the wine as perceived in the mouth.

NOSE: The smell or aroma. See also *bouquet*.

OAKY: Retaining a good deal of flavor and/or aroma from the oak barrels in which it was aged. In the right amount, oaky flavors can positively refer to a toasty, vanilla, dill, or smoky quality, but in the negative can be referred to as burnt, green cedar, or plywood.

OFF: Flawed or spoiled.

OFF-DRY: Slightly sweet.

OXIDIZATION: A condition that occurs when wine is overexposed to air during its making or aging process, resulting in a stale or vinegary taste.

PRECOCIOUS: A wine that has matured quickly with a round softness typically found in much older wines.

ROSÉ: A type of wine made from red grapes, with a lighter pink or salmon hue due to a very short exposure to its dark-colored grape skin during fermentation. Also known as blush wine.

ROUND: Having a smooth, velvety mouthfeel, often due to a lack of tannins.

SEC: (French) Dry, or not sweet.

SOFT: Easy-drinking, low in acid and/or tannins.

SULFITES: Refers to sulfur dioxide (SO_2), a preservative used in all winemaking countries to clean equipment and prevent spoilage. Sulfites also occur naturally during the fermentation process.

TANNIC: Causing a mouth-puckering sensation created by concentrated tannins.

TANNINS: A chemical compound found in grape skins, seeds, and stems. These break down with age, lending older vintages a softer, less astringent edge.

VARIETAL: A wine sold by the name of the grape from which it is made.

VINTAGE: The year in which the grapes were grown and/or harvested.

VINTNER: A wine maker.

YOUNG: Of recent vintage.